PAUL VANDORN

INAKI

COLD FRONT PUBLISHING, LLC

First edition

ISBN: 978-1-7379662-0-3

This book was professionally typeset on Reedsy.
Find out more at reedsy.com

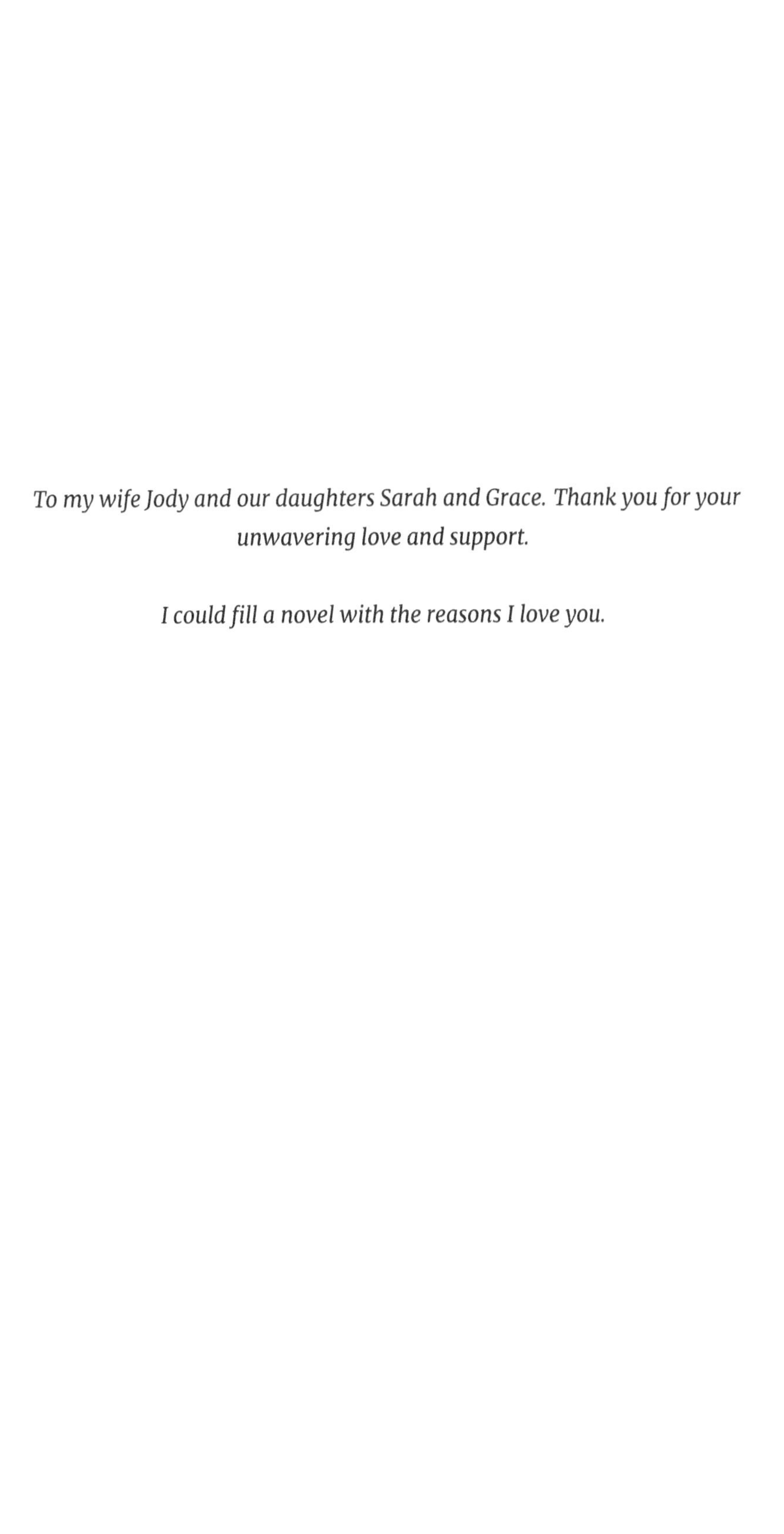

To my wife Jody and our daughters Sarah and Grace. Thank you for your unwavering love and support.

I could fill a novel with the reasons I love you.

Acknowledgement

Special thanks to Tina Kott and the pros at Kott Shot Photography. Jody says it's the best picture I've ever taken. Follow Tina at https://www.facebook.com/KottShot/

I

Part One

The history of this country is rich with mysterious disappearances, from individuals like D.B. Cooper, who in 1971, parachuted out of a plane and vanished near Mount Saint Helens, to Dorothy Arnold, who disappeared in 1910 while walking through Central Park. From entire settlements like the lost colony of Roanoke who settled on the east coast, the Anasazi who roamed the great Southwest, to the Cahokia who thrived in the Midwest.

So, what's one more, right?

1

Thanksgiving
November 28th. 1985

I t was faint, but it was there. It mingled with the fading smells of turkey, stuffing, and the malodorous torrent of perfumes that rushed in like high tide when his aunts arrived, but it was there. If he inhaled just right, Nick Ryan could parse it out from the other smells that clung to the air. The smell was strongest on the back porch, a little too strong, and Nick had always been sensitive to strong smells. The detergent aisle at Burton's General Store, BGS to the Red Hook regulars, would just slam his intake shut. But in the sitting room, tucked between the kitchen and the living room, it was just right. There he could pick up the ghostly tendrils of the fine Turkish tobaccos used to make Camel cigarettes, the chosen brand of the Ryan Clan.

Maggie Ryan, Nick's mother, didn't allow smoking in the house except on special occasions, and Thanksgiving certainly qualified. They were over forty strong when they all showed up, and to the Ryans, Thanksgiving, Christmas, Easter, and the Fourth of July were all days of familial obligation.

Maggie set two tables, one in the kitchen and one in the dining room, each with twelve places, and even then, they had to eat in waves. The back porch, a kind of three-season room, was used as a makeshift chow line. The guests would grab their plates at one end and then proceed down the line where Maggie and Nick's aunts would dish out heaping portions to the first-wave diners. Then Nick's father, Tim, and Nick's uncles would take their place and serve the second wave, all the while complaining about their full bellies.

As soon as dinner was over, the dining tables were cleared, and the serving tables on the back porch were converted into poker tables. The men would sit out there for hours, playing cards for nickels and dimes and smoking cigarettes.

Nick sat alone on the old wagon-wheel-framed couch in the sitting room and listened to the sounds coming from around the house. From the living room—or *frunchroom*, as his family from Chicago called it—he could hear his cousins bickering as they sat around the Christmas tree deciding on which newspaper-wrapped box they would be trying for. It was a Ryan family tradition to have the kids decorate the tree on Thanksgiving, and then, after dinner and the big card game, the kids would exchange white elephant gifts. About once every three minutes, one of his cousins would yell, "Is it time yet?" This was always followed by the same refrain, which came from the kitchen amid a cacophony of running water, clanging plates, and jangling silverware: "If you ask again, we are just going to forget the whole thing." Except they never forgot. Nick thought that the adults enjoyed the frenzied exchange even more than the kids. But being an only child, Nick had learned to entertain himself and quickly grew tired of the chaos that came with large family gatherings. He was sure his cousins thought he was weird. He could see them whisper and cast cautious glances his way, but he didn't care. He was happy and content in his little family of three.

From the back porch came booming laughter and constant ball-breaking—at least that's what his father called it, though, to Nick, it sounded like things that would get you punched in the mouth if said in public. Every so often, a swear word would sneak out, which garnered stern warnings from the kitchen. The back porch was where Nick really wanted to be. He couldn't wait until he was old enough to join the card game. It was a rite of passage for the Ryan boys. His cousin Kevin had just turned eighteen and had been allowed to make the crossing, and Nick was green with envy. He had three more years to wait, but it might as well have been thirty. For now, he would have to be content to sit and listen.

At the end of the evening, when all the guests had been matched up with their hats and jackets, and the last of them was out the door, Maggie went about putting up the dishes. Tim grabbed the margarine and the plate of turkey out of the fridge, pulled the loaf of Wonder Bread down off the top of the fridge, and made himself a sandwich. He slid a chair out and sat at the kitchen table just as Nick came following his nose into the kitchen.

"Smells good, eh, Champ?" Tim held his sandwich and waved it like a fan. "I left the stuff out for you."

Nick loved his old man. To him, his father was Indiana Jones, and Bruce Springsteen rolled into one. He wasn't hungry, but he made a sandwich and sat down next to his dad at the yellow-and-white Formica table while his mom washed the dishes.

"Put a little horseradish on there. It'll put hair on your chest," Nick's father said, and slid the jar over.

Nick removed the lid, sniffed it and, his eyes began to water. If anything was capable of smelling hot, this was it, he thought, as he dipped the tip of the knife into the spicy concoction and touched it cautiously to the bread.

"When you're done eating, we'll help your mother put up the dishes."

Nick sat there feeling content and loved in the little house on Sugar Maple Lane. Tim built the house as a wedding gift to Maggie on their special day. He'd built it with his own two hands, and Maggie cherished it as if it were an everlasting symbol of their love. The Ryan's Cape Cod looked right at home on the Red Hook River. A few other houses had popped up along the road, and while most of them were bigger, none were as nice or as well-kept as 289 Sugar Maple Lane. Nick would always remember sitting at that table, with his eyes watering from the horseradish and his heart feeling fuller than his belly, as the last truly happy moment they would ever share in that house.

Tim leaned back in his chair, patted his flat stomach, and let out a seismic belch. Nick tried, but he couldn't stifle his laugh. Maggie, who it seemed was no better than Nick at stifling laughs, tried to scold her husband.

"Timothy Michael Ryan," she said with a lilt in her voice.

Tim jerked his head back and flared his eyes. "That was Nick."

"I'll Nick you," she said, and they all busted out in laughter.

That was a common Ryanism: to take the last word of a sentence and make it a verb, as in, "If you're running to the store, grab some bread," and in response, "I'll bread you!" No one had ever nicked or breaded anyone as far as Nick knew, but like his dad always said, anything is possible. Nick had always loved the uncertainty, the unknown that came with that statement, *anything is possible,* or at least he did until that night. Nick sucked in air to try and top his father's ripper, but Tim shot him, the *'don't push your luck look,'* and Nick swallowed the burp.

"Dinner was so great, mom."

"Aw, thank you, honey." Nothing beamed so bright as a mother receiving her child's appreciation without having to ask for it.

Nick hugged his mother, kissed her on the cheek, and spun for the living room and his Commodore 64, where he would play *Lawman of the West* until it was time for bed. He'd almost reached the threshold when his father's voice stopped him in his tracks.

"Where do you think you're going, Champ?"

Nick's shoulders slouched; his escape had been thwarted. He'd almost made it, but almost only counts in horseshoes and hand grenades, as the saying goes. Nick trudged over to the sink and grabbed the dishtowel.

"That's my good boy," said Maggie.

"Good boy, my eye. He was headed to play his computer games if I hadn't stopped him."

"Well, here's another towel if you want to help." Maggie tossed a dish towel at Tim.

Tim released an airy burp and patted his stomach. "Mags, baby, I'm so full, I couldn't move a muscle."

Maggie rolled her eyes, and she and Tim shared a soft laugh, but not Nick. Nick stood as still as a statue, staring out the window.

"Did you hear that?" he asked.

"Hear what?" Tim asked, still smiling at the exchange with Maggie.

"I don't know; it was a sort of crack."

"Never mind cracks," Tim pushed himself away from the table. "You help your mother, or I'll *crack* you."

Nick scanned the backyard and went back to drying. The quicker he finished, the quicker he could tend to the outlaws and gunslingers in the Old West.

***

Tim walked down to the river's edge to grab a quick smoke, just as he did every night after dinner, and glanced at the glowing face of his Timex. It was 9 o'clock, and the Red Hook Valley was quiet. It was always quiet this time of year. Quiet and still. The winter winds wouldn't kick up for another month. And even though the fishing season was coming to an end, Tim had to admit that there was something beautifully serene in the silence that fell over the valley in late fall and early winter.

Tim looked back at the house and at Maggie, who stood at the kitchen window still doing the dishes. The yellow from the light above the sink fell over her auburn hair as gently as winter's first snow, and he thought that she looked like an angel. He had loved that face for nearly twenty years. Her warm chestnut eyes, almost too big for her cherubic face, full lips, always soft and pink, and her small, slender nose. Tim looked up into the night sky. "You really outdid yourself when You made my Maggie," he said, and glanced back down at her. She must have caught him staring because she flashed a warm, coy smile that cut through the crisp November air and brushed against his cheek.

He took a satisfying drag on his cigarette. *Son-of-a-bitch, you really made it*, he thought to himself and jetted smoke out through his nostrils. A beautiful wife, a pretty damn good kid; he knew Nick wasn't a reefer-head like his buddy Mickey Donovan's kid. That poor bastard had to hide his wallet and car keys at night. Tim shifted his gaze. He looked at the house he had built. Brick on all four sides, good watertight foundation. No basement—not this close to the water—and no basement meant no flooding. *Hell, Nick's grandchildren's grandchildren could raise their kids in this house*, he thought to himself. On top of all that, his recent promotion with O'Kray Construction meant loosening the purse strings. Yes, he really had made it.

Tim finished his first cigarette and tossed the butt into the water, where it died with a satisfying hiss. He glanced over his shoulder to make sure

Maggie wasn't looking as he shook another from the pack and placed it between his lips. She'd recently cut him back to one-a-night after dinner. He pulled a stick-match out of the box and struck it with his thumbnail. But instead of the comforting pop and flare, Tim heard the unmistakable creek and crack of a screen door opening and slamming shut. The sound came from the Ironweiler's place across the river. Tim looked over, expecting to see Mark Ironweiler, but what he saw instead sent a chill down his spine. Six-year-old Josh Ironweiler, the only child of Sadie and Mark, was walking toward the river in his footie pajamas with his stuffed purple giraffe in one hand and his blue blanket in the other.

"Josh!" he yelled. "Boy, what are you doing?"

Josh, an attentive and respectful child, didn't respond, even though Mark was sure the boy heard him. The river was barely moving, and except for the crack of the screen door slamming shut, the night was perfectly silent.

"Josh! Hey Josh!"

The little boy reached the water's edge and stepped in.

Tim cupped his hands around his mouth like a megaphone. "Josh! What the hell are you doing, boy?"

Josh was past his knees and almost up to his waist in the frigid Red Hook River. Tim dashed across the dock to his rowboat *Gypsy Soul*. He'd taken the name from Van Morrison's *Into the Mystic*, the song that played as he and Maggie shared their first dance as husband and wife. He untied *Gypsy Soul* and bent hard into the ores. Tim had to keep looking over his shoulder so as not to lose sight of the boy.

"Josh! Turn back, you hear!"

But Josh kept walking. There was no way the boy was sleepwalking; the water was cold enough to snap a man out of a coma. He looked back again. Little Joshua Ironweiler was in past his shoulders.

"Maggie!" he screamed back at his house, but she was no longer at the window, and suddenly the night seemed colder.

He glanced again over his shoulder, but Josh was gone. Standing on the shore where the boy went in, Tim saw a small man in a black suit.

"Hey buddy, go bang on that door! Tell them their kid is in the river!"

1

The man didn't move, and as Tim filled his lungs to shout again, the man vanished into vapor. Tim blinked and refocused, but the man was nowhere to be seen. He dismissed the apparition—*must have been a bush or tree branch, or something*—and kept pulling on the oars. When he reached the spot where he'd last seen Josh, Tim plunged his arm into the cold, still water. The water quickly soaked through Tim's heavy flannel jacket and attacked his flesh like frozen needles. The pain was exquisite, and Tim ripped his arm from the water and blew warm breath on his hand.

Tim knew the Red Hook—he had ice-fished on this river, but he never remembered the water being this cold. *How could Josh have walked so slowly, so deliberately into this?* He plunged his arm back under the surface and groped around in the water as long as he could stand it, then ripped his arm out again.

He was about to yell back at the house for Maggie when he heard his son's voice.

"Dad! What are you doing? What's wrong?"

"Nick, go into the house and tell your mother to call 9-1-1!" Tim didn't have to yell. His voice carried easily over the still air, but he couldn't help it.

"Why, what happened?"

"It's Josh. He's in the water!"

"What?"

"Now, Nick!" And without another word, Nick turned and ran for the house, pausing only once, to swat at a bird or, more likely, a bat that swooped at his face.

Tim pawed at the buttons of the thick flannel with numb unresponsive fingers. Failing at the buttons, he grabbed hold of each side and pulled, snapping the thread that held them in place. He saw the black quarter-sized plastic discs pop off the jacket and go rolling across the sole of his little boat.

"I'm going to have to ask Maggie to fix that," he said as he threw the flannel off and jumped into the water.

The icy plunge stole his breath, and he could feel his heart pounding in his throat. Tim caught what breath he could and went under. He thrashed around, groping wildly in the dark, cold water, but time and again, he came up empty-handed. As he surfaced for the last time, he saw the *Gypsy Soul* floating away downriver and knew he would lose her to the churning water of the boil. With his own strength beginning to fail, he swam for the east bank, pulled himself out of the water, and ran for the Ironweiler's house. He crashed through the back door yelling for Mark but got no response.

Maggie stood on the dock, holding Nick and calling her husband's name in the cold night, but if he heard her, he didn't respond.

The house was quiet and dark, except for the moonlight that filtered in.

"Mark! Sadie! Where the hell are you? Your boy's in the river!"

Tim ran through the first floor, calling for them, but there was no response. He bolted up the stairs to the second floor and stopped dead in his tracks at the master bedroom. Mark Ironweiler sat slumped against the wall. Head cocked to one side. One eye half shut, the other wide open and crossed toward his nose. His jaw, or what was left of it, hung unhinged and caked in a wad of black pulp. Blood and brain matter slid down the wall behind him, and a sawed-off shotgun lay across his legs, his right thumb still caught in the trigger guard.

"What the fuck, Mark?" The question was rhetorical.

There was nothing he could do for Mark Ironweiler, but he might still be able to save Josh. Tim turned out of the room, flew down the stairs, and tore through the house. On the counter near the back door sat a yellow waterproof 12-volt Eveready flashlight. Tim grabbed it as he burst out the back door and sprinted toward the river. Tim clicked the light on and shined the beam over the water's surface. Still no sign of the boy. He waded out to the spot he saw Josh go under. The water seemed colder now. He ducked under the water, flashlight in hand, and began searching. Tim stayed under for as long as he could before the cold drove him back up. He continued reaching under for the boy, but his body was going numb again, and his hands turned back into blocks of frozen flesh. The flashlight slipped from his grip, and he watched it sink to the bottom, where it kicked up a plume of silt. The beam cut through the clouds of sediment across the cold dark river bed, and Tim saw something move. He grabbed a gulp of air and dove deep one last time. As he reached the bottom, he saw him. Josh Ironweiler's eyes were filled with fright. Tim reached for him, but he lost the boy in another cloud of silt. The sediment settled just in time for Tim to see the riverbed throb and Josh slip beneath. Tim's body, acting independent of conscious thought, clawed its way to the surface in search of oxygen.

As he broke the surface, his lungs began forcing air in and out of his body, and he became acutely aware of his level of fatigue. Tim fought for every inch until he reached the shoreline, where he paused to catch his breath. He needed a moment before he could dive back under to continue his search, but before he could slow his breathing, something gripped his leg and pulled him back under. As he went under, Tim swallowed a gulp of cold river water. In a panic, he reached down and clawed at whatever had seized his ankle. The grip tightened, and when he looked down, he saw it. Summoning every last bit of strength, Tim tugged hard and broke free. He reached the surface and coughed hard, trying to clear his airway. Sirens, which only seconds ago bleated helplessly in the distance, now ripped through the night as the first police cruiser slid to a stop in the grass a few yards away from the riverbank.

***

Officer Fisher jumped out and swept his light around in the darkness. From across the river, he heard Nick and Maggie.

"Fred! It's Tim. He's in the water!"

Fisher turned his light on the water and saw Tim about fifteen feet out and struggling to stay afloat. Fisher snapped his belt-keepers and let his gun belt drop onto the grass as he ran into the Red Hook. He grabbed Tim around the wrist and pulled. Exhausted, Tim fought his rescuer, but Fisher overpowered him and dragged him to the bank.

"What the hell happened, Tim?" the officer asked.

"H-h-h-h-helppp m-m-m-me f-f-f-f-find h-himmmm, it's g-g-g-g-got h-himm," Tim sputtered.

Fisher pulled Tim onto the grass just as other rescue personnel sprinted toward the water.

"Fred, there's s-s-s-something d-d-down there. There's s-s-something down there." Tim Ryan clawed at the officer as he spoke.

"What's down there?"

"I d-d-don't know, it's got, Josh."

Tim Ryan's eyes began rolling back in his head, he was shaking like a leaf, and his speech was terribly slurred. Fisher knew hyperthermia when he saw it and called for the paramedics.

Tim struggled and cursed wildly as they loaded him onto the gurney. "G-g-get off of me! G-g-get the f-f-fuck off of me! There's something d-d-down there, and it's got J-j-josh!"

Between the medics and several officers, they were able to strap Tim Ryan down and load him in the back of the ambulance.

"I've never seen him like that," said Fisher.

"He's going into shock," said one of the medics. "We have to get him to the hospital."

Fisher closed the doors, and the ambulance sped off into the night. Over the next several hours, a tragic story would unfold. The police found Sadie Ironweiler's body hung from a rafter in the garage. It was clear from the intrusions cut into the wood by the rope that she was dragged up there by her neck, likely struggling the whole time. Mark was found just as Tim Ryan had left him. According to the Herrington County Coroner, the death resulted from a single projectile having penetrated the superior turbinate bone, entering the frontal lobe, passing through the temporal and occipital lobes, and exiting the rear of the skull. To the cops talking outside, Mark Ironweiler blew his brains out. The detectives on call took the rope-burn marks on his hands as evidence that Mark was the one who pulled Sadie up into the garage rafters, where she hung by her oddly elongated neck. As for six-year-old Josh Ironweiler, the working hypothesis was as follows: likely having witnessed the violence in his home, the young male subject walked into the river in a state of shock and drowned. His body was never recovered.

2

September 16th, 1995

Scott Waters signaled and took the second exit for the town of Red Hook. The cream-colored 89 Jeep Wagoneer with its wood-siding looked right at home as it left Interstate 39 for Grove Road, two lanes of smooth black-top flanked by centuries-old Tamarack trees. Connie Waters lowered her window and took a deep breath.

"You guys smell that?"

"Yeah, mom, it smells like dad's air freshener." Frankie stuck his head out of the back window and looked up. "Hey, dad, how tall do you think these trees are?"

Scott pulled himself up with his steering wheel and twisted his neck to take a look. "At least fifty feet. You seeing these trees, Levi?"

Levi wanted to look, but he had to maintain the proper level of apathy for a young man entering high school. "Who cares about some dumb old trees."

"They're so awesome, dad!" Frankie shouted, his body half out of the car.

"Levi, keep an eye on your baby brother," Connie ordered.

"Jeez, mom, I'm eleven years old. I'm not a baby," Frankie Waters whined.

"You'll always be my baby, sweetie."

"Yeah, sweetie," Levi teased as he grabbed his brother by the shirt and yanked him roughly back into the car. "Buckle up, stupid; you want to fall out and splatter your brains all over the road?"

Frankie buckled in but still managed to crane his neck and poke his head out the window.

"What road am I looking for, babe?"

Connie glanced down at the directions Scott had jotted down. "Square Barn Road. There it is," she said, pointing a delicate finger at the road sign just ahead. "Take a left."

Nearly missing his turn, Scott cut the wheel hard, and the Wagoneer rocked. "Jesus Jones! Nice navigation Columbus."

"Oh, shut up. And what did I tell you about using the Lord's name in vain?"

Scott held up an apologetic hand. About a mile down, just over a crest in the road, the Waters boys got their first look at the Red Hook River. Even Levi couldn't hide his wonder, and both boys responded with oohs and aahs usually reserved for fireworks. The Wagoneer's tires hummed as Square Barn Road bent to follow the river. Ahead on their left sat a serene riverside picnic grove with a large wooden sign that read, *Welcome to Red Hook.* Below the powder blue letters was an artist's rendering of what the place must have looked like back in the 50s. A bright yellow Ford Woody sat parked along a sparkling river with a couple of families picnicking in the grass. The women were dressed in skirts and button-down blouses, the men in short-sleeved button-down shirts, worn tucked into pleated pants. Across the bottom in the same delicate cursive hand as *Welcome to Red Hook*, read, *You May Never Want To Leave*, only some joker had painted over "Want To" with black paint.

"Did you guys really dress like that back then, mom?"

"How old do you think we are?" Asked Scott.

"No, baby, that was more your grandparent's era. Dad and I wore acid-washed jeans and Zubas."

"What's Zubas?"

"Oh, and don't forget Swatches, babe."

"How could I ever forget Swatches," Connie said wearing a nostalgic smile.

"Man, I loved your Pat Benatar phase," Scott glanced over with pervy eyes.

"Scott!" Connie screamed and grabbed the dashboard.

Scott's eyes shot back to the road as his foot automatically hit the brake pedal. A huge black bird swooped up, just missing the Wagoneer's windshield.

"What the hell was that?"

"I think it was a vulture, dad."

"Seriously, Frankie?" Levi asked. "Vultures live in the desert, stupid."

Scott glanced in the rearview mirror as a massive black crow settled back to feed upon the carrion in the middle of the road.

"Well, whatever it was, thank God we didn't hit it," Connie said, in her most calming tone.

"Hey, mom, what's Zubaz?"

"Zubaz were like parachute pants."

"Stop, Hammer time," Scott said.

"What's parachute pants?"

"Will you shut up about clothes, Frankie?" Levi snapped.

"Fine, sorry, jeez," he pouted, but only for a moment. "Whoa, what's that?" Frankie asked, pointing at a large structure in a field across the river. The town's water tower stood like a sentinel watching over the sprawling valley below. Frankie read the words stenciled across the side that faced the road. "Welcome to Red Hook. Home of the Rivermen. 1945 IHSA State Basketball Champs."

"That's a water tank, baby," Connie answered. "The town stores water up there in case of an emergency."

"What kind of emergency?"

"A water emergency, dummy," Levi answered.

Scott shot Levi a quick disproving glance in the rearview mirror. "They're going to have to repaint that thing now that Levi *the Cannon* Waters is in town," Scott said. "Next year, it will say Home of the Rivermen, 1995 IHSA State Football Champs!" He was beaming.

"Dad, I've already missed a month of two-a-days. The coach probably won't even let me join the team this year."

"Bullshit!"

"Scott Waters, you watch your mouth!" Connie scolded.

Ignoring her rebuke, Scott said, "I already talked with Coach Duncan. He said he got a call from Coach Mills about that arm of yours. Once he sees you in action, you can bet your ass you're gonna play." Scott's grin widened.

"I hope so, dad."

"Besides, your old man is the new vice-principal. If that guy wants to keep his job, he'll make you his starter."

Levi rolled his eyes and turned his gaze back out the window. As Square Barn bent back away from the river, they found themselves, once again, driving in the shade of the tamaracks.

"Are we moving into a forest preserve or something?" Levi muttered.

"Yeah, dummy, we're going to live in a hollowed-out tree like a family of owls."

"Don't listen to your father," said Connie.

Just over the next hill, the trees broke, and a picturesque little town appeared below.

"That's where we're going to live," Scott said, sounding very satisfied with himself. "That's Red Hook boys, our new home. And see there?" Scott pointed across the river. "That's the Red Hook High School. That's where your old man will be working."

"Assistant Principal Waters," Connie said, halting after each word to emphasize their importance.

"Yep," Scott said, not sounding nearly as impressed with himself as his wife seemed to be. "And over there," he thrust his chin toward the football field. "That's where we're going to spending our Friday Nights," said Scott in a tone that almost sounded nostalgic.

Riverman Stadium stood as a monument to the importance placed on high school football in the region. Newer looking than the rest of the school, the stadium was surrounded by a six-foot-tall chain-link fence, with ticket booths at three gates. Two small buildings marked CONCESSIONS sat at either end of the verdant field, and brilliant, aluminum bleachers glistened in the early afternoon sun. Over the north endzone, there flew an enormous American flag, bigger than any Levi had ever seen. Next to it, flying lower by half, flew another flag. This one featured a crimson colored hook set sideways on a navy-blue field. The sight of it seemed off to Scott. It seemed harsh and contrary to the countryside's natural aesthetic, but the feeling was fleeting as his eye was drawn back to the glistening bleachers.

"They're going to be chanting your name from those seats, son."

Connie shot Scott a look. "We just want you to play and have fun. Don't let your father put any pressure on you."

"It's okay, mom. Like I said, I probably won't even play this year.

"Bullshit!"

"Scott!"

The Wagoneer crossed the McKinley Avenue Bridge, turned right onto Sugar Maple Lane.

"There it is," said Scott.

The little Cape Cod sat baking in the warm summer sun. Scott had barely put the car in park before Frankie hopped out and ran toward the river.

"Frankie Waters, you come back here!"

"Mom, look, it's the river," he called excitedly.

"Scott, I don't want him down near the water by himself."

The rear passenger's side door squeaked open, and Levi slid out of the back seat gripping his football. "I'll get him, mom."

Levi called for Frankie to button-hook right and heaved the ball through the air in a tight spiral. The ball hit Frankie's hands but dropped and rolled in the warm grass. Frankie tumbled on the ground like he was recovering a fumble and threw the ball back toward his brother. The football wobbled and fell about five feet short.

"Not bad for a little kid," Levi shouted, sending Frankie into a full charge.

Levi bent to pick up the ball and braced himself for impact, but the impact never came. Something else had captured Frankie's attention. About a hundred feet south of the main house sat a detached garage with a turret-style lookout built into the roof.

"Wait up, Frankie," called Levi.

"You be careful," Connie called after her sons as they disappeared from view. "Do you think they'll be okay in there?"

"They're fine, babe," Scott assured her.

***

The garage was huge and immaculate and as dull as dirt as far as the boys were concerned. Wall to wall nothing. Nothing that was, except for the wooden stairs that ran up the far wall to a door leading to a room that surely led to the walkout. They ran up the stairs; Levi took them two at a time and reached the oblong brass knob first. He gave it a twist, but the door wouldn't budge. He squatted down and put his eye to the keyhole but saw only darkness on the other side.

"I've never seen a keyhole like this," Levi said as he studied the lock.

"It looks like the skeleton keyholes at grandma's house," said Frankie.

"Sort of, but it's different, see, it's like a plus sign."

"Can you pick it?" Frankie asked, hopefully.

"Heck yeah, I can pick it, but I need an allen-wrench. We'll have to wait until dad unpacks his tools."

Temporarily defeated, the boys walked down the stairs and started back for the house.

***

A woman in a tight-fitting pencil skirt and white blouse stood talking with their mom and dad back near the house. Levi had recently begun noticing things like tight skirts a lot more. Janice Crenshaw of Crenshaw and Crenshaw Realty smiled at Levi, having caught his blatant stare at her legs.

"As I was saying, Mr. Ryan kept a meticulous home."

"Dad, there's a room above the garage," Frankie said, and puffed out his lower lip, "but the door is locked."

"Don't act like a baby, Frankie."

"Aw, leave your little brother alone," Janice tussled Frankie's hair. "But your son is right. The door is locked, and we don't have the key. I've been trying to reach Nick—excuse me, Mr. Ryan, but he hasn't returned my calls."

"That's alright; I'm sure I can jimmy it open."

"It's such a lovely old lock, Mr. Waters. Wait till you see it. I'm sure you would hate to see it damaged. Besides, I'm sure Mr. Ryan will be in touch."

"Speaking of Mr. Ryan," Scott said. "Why wasn't he at the closing? I mean, isn't it customary for the seller to be at the closing?"

"Oh, that, well, Mr. Ryan, is attending the University of Chicago. He's working on his Ph.D. in astrology or archaeology or something. He inherited this beautiful place when his parents died."

Connie Waters's eyes widened. "They didn't die in the—"

"In the house? Oh, heavens, no. The late Mister Ryan died about five years ago over at Saint Anthony's Hospital. *Pneumonia.*" She whispered pneumonia as if anything above a whisper would invoke the sickness upon herself.

"And Mrs. Ryan?" Connie asked.

"Poor dear, she died last year—*of the cancer*," again in a whisper. Nick tried to care for the place, but with all of his work keeping him in the city, he could hardly make the long drive back home often enough to make the house worth keeping. Well," in a suddenly vibrant tone, "his loss is your gain."

All three froze. "Oh my, I mean the loss of the house, not of his parents."

Scott cleared his throat. "Right, so if you'll excuse us, we have to get ready for the moving men."

"Certainly, and you have my number. You call if you need anything, ya hear?"

"We sure will, and thank you," Connie shook her hand. Scott waved over his shoulder as he headed for the front door.

"Connie! Chop chop babe, I gotta carry you over the threshold."

Connie held her hands up in a, *what are you gonna do,* gesture and hurried toward the house.

"We'll be in touch, Mr. Waters," Janice called as she set off for her car. Scott scooped Connie up into his arms, set her down in the foyer, and kissed her long and hard.

"God! Get a room, guys!"

"Frankie! What have I told you about that?"

"Sorry, mom, I meant gosh."

"Besides, we're in a room," Scott pointed out.

"Yeah, dad, but I meant your own room."

"These are all my own rooms, my man, and if you don't watch your ass, you'll be sleeping in the garage."

"Cool! Can I, mom?"

"Absolutely not!"

"Absolutely not what?" Levi asked. He hadn't heard the conversation. He was distracted by the Realtor walking back to her car.

"Never mind, you boys, go check out your room."

"But there's a room above the garage."

"I know, son, that's going to be the dog house," Scott said with a smile.

"We're getting a dog?" Frankie asked excitedly.

"No, Frankie, that's just an expression. The dog house is where dads go when moms get mad at them," Scott smiled and winked at his wife.

"Are you sure I can't sleep in the garage?"

"Yeah, dad, let us have our room up there. The dog can sleep in the house," suggested Frankie.

"What do you mean, our room? You're not sharing my room," Levi snapped.

"See what you started?" She gave Scott a stern look. "No one is sleeping in the garage."

"Well, what about the dog?" Frankie asked.

"No dog and no garage," Scott said in a lightly authoritative tone.

"Well, it's locked anyway," said Levi as he took off running down the hallway.

Frankie gave the raspberries and ran to catch up with Levi, already halfway down the hall.

"First dibs on the beds!" Levi shouted. It didn't matter that the furniture hadn't even arrived yet.

"No fair!"

Levi grabbed the frame of the door and cut hard, swinging himself into the room. Frankie tried to put on the brakes but went sliding on stocking feet across the dark oak floor right past the door. Scott and Connie watched as Frankie regained traction and joined his brother in their new bedroom.

"There go our most precious possessions," Connie said with a smile.

"Speak for yourself; I'm buying a fishing boat."

Connie slapped his shoulder. From where they were standing, they could see clear through the house to the river out back. Scott wrapped his arms around her and kissed her head.

"We did it, babe," he said, an uncontrollable smile springing up.

"Can you believe this is all ours?" She said.

"Well, it will be in 30 years," said Scott.

A great whoosh of air from its brakes announced the arrival of the moving truck, and in no time at all, the men unloaded the rest of the Waters's possessions into their new home. That evening, the Waters family sat surrounded by moving boxes and ate their first meal in their new place.

The next few days were consumed with unpacking and breaking down boxes, tedious and boring work, but every night, the boys helped their father burn the cardboard boxes in the fire pit down near the water. On Friday, Scott ran into town and picked up a bundle of firewood. Connie boiled hotdogs and put them on sticks so the boys could roast them. After the hotdog dinner, they took a walk down to the river.

"Would you look at that? We got a dock. You know what that means?"

"What does it mean, dad?"

"Well, Frankie, it means that we have to get a boat!"

"Scott, you've never even been in a boat."

"Sure, I have, down at Lincoln Park."

"That's a four-foot-deep lagoon. This is a river, a big river."

"Water is water. Take it from mister Waters himself," Scott said, laughing at his own dumb joke.

"No boat, end of discussion. Now can we just enjoy a nice quiet evening?"

"We would keep the boat outside, mom," Frankie begged.

Levi rolled his eyes, having no interest in the conversation.

"See what you started? Now I have to be the bad guy."

"Okay, that's enough. Leave your mother alone." Scott said, bringing an end to the boat conversation. "Did you notice that the grandfather clock isn't working?" Scott asked Connie.

"Yeah, must have happened in the move."

"Of course, it happened in the move. It was fine before we left Chicago. I am going to sue those idiots. That clock has been in my family for sixty years."

"What about that clock shop we passed coming into town; it had a magician's name..." she scrunched her face trying to remember.

"Was it Marshall Brodine's clock shop? Clock repair is easy once you know the secret," he said, recalling the old commercials.

"No, shut up, it was," Connie scrunched harder. "Merlyn's," she said triumphantly. "It was called Merlyn's. Why don't you go see him before you get all litigious?"

Scott shrugged. "I guess," he said, and then his tone hardened. "But I just hope for their sake..."

"Yes, I know, the big bad assistant principal is gonna sue," she said, in a baby voice, and settled back into his arms.

3

Nick Ryan pulled the heavy wooden door open and sprinted up the creaking stairs to the third floor of Kresge Hall. Kresge was one of the oldest buildings on campus, so it seemed only fitting that it housed the archaeology and anthropology departments. He glanced at his watch, 10:10, as he hurried down the hall, already ten minutes late for his meeting with Jinan Bondiani. Nick grabbed the newel post as he crested the stairs and hooked a hard right.

"Shit, shit, shit.."

Nick turned the knob with one hand and shouldered the door sending it into the wall with a thunderous crack. Dr. Bondiani, a striking but serious-looking woman, sat with her hands folded neatly atop her desk and gently cleared her throat.

Sheepishly, Nick began his apology. "Dr. Bondiani, I am so sorry. Traffic was insane and parking on campus," a nervous laugh escaped him, "well, you know."

Dr. Bondiani held her hands out in a gesture that suggested to Nick that he wasn't in any serious trouble. "Mr. Ryan, as your dissertation committee chair, it is my job to advise you on the subject of your dissertation." Dr. Bondiani offered a fleeting but disarming smile, and Nick smiled in return, feeling the noose loosen a little more. "Nowhere, in my job description, does it say that I am responsible for imparting advice on making sound life choices."

Nick swallowed hard. Dr. Bondiani leaned back in her chair and tented her fingers as the smile faded from Nick's face.

"However, it is in that vein that I offer this nugget. When you have an appointment, allow extra time so that you might thwart traffic, or parking, or whatever diabolical plan fate might have in store to keep you from your appointed task."

"Again, Doctor Bondiani, I am so sorry—" She held up her hand to halt his apology.

"Do you see how ineffective apologies and excuses are as tools for proper time management? That is, of course, operating under the assumption that your goal is, in fact, to be on time."

At thirty, Jinan Bondiani, a prodigy, was the youngest professor on staff at the university and perhaps a little more forgiving than her counterparts. The other two members of Nick's committee, Dr. Belifuss, and Dr. Weiss, both in their mid-60s, would have locked office doors at ten on the dot, and Nick knew it. So, he sat silent, hoping muteness would adequately convey his remorse, except he noticed that she, too, was silent. Jinan Bondiani seemed to be staring right through him. Beads of sweat began to form on his upper lip as his eyes dropped to the center of his chest. *So-of-a-bitch!* He had forgotten his tie clip. While rushing out the door, Nick shoved a piece of toast down his throat and dropped a dollop of blackberry jam on his white shirt. It was a small stain, about the size of a dime. He'd planned to change shirts at his earliest opportunity, but in the meantime, he thought his tie would do nicely to hide the splotch. And it would have if only he'd remembered to affix his tie clip. Nick began rubbing the pads of his thumbs against the pads of his middle fingers, the self-soothing exercise he'd picked up from his father. It was Tim Ryan's only poker-tell, and he did his best to keep his hands under control when he played.

Jinan cast a disapproving look at Nick's busy fingers, cleared her throat, and continued. "While I cannot say that I condone your personal habits, I found your subject matter fascinating and your prospectus quite compelling. A dissertation on the Mooka'am is a bold undertaking, and while I often find it necessary to insist on a narrowing of scope, in this case, I believe you have full reign. The Mooka'am vanished over 300 years ago. And, as far as I am aware, very little research material exists on the people, and virtually nothing pertaining to how or why they vanished."

Nick smiled; it seemed he had made it through his dressing down. And then she continued.

"Frankly, I'm not sure you're up to the challenge, and as your advisor, I would *advise*," she stressed the word advise, "that you reconsider; lest the stink of your failure rub off on me, and even worse, on this great institution."

"Doctor Bondiani, I assure you—"

Jinan raised a hand, and Nick shut his mouth. "But I know you will not heed my warning," she continued. That is why I intend to be on you like a jelly stain on a white shirt." She paused but did not break eye contact. "Would that be grape?"

"Um," he glanced down, "blackberry actually, and I just want to say—"

Again, she raised the silencing hand. "I'm not interested in apologies or platitudes, just good sound research."

"Understood," Nick gave a sharp nod.

"I will be submitting your prospectus to the program director for approval, and we will begin work on your dissertation description."

At times Bondiani was rude; at other times, she was merely patronizing. Nick preferred patronizing, but oddly, he enjoyed her company either way. Oddly, because Nick didn't enjoy anyone's company. Being an only child, Nick had learned to appreciate solitude to companionship. It was a trait that his mother recognized in him at an early age. Maggie Ryan signed her son up for every activity imaginable, from little league and Pop Warner football to band and the high school's drama club. Nick hated the latter but enjoyed, even excelled at sports. But after a big game, when the team went to Gert's for ice cream, Nick had to be dragged and usually sat with his parents despite his teammates' efforts to have him join them.

It wasn't that he disliked people; on the contrary, he found them fascinating, something to be studied and cataloged. His enjoyment of sports carried over to college, where he lettered in rugby and baseball. Still, just as in his early years, when the activity was over, and everyone wanted to go grab a beer, Nick would retire to his dorm, more recently his apartment, and resume his research. To quell his mother's nagging, "Nick, when are you going to bring home a nice girl?" Nick tried dating during the second semester of his freshman year, but that was a bust. His girlfriend, an undeclared psych major, said that he had commitment issues—her undeclared professional diagnosis.

With his mother gone, and with her the guilt-trip that only a mother can lay, Nick Ryan was free to focus on his work. Nick was an outstanding researcher and well above average when it came to presenting his ideas on paper, and he knew it. In a perfect world, Nick would be allowed to lock himself in a study and submit brilliant articles on the topics he chose to research. Sadly, it wasn't a perfect world, and his upcoming oral presentation hung like the Sword of Damocles above his head. But for now, he was well within his wheelhouse, and that caused him to smirk involuntarily.

"Something amusing, Mr. Ryan?"

"I have it now if you'd like to see it."

"You have what, Mr. Ryan?"

Nick caught the emphasis on Mr. and read it as a not-so-subtle way of putting him in his place. He set his briefcase on his lap and snapped open the latches. Loose notes, a half-eaten sandwich, and a browning banana greeted him, and he felt his stomach tighten. *Please tell me I didn't leave it on the kitchen table!* Pushing aside papers and produce, he found what he was looking for. He removed his dissertation description, snapped his briefcase shut, and set it on her desk. The smirk grew into a smile.

Doctor Jinan Bondiani opened the folder and began reading. About the middle of the third page, she narrowed her gaze. By the middle of page six, she began to chew her lower lip, and by page ten, she brought her hand to her chin and massaged it with her thumb. Nick sat, smugly silent, while she finished reading. Jinan placed the folder on her desk and regarded Nick Ryan in his jelly-stained shirt.

"This is excellent work, Nick. Of course, it will need some fine-tuning, but we may make a decent academic of you yet." She tossed the folder on her desk, and Nick scooped it up.

"Thank you, Dr. Bondiani," Nick picked up his folder and turned to leave.

"On time next week, Mister Ryan," she called behind him.

Nick exited her office without a word, shot down the hall, down the stairs, and out the door. He parked in a No Parking zone and hoped to make it back before parking enforcement slapped a $30 ticket on his window.

"Son-of-a-bitch!"

He snatched the ticket out from under the windshield wiper of his powder blue 1971 Ford Bronco and tossed it into his glove compartment with about a half dozen others he'd accumulated. His mother would never accept help from the family, but she couldn't refuse a gift given to Nick. The Bronco had been a graduation present from his aunts and uncles. His cousin Kevin picked it out for him and drove it to Red Hook for his party. It was an off-roader's wet-dream. Massive knobby tires, a spare mounted to the rear tailgate, a reinforced roll bar, and a Baja light bar. Nick didn't care about all of that; he just loved the freedom it represented.

Nick shoved the tickets aside and grabbed his bright yellow Sony Discman and the cassette player adapter. Five months ago, he heard a band called The Tragically Hip for the first time, and two months later, he was following them around the Midwest on a five-state tour. Ohio, Illinois, Iowa, Wisconsin, and Minnesota, he called it the Tragic-Tour. Nick hit play, and Nautical Disaster poured out of his speakers. He put the Bronco in gear, drove off-campus, and headed south on Lake Shore Drive. To his left, waves crashed against the beaches of Lake Michigan's west coast; to his right, stately old brownstones sat scattered among towering skyscrapers. Alone in his car, Nick breathed in deeply and felt that all was right with the world. The top was down, and the sun was merciless. The Bronco's air conditioning stopped working the previous summer. He had tried to get it into the garage, but it seemed everyone's air conditioners went on the blink at the same time, and he was just shit out of luck. No matter, there was a cool lake breeze, and he was feeling fine.

Nick undid his tie and slipped out of his jelly-stained shirt. The maneuver caused him to swerve, and his less than perfect driving garnered blaring horns and hand gestures from other drivers. Some guy in an old Datsun B210 called him an asshole and flipped him the bird. Nick took the exit for

I-55 South and settled in for the long drive to Chesapeake Station. As he left the urban sprawl for the peaceful countryside, he felt a certain sense of nostalgia, and then the seller's remorse crept upon him.

"Keeping the house in Red Hook would have been impractical," he told himself. "Besides, you needed the money for school, and whoever said that you had to be born and die in the same place?"

Actually, an article he'd read in some magazine or other claimed that 60% of the people who lived in the Midwest never moved out of their state. The author wrote that 1 in 10 never moved out of the town they were born in and that 1 in 17 had never left their home state. Not to travel, not for business, not even for a relative's wedding.

"Well, at least I'm not one of the 1 in 17." He cranked the knob on his radio to drown out the sound of his tires whirring against the pavement.

4

Frankie and Levi woke up early the following day. To them, Saturday morning cartoons were just as sacred as Sunday morning church was to their parents. They had been glued to the local FOX affiliate all morning long, but when the X-Men cartoon was over, it was time to go out and play before their mother found work for them. It was mid-September, but stepping out of the comfortable air-conditioned house into the yard was like passing through a wall of fire. It had been a brutally hot summer. In Chicago, the heatwave claimed the lives of 739 people during one week in July when temperatures reached 102 degrees.

"Jeez, Levi, it even smells hot," Frankie whined.

The air smelled of baking grass and melting asphalt. It was too hot to play, but there was no way they were going inside to be put to work. Frankie followed Levi into the garage, where Levi began sifting through his father's tool bag.

"What are you looking for?" Frankie asked his brother.

Levi didn't answer him; instead, he held up the objects of his search. Two allen wrenches. It was cooler in the garage than outside, but just a little, and the sweat dripped down Levi's forehead and into his eyes as he fumbled with the skeleton key lock. A quick lift with one wrench and a slide with the other, and one part of the lock snapped open. Same for the second lock, and the third, and the fourth, or so he thought. Levi blew on his nails and polished them against his shirt.

"Told you I could pick it."

Levi grabbed the knob, gave it a turn, and pushed on the door, expecting it to fall open, but it didn't budge.

"Told you I could pick it," mocked Frankie.

"What the hell? I don't understand it. I picked the locks," Levi said, speaking more to himself than to Frankie. He began twisting and turning the knob and shoving his body against the door, but it would not budge. "What the hell?"

Levi and Frankie shouldered the door a few more times but eventually gave up and went back outside.

Levi grabbed his football off the grass and cocked his right arm. "Go deep Frankie!"

Levi pump-faked once and let it fly. Frankie looked back over his shoulder for the ball, but the sounds of splashing and laughter drew his attention out toward the river. There, floating without a care in the world, were two rafts full of kids. The ball hit the ground a few feet ahead of him, but he didn't seem to notice; the rafts had his attention.

"Nice catch, doofus," Levi called as he ran toward his brother, not immediately noticing the rafts or the kids riding in them.

"Hey, guys!" Called one of the rafters.

Levi's eyes drifted slowly from the back of his brother's head out toward the water. It was a girl with long dark hair in a bright yellow bikini top, and she had just snatched Levi's brain right out of his head. It wasn't as if he hadn't seen girls in bikini tops before; he and Frankie had spent countless summers at Oak Street Beach. He'd just never really noticed them until recently, and now it seemed like it was all he could think about. The drivers paddled the rafts to shore and tossed ropes out to Levi and Frankie. The brothers pulled, and the rafting party disembarked. First off was a short kid. He was thin, and he had no definable muscle structure, not unlike Frankie.

"Hey, I'm Stan Howard. This is my little brother Finn," he said, jutting a thumb.

But there was nothing little about Finn. He was maybe two inches shorter than Levi and perhaps 15 pounds lighter, but he was only in the 7th grade.

"That there is Stevie and Lonnie Johnson. They're brothers."

"Duh, Stan, what else would they be with the same last name?"

"That's my stupid sister, McKenna. They could be cousins, dummy."

McKenna folded her arms and glared at Stan. Levi guessed she was about fourteen, his age. She had curly red hair that blew across her face. The girl with the long brown hair and the yellow bikini top stood next to her and mimicked her pose.

"You're such an asshole, Stan."

"Oh, sorry, that's my sister's stupid friend, Kaylin."

"Hey," Levi gave a quick head-nod. "I'm Levi. This is my brother Frankie."

"How do you guys know, Mister Ryan?"

"Who's Mr. Ryan?"

"The guy who owns this place, dummy," said Stan.

"We own this place, dummy. My mom and dad just bought this house."

Stan's brow furrowed, and he exchanged glances with the other rafters. "You're kidding, right? I mean, you guys know about the murder house, right?"

"The what?" Frankie squeaked from behind Levi.

"Don't listen to him, Frankie. He's just screwing with us,"

Nervous glances and soft murmurs passed through the group.

Stan shook his head and exhaled hard. "Look," he pointed across the river. "See that house? A whole family was slaughtered there."

Levi raised his hand to his brow in a sloppy salute to shield his eyes from the sun. On the east bank of the Red Hook, like some antebellum relic, sat a timeworn colonial. You couldn't see the house unless you were down on the dock. The huge willows along the eastern shoreline blocked it from view up at street level.

"Big deal, it's an old abandoned house."

"An old abandoned house where a family was murdered."

"Bullshit," said Levi.

Frankie's eyes bulged, and he glanced back toward their house. Probably to make sure their mom hadn't stepped out into the yard and heard his brother swear.

"Then let's go check it out," Stan challenged.

"How are we supposed to get over there?"

"In the rafts doofus."

They might have squeezed Frankie into one of the rafts, but Levi was a big kid. Just starting high school, he was already 5'10" and 180 pounds.

"We can't all fit in those things," Levi gestured toward the rafts.

"Why don't you take your boat?" Kaylin asked, pointing toward the river.

"We don't have a bo—" The word boat trailed off as Levi spotted the weather-beaten rowboat tied to their dock.

"Where did that come from?"

"Beats me," said Frankie.

"So, what's the holdup?"

It was obvious to Levi that Stan Howard was the shot caller for this group, but Levi had never been a follower.

"That's not ours."

"Well, it's tied to your dock."

"How do we know if the thing is even safe?" Levi hoped he didn't sound as nervous as he felt.

"Is there any water in the bottom of the boat?"

Levi looked into the boat and, to his disappointment, saw that it was bone dry. "No."

"Good, then it's safe, so let's go." Stan was already walking toward his raft.

Levi was about to step down off the dock and into the boat when he stopped. "Hey, hang on. My brother can't swim."

"No problem," Stan tossed Frankie a life jacket. "Put that on, squirt."

Frankie slid into the orange jacket and cinched the strap.

"How about you? You need one?" Stanley tossed a life jacket to Levi.

"Heck no, I don't need it."

Frankie tugged at Levi's arm, "I can swim, Levi, you're the one..."

Levi glared at him. "Shut up," he said through clenched teeth. "I'll just hang on to it for you," he said to Stan.

"Whatever, let's go!"

The group shoved off and paddled across the Red Hook. As they neared the shore, McKenna noticed something floating in the water but not moving with the current.

"Hey Finn, what is that?"

"I don't know," he answered, squinting against the sunlight bouncing off the water.

"Well, get closer, so I can grab it."

Finn maneuvered the raft toward the object, and McKenna plunged her arm into the water and screamed.

***

Scott Waters kissed his wife goodbye and got into the hot car. The Wagoneer's vinyl seats were hot enough to grill a cheese sandwich, but Scott closed the door without opening the windows. At first, the heat in the car felt good. It was the kind of heat you can feel deep in your bones. But by the time he reached McKinley Avenue, it had become stifling. As he crossed the bridge, Scott lowered the windows and signaled his right onto Main Street. A man in an old Ford LTD waiting to make the left off of Main greeted Scott with a smile and a wave. Scott returned the gesture and smiled back. Merlyn's Clock Shop was four blocks down on the left at the corner of Main and Pine. As he drove, Scott Waters felt a sense of calm wash over him and his smile grew. In the distance, he could hear the sound of lawnmowers as homeowners manicured their lawns. He could hear birds singing in the trees that lined the parkway. A man was sweeping the sidewalk in front of the BGS, and all of it called to mind the old Monkeys' tune *Pleasant Valley Sunday.*

"You did it, Scott, you son-of-a-bitch, you made it," he said to himself.

Scott parked the Wagoneer, slid out, and approached the shop. He could feel the heat coming off the old wooden door even before he reached it. Scott turned the knob and stepped inside. The place smelled old, not musty but aged, like a library. As he walked, Scott ran two fingers over the surface of an antique-looking table displaying several desk clocks and marveled at how clean the place was. Not a speck of dust. Beautiful old regulators filled the walls, and grandfather clocks stood like guardians around the shop floor. Scott snaked his way past the clocks to the front counter, where a gray-haired man labored, with tiny tools, over the inner workings of a timepiece.

"Mr. Merlyn?" He asked in as soft a voice as he could manage.

"Just Merlyn, please. I'm not a magician," replied the proprietor without looking up from his work.

"Of course. My name is Scott Waters. My family and I are new to the area."

"Welcome to Red Hook, Mr. Waters," he replied, still laser-focused on his work.

"Please, call me Scott."

"Right, what can I do for you, Scott?"

Scott looked around, suddenly surprised at the silence in the clock shop. No ticking, no chiming, no music or sound of any kind.

"Sure is quiet in here."

"Yep, need quiet when you're working with gears and springs the size of a baby's eyelash. Besides, you wouldn't want to be here at noon if all the clocks were running."

"Good point," agreed Scott. "Say, I was wondering if you make house calls?"

"Sure do," he replied, finally setting the spring in place and coming up to face Scott Waters and waving a hand in the direction of the Grandfather Clocks. "Folks don't want to have to drag these monsters into the shop for repairs."

"I bet, well, we just bought the old Ryan place, and the movers did something to our grandfather clock, and now it won't work."

"Did you remove the foam blocks above the pulleys?"

"The foam blocks above what?"

Scott's face screwed up in such a way as to indicate that no further discussion on this topic was necessary.

"I can be out later this afternoon. I promised Gianna Jensen I would deliver her parents' anniversary present while they were out to dinner. I can swing by your place in a little bit if you have time."

"You know where our house is?"

"Everyone knows the old Ryan house. One of the nicest houses in town. Real shame what happened to him."

5

Nick Ryan had been back on the road for about an hour, having stopped for food and gas, when he saw a sign that read, NOW ENTERING CHESAPEAKE COUNTY. As he crossed the county line, he began to notice a change in the landscape. All along the highway to that point, the fields were full and lush. Corn as high as an elephant's eye as the saying went. But here, in Chesapeake, the corn looked a sickly gray, and it wasn't even up to his knee. And the deeper into Chesapeake County he drove, the worse the crops looked until the fields were completely bare. Patches of brown and black earth that looked more like roped scars and scabs than fields.

Nick exited I-55 at Black Horse Road and followed the signs into Chesapeake Station. As he drove, he began to notice dozens of flyers stapled to trees and fence posts and slowed to take a closer look. There was a picture of a young woman and a caption that read....

TAKEN

SEPTEMBER 1st.

JESSICA UPSHAW OF MILLBROOK,

$10,000.00 REWARD

FOR INFORMATION LEADING TO HER SAFE RETURN.

Jessica Upshaw, blonde hair pulled back in a tight ponytail, slim facial features with dark-colored eyes, looked to be in her mid-twenties. She wore a flannel shirt that gave the impression that she could be anyone's family member, but the carat plus diamond earrings she wore suggested otherwise. She obviously came from money, Nick thought, but he didn't dwell on the missing woman. He didn't have time. A short distance from the exit ramp, Nick spotted the sign and turned into the unpaved parking lot for the Pleasant View Motor Lodge. Not a typical motel, the Pleasant View Motor Lodge, was a series of tiny cabins laid out campground-style off the main house, which served as the rental office, and a small grocery store. Nick climbed out of the Bronco and stretched his back, which responded with appreciative pops and snaps. A powder blue and white Pepsi Cola vending machine that looked like something out of the '50s hummed next to the door with the small green and white ceramic sign that read OFFICE. The bell above the door to the motor lodge office jingled when he opened it, and a woman who reminded him of his mother, not so much in stature as in dress and mannerisms, welcomed him.

"Welcome to Chesapeake Station, sweetie," she said as she looked past him to the parking lot. "Are you traveling alone?" She spun the sign-in-book around to face him and placed a pen in the book's gutter.

"Yes, ma'am."

"Bet you came to see John Henry?"

"Who's John Henry?"

"John Henry's not a who, dear, John Henry's a what. Our old Steamer?"

Nick cocked his head. "Your old what?"

"Steam-powered locomotive, dear, it's one of the oldest in the country."

"No. I—"

"Well, you're 2 months too late for the Pickle Festival," she said, interrupting him. "And a good month too early for the Fall Harvest Festival, though I suppose we will be forgoing that again this year," her welcoming smile faded.

"No, ma'am, I'm here to study the disappearance of people that used to live around here."

The woman's eyes widened. It was only for a moment, but Nick caught it. She looked frightened.

"Oh! Well, I don't know nothin' about that," she said, offering a nervous smile. "So you're a policeman?"

"No, nothing like that. I'm working on my doctoral dissertation."

"Well, that sounds pretty interesting," though it sounded like innerestin.

"Yeah, so If I can get some privacy?"

"Tell you what, I'm gonna put you in cabin number 11. That's all the way down toward the end, and there ain't no one in 9 or 10, so it should be nice and quiet for you. Now, if you should need anything at all, you just dial 0 on your room phone, and me or Phil, that my husband; we'll be at your service. We live right here on the property," she gave a quick head tilt toward the door behind her, so it's no bother, no matter what time it is. We'll be more than happy to help. My name is Margie Reuss, by the way," she spun the book back to face her. "Nick Ryan, say, that is a nice name."

"Thank you, ma'am."

"The room is $45.00 per night, and we offer a weekly rate of $40.00 per night but don't you worry, we can square up when you're ready to check out, Mister Ryan."

"Just Nick, if you don't mind," he said and thanked her.

He'd been living in Chicago for the past 4 years and forgot how friendly strangers could be. Hell, he barely knew the people who lived on his floor, let alone the other eighteen stories in his apartment building. There were a handful of people on campus that he knew well enough to say hello to, and that was more than enough for him. Nick Ryan had never been one to cultivate friendships. His work kept him busy, and he was good with that.

As he turned to leave, he stopped. "Can you point me toward a restaurant?"

"Well," she tapped her pointer finger against her lips to give the impression that she was giving it a good, hard think. "The Country Dumplin' is about the best place around, just up the road, and turn left at the first stop. You can't miss it. Good home-style cooking, none of that pre-made slop like they serve at the Triumph Diner. Now you take my advice and avoid that place like the plague, or you might just end up with it," Margie smiled and chuckled to herself.

Nick thanked her again and headed to his cabin to freshen up. The motor lodge grounds were immaculate, not a thing out of place. Each little cabin was painted in a different pastel color, with a large front window decorated with lace curtains. A flower box hung just below the window, and each cabin had a small café' table and two chairs set beneath the flower box. Nick walked the concrete path to his cabin and turned the knob without thinking, and the door opened, *not even locked,* he thought and rolled his eyes. Inside there were two twin-sized beds and another small table with two chairs near the window. Across the small room was an even smaller bathroom with a stand-up shower. Opposite the beds was a wood-burning stove, probably how they heated the rooms in the winter months. No frills, but he didn't need frills, just a place to sleep and work.

Nick looked around for a phone jack to connect his computer to dial-up. He found a black, rotary dial phone on the nightstand between the beds and pushed it aside. "Shit," it was hardwired into the wall, so he couldn't access the internet. Not a big deal considering there wasn't much on the world-wide-web about the Mooka'am, but still, it would have been nice to have access. A slight chill ran the length of his spine. It would be *his* work that future generations, those curious about the Mooka'am, would be looking up online. At least he thought they would if the web actually caught on.

He gave his face and neck a good scrubbing in the bathroom sink and put on an old Property of Red Hook High School Athletic Department T-shirt. The navy blue faded to a sort of slate blue, and the once bright crimson lettering looked more orange. It had a few holes in it, but it was still his favorite shirt. Besides, he thought his biceps looked bitchin in the tight sleeves. He changed out of his dress pants and shoes. Nick threw on a pair of jeans and well-worn work boots and exhaled long and satisfied as he wiggles his toes and felt their familiar comfort.

Nick grabbed his laptop and locked the door behind him. Nothing but some clothes and toiletries left in the room, but old habits die hard. Still, he felt a little guilty and considered going back to unlock it, but he was already in the Bronco, and besides, who would be going to his room to check? Turning the key in the ignition, the truck fired up, and he was headed out of the parking lot, awkwardly returning Margie's wave before turning left and heading down Black Horse Road. He must have been flipping through songs on his Sony Discman when he rolled right through the second stop sign. He hadn't realized it, but by the time he looked back up, he was past his turn. Nick kept driving until he saw a sign for the Triumph Diner. He considered Margie's warning, but he was starving, and he needed some grub. He pulled into one of the diagonal parking spots out front and walked into the diner.

Another door and another jingle from the bell mounted above it. The place reminded him of the No Finer Diner back in Red Hook. Red vinyl chairs and booths, and a long lunch counter. Nick looked at his watch; it was 4:30. A little too late for the lunch crowd and a little too early for the dinner rush, the place was almost empty.

"Sit anywhere you like, sweetie," called the waitress.

Nick plopped himself down in a booth. The waitress had a deep tan, long legs, and long blonde hair that she didn't bother to put up. She wore a tight gray shirt with a cartoon mouse stretched tightly across her ample but not too ample chest. As tight as her shirt was, it looked like a comfort cut compared to her shorts. Shorts that were so short that the front pockets hung out below the hem-line. She stood in front of him, open-mouth chewing a wad of gum. Nick couldn't help but stare.

"Like what you see?"

Her voice called him out of his trance. "What? No, I was just—"

"Name's Babe, and I'll be taking care of you. What'll it be, darlin'?"

"Babe?"

"The only thing Abraham Adams loved more than mama was baseball."

Nick nodded, "Babe Ruth, I get it."

"Babe Adams," she said with a wink, "but yeah."

"Well, it's a pretty cool name."

"Ya think? Just try to find a pair of mouse ears with Babe on them. No easy task, I can tell you."

"A pair of...?"

Babe waved her hand back and forth across her chest.

"Right, mouse ears."

"Say, what happened there? Bar fight?" Babe asked, passing her finger back and forth over her own cheek to make her meaning clear.

"Oh, that? That's nothing."

"Nothing, huh?" Babe regarded him with lighthearted suspicion. "So, what can I get you?"

"How's your cheeseburger?"

"Fine, how's yours?" Babe said and laughed.

"You get to use that a lot?"

"Not as much as you would think," she winked and gave him a little hip check on his upper arm. "Medium?"

"Um, medium-well, lettuce, tomato, grilled onions, and cheddar if you have it."

"Fries and a Coke?"

"Do you have root beer?"

"You bet we do, root beer, cream soda, Green River, and all the regular stuff."

"Root beer and fries," Nick said.

Babe tapped her pencil on her order pad. "Back in a jiff."

Nick watched her walk away but did his best to be cool about it. She was a little older than he was, probably closer to thirty, but with a sort of retro 1950s, American Beauty look about her. She reminded him of someone, but he couldn't put his finger on it. He shrugged the question away, flipped open his laptop, and scrolled over to the folder marked Chesapeake Station. Nick stopped on the tab marked Chesapeake Station Historical Society and clicked on it. The screen filled with more folders, and he clicked on the one marked Address and Contact. That file contained all he needed to make contact with Colt Cooper, president of the society, everything but a way to access his dial-up internet connection. He looked at his watch again, almost five o'clock. Odds were good that the historical society would be closed before he finished eating.

"Excuse me, um, Babe?" Nick called across the nearly empty restaurant. He felt strange, using such a familiar term with a perfect stranger.

"Be right there, sweetie," she bounced back over, chewing and popping the wad of gum. "What do ya need?"

"Can you tell me where your local historical society's office is?" Nick asked as he scrolled through the saved files and stopped on an article he wanted to finish reading.

"Down at the Chesapeake Station Depot. They moved over there from the library after the remodeling. They're open till 7 tonight."

Nick's jaw dropped a little.

"I know, all this and brains too," she said with a coy smile. She popped a bubble and fluttered her lashes.

"No! Not at all," he said.

She frowned and put her hands on her hips.

"No! That's not what I meant," Nick stammered.

"Relax, sweetie, I'm just giving you a hard time. Say, where are you from, anyway?

"A little town called Red Hook."

"Never heard of it."

"I'm not surprised," Nick said, and turned his attention back toward his laptop.

"You got family there?"

"What?" Nick was getting annoyed but tried to be polite. He loathed chit-chat. To Nick, small-talk was as annoying as a mosquito buzzing around his ear.

"Family, you know, a mom, dad, brothers or sisters."

"Sorry, I'm just trying to finish this article," he said, hoping Babe would take the hint.

But she didn't. She stood there bright-eyed and chomping away on her gum. "So?"

"No, no family." He said curtly.

"Girlfriend?"

Nick couldn't pretend any longer. He pushed himself away from his computer and sucked in some wind to let her have it when the cook's bell rang.

"Hey, Betty Boop, order up!"

She smiled, sprung up on her tiptoes, and popped her bottom like a 1930's flapper.

"Be right back, doll," she said, in her best Boop voice.

The annoyance that Nick had been feeling like a tingling at the back of his neck vanished as he suddenly flashed back to hot summers working on cars with his grandfather. "That's it!"

Babe stopped in her tracks. "What's it?"

"I just thought of who you remind me of."

"And who might that be?"

"Betty Brosmer."

"Betty, who?" Babe tilted her head.

"Brosmer, my grandfather had her picture in his garage. More the face than the body," Nick's inner dialogue was slipping out as commentary.

"Hmm, you don't say."

"Not that there's anything wrong with your body!"

"Well, thank you," said Babe with a look that Nick read as confusion.

"She was a pin-up girl back in the '50s."

The little voice in Nick's head was screaming, '*abort, abort, abort!*'

"Okay," Babe said, sounding more like a question than a statement.

"I mean, I'm just saying you have a body... and Betty Brosmer... she had a body," Nick was stammering.

"Sweetie, a bit of advice?"

Nick swallowed hard and nodded.

"My daddy always said that the first step to getting out of a hole was to put down the shovel."

Nick nodded, shut his mouth, and the cook rang the bell again.

"Babe! Your order's up!"

She gave Nick a wink, and he knew he was off the hook. "Be right back, sweetie."

Nick just shook his head. He felt stupid. He supposed it said something about him, that he even recalled the pin-up's face. Betty Brosmer was beautiful; he doubted there was a person alive who would argue that, but that wasn't what she was known for. She was the girl with the impossibly tiny waist. Nick had spent many days and quite a few nights thinking about that tiny waist and the territories north and south. Babe returned with his order, interrupting his train of thought.

"Here you go, sweetie."

"Look," Nick said. "I'm not some kind of creep or something; I'm actually working on my doctoral dissertation," he said, smiling proudly.

"Well, that's just fine as frog's hair," she said, affecting a thick drawl.

Nick got the message. "Sorry, that came off snooty. I'm just saying that I didn't mean anything by the Betty Brosmer comment.

"Not to worry," she assured him. "I can banter with the best of them."

"Say, can I—" He was going to say, ask you a question, but a loud crash from the kitchen cut him off.

Babe set his plate down on the table, "Sorry, sweetie, be right back."

Nick slid his laptop aside and moved the plate front and center. The burger was huge, a real two-hander, and he took a bite. Warm juice slid down his chin, and the flavor exploded in his mouth. Hooked from the very first bite, Margie didn't know what the hell she was talking about. Nick hadn't had a burger that good since he was a kid, and his dad grilled them over the coals on the Weber back home. In fact, this burger put his old man's burger to shame. By the time Babe made it back to check on him, Nick had almost finished his burger and was halfway through his fries.

"Sorry about that, sweetie, he's a good cook, but he's all thumbs when it comes to doing dishes. Did you need anything else? It sounded like you were going to ask for something."

Nick looked up at her, his mouth still full of french-fries, and gave her a wave suggesting that she need not worry.

"Hope everything's to your liking," she said, with what Nick could only assume was her most flirtatious smile.

He swallowed and smiled back. "Babe, this is the best burger I've ever had. My compliments to the chef."

Babe smiled. "Artie, a chef? Hey Artie! This guy called you a chef!"

"Finally, some respect," said the gravelly voice from the kitchen.

"Can I ask you something?" Nick asked.

"Anything, sweetie."

"Have you lived here all your life?"

Babe gave a sharp nod. "Chesapeake Station, born and raised up into the woman you see before you."

"Have you ever heard of the Mooka'am? Like I said, I'm working on publishing a paper on them and..."

The color faded from her face. "Mister. Um..."

"Nick, Nick Ryan," he offered.

"Sorry, Mister Ryan, I can't help you," she said, glancing around nervously.

"If there's nothing else," Babe ripped the bill from her pad and placed it on the table.

The one-eighty in Babe's demeanor threw Nick, and for a moment, he didn't know quite how to respond. The lady at the motel didn't bat an eye when he mentioned the Mooka'am, and he was almost sure he had. *Hadn't he?*

"I'm sorry, did I say something wrong?" Nick asked in a whisper.

Her face softened. "Sorry, sweetie, that's just not something we talk about here."

"I don't understand," said a perplexed Nick Ryan.

"If that's what you are going to the historical society for, you can forget it. Babe looked around and lowered her voice to a whisper. "They won't tell you anything more than what I'm assuming you already think you know."

Nick's brow furrowed. "Sounds like *you* could tell me more."

"You said that you're a writer?"

"Well, I'm working on a paper that will be published, yes."

Babe glanced around, "I get off at 7, write down where you're staying, and I'll stop by."

More than a little perplexed, Nick wrote *Pleasant View Motor Lodge, room 11,* on the back of the bill and handed it back to Babe.

"You can pay me here, sweetie," she said, looking around as some of the regulars started filing into the diner.

Nick handed her ten dollars and told her to keep the change. Babe folded the check and stuck it in her tight front pocket, and carried the money off to the register. Nick walked out to the Bronco, still puzzled by Babe's response. All the research that had been done on the Mooka'am suggested that they were simple farming people who never really made a mark in history. There was nothing to suggest that they were great warriors, like the Apache, nor were they known to have any great tribal leaders, like Red Cloud or Sitting Bull of the Lakota Nation. Just a simple people whose existence might have gone entirely unnoticed by the modern world if not for a few letters discovered among artifacts uncovered by a team of anthropologists and archaeologists studying the tribes of the Illinois Confederacy. The letters, which made brief reference to the Mooka'am, had been written by Jesuit missionaries around the time of the Great War that saw the end of the Illinois Confederacy.

Nick drove into town and spent some time scouring the old microfiche films at the local library. Try as he might, he couldn't find a single article on the Mooka'am. At closing time, Nick made his way back to his cabin. He laid back on one of the beds and kicked his boots off. History was full of mysterious disappearances; Amelia Earhart, D.B. Cooper, the lost colony at Roanoke, but how many colonies or tribes like the Mooka'am may have wholly escaped notice. No one to know that they lived and died, not mattering to anyone once they were gone. No stone to mark their graves, no mention in of them in the history books. It seemed a great tragedy to Nick that a people could come and go without notice. Suddenly, he felt a tremendous weight, an enormous burden of responsibility. He was an anthropologist. That made finding the Mooka'am and securing their place in history his cross to bear. But how was he supposed to do that? *Could it be that a waitress in a diner in the middle of nowhere knew something all of the researchers had missed?* Nick didn't see how that was possible? His train of thought was derailed by a knock on his door.

6

"What the hell are you screaming about?" Stan Howard asked. McKenna stared at the stuffed giraffe. "The water, it's freezing."

"You're high. It's almost a hundred degrees out. The water can't be less than seventy degrees," Stan said, as he shoved his hand into the water to prove his point.

"See, warm as piss."

McKenna stuck her hand back into the water. "I don't understand it. I swear, guys, it was a cold as ice a minute ago. It felt like needles going into my hand."

"Give me some of what you're smoking, dude."

"Shut up, Lonnie, you burnout," snapped Kaylin.

The rowboat's bottom scraped along the gravel as Levi ran aground. The two rafts followed, and the travelers climbed out. Like the west bank of the river, the shore was mostly sand and pea-gravel, but unlike the Waters's well-kept lawn, this property looked like it hadn't seen a lawnmower in years. The path leading to the house was overgrown with tall fescue and burweed that grabbed and scraped their legs as they walked. Even in the bright afternoon sun, the house up ahead looked like something dreamt up in a nightmare. Sun choked slat board planks wrapped themselves around the two-story colonial, looking like exposed ribs, and every window on the river-facing side of the house had been broken. Curtains sun-burnt and yellowed floated like ghosts in the windows on the second floor, and the back door stood open a crack as if it were inviting unsuspecting travelers

47

inside.

"Bet I can put a rock through the attic window," Stanley Howard said.

Stevie Johnson made a sun-visor with his hands and looked up at the gable. "No friggin way, you can throw that high, Stan."

"Wanna bet?"

"Hell yeah, I got fifty cents that says you can't do it."

"I want in on that action," said Lonnie Johnson, digging deep into the pocket of his cut-off jean shorts.

"You're on dick-head," said Stan, picking up a goose egg-sized rock and rearing back to take his shot, and then he froze. "Where the hell did that thing come from?"

A massive soot-colored raven sat perched in the window frame of the gable.

"That's one big-ass bird," said Stevie.

Stan set his bead on the old passerine and chucked the rock. It sailed into the air and struck the slat board two feet below the gable.

"Stan, you ass, you could have hit that old bird!"

The rock hit the wall with a solid crack, but the raven paid it no mind.

"Don't worry about it Kaylin, he's lucky he even hit the house," Finn said.

Stevie and Lonnie doubled over in laughter, which pissed Stan off, more than missing the bird.

"Yeah, big shot? Let's see what you got!" He challenged his brother.

"Finn, don't you dare," McKenna said sternly.

Finn hemmed and hawed, but it seemed the pressure was too much to bear when Stevie and Lonnie laid into him. Finn grabbed a rock and hurled it at the old gray bird. His arm was stronger, but his aim was as piss-poor as his brother's. The rock struck the roof next to the gable, and still, the bird did not react. The laughter resumed, and the mocking picked up.

"How about you, new kid?" Lonnie challenged.

McKenna and Kaylin both folded their arms and exhaled, clearly exasperated by the stupidity of the male of their species.

"I'm not going to hit a bird with a rock. That's stupid," said Levi.

"Because you know you can't," said Stevie, and soon Lonnie, Stan, and

Finn all joined in.

Hearing the guys tease his brother, Frankie came to his defense.

"He could too hit it! Go on, Levi, show em."

Levi glanced at Kaylin, who just shook her head. Then he looked at Frankie and saw the confidence in his little brother's eyes.

"How about if I hit the gable above its head?"

"Hell," said Lonnie, "Finn can do that. Hit the bird!"

Levi shook his head, picked up a stone, and pegged the bird right in the center of its chest. The rock clattered down the roof and onto the ground, but still, the bird sat there.

"Holy crap! Great shot," Lonnie held the sides of his head as if he'd just had his mind blown.

Stevie joined his brother; "Yeah! You gotta go out for the baseball team."

"Hey, Stan, how come the bird didn't fly away?" Finn asked.

"Maybe It's dead," said Stevie.

"It's not dead stupid; it's fake," said Stan. "If it was dead, it would have fallen over. That was a solid hit. The feet have to be nailed to the window frame. Probably the stupid upperclassmen."

"Yeah, it was," the rest of the guys agreed.

"I guess it is fake," said Levi, sounding relieved.

No sooner were the words out of his mouth when the big black bird slowly and deliberately turned its head and fixed its eye on Levi Waters. The whole gang jumped back.

"Holy shit!" Stan exclaimed. "That scared the shit out of me," he clasped his hands on his knees and bent over laughing.

"That's it, Stan, we're out of here," Lonnie said.

"Come on, I knew you were a wuss, Lonnie Johnson, and so is your brother."

"I'm no wuss," said Stevie.

"Good, then let's go in." Stan was like a strange little general, leading his troops into the unknown. "Who's with me?"

Levi was still watching the bird watching him.

"Come on, Levi, it's just a dumb bird," said Stan. "The thing was too stupid to move after you pegged it!"

Levi moved forward, and the bird's eye moved with him.

"Well, we aren't going in that stupid house," said McKenna, speaking both for herself and Kaylin.

"Suit yourself. Maybe the old bird up there will swoop down and peck your eye out of your stupid head," said Stan.

The girls looked at one another and followed a few steps behind the boys as they made their way toward the house. By now, the bird's head was turned sideways and down as it watched Levi Waters pass below. Even for a bird, the movement looked unnatural. Levi tried to ignore it, but he could feel the bird's eye following him.

Stan reached the door and turned the knob. The door screeched on rusted hinges but opened to receive its guests. They stepped into the small mudroom and then to the kitchen.

"Welcome to the murder house," said Stan.

The kitchen was old, dusty, and cobweb-covered, but otherwise just an average kitchen.

"What happened here?" Frankie asked timidly.

"Some guy went nuts and murdered his family," said Stan.

"How?" Levi was surprised by his brother's question.

"What do you mean, how? He blew their heads off with a shotgun."

"How do you know?"

"We really don't know," said McKenna. It's just what we heard from the older kids."

"Yeah, we do. I saw pictures."

"No, you didn't, liar," McKenna challenged.

"Well, I didn't, but I know a kid that did."

"Bullshit," said Lonnie.

"Whatever," Stan said, dismissing the doubters.

"Man, I thought there would be blood all over the place," Stevie Johnson said.

They expected to find the whole place painted in dried blood based on the rumors they had all heard, but it wasn't like that. It was just a house.

Abandoned and run-down, wallpaper hanging like ancient scrolls halfway down the walls, and it smelled a little dank and musty, but that was all. They walked through the whole first floor and found nothing more frightening than a spider in its web in the door jam leading from the hallway into the living room. The group made their way upstairs and walked into what had been the parent's room. Frankie was the first to see the faded red stain on the wall near the bed.

"Look," he whispered and pointed.

The whole group gasped.

"Damn, there really was a murder here," said Finn.

"See, I told you!" Stan said, almost indignantly.

"Okay," said Kaylin, "we've seen the bloodstain. Can we please get the hell out of here?"

"Hang on," said Stan. "There's just two more rooms up here. We can't leave without checking them out."

"The hell we can't," said McKenna, still holding the little stuffed giraffe in her hand.

"Shut up and come on," Stan said. "It'll only take a minute."

The floor creaked under their feet and gave them a slight start, but the next room was just a room. It looked like a study, there were bookshelves but few books, and the ones that remained were strewn about the floor. All-in-all a pretty dull room. They moved down the hall, and Stan pushed open the door to the last room. It was a child's room with a rocking chair in one corner and a small bed against the wall near the room's only window. A dresser and an empty toy box, but that was it. McKenna walked over and stood next to the toy box.

"Guys, I don't think we should be in here," she said, and then she screamed. "Son-of-a-bitch!"

McKenna dropped the giraffe and looked at three small puncture marks in her hand. She remembered a similar injury when she was younger and went fishing with her dad. She caught a sunfish, and in her hurry to free it from her line and toss it back into the water, she grabbed over the top of its dorsal fin and took the tines in her hand.

"That's it, Stan, we are out of here." McKenna turned and stormed down the stairs.

"You're a real jackass Stanley Howard," said Kaylin as she followed her friend.

"What? What did I do?"

"Yeah, McKenna's right. We shouldn't be here," said Finn, and he followed down the stairs.

Lonnie, and Stevie, looked at one another, shrugged their shoulders, and followed Finn. Stan hung his head in exasperation, and he and the Waters boys made their way down to the first floor and out the door. As Levi stepped back into the yard, he could feel the crow's eye on him.

"Frankie, is that crow still staring at me?"

Frankie looked up and confirmed his big brother's fear.

"I'm sorry I made you throw that rock Levi," whispered Frankie.

"You didn't make me throw it, Frankie; I'm in high school, I'm responsible for my actions. Isn't that what dad always says?"

"Yeah, I guess, but I'm still sorry."

They followed the group to the shore.

"Nice going, dumb ass. You didn't drag your boat far enough out of the water."

Levi had enough and moved toward Stan, with fists balled up and his chest expanding as he drew in a deep breath. Frankie grabbed his brother's arm.

"No, Levi, don't, you'll hurt him."

Stan's eyes looked like saucers, "easy big guy, I was just kidding."

Levi exhaled loudly, and so did the rest of the group as Stan avoided a beating.

"But seriously, man, your boat, it's gone."

They looked downriver, expecting to see it floating away, but it really was gone.

"Great," said Levi. "Now what?"

Stan, eager to rebuild some goodwill, offered a solution. "You wait here. We'll take Frankie back in our boat and then come back for you."

"No," protested Frankie. You can't stay here, Levi."

Levi placed his hand on Frankie's shoulder. "I'll be fine, you go ahead, and I'll wait right here."

Frankie didn't move.

"Go on, Frankie, you go back with them, and I'll be right there."

The rest were already loaded into the rafts, and Frankie climbed aboard the Howard's raft.

"You guys take care of my little brother."

They pushed off, and Stan called back. "He'll be fine, just wait right there, and we'll be back."

Levi watched as the rafts pushed upriver, where they would eventually let the current carry them back. As he watched, he heard what sounded like a child crying. He shook it off, sure he imagined it, but it only grew louder. The sound was coming from the house, and the child sounded scared. Levi took off at a dead run, forgetting for the moment about the crow, the murders, or anything else.

He paused as he entered the kitchen. The cries were coming from the second floor, and Levi sprinted up the stairs and followed the sound back into the child's room. It was coming from under the bed. Levi bent over with one hand on the soiled mattress and one on the floor to steady himself. He moved the dirty old dust ruffle and peeked beneath the bed. It was black as pitch under the bed, but in the sparse light that spilled through the window, Levi could see the stuffed giraffe that McKenna had dropped near the door. He reached his arm into the darkness, pushed the giraffe aside, and a pair of pale eyes stared back at him.

"It's okay, come on out, I can help you."

Levi felt a cold, wet hand swipe at the back of his neck and spun on his ass, but there was nothing there. He placed his hand on the back of his neck, making sure that he had just imagined it, but his neck was still wet. Levi spun and darted in a crab-walked toward the door. He was breathing hard, trying to calm himself, determined to get the kid out from under the bed, but when he looked again, the little boy was gone, and so was the purple giraffe. Levi looked around in a panic and then bolted out of the room. As he made his way out, he heard a scratching sound from above and looked up to see the old gray crow watching him through a hole through the roof. Levi ran down the stairs, out the back door, and down to the river. He was in past his knees before he remembered that he couldn't swim. Levi scrambled to the shore and glanced nervously from the river to the house as he watched for the raft to return. He looked upriver and saw a foot-bridge about a quarter-mile away and took off running for it.

"Hey!" Stan yelled from the raft. "Where are you going?"

Levi stopped. Stan and Finn were paddling upriver to catch the current back.

"I was just trying to make it easier," Levi offered.

"Well, you're not, so just stay put!"

Levi stopped and looked back at the house. The crow had returned to the gable. That made Levi feel a little better, but he still needed desperately to get back to his side of the river.

"Come on, guys," he whispered to himself.

7

Nick opened the door and held tight to the knob as he took her in. She was the same girl he'd seen at the diner, but something was different. Maybe it was the way the soft purple of the evening sky danced at the tips of her hair, or perhaps it was the fullness of her lips. He hadn't noticed it earlier, probably because she never stopped talking or chewing that wad of gum. Whatever the case, he certainly noticed it now. There was a tenderness in her face, a tenderness that belied her body. He didn't want to, but he couldn't help himself. Nick's eyes fell from her lips to the round flesh of her breasts that peeked up and over the sloping neckline of her mid-drift tank-top. From there, his eyes found her tan, firm, but not too firm stomach. Just the slightest swell to show that it would be soft and nice to touch. She had exchanged her too-tight shorts for too-tight jeans and a loose-fitting brown leather belt with a peace sign belt buckle. Nick's high school brain imagined pulling that belt like a starter cord on a mower and then leaning back as he watched her peel the jeans down over the curve of her hips.

"You done eye-banging me?"

"What? I wasn't."

"Bullshit, you *wasn't*."

Nick blushed.

"Eye-banging is going to have to wait. We gotta go."

Nick swallowed hard. "Go, go where?"

Babe looked from side to side and then back over her shoulder toward the office of the Pleasant View Motel.

"What's wrong?" Nick could tell that she was nervous.

"Nothing, nothing's wrong. Come on, there's someone you need to meet," Babe said and licked her lips.

Nick read it not as a seductive act but as the act of an anxious person with a dry mouth. An act that made Nick very uncomfortable.

"Why didn't you just bring them here?"

Babe's eyes darted from side to side again, and she forced a smile that made Nick's asshole tighten. "Because it's not safe," she whispered, her tone ripe with urgency.

Something wasn't right, but Nick couldn't put his finger on it. He was about to call the whole thing off. Then he thought of Jinan Bondiani. Five-foot-six, 120 pounds soaking wet, but as battle-tested as they came. From the frozen lands of Oymyakon, Russia, where the temperature in the winter averages 40 degrees below zero, to the rain forests of Papua New Guinea, where the temperature wouldn't kill you, but the cannibals might. Jinan embedded herself in some of the most dangerous places on earth in her pursuit of research. Nick shook his head. Here he was, six-foot-two, 225 pounds of lean muscle and afraid of a girl, a girl smaller than Jinan.

Come on, Nick, man up! If you can't do fieldwork, you have no business in anthropology. He decided that he would ignore the butterflies in his stomach and head out into the unknown with this complete stranger. "In for a penny, in for a pound."

"What?" Babe asked.

"Nothing. We taking your car?"

"Let's take yours. I've always wanted to ride in one of those."

"Whatever you say."

"A man who knows his place; I like that," Babe said with a smile.

Nick was glad that she wanted him to drive. It gave him a greater sense of control. Babe popped into the passenger's seat of the Bronco and clicked her seatbelt, the strap crossing tightly between her breasts. Nick couldn't help but notice as he climbed in and fired up the engine.

"Head back toward the diner. I'll tell you where to go from there and keep your eyes on the road," she said with a smirk. "Swear you'd never seen a pair of tits before."

"I—"

Babe waved the back of her hand dismissively. "Just drive, pervert," she said, her smile widening.

Nick offered an uneasy smile in return and pulled out of the parking lot. Gravel crunched under the Bronco's tires as they drove out past the office.

***

Margie Reuss snapped the blinds shut. Lifted one of the slats and peeked out. Phil, Margie's husband of more years than either of them cared to recall, adjusted the rabbit-ears on top of his trusty old 19-inch RCA.

"Margie, dammit, woman; didn't I tell you not to fiddle with the ears?"

She didn't answer him. Margie was busy scratching something down on a piece of paper. Phil murmured and cursed as he worked to dial in the Cardinal's game. When the picture finally stopped running, he plopped himself down on a couch and pulled his TV tray over. He peeled back the foil on his Hungry-Man fried chicken TV dinner and stuck his finger in the mashed potatoes.

"Damn-it Margie, the mashed potatoes are cold!"

"Well, they wouldn't be if you hadn't fooled with that television for so long."

"I wouldn't have to fool with it if you would just leave the damn thing alone! What are you doing anyway?"

"I was watching our new guest, Mr. Ryan," she said, sliding into the doorway that connected the motel officer to their living quarters. "He just left with Babe, that little hussy from the Triumph diner."

"Good for him, now mind your own business and heat up these potatoes!"

"Heat up your own damn potatoes," she snapped, and then is a softer voice. "Phil, honey, he said that he's down here looking into missing people."

Phil set his knife down and regarded his wife. "He said that? He said, looking into missing people?"

"Uh-huh."

"Well, did he mention the Upshaw woman?"

"No, not in so many words."

Phil stroked his chin. "Well, maybe you should put a call into Sheriff Tucker, just to be safe."

***

Cyrus Tucker answered the phone on the second ring. "Tucker, here," he said, speaking through a mouth full of food. Like Phil, he too was plopped in front of his television, working on a TV dinner. He listened a moment and chased his Salisbury steak with a swig from a beer bottle.

"Sheriff, this is Margie over at the Pleasant View."

"What do you want, Margie?" He said, sounding perturbed. "I'm trying to watch the game—son-of-a-bitch!" Tucker exploded. Mark Grace sent one out of the park on a Rich DeLucia change-up.

"Well, I'm sorry to bother you, Sheriff, but I have a young man staying with us."

"Yeah, so what?" Cyrus Tucker slammed his bottle of bear down on the tin tray with a bang.

"Tighten your shit up, DeLucia!"

"Sheriff, he said he's here about a missing person," she said and paused. "Or was it missing people?"

"Well, which was it?" Tucker barked into the phone.

"People," she said, trying to sound confident. "Missing people."

"What did he look like; did he look like a Fed?"

"I don't know, I mean—well, he looked kind of," she paused, groping for the right word. "Normal, I guess."

"What the hell does that mean? You mean normal for a Fed or normal for a pig butcher?"

"Just normal, like a regular person."

"Christ-almighty, woman."

"Sheriff, do you think he's here about the Upshaw girl?"

"How the hell should I know," Tucker clamped a meaty palm onto his forehead and massaged it with his fat fingers. "Son-of-a-bitch, we sure as shit don't need any Feds snooping around. Not now. It's almost time!"

58

"That's why I decided to call, Sheriff."

"Well, you did the right thing, Margie. Could have been a little more inquisitive, though."

"And Sheriff, there's one more thing. He had a visitor to his room," Margie said and paused.

Tucker waited a full five seconds. "Cripes Margie, am I supposed to guess?" Tucker barked.

"Babe, from the Triumph. Little hussy," she muttered the latter under her breath. "She must have left her car on the road cause I don't see it in the lot."

"What's he driving?"

"It's a blue car or truck thing. No top on it."

"You mean like a Jeep?"

"I guess; I was focused on something else. I got the license plate number. I wrote it on a slip of paper so I wouldn't forget it." There was a lilt of satisfaction in her voice.

"What the hell am I supposed to do with that?"

"Well, don't you have some kind of computer that can tell you who owns the car?"

"Three problems with that, Margie," he held up three sausage-like fingers and folded them down as he listed them off. "First of all, we already know his name, unless you were too stupid to have him sign the register,"

"Well, no, I—of course, I had him—"

"Second of all," he said rolling another pudgy digit down on itself. "If he is with the feds, the car ain't going to register to the F.B.I. cause I'm sure they don't put their agents in Jeeps."

"No, I don't suppose they do."

"And third, if I run that plate, there is going to be a record of me running it. And let's just suppose your guest meets with some unfortunate accident while visiting our beautiful little town. Now, how's that going to look, me running his plate before his—accident?"

"I'm sorry, Sheriff, I—"

Tucker cut her off with an airy burp, "I'll send a car out to the river," he said and hung up without so much as a thank you or a goodbye.

Tucker thumbed the receiver cradle and punched in the number to the station, careful not to mash more than one button at a time. The phone at the sheriff's office jumped to life in the empty building. After eight rings, Tucker slammed the receiver down and chuffed, like some great bellow stoking a blast furnace. "Son-of-a-bitch. It's getting to be where a man can't enjoy a game without bullshit starting up." The fat old sheriff shoved his TV tray aside. "So-help-me boy, if you're snoozing somewhere, this one's going to cost you some ass flesh."

Tucker pushed out of his chair with a chorus of grunts, uttering several more curse words, and lumbered across his living room. The buttons on his uninspired tan uniform shirt fought to hold back the massive gut that cascaded over his belt buckle, and the laces of his untied boots dragged on the floor as they had for the better part of twelve years. Tucker stomped out to his patrol car and opened the door where no less than a dozen pine tree air fresheners hung from the rearview mirror in a failed attempt to hide the smell of the food that had fallen to the floor over the years and had been left to rot.

The springs and tie rods on the old Crown Vic prowler, something he put on more than got into, groaned as he settled his fat ass onto a driver's seat. A seat that had been flattened by years of abuse. He started the car and made no attempt to fasten his seatbelt. It had been more than a decade since the strap had been able to make the trip around his massive gut.

Tucker grabbed his police radio and keyed up. "Abernathy, come in."

The radio crackled. "Go ahead, Sheriff."

"Where the hell you been, boy?"

"Sorry, Sheriff, I was out to the pumps for gas."

"Well, get your ass out to Consumption River. Margie from the motel called. She said some guy from out of town is snooping around with that bitch from the Triumph Diner."

"Copy that sheriff, on my way."

Tucker hated his job, mostly because he hated being bothered, but since he'd already gotten into the car, he decided he might as well head out to the lake to make sure Abernathy didn't screw anything up. He flicked on the AM radio and tuned in the game so he could listen as he drove.

8

Without asking, Babe reached over and flipped on the radio. Beautiful Girls by Van Halen came on midway through the first chorus, and she turned it up. Nick turned to chew her out. He hated it when people messed with his radio. His mouth fell open, but nothing came out. Babe had her eyes closed as she bobbed her head rhythmically to the music. There was a gentle breeze that blew her hair across her face, and Nick couldn't speak. She was probably the hottest girl at Chesapeake Station High, he thought.

"Nick!"

He snapped out of his daydream just in time to keep from blowing the stop sign.

"Oh my God, you are the worst driver!"

"No, I was just—"

"Turn left here," she said, rolling her eyes.

It wouldn't have been the first time he'd blown that stop sign. The turn took him out past the Country Dumplin'.

"Hey! That's the place Margie, the lady at the motel, recommended, but I must have missed the turn and ended up at your place."

"Imagine that," Babe said, the words dripping with sarcasm.

"Hey, I'm a good driver."

"I'm sure you are. Take the next right, sweetie," Babe said, smiling softly.

Nick signaled. "Where are we going anyway?"

"You'll see."

"Can't you just tell me?" Nick was doing his best not to sound nervous.

"You said you wanted to know about the Mooka'am, well, I'm taking you to see a friend of mine. He's an expert on the subject."

"And he lives out here?"

"Not exactly," she said cryptically.

"Then where are we going??"

"Nick, sweetie, just shut up and drive," her soft smile never fading.

After about half an hour, they arrived at a dirt road cut into a row of towering Blue Spruce. Perhaps sixty feet tall and almost twenty feet wide at the base, the grove of trees planted by the Cavanaugh family generations ago provided a perfect barrier from the once heavily traveled road. Nick breathed in the combination of river water and fresh pine.

"I love that smell. It reminds me of home."

"Enjoy it while you can, sweetie."

"Why's that?" Nick asked, but Babe didn't need to answer. Just beyond the trees, the smell hit him. A pungent cross between rot and swamp gas flooded his olfactory. He held the back of his hand to his nose; the faint smell of the hotel soap lingered but failed to blot out the stench.

"What the hell is that smell?"

"You'll get used to it," said Babe.

"I don't want to get used to it."

To call it a road would have been a gross exaggeration. It was nothing more than two ruts cut through overgrown grass that weaved in and out between enormous trees with twisting branches that all but blotted out the moonlight.

He missed the butterflies he felt earlier. Apparently, they'd been eaten by the bats. He began looking for a place where he could turn the Bronco around on the narrow dirt road. He doubted even the fearless Jinan Bondiani would have gone down some creepy, dark, deserted road with a complete stranger. Nick's mind whirled. What had he been thinking? He flashed back to his conversation with Babe back at the diner. Nick recalled it vividly because he hated small talk. She had asked him if he had family if he had a girlfriend. No one to come looking for him if he disappeared. He considered backing out, but it was too late.

"Okay, stop. We're here."

Nick hit the brakes. Ahead of them, in the Bronco's pale headlights, stood a large barn, the once bright red of its slat boards, or at least what was left of them, timeworn to a sort of muddy dried blood color. Nick was sure it was abandoned or, if not abandoned, no longer used for its intended purposes. Though he was sure, it still served as a perfect spot for local kids to hide away from grownups and their prying eyes. A place where they could make-out, drink beer, smoke pot, and screw. So long as their senses weren't easily offended.

A huge bald man stood in front of the barn wearing a dago-tee and carrying a messenger-style bag over his shoulder. By anyone's estimation, Nick was a big dude, but the man standing by the barn made him look dainty. Almost a foot taller and at least fifty pounds heavier, his thick neck and arms were covered in tattoos of strange tribal art interwoven with animal images. Ropey flesh stood raised on one forearm, where he'd been branded; a brand that struck a familiar chord with Nick, though, at the moment, he couldn't seem to place it. Nick swallowed hard and joined Babe in the Bronco's headlights. *I'm walking into a fucking setup*, he thought to himself as he worked to control his breathing.

"Nick, this is Achak."

Nick had to look up. "Achak?"

"Achak," croaked the big man.

The giant was clearly Native American, but Nick detected no hint of an accent, at least not in the one word he'd spoken thus far.

"This man knows everything there is to know about the Mooka'am and why they vanished. And he's the only one who truly knows about the Inaki."

"Babe!" Achak's tone was harsh, and he shot her a disapproving look that was not lost on Nick. He found the exchange comforting. If they planned on robbing him, they would have already done it, and they probably wouldn't have bothered with a back story.

"Wait," Nick said. "the what?"

"It's not safe to talk out here; pull inside," Achak said, looking around uneasily.

Nick ignored the slight tingle up his spine and pulled the Bronco into the back corner of the barn, where he watched with growing unease as Achak stacked hay bales and planks to hide the truck from view. Maybe they *had* planned on killing him.

"This way," Achak said, climbing a ladder up to the hayloft.

What the hell am I doing? Nick chuffed air through his nostrils and followed Babe up the ladder.

Pale, yellow moonlight spilled through holes in the battered old roof and through the massive hayloft doors, which hung open on rusted failing hinges. Nick brushed his hands together absentmindedly.

"It's pretty dusty up here," said Babe, apologetically.

"Yeah," Nick agreed. "So, what's the big secret? Why couldn't you guys just come to the motel?"

Achak ignored his question and asked one of his own. "What can you tell me about yourself, Nick?"

Nick rolled his eyes; more small-talk, but he would suffer it if it meant finding answers. "What's to tell? I'm a college student working on my dissertation to get my Ph.D. in anthropology."

"Where are you from, Nick?"

"I'm from a small town about two hours north called Red Hook."

"Along the Red Hook River, yeah, I'm familiar with it."

Nick was surprised. "Then you know it's a pretty small town where nothing much happens. Anyway, after my parents died, I went off to Chicago to attend college, and now I'm here."

"I'm sorry for your loss."

Nick's face pinched into a furrow; he hadn't thought about his loss in some time. "Thanks."

"What happened to them?" Achak asked.

"What, my parents?" Not one for dumping his purse, Nick answered simply. "Pneumonia took my dad, and cancer took my mom."

"Babe rested a hand on Nick's shoulder. "I'm so sorry, sweetie."

"Yeah, anyway," Nick redirected his attention toward Achak and the purpose of their meeting. "Babe said that you can tell me what happened to the Mooka'am."

"What do you know of the Mooka'am, Nick?"

Nick rolled his eyes. He already knew what *he* knew about the Mooka'am. He wanted to know what Achak knew, but not letting his frustration get the better of him, Nick answered Achak's question.

"Not much, no one does—except for you, maybe."

"Suppose you tell me what little you do know."

"Well, as I understand it, the Mooka'am were farmers, but they were also known as great healers. They openly traded with the French and the British and managed to keep from taking sides during the French and Indian War. Sometime between the end of the war in 1763, and the turn of the century, they were gone. They lived in this area, somewhere along the waters of Consumption River. Mostly we know that one day they were here, and then they weren't. There is no record of illness in the region—at least none that affected the other tribes to any great extent. Certainly not to the point of extinction. We considered some kind of natural occurrence—say a flood, but the only major flood we have a record of was the Great Flood in 1927 when the Mississippi slipped its banks, and we assume the Mooka'am were gone long before that. Otherwise, I think we would know more about them.

"Most of what you say is true, Nick."

"Exactly!" Nick exclaimed. "Which is why their disappearance is so strange."

"I said most of what you say is true. The Mooka'am were not at war when they vanished, and it was not illness or disease that took them."

"Then what?" Nick asked impatiently.

"The Mooka'am starved and froze to death. Come here. I want to show you something." Achak, who was standing near the open loft doors, motioned Nick over. "See that islet in the middle of the river?"

"Sure," Nick said.

"Yes, well, that is where the Mooka'am met their end."

A rocky islet, about an acre in size, sat in the middle of the river. The entire area was covered in jagged stone except for one bare twisted tree trunk that seemed to grow right up through the rock, dead center on the islet.

"That islet was once lush, and its trees were home to many birds."

"I don't understand. What were the Mooka'am doing out there?" Nick asked.

A loud crack from outside sent Achak quickly away from the opening, grabbing Nick as he went. Nick almost lost his footing but reset and pushed against Achak in an attempt to create distance.

"What the hell, dude?"

"Shh," Babe was hunkered down behind the hay bale. "Lower your voice," she said in a harsh whisper.

"Why? He's the one..."

"Please, Nick," fear replaced the harshness in her voice.

Nick lowered his voice. "What's going on, guys?"

Neither answered. Both Achak and Babe strained to listen for follow-up sounds to the crack. After a few moments, Achak stood up with an exhalation of relief. "It must have been a deer."

"What must have been a deer? What's going on?"

"Nick, Achak is putting his life in danger just by meeting with you."

"What?" Nick said incredulously.

"There are people who would like to see him dead because of what he knows."

"About the Mooka'am?"

"About the Inaki," Achak said.

"Who the hell are the Inaki? Babe, you told me that this guy knew what happened to the Mooka'am."

"I do," said Achak.

"Yeah, you said they died because they were trapped on that island and froze to death. Sad, but hardly earth-shattering, and completely useless to me if you don't have proof." Nick rubbed his forehead in frustration. "Even if you do, how the hell am I supposed to stretch that into a full dissertation? Fuck!"

"They weren't trapped there because of the weather, Nick. They were trapped there by French soldiers. When the last of the Mooka'am had perished, the soldiers crossed the frozen river. They piled the bodies by the tree in the center, lit torches, and burned them. The whole islet went up, killing the Mooka'am and the soldiers alike. The only thing left was that twisted trunk."

The wheels in Nick's head started spinning. "Okay, maybe that's something I can work with. But why? What did they do?"

"You're going to have to keep an open mind if you want to understand, Nick."

Nick held up his hands in acquiescence.

"There was a woman. Her name was Evangeline Reaume."

"Never heard of her."

"Of course, you haven't. Not many have. But she is the key to the disappearance of the Mooka'am. It was her pain and anguish that summoned the Inaki."

"Wait, I thought you said the French killed the Mooka'am. Who are the Inaki?"

"The Inaki isn't a who; It's a what. It's a soul reaper, Nick," said Achak.

"A what?"

"A soul reaper."

"Wait a minute; I came here to do serious research. I came here to find out what happened to the Mooka'am, and you're going to tell me ghost stories?"

"It's not a ghost story. The Inaki is a creature of pure evil, as alive as you or me, and it stalks that river out there."

Nick threw his hands up. "Okay, well, this has been fun, but I got shit to do, and I don't have time for campfire stories and urban legends."

From outside, a spotlight passed over the barn and through the trees. Achak placed his meaty hand on Nick's shoulder and pushed him down. Nick crumpled to the floor; he couldn't have fought it if he'd tried.

"Shh," Achak said, clamping a hand over Nick's mouth.

Nick shoved his hand away. "Get the fuck off me!"

Babe scrambled across the loft floor and pressed fingers over Nick's lips. "Please, Nick, please," she begged and pressed herself against him.

He'd had enough but remained silent and listened as tires crunched up the gravel road and slowed to a stop. Nick could feel the quick rise and fall of Babe's chest against his arm. He could feel the pounding of her heart as she clung tighter and tighter. She was scared, and something in Nick made him want to protect her. The car was right outside the barn. Nick could hear the door open, and leaf springs creak in relief as the driver, amid a chorus of grunts and groans, separated himself from the vehicle. Through the gaps in the floorboards, Nick could see an obese man in a sheriff's uniform waddle into the barn and begin washing over the space with the beam from his flashlight.

"It's just a cop," Nick whispered.

Babe didn't answer. She just shook her head, her eyes wide with fear.

The barn was large but empty for the most part, and it didn't take much to clear the area. The rotund cop approached the ladder and shined his light up into the hayloft. The beam hit the ceiling and lit up a small area in the loft. Moving away from the gap, Nick pressed his eyes shut. *"No way he's climbing his fat ass up that ladder,"* he thought. The first rung of the ladder snapped like kindling under the weight of the sheriff's right foot.

"Old piece of shit," Tucker said and planted his foot back on the ground.

Nick peeked down through the gap again. Achak did an excellent job of hiding the truck, but it wouldn't take more than a cursory search of the area to find its hiding place. As Nick watched, the lawman pulled a handkerchief out of his pocket and dabbed at his brow, and then used it to cover his mouth and nose.

"Place smells like slow-roasted shit," Tucker said and moved toward the corner of the barn.

Now Nick could feel his own heart pounding. Ten feet away, then three, then a foot, and then the squad's radio crackled to life, "Sheriff, this is Deputy Abernathy, come in."

The sound in the silent barn startled Nick, who moved just enough to cause a little dust and debris to fall through the crack onto the ground behind Tucker. Tucker turned and paused. He shined his light on the floor and then up at the loft. Nick was sure they were busted.

"Sheriff, come in, Sheriff."

"Son-of-a-bitch!" Tucker grunted and walked back to his cruiser.

"Sheriff, It's Abernathy here; come in, please."

Tucker grabbed the mic. "Tucker here," he barked.

"Sheriff, someone has been out to the Kramer's cottage. The kitchen window looks like someone tried to jimmy it open."

"Did they get in?"

"I don't think so," said Abernathy.

"What do you mean; you don't think so? You better make damn sure, boy!"

"Sorry sheriff, I mean I looked, and I —"

"Don't touch nothin'; I'll be right there. I'm on the other side of the river at the old Cavanaugh barn. If anyone comes out of that cabin, you shoot 'em! Got it?"

"Yes, sir," the voice on the other end of the radio cracked.

"Son-of-a-bitch, I don't need this shit. Not now."

With that, the sheriff crammed himself back into the creaking Crown Vic and hit the gas. Dirt and gravel ricocheted around in the cruiser's wheel wells and sprayed the foliage, making a sound like falling rain as the sheriff drove away. Achak held a large finger to his lips in a *hush* gesture. After several moments everyone took a deep breath and exhaled.

"See?" Babe said.

"See what?" Nick challenged, still pissed about being manhandled. All I saw was a sheriff doing his job. We're trespassing, aren't we?"

Nick looked out of the large door in the hayloft and saw a squad car's headlights bounce across a wooden bridge that spanned a narrow section of the Consumption River.

"Did you hear him tell his deputy to shoot anyone who came out of that cabin?" Babe asked.

"I'm sure he didn't mean for the deputy to literally shoot them."

"We're wasting time, Babe. We'll never convince him," Achak said.

"Nick, listen to me," Babe said, her voice sounding desperate. "This town has a secret, a terrible secret, and Achak is willing to tell you the whole story. But you have to understand, he is risking his life."

"So why not call the police?"

"If the sheriff had found us, we'd probably all have bullets in the backs of our heads by now."

"Oh, come on!" Nick raised his voice.

"Shh! Not so loud," cautioned Babe. And it's not just the sheriff. Most of the influential people in town are in on it."

"In on what, your ghost story?"

"Let him go, Babe. He can't help us."

9

evi watched anxiously as Stan and Finn turned their raft to ride the current back toward the east bank. Having put a little more distance between himself and the house made him feel a little better. Levi worked to slow his breathing and stretched his neck muscles. He worked his fingers, which he had clenched into tight fists at some point, and could feel the pounding in his chest beginning to slow. And then he glanced back at the house. The gable window stood empty, and the pounding in his chest quickened again and moved into his throat and ears. Levi's eyes shot upward as he searched the sky, certain that he would see the crow streaking toward him, but the sky was clear. He took his eyes off the sky for a moment to look for the raft but spun on his heels when he heard the long slow, raspy caw behind him.

It was almost as big as he was, with a soot-black head, not shiny like most crows he'd seen. It had maggot encrusted eye sockets, hollow except for the smoldering red glow that shone from deep inside the thing. It exhaled long and slow, and Levi could feel the ice-cold breath hit his face. The razor-sharp beak drew closer to him, but Levi couldn't move. He'd only had this feeling once before. It was last summer when a junkie pulled a gun on him and his dad one night in the parking lot of a grocery store. His dad rushed the junkie and told Levi to run, but he couldn't. Just like now, he froze, dead in his tracks. The junkie pistol-whipped his dad and took his wallet. The whole thing was over as quickly as it had begun, but the trauma lasted for months.

His parents sent him to see a psychologist who helped him work through his experience. The psychologist explained how the body's parasympathetic nervous system works like an emergency brake when there is a perceived threat. How it allows the autonomic nervous system to decide if you should run or fight. And here it was again, on full display, rooting his feet to the ground against his will, only the fight or flight response never came. Just the emergency brake.

"Not this time mother-fucker!" Levi swung a fist catching nothing but air, but the action freed him from his paralysis, and he turned and ran. He'd taken about four steps into the Red Hook when the riverbed dropped, and he found himself flailing his arms and slapping wildly at the water. He would have drowned, but Stan steered the raft next to Levi, and he and Finn reached down and pulled Levi into the raft.

"Jeez," Stan said. "Could you give a guy a minute?"

Levi didn't say a word. He just lay in the bottom of the raft, white as a sheet and panting heavily.

"You, okay?" Finn asked.

Levi didn't answer.

"What's wrong with him, Stan?"

"How the hell should I know? Just help me paddle."

When they neared the western shore, Stan threw a line out to the Johnson's, who pulled the raft ashore. Levi scrambled out of the raft and dropped into the grass. He lay on his back, blinking at the sky but still not speaking.

"What's wrong with him?" Kaylin asked.

"Beats me; he's been like this since we picked him up," Stan told her.

Frankie knelt next to his brother. "Levi, what's wrong?"

Levi didn't answer, and Frankie's eyes welled up.

"Come on, Levi, you're scaring me."

Slowly, Levi stirred from his state.

"I don't know, Frankie, something happened back there."

"What, Levi? What happened?"

Levi became aware that everyone was staring at him, and suddenly he felt more embarrassed than scared.

"Levi, what happened?" A pleading in his little brother's voice.

"What? Nothing, nothing happened. I'm fine. I just tried to wade out to the raft, and the riverbed dropped faster than I thought, and I swallowed some water."

He hoped he sounded reassuring, but he could tell they weren't buying it.

"Jeez, guys, I'm fine."

Kaylin knelt next to Frankie. "I'll stay with him; you go get your mom."

Frankie started to rise, and Levi grabbed his arm. "I'm fine, Frankie; mom will just freak out."

He wasn't feeling fine, but his mother would only make things worse. He didn't know what she would do exactly. He only knew it would be more embarrassing than what he was already dealing with. Levi raised himself to a sitting position. "See, guys? I'm fine."

"What happened over there, Levi?" Frankie asked.

"Nothing, I don't know," he stammered.

"Bullshit," Stan said. "Something happened. What was it? Did you see something?" A devilish smile crept onto his face. "Guys, he saw something! I told you that place was haunted! What did you see?"

"Leave him alone, Stan," Kaylin demanded.

"Nothing, I didn't see anything. I got a headache, guys; I'm gonna go in and lay down for a while."

"C'mon, dude; you have to tell us," Stevie demanded.

"Leave him alone," Kaylin snapped. "He'll tell us when he's ready."

Connie Waters had just stepped out into the backyard to see what her boys were doing when she heard the raised voices.

"Everything okay, boys?"

"Yeah, mom," Frankie offered.

She looked at Levi.

"Levi! What happened? Did you go in the water?"

"No, mom," he said, his eyes pleading with her, not to embarrass him.

"Why are your clothes wet? You have no business going in the water!"

She was going to say it. He knew she was going to say it, and there was nothing he could do to stop her.

"You know you can't swim, Levi Waters. You promised you would stay away from the water," Connie chastised.

Levi hung his head in shame, forgetting the incident in the child's room and his encounter with the man-sized crow. Kaylin, seeming to sense Levi's embarrassment, chimed in. "I'm sorry, Mrs. Waters, I leaned too far out of my raft, and Levi ran in to pull me out. He didn't go in too far, only up to his chest, but he saved me."

Connie's expression turned from a frown to a smile.

"And you are?"

"Kaylin, ma'am. Kaylin Vaughn"

Connie looked at the rest of the group, who all added their names in introduction to the adult.

"Well, it's very nice to meet you all. Levi, we will talk about this later."

Levi, thoroughly exasperated, sighed, and Connie headed back to the house, but before she went in, she made sure to yell good and loud, "You stay away from the water Levi Waters."

"Dude!" Stan said. "Your name is Waters, and you can't swim? Ha!"

"Maybe I can't swim, but I can beat your ass." Levi rose full up; his chest expanded fists and jaw clenched.

"Jeez! Why so hostile, man? Does everything have to turn into violence with you, jocks?"

"Shut up, Stan," Kaylin said.

"You can be such an ass," McKenna added.

"I'm just messing with the guy."

Levi turned for the house. "I have a headache; I'm going in to lay down. I'll talk to you guys later."

Frankie followed his brother up toward the house.

"What's up his ass?" Stan asked.

Finn shook his head. "McKenna's right Stan, you can be a real asshole."

"Um, correction," said Stan in a Sylvester the Cat voice. "She just said ass; there was no hole."

"You're the hole," Kaylin said, obviously pissed off.

They all loaded back into their rafts to paddle back up the river.

"What's up her ass?" Stan asked earnestly.

"She likes him, dummy," McKenna said, waiving to Levi, who watched them leave.

***

Levi let the screen door slam behind him, not bothering to hold it for Frankie, who was following as quickly as he could manage. Frankie caught up to his brother in the hall, where they came upon a stranger doing something to their father's beautiful antique grandfather clock.

"Hey, who are you?" Frankie asked.

"Name's Merlyn."

"Cool! Like from King Arthur?"

"Yup, something like that. I'm here to fix your dad's clock."

"I'm Frankie, and this is my big brother Levi."

Levi stood there, scowling, not saying a word.

"Something troubling you, son?" Asked Merlyn.

Levi didn't reply, which made Frankie uncomfortable. You always answered when adults spoke to you.

"He's mad because he can't swim, and now the girl he likes knows it."

Levi shot Frankie a look that let him know that he was in for a beating.

"No kidding," said Merlyn. "I never learned to swim either. Never saw the point. We got three bridges in town if I need to get across the river. And there ain't nothing you can do in the river that you can't do out of the river. Nothing worth doing anyway." Merlyn smiled and gave Levi a wink.

"You can't swim out of the river," offered Frankie.

"Sure you can, in a pool," corrected Merlyn. "If you were so inclined."

"Inclined?" Asked Frankie.

"Had a mind to," Merlyn said.

"Yeah, dummy, you could swim in a pool if you were inclining to," said Levi.

"Well, inclined, but look. Your brother isn't a dummy. He just didn't think it through," said Merlyn seeing Frankie's hurt face. "Besides, what's so great about swimming in the river? You know fish do their business in the river, don't you?"

"I guess so," said a slightly defeated Frankie, and then his face lit up. "I bet kids pee in pools too!"

"Touché" said Merlyn.

"Touché?"

"Yes, Frankie, it's a fencing term. It means, you scored a point."

Frankie smiled, still not exactly sure what Merlyn meant but liking the idea of scoring a point.

"So, what's wrong with our dad's clock?" Asked Levi.

"Your dad forgot to remove a few foam bumpers, and he hung the weights in the wrong places. Look, I'll show you," Merlyn held one of the weights in a piece of cloth so the boys could see the bottom. It was marked *center*, but there was a weight hanging in the center spot. They're all weighted differently, so it's important to get them back in the right place."

"Can I ask you a question?" Asked Levi.

"Sure, ask away," Merlyn answered.

"What do you know about crows?"

"Crows? I know lots about crows. One of the smartest creatures on God's green earth," Merlyn considered his idiom. "Or God's blue sky, if you prefer."

"Are they dangerous?"

"What do you mean by dangerous? Are you asking if they can hurt you?"

"Yeah, like, do they ever attack people?"

"Well, if you wrong a crow, he will never forget it. They will remember your face and occasionally dive-bomb you, but they can't really hurt you."

"They can remember your face?"

"Sure can." Merlyn carefully hung the first weight in its correct position.

"How big do they get?"

"Well," said Merlyn, taking a moment to think. "They only weigh a few pounds, and I don't think I've ever seen one more than...oh I don't know," He held out his hands to gauge the size, "say about a foot long."

"So, there couldn't be one the size of a man, right?"

"Not that I've ever seen, but I suppose anything is possible. Some birds can get to be bigger than football players."

"Really?" Frankie leaned in.

"Oh yeah, like the ostrich. An ostrich can grow to over nine feet tall and weigh over 300 pounds, but we don't have any wild ostriches around here," he said, hanging the final weight and handing the winding key to Levi.

"Here you go, son, the movers taped this to the back of the clock."

"What is it?" Levi asked.

The wood and brass tool looked like the crank on top of a coffee grinder.

"It's the winding key," Merlyn said. "When it winds down, you put this in the keyholes," he pointed at the three holes in the clock face, "and give them each a few turns. But you be careful not to over-wind her."

"It's not a her; it's a him," said Frankie.

"It is?" Asked Merlyn.

"Yes."

"And how do you know that?" He probed.

Again, a smile lit his face. "Because it's a grandfather clock, not a grandmother clock."

He could have corrected Frankie and told him that they were actually called longcase clocks, but instead, he tipped his head and said, "touché again, young man," garnering another smile from Frankie. "Well, you be careful not to over-wind him. The old man was built in 1922. You know how old that makes it?"

Frankie's face scrunched up.

Levi turned the key in his hands, and almost as an afterthought, said, "73 years old."

"That's right, son," said Merlyn. "It's almost an antique."

"Levi," said Frankie, "do you think that would open the door in the garage?"

"No, not like this, but I bet we could rig something up."

"Boys, it's none of my business, but if your parents have a door locked in the garage, it's probably for a good reason," cautioned Merlyn.

"Oh, it's nothing like that; we just don't have a key for it," said Scott, who had entered from the kitchen.

"Hey there, Scott, got it going for you."

Scott looked amazed at the swinging pendulum.

"How'd you do it?"

"Your boys can explain," Merlyn said with a smile.

Levi and Frankie smiled back.

"What do I owe you?"

"Not a thing, just promise me that if this grand old clock ever needs real fixing, you'll call me first."

"It's a deal," replied Scott.

"Well, that didn't take near as long as I thought it would. You want I should take a look at that lock for you? I've been known to pick more than a few in my day," Merlyn offered.

"Sure, if it's not too much trouble. I've been meaning to get a look up there."

The boy's eyes widened, and they followed the adults out to the garage. The staircase was too narrow for all of them to fit, so the boys waited at the bottom. Merlyn held a jeweler's loupe to his eye and illuminated the lock's inside with a penlight to study the thing. He let out a short whistle and folded up his works.

"I've only seen one other like it," he said, rubbing his chin, "but that better than 30 years ago. A man came in with a box that needed a four-headed key to open it. I mean, it's not the kind of thing you take to the local hardware shop. You need a skilled craftsman, someone like yours truly," he said with a wink. "It's brilliant, really. Three locks in one, and it can't be picked."

"No shit," Levi whispered to Frankie.

"You mean we'll never be able to get in there without breaking the door down?" Scott asked.

Merlyn gave the door a rap with his knuckles. The skin responded with a ping.

"Steel door, it would be easier punching a hole up through the floor, assuming he didn't line the floor with steel too. Old Tim Ryan went kind of loopy near the end."

Merlyn sat down on the top step. "A real shame what happened. The whole thing was just a damned shame."

"Boy's, get in the house," Scott ordered.

***

After dinner, as they stood at the sink doing the dinner dishes, Connie told Scott about the incident at the river, in as much as she understood it. Scott agreed to pick up life jackets the next time he went into town. Connie folded her arms and gave him a look.

"Fine, first thing in the morning."

Connie smiled; she'd grown accustomed to getting her way.

"Connie, I don't think the Realtor told us everything," said Scott, drying and putting away the dishes.

"What do you mean, didn't tell us everything?" She dropped her sponge in the sink.

"Mr. Ryan didn't die of pneumonia."

"What?"

"Well, I mean, maybe he died of pneumonia, but he went crazy first," Scott corrected himself.

"You know Merlyn, the clock guy?"

"You don't have to say 'the clock guy,' it's not like there are a lot of Merlyns running around," she said impatiently.

"Anyway, Merlyn told me that there was a family that lived in the house across the river."

"What house across the river? All I saw out there were trees."

"There's a house behind the trees," he said, jutting a hand toward the river. "You have to walk down to the dock to see it. Now, do you want to hear this or not?"

Connie held her hands open in a gesture indicating that he should proceed.

"So, about ten years ago, a little boy, his name was Josh Ironweiler, he drowned in the river! Right out there!" Scott said excitedly. "Well, Tim Ryan swam out to save him, but he was too late. The boy drowned, and they never found his body!"

Connie clamped a hand to her mouth. "Oh my god, that's terrible."

"And that's not all. The kid's parents were murdered in the house."

Scott whispered the last part so the boys wouldn't hear, but it didn't matter. They already heard the whole story from Stan. They'd seen the place where it happened, with their own eyes, and now, with their bedroom door cracked just enough, they heard their own father telling the same story. It was all the proof they needed.

***

That night, Levi woke with a start from a restless sleep, middle finger and thumb working madly in a newly acquired self-soothing gesture. Levi could feel his heart pounding in his ears and throat. In his dream, he saw the mottled old crow. As he watched, the crow's milky black eyes faded into vapor, and in their place, he saw glowing darkness, like the light from a burning black fire deep inside the bird's body. His eyes locked on that darkness and felt it begin to drag some part of himself out of his body. *"My soul, it was trying to take my soul,"* he thought. Levi tried to break the gaze that held him firmly in place in the dream, but it was no use. His mouth was forced open, and he could feel something pushing its way down his throat. Levi raised a hand to his neck at the memory. He remembered wanting to scream to wake Frankie, but he couldn't. *"It was just a dream,"* he told himself and pulled his covers up.

Levi wanted to fall back asleep and try to dream of something pleasant. As he pictured Kaylin, her tanned body in her blue jean shorts and yellow bikini top, he smiled and drifted off to sleep. But as soon as sleep took him, Kaylin's image faded, and his nightmare returned.

The thing in his throat was back and pulling his soul from deep inside his body. Levi was asleep, but he could feel himself slipping into a deeper state of unconsciousness. He began to claw at his throat and gulp for air, but he was losing the battle. As Levi felt his brain shift into a lower gear, he began hearing voices speaking in a language he did not understand, and the sound overpowered his inner dialogue. Then, just as his own voice, and with it, his own self was to be lost forever, Levi felt a cold, wet hand on the back of his neck that startled him awake. He reached back, fully expecting to feel his mother's hand holding a damp cloth, waking him from his nightmare, but there was nothing there. Levi rubbed the back of his neck in a soothing motion and closed his eyes again, but it was no use. He couldn't get that damned bird out of his head.

Levi sat up, swung his legs over the side of his bed, and slid his feet into his slippers. Connie Waters was old-school. Pajamas, which she called bedclothes, and slippers. "No dirty feet in bed," she always said. He crept down the hall and into the kitchen.

Levi grabbed a flashlight out of the junk drawer in the kitchen and crept out into the yard. The moon was full and bright as he made his way to the garage. Once inside, he breathed a sigh of relief. Sweeping the beam of the flashlight around, Levi found the box marked *Scott's Stuff*. Lots of old baseball trophies and a couple of old jerseys. Some cassette tapes, one marked Scott and Connie's Baby Making Music. He shook off the image, trying to keep it from fully forming in his head. Pushing that piece of Waters's Family history aside, he dug deeper and found the object of his search. His father's binoculars were old but well cared for. At least they had been before ending up at the bottom of the box marked *Scott's Stuff*. In their apartment in Chicago, Scott Waters hung them on the inside of his closet door, and no one, absolutely no one, was allowed to touch them. The penalty for violating this one simple rule? A boot in the ass.

Still, the bird worried him more than his old man, so boot in the ass or no boot in the ass, Levi reached down and pulled the binoculars out of the box. He would already be in trouble for sneaking out in the middle of the night if he got caught. Violating the don't touch my stuff rule wasn't likely to add much time to his sentence. Levi passed the light up the staircase to the door that still barred access to the loft. Levi wanted, no, he needed to know what lay on the other side of that door, but there was nothing he could do about that now. He walked out to the river and held the binoculars to his eyes, and peered across the water. The trees at the water's edge were leafless, but the branches made seeing the gable window impossible.

Levi moved out onto the dock and inched his way to the edge. Stepping on the last board in the dock, he heard a snap and then the thunderous beating of duck's wings on the silent night air as they flew off from where they were sleeping below. Levi staggered backward and sat down hard on the wood, lost his grip on the binoculars, and watched as they tumbled off the edge of the dock.

10

The air in the loft was hot and thick, and the smell was nauseating. Feeling that he'd wasted enough time, Nick got up and walked toward the ladder. But just as he was about to descend, something made him stop. Nick was a grown man, an educated man, and he didn't believe in monsters. But, and in his line of work, there always seemed to be a but, what if Achak was right? Not about soul-stealing monsters, but about the Mooka'am being herded onto a small islet and left to die. And what if even the reason was true. Not true in the sense that there really are monsters, but that the people responsible for trapping them there believed there were. The last line of his paper popped into his head, *and in the end, perhaps men and mankind are the real monsters.* Nick dismissed it immediately for the cornball tripe that it was.

Nick hung his head and considered what he thought he knew. He knew that Babe, the overly friendly waitress, became very unfriendly, even cold, when he mentioned the Mooka'am. He knew that she was genuinely terrified when the fat sheriff was lumbering around the barn. He knew that neither Babe nor Achak had planned on rolling him. If that had been the case, he would have been out one wallet and probably tossed into the river by now. Nick considered the eight bucks in his wallet and smirked. *Man, they would have been disappointed if that had been their plan.*

"Fuck," Nick shook his head and exhaled hard. "Okay, I'm listening."

Babe smiled, "I told you he would help us. I just knew it; I could see it in his eyes."

"Right," Nick said. "So, tell me your ghost story."

"I told you," began Achak.

"Right, you told me that it's not a ghost story, so how about you tell me what it is then?"

"Please, sit," Achak said, motioning to a hay bale.

Nick slapped his hands against his thighs and plopped down. Babe settled in right next to him, and Achak began.

"My grandfather's grandfather, Makadewa' Mahingan, the Black Wolf, was an Aakwaadizi scout. Have you heard of the Aakwaadizi?"

"Sure, they were a warrior tribe."

"Scouts and hunters, but close enough. The Aakwaadizi were allies of the French during the French Indian War, and my great-great-grandfather scouted for them," Achak dragged his large hand down over his chin and sat on a bale across from Nick and Babe.

"He was a great man, Nick. My great-great-grandfather could hunt or track anything. When I was a little boy, my dad told me stories about him. My father was an earnest man, a solemn man, Nick. So, when he told me what I am about to tell you, I had no reason not to believe him. Even though, just like you, my first reaction was one of, shall we call it, cautious skepticism."

"No disrespect Achak, but I'm here to find out about the Mooka'am, not your family history."

Babe placed her hand gently on Nick's forearm, a gesture suggesting patience rather than affection.

"My family history is intertwined with the Mooka'am and, more specifi-cally, with the Inaki. To understand what happened to the Mooka'am, you must understand the Inaki."

Nick raised his hands. "Whatever, man, I said I'd listen, so I'm listening."

Achak shot Babe a look that Nick read as exasperation.

"Fuck it," said Achak.

"Achak, please. We have to try. We're running out of time."

"There has to be another way, Babe."

"What other way?" Babe raised her voice. "We can't go to the cops, and the guy at the newspaper laughed me out of his office. So, if you have another idea, please—by all means, let me hear it."

Achak shook his head. "I just don't see how this asshole can help us."

Nick took umbrage, but not so much that he would risk a beating.

"He can publish his paper in a serious scientific magazine. He will have the ear of the anthropology community, and even if he's too close-minded to believe, maybe one of his colleagues will."

Achak let out a stifled roar. "Fine! Look, I know you don't believe in ghosts; you have made that abundantly clear, but do you believe in God?"

Nick shrugged his shoulders. "I was raised Irish Catholic."

"I'm not asking if you have heard of God. I'm asking if you believe in God."

"Of course, I believe in God."

"Then you must also believe in the devil, correct?"

"You're looking at a lifetime of Catholic school education here, buddy."

Achak shot Babe another look. Nick knew that look. It was the same look Jinan Bondiani had given him on several occasions. It was a look that meant that he was pushing his luck. Babe responded with a pleading look, and Achak cast his eyes upward and shook his head.

"Let's do this another way. You're an anthropologist, right?"

Anthropology student," Nick corrected.

"Fine, but is it safe to say that you believe in science?"

"Sure, I mean, what's not to believe?"

"Okay, then maybe I can explain it in more scientific terms."

"Explain what?"

"Just hear me out," Achak said.

"Fine," Nick said, raising a hand.

"I'm sure you're familiar with transpiration."

"Of course, the sun heats the water; the water evaporates into the air and collects in clouds, blah-blah-blah."

"Right, then the clouds drop the water back to earth, transferring the life force of the water into the growing grass and trees. The trees transfer that life force into oxygen, which connects to hydrogen atoms, and that energy creates water, which then evaporates. Harmony in nature."

"Yeah," answered Nick, not even trying to hide his annoyance. "I understand transpiration. But what does this have to do with your ghost story?"

"Patients, Nick. Now tell me this. Can you destroy water?"

"You can boil it away," Babe offered.

"No," said Nick. "Boiling it only changes it. It's the Law of Conservation of Matter."

"Exactly! And all of nature works this way. For you, it might be called God's grand design. For my people, it was the way Mother-Earth provided for her children. If someone or something were able to destroy matter, it would be an act against nature, an act against God's grand design. And that, Nick, is what the Inaki is; a disruptor to that grand design.

No longer annoyed, Nick was merely confused. "Dude, you're giving me a headache. So, you're telling me that the Inaki has a way to destroy water?"

"Not water, Nick, something far more precious. The Inaki destroys souls."

Nick's brow furrowed.

"Your people believe that God has given each man a soul. It is your connection to God. My people believe that the Great Spirit has given each man two souls. One that governs while he is awake and one that travels the night living out dreams while he sleeps. The Inaki devours the waking souls of its victims, extinguishing the life force and trapping the sleeping soul in a kind of limbo. The Mooka'am summoned the Inaki, and it was for this act against nature, against the Great Spirit, that aapijinazh was ordered."

"What's aapijinazh?"

"The cleansing of the Mooka'am from this planet."

"So, because your ancestors were superstitious, they ordered the extermination of an entire tribe, a fucking genocide?"

"Is the belief in God any less superstitious?"

"It's not the same thing. Believing in God is an act of faith."

"It's *exactly* the same thing. Or are you so arrogant that you believe you have the only proper way to understand God?"

Nick held his hands up in acquiescence. "Look, we're getting off-topic. I don't want to argue religion with you."

"Fair enough. Nick, have you heard of Dakib-Jiibay, the Water Ghost?"

Achak asked.

"Yeah," said Nick. The zombie cannibal of the Wabanaki. Another Native American ghost story."

Achak held a hand up, conceding the point. "And have you heard of Wendigo?"

"Of course," replied Nick. "But I don't believe in either of them. I told you, I don't believe in monsters."

"You don't have to believe in evil for it to exist."

"I didn't say that I don't believe that evil exists."

"Then we have a starting point because that is what the Inaki is; pure evil."

Achak leaned forward and let his head drop for a moment as if in contemplation. Slowly he raised his head and rested his elbows on his knees, and folded his big hands. Nick thought he looked exhausted.

"How long have your ancestors been in this region, Nick?" Achak asked.

"My parents were both born here, but their parents came over on the boat."

"My ancestors have been here since the beginning of time. They believed that this land was given to us by the Great Spirit. This land is our mother. That's why we honor her the way we do."

Nick nodded, "Mother-earth, I get that. But what does it have to do with the—"

Achak raised a halting hand. "I'm getting to that."

Gently rebuked, Nick sat back and listened.

"As old as *Mother Earth* is, the Inaki is older. It existed before God created the heavens and the earth. The book of Genesis says that a great groaning came from deep in the dark void, and then God spoke the world into existence. It says that God and His angels watched from Heaven, and God said that it was good."

"Yes," Nick said impatiently. "I'm familiar with the story of creation." And then, softening his tone, added, "Like I said, this is twelve years of Catholic school education you're looking at here."

"Then you know that God cast Lucifer, the son of the morning star, out of heaven and down to earth."

"You're saying that the Inaki is Lucifer?"

"No," Achak said. "But with Lucifer, God also cast down one-third of the angels in Heaven. The fallen angels, thirty-three million strong. The Inaki is one of the thirty-three million. As is Wendigo and Dakib-Jiibay."

The thought of thirty-three million fallen angels set loose to roam the earth caused a lump in Nick's throat.

"Now that it has been awoken, the Inaki seeks only to survive until what you in your faith call Armageddon when it will rise up with the other thirty-three million and their Dark Lord to battle for dominion over the earth. Nick, the Inaki will do whatever it takes to stay alive until that time."

Nick massaged the back of his neck.

"This region was settled, by your people, in the early 1700s," Achak said. "The French came. They set up a military outpost about 20 miles downriver at the south end of what is now Chesapeake County."

"Yeah, well, I'm not French, but I get your point."

"Among the first settlers to arrive and carve out their own piece of my ancestor's land was Jules and Evangeline Reaume. Jules was not what you would call a capable man. He could not hunt, was not adept at farming, and had no stomach for soldiering. But he had money, and he used that money to set up a successful trading post. By all accounts, Jules was a good businessman, and it wasn't long before the Reaumes decided that they were ready to start a family. Evangeline became pregnant twice, but both times, the children were stillborn. They were devastated and had all but given up the hope of ever being parents. Then Evangeline became pregnant for the third time and carried to term. In the Winter of 1752, Evangeline gave birth to a son."

"Time out," Nick said. "Where are you getting your information? What are your sources? Because none of this is worth a shit if I can't back it up with sources."

"Show it to him, Achak. It's the only way he's going to believe it."

"Show me what?" Nick asked.

Achak reached into the messenger bag he'd been carrying and pulled out an old-looking book of some kind. Bound in leather and less than an inch thick, Achak told Nick that it was the diary of Jules Reaume.

"This book has been in my family for eight generations. No one outside my family, not even Babe, has so much as touched this book, let alone read it. In it is the story of the coming of the Inaki and the genocide of the Mooka'am.

Instinctively, Nick reached for the book, but Achak pulled it back.

"Not so fast," Achak said. "There are two things you need to understand. Number one, if I hand you this book, you become part of its history. You are responsible for the consequences of whatever action you take or choose not to take."

"And second?" Nick knew he sounded eager, but he didn't care.

"You may read it, but you cannot take it from me. It must remain in my possession."

"But I'm going to need it to show where the information came from. Otherwise, it's just my word, and science doesn't work on the honor system."

"When the time comes, I will make it available for review by anyone you choose, with the same stipulations."

Nick knew he would have agreed to just about anything to finally hold his holy-grail, the thing that seemingly no living person outside that dust and dirt-filled hayloft had ever seen.

"You have a deal," Nick said.

Achak glanced at Babe once and then handed the manuscript to Nick, who took it as gently as if it were made of air. The book was covered in an aged leather binding and bore the name Jules Reaume. Nick breathed in the warm smell of the leather and turned to the first page. In keeping with the time, the text was written on vellum in ink from a feather pen. If this was a hoax, it was an elaborate and likely expensive hoax. And for the life of him, Nick couldn't figure a logical endgame to such a prank. Nick settled against the wall next to the open hay door and read the document by moonlight.

11

The Diary of Jules Reaume
Introduction and Part 1

My name is Jules Reaume. It is the winter of 1760 as I sit here at my kitchen table in what is left of our small home along the banks of the Consumption River in the Illinois Territory. Though it is the coldest winter that I can recall, there is no log in my hearth, nor is there warmth in my soul. My beloved Evangeline and the son she bore me are both gone. I have only to pen this memoir before I go off to join them in whatever awaits after I close my eyes for the last time. Though I would not have you think me brave or even a romantic. You see, the death that awaits me isn't of my choosing; instead, it is the reaping of what I have sewn.

The men who will mete out my sentence have granted me, through their good grace, the opportunity to put my story to vellum. I prepare these papers as a record of our lives, mine and Evangeline's. From the birth of our son to the time of my death. And as you will undoubtedly find in reading, this is no self-serving exercise but rather a confession of sorts to the evil that I fear we may have unleashed upon the Earth. Additionally, please forgive me if I stray from the job of the narrator and let my emotions run unbridled from time to time. For terrible and traumatic events will be revealed in this writing.

Part 1- The Birth of Our Son

Evangeline and I came to the Illinois Territory in late spring 1747. We set up home in this humble cabin, and it was our intention to raise a family here among these good people. Our son was born on a cold January night in 1752. The icy northern wind howled through the trees and through every weakness in the cabin I had built for Evangeline and me. I'd spent the fall collecting and storing wood for the hearths, and even with the fires going day in and day out, a chill clung fast to the air. Our village consisted of twenty-two families and a garrison of ninety, and I doubt many in the encampment slept that night whether kept awake by the shrieking of the wind or Evangeline.

I stood just outside our bedroom door, calling words of encouragement while my beautiful wife labored for 33 hours, resting only when she did. By her side were several women from the Mooka'am, a local tribe. Having previously delivered two babies stillborn, the village midwife refused to assist Evangeline in the birth stating outright that God Himself did not want her to bear a child. May she be stricken dead.

The few townswomen who had offered to help had all been driven away behind the lash of Evangeline's tongue. Some had offered their own supplies of opium to ease her pain, but Evangeline refused. When it was done, and our son was born, Evangeline lay bedridden and clinging to life. The women from the village returned bearing food and tending to the new mother and our infant son. Evangeline named him Ezra after her brother, who drowned in the River Arnon near their childhood home in Saint Baudel. I wanted to oppose, but having seen what she'd gone through, I felt that it wasn't my place. I've never been one for burdening a child with the name from the dead should they be kin.

Evangeline groused about the women from the village wanting to return after having fled during the storm. She said she preferred the Mooka'am women to our own, but I put my foot down. After all, we had a business to run, a business that, like our lifestyle, depended on money, not beads and trinkets. I ordered my wife to allow our own kind to care for her, and Evangeline, being too weak to put up much of an argument, acquiesced.

As the months went by, Evangeline grew stronger. Ezra was a happy baby. Not given to fussing or crying, the child never caused his mother a sleepless night. Evangeline said that he was her perfect little lamb delivered by Winter's roaring lion. At the time, I agreed.

In the late fall of his first year, Evangeline carried Ezra to the river to bathe him and gather water. As she filled skins to carry back to our home, she was approached by a French soldier. He greeted her with, "Bonjour, mademoiselle." The heathen, he'd have been a fool not to know that she was a Madame. She was, after all, with our child. Evangeline said that he asked if he might be of assistance. Evangeline corrected the ill-mannered brute. "It's madame, Madame Reaume, and thank you, but I can manage," she told him.

Evangeline said that as she stood and turned, the soldier stepped forward onto her path. She said that he smelled of spirits and appeared unkempt. Evangeline tried to step around him, but he pushed forward, pressing his chest against hers as he leered ravenously. Evangeline dropped the water skins, wrapped both arms around Ezra, and tried to push past, but the soldier grabbed her by her hair and dragged her to the ground. Evangeline clung desperately to our son, but the animal ripped him from her arms. She dug her nails into his face and pulled her knife from her boot. The blade cut into his forearm, but she said that he didn't seem to notice. He struck Evangeline and knocked her to the ground. She swung the knife again and pierced the soldier's hand. She said he looked at the blood pouring from the wound, and his eyes filled with rage.

Evangeline said that she moved to pick up our son, who lay crying on the ground where the soldier had carelessly dropped him, while at the same time trying to hold the soldier bay with her knife. She only took her eye off him for a minute while she bent to pick up Ezra. That was when he grabbed her wrist and forced the knife from her hand. She said that she recalled his head flying toward her face and, mercifully, that was all she remembered of the attack. But that would be the only mercy we would ever receive.

Evangeline woke to find her bodice torn open and her dress pushed up around her waist. Ezra lying face down in the wet sand next to her. Evangeline scrambled to her knees and took Ezra in her arms. His head fell back, and she knew at once that he was dead. That was where I found her, collapsed, rocking back and forth and absent expression while clinging tightly to our dead son. Through agonizing groans and shuddering tears, she told me what had happened. I swept my wife into my arms and carried her home, where I cleaned the blood from her face and hair and laid upon our bed. She would not release Ezra.

Once she was asleep, I grabbed my flintlock pistol and went out to hunt the animal who destroyed our world. I searched the entire encampment to no avail. I was forced to admit the atrocity and called upon the captain of the guard. I explained the attack as it had been told to me by Evangeline. The captain informed me that all of his men were uninjured and accounted for. He suggested that perhaps it was one of the savages in a French soldier's uniform.

"Impossible!" I shouted.

The captain leaned forward in his chair and placed his palms on his desk, and said, "Monsieur Reaume, my men are men of honor. To question their integrity is to question mine. I beg you, choose your next words carefully."

Admittedly, I am not one for physical confrontation, having been born with my mother's narrow shoulders. I was well aware that I could have been bested by any man in the room and spoke my words through clenched teeth. "Captain," I said. "I assure you that my wife knows the difference between a Frenchman and an Indian."

This brought laughter through the ranks. I spun on the man closest to me and shouted. "Was it you?" The soldier held up his hands to show that he was uninjured.

"Monsieur Reaume!" The captain bellowed. "I will not have you accusing my men of something so foul, nor will I allow you to rebuke them in my presence!"

My temper was getting the better of me. I told the captain that I would do more than rebuke his man when I found him. Then I saw the corner of the captain's mouth turn up as to smirk, and my blood began to boil. When he spoke, I lost all control. He dared to ask if I had considered that my wife may have voluntarily laid with one of his men. He could see that his insult provoked me, and his smile grew more vulgar.

"Perhaps Madame Reaume made the story up to protect her should she become pregnant?"

I felt something break inside me. I pulled my pistol, leveled it at the captain, and pulled the trigger. I could see the spark as flint struck steel, and I saw the flash of the primer in the pan and braced myself for the weapon's recoil, but it never came. The spark had failed to ignite the main powder charge, and the ball sat unspent in the barrel. Time stood still, and the room fell deadly silent, and then my world turned black.

When I finally opened my eyes, I found myself staring up into Evangeline's beautiful face. I had to blink several times to bring her into focus.

"Jules, you have come back to me," she said.

I have no words to express the shame I felt at my inability to revenge my wife. I pushed myself up, first onto an elbow, and then sat with my legs off the bed. As the rest of the room came slowly into focus, I saw that I was home. Evangeline said that the Mooka'am found me down by the river and brought me home. I got to my feet and demanded my pistol but collapsed dizzily to the floor. I rubbed at the back of his head. I could feel the knot that had formed where I had been struck and picked flakes of dried blood out of my hair. As I came out of my cloud, I noticed the bassinet next to our bed. Ezra lay there, swaddled and peaceful.

"He looks like a sleeping angel," I said.

"He is." Evangeline smiled wanly, sweeping the tiny body up into her arms. "You should rest, Jules."

I told her that I did not want rest. "Evangeline," I screamed. "I want revenge!" The sound of my own voice split my head like an ax blow.

She sat next to me on the bed and rested her head against my chest. She brushed lightly at Ezra's hair and said, "I don't care about vengeance, Jules; I just want our boy back." Then she began to cry softly. Not a cry of pain or anguish, but a cry of brokenness.

I held her all through the night while she cradled Ezra's lifeless body in her arms. That night lightning flashed, thunder crashed, and rain fell in sheets as nature itself joined in mourning the loss of our child. When morning broke, everything outside felt fresh and new, the old washed away, replaced by the promise of a new day. All through the encampment, life went on as usual. I suppose we resented that more than anything.

Evangeline paced the floor, still holding Ezra. "Why should everyone continue on as if nothing happened?" She screamed. Evangeline tore at her clothing and ripped out a clump of her hair in her anger. I grabbed her arms to stop her, but that only sent her deeper into a rage. "Don't touch me!" She screamed, and she lashed out, carving deep grooves in my face with her nails.

I threw my hands up and begged her to calm herself.

"Calm down? How can you say that?" She screamed. "Our child has been taken from us, and yet the world and all that trod upon it continue as if nothing has happened!"

I told her I understood that. "Evangeline," I said, "I love you, and I loved our son, but he's gone."

She held his body out to me. "He's not gone," she said. "He's right here."

The look on her face broke my heart. She almost looked happy, like she was opening my eyes to something I had failed to see, but I had to hold firm. "We should see to his burial," I said.

The tenuous expression of joy slipped from her smile, and she bared her teeth at me. She said that she would not see our son placed in a box and buried in the cold ground. I told her that we must bury him or he would not find peace in the arms of God. Evangeline's eyes flared.

"Don't you dare speak to me of God, Jules Reaume! Where was He when our Ezra was murdered? Where was He when that animal mounted me?"

Truth be told, the same questions had occurred to me, but I would not allow the thought to germinate, nor would I allow my wife to tread that dangerous path. I took her by the shoulders and shook her. "Evangeline," I scolded. "You are grief-stricken; you don't know what you're saying!"

"You're wrong Jules, I know exactly what I am saying," she said.

I tightened my grip. "Evangeline," I said. You are my wife, and you will obey me, and we will honor God in this house!"

She drew in a breath to offer a retort, but a knock at the door interrupted, and it was just as well with me. I was losing my temper and had come perilously close to saying something unforgivable. I was about to tell her that I wouldn't risk my immortal soul for a dead child or a living wife. Looking back, I wish I had.

I opened the door to find the old Mooka'am woman that we had taken to calling Ookomisan, a word meaning grandmother. She stood there holding a bouquet of purple flowers.

"Oniijaanisan," she said. Her people's word for, child. "What is wrong?"

Ookomisan visited at least once a week. She would sit with Ezra so that Evangeline could nap to keep up her strength. She was a savage but still a gentle caregiver and could not have acted more grandmotherly toward Ezra.

Tears poured down my face. "Ookomisan," I said. "It's Ezra. He's dead."

Evangeline stood holding Ezra. "He's been murdered," she shouted. "The way you say it almost sounds pleasant."

I couldn't take being in Evangeline's presence one second more. I stepped past Ookomisan and paused. "There is a matter at the shop. Something that I need to attend to," I said. "When I return, we will resume our conversation and make arrangements for our son."

As I closed the door, I thought that I had read something in the old woman's face, something sinister, but I felt that it was just my exhausted mind playing tricks.

12

Part 2 The Pact

I returned home just as the twilight had fallen. I hadn't intended to stay away for so long, but I had fallen asleep on a bale of cotton in the storage room at my shop. While still a good distance away, I noticed a commotion around my home. I hurried my pace and was shocked to find several Mooka'am carrying our belongings away. I struck one of the burglars with my fist, knocking him to the ground, but he took no umbrage.

"Evangeline," I cried out as I ran for the door.

I couldn't make sense of what I was seeing. Were we simply being robbed, or was it something more, something worse? Had the Mooka'am done something to Evangeline?

"Evangeline!" I cried again. Ookomisan stood in the door. Seeing her eased my mind. I asked her what was happening, but she just grinned at me. I tried to push past her, and it seemed like she had been nailed to the floor. I outweighed her by no less than forty pounds, but I could not move her.

As I stepped back and regarded her, a knot formed in my stomach. The old woman's wrinkled skin turned from golden brown to the color of ash. Her eyes, tired but always warm, had turned obsidian black, inclusive of the white portions, looking like two black eggs.

"Step aside, Ookomisan! I must see my wife!" I screamed and tried again to push past her. But again, she barred my ingress as un-passable as a stone blocking the entrance of a tomb. When I threatened to strike her, she blew a purple-colored powder in my face.

I coughed and brought my arm up, but it was too late. I could feel the paralysis overtaking me. It started slowly, down at my feet and climbed up my legs like clinging ivy. I tried to step back, but my legs would not obey. And then the thing that used to be the ookomisan spoke in a voice that caused my bladder to release. It was a sort of low growling that came from somewhere deep inside the old woman. I could feel it reverberate in my chest. I have never heard Satan speak, but I'm sure that I now know his voice.

The growling rose, and the old woman we had known as Ookomisan began to shake and jerk as if she'd been stricken with St. Vitus Dance. Then, in an instant, she stopped and threw her head back. There she stood with her mouth open like a baby bird waiting to be fed.

The paralysis clawed its way up through my intestines and into my neck. I tried to take in a breath, but I could feel the fibers of the poison taking root in my lungs.

The thing that once was the ookomisan began to laugh and then fell to dust before my eyes, and I was alone. Twilight became night, and night became day, but still, I could not move, nor could I speak. I stared through the open door of my home to the emptiness inside.

Two more days passed, then, on the morning of the third day, I found myself lying on the ground. It took several tries, but I got to my feet. My whole body ached as I stumbled through the house, calling for Evangeline. It took no time to search the house. All that remained was the table at which I now sit. Every stick of furniture, every morsel of food, every stitch of clothing, gone.

I ran out to the barn. Perhaps Evangeline had gone there to hide. But alas, she was gone, and like the house, the barn too was stripped clean. Where was she? Where was my wife? I ran into town and met with the farrier. He'd been shoeing our horse, Louis, a stroke of luck lest he'd have been taken by the heathen Mooka'am as well.

For what reason, I cannot say, but my gut told me that Evangeline had gone north, so north would be my direction. I rode a full day before I picked up a trail. I couldn't be sure it was Evangeline's and wrestled with the idea of heading back. I was so hungry, and I hadn't thought to gather supplies. But I was so confident that she had gone north that I pressed on. I put my trust in God, and that evening my prayers were answered, or so I thought.

I came upon Evangeline in a clearing near a small creek. Caked in filth, her dove white skin reddened by the sun; she'd always taken precaution against the darkening effects of the sun. I watched as she foraged on the ground. She twitched like some feral animal. As I moved to improve my position, a twig snapped beneath my foot. Evangeline snapped her head around. Her eyes shone with a ravenous glare as she peered into the tree line where I remained perfectly still. I had spent three days trying to find her, and now I questioned myself for the undertaking.

She turned back away from me and dug in the soft ground near the water. I was just about to call out to her, but something stopped me. I watched for another minute as she pulled a worm out of the ground. I had never known my wife to fish, but perhaps she'd acquired a new skill for survival. I smiled, feeling a little proud of the capable woman I'd married, and then my smile faded into stunned dismay.

Evangeline threw her head back and dropped the wriggling thing into her mouth. I almost gagged as she chewed the worm into a paste, and then bird fed the bolus to Ezra. The food fell from Ezra's slacked dead lips, and Evangeline scooped it off the ground and tried again.

"Evangeline," I cried, as I ran to her. "Stop! Have you gone mad?"

Evangeline turned. "Jules," she crackled. "You came for us." She threw a limp arm around my neck. The pride I felt only a moment ago turned to shame and revulsion. She smelled horrid, and I could see mud and bits of worm pulp in her teeth.

"What in God's name has happened to you?" I asked, but she didn't answer. I caught her as she fainted, exhausted, and starved, and I thought, quite mad.

I pulled the saddle and blanket from my horse and made a place for her to lay. I collected Ezra from the ground with considerable disgust, where she dropped him upon fainting and set him next to his mother. I used my hat to gather water from the stream and slowly dripped it into Evangeline's mouth. I managed to trap a squirrel in a deadfall and prepared the meat for supper; Evangeline hadn't yet regained consciousness, and I devoured the thing. After supper, I used my shirt and water from the creek to clean Evangeline's face. With the black sky above, looking as vast and desolate as the ocean we had crossed to begin our new life in the new world, I settled in next to my wife and closed my eyes.

I woke the following day to the smell of earth and pine. Evangeline had hollowed a small pit in the ground and laid Ezra's body in it atop a bed of pine branches. I walked over to her side, placed my hands on her shoulders, and whispered in her ear. "It's for the best, Evangeline."

She smiled brightly. "I know it is." Her words were soft and pleasant. At last, it seemed that my wife was coming to her senses.

After setting Ezra down, Evangeline stripped her clothing and walked into the cold running stream. I watched her bathe and studied the perfect curve of her hips and the roundness of her breasts. The cold water from the stream raised goose flesh on her breasts and her flat stomach, and I could feel a stirring in my body. Silently, I scolded myself for having such a reaction even as we were preparing to bury our son. But I could no more control my body's response to seeing Evangeline's beautiful form than could I stop the rain from falling or the wind from blowing.

We hadn't laid together as husband and wife since Ezra's birth, and truth be told, I yearned for her. Evangeline stepped from the creek, water dripping from her body, and I tugged at my trousers and turned away. I could hear her approaching footsteps.

"Stay with our boy," her voice fell breath against the back of my neck, and she kissed me there. "There is something I need to do," she said. "I won't be gone long."

Her lips on my neck re-aroused the stirring on which I will not elaborate. Suffice it to say that I found myself unable to speak. Evangeline dressed and started off into the woods. While she was gone, I went to the stream and splashed my face. Returning to our camp, I looked at my son's lifeless body and took heart knowing that we could finally put him to rest. I gathered wood and built a small fire to stave off the dampness in the morning air. I caught another squirrel in the deadfall and roasted it over the fire for Evangeline to eat upon her return. I gathered wood and kept the fire burning as dusk began to fall, soft and purple in the western sky. Still, she had not returned.

I found myself pacing nervously. Thoughts that ranged from wild animals to wild savages to an array of accidents ran through my mind. Then, just as I was about to go after her, Evangeline wandered back into camp carrying a large black crow.

"I already prepared food," I said. I had eaten the first squirrel but had caught and prepared another. I suggested keeping the bird for later, but Evangeline did not answer and continued past me.

The bird's head lolled as she walked. Evangeline knelt next to Ezra's body and gently laid the bird next to him. "What in God's name are you doing?" I asked.

Her voice was soft and sweet. "We are going to be a family again, Jules."

Unsure what she meant, I demanded an explanation, but she did not speak. Instead, she bowed her head just as the Mooka'am woman we once called grandmother stepped out of the deep purple of twilight.

"You!" I cried. "I saw you fall to dust!"

The old woman walked toward me, reaching into one of the pouches that she wore around her neck.

"You're a witch!" I screamed and pulled my knife from my belt, but it was too late. The witch blew more powder into my face, and I felt my feet bolt themselves to the ground as before.

"Oniijaanisan, children," she said, addressing us both. "Your young one is to be a vessel. Through him will come the time of the Inaki."

Nick paused and looked up from his reading. "Inaki," was all he said, and then cast his eyes back to the book.

Evangeline's face hardened. "What do you mean, through him?" I could see that she was taken aback by the witch's words. "You said you could return my son to me!"

12

"And I am," said the old witch, in perfect English. "Your son will return as a god!"

"Evangeline!" I cried, as the paralysis began to seize my vocal cords. "What have you done?"

Unable to raise my voice in protest, I watched the unholy ritual play out before my eyes. I heard Evangeline's cries of anguish and felt some relief that the sound was muffled by the paralyzing poison that crawled through my body and filled my head like some spidering ivy.

The witch blew the same powder into Evangeline's face and then laid her down next to the stream. I could see her limbs begin to stiffen and knew the fear and confusion she felt. The witch cut Evangeline's clothing from her body. I did not react the way it had earlier to the sight of my wife's naked form. The witch lifted Ezra out of the pit and placed his small lifeless body on Evangeline's stomach. She did likewise with the bird.

Then she reached into one of the other pouches; she wore several fastened by leather thongs around her neck and retrieved several berries. She used her knife to cut Evangeline's hand and let the blood drip onto the ground. She spat on the ground, added the berries, and mixed the concoction together as she began to undulate and chant in the same demonic growling I had heard earlier. Evangeline pitched her eyes as far down as she could. I could see her straining to try and see what was happening. Failing that, she began to dart her eyes around like a frightened animal caught in a hunter's snare. Oddly, I thought of the squirrel that had been my dinner.

I knew that Evangeline wanted to see what was happening to her, to her baby, but it was better that she could not. I, on the other hand, had nothing to obstruct my view. The witch scooped the blood and berry paste into her hand and lapped it into her mouth, and then dribble it into the bird's beak. The bird, its neck was still broken, flapped madly, and the witch snapped its wings. Then she picked up Ezra's lifeless body.

In my head, I raged and cried out, but my body remained still as stone. Indifferent to my torment, the witch spat the potion into Ezra's mouth, and my dead son began to fuss and cry. I looked at Evangeline's face. A battle between joy and horror was waging there. If I could hear the muffled cry,

I was confident that she could as well. Still unable to move, Evangeline's eyes bounced maniacally, trying to see her son.

As I could no longer bear to look upon Evangeline's tortured face, I looked back at the old woman who was in the process of splitting the bird's chest open and removing its heart. The tiny organ, it looked like a small black rock, pulsed in her hand.

She must have sensed that I was watching her because she turned her gaze toward me and smiled knowingly. I watched as she split Ezra's chest from the base of his neck to the middle of his stomach. I could feel the tendons in my body on the verge of snapping as I strained to break the paralysis. The witch kept her eyes on me even as her hands worked, and I could see her enjoyment intensify as Ezra let out a wet and blood-curdling scream. Then she broke her gaze as she removed my son's heart and tossed his body onto the fire. Evangeline's eyes shot to the right, where the fire sat in clear view, and we both watched as our child's body burn.

I fixed my eyes on Evangeline, not wanting to watch. I pitied her and hated her at the same time. Evangeline turned pale white and her eyes filled with blood which ran like tears down the side of her face. I feel no shame in admitting that some strange satisfaction came over me, but it was short-lived. The witch placed Ezra's beating heart into the body of the crow and sealed the wound with her fingertip. The bird lifted its head, flapped its healed wings, and flew onto the old woman's shoulder. Then she took the crow's small stone of a heart, which she still held, and placed it on my wife's stomach. She covered the heart with her horribly gnarled hands and pressed hard against Evangeline's flesh. Evangeline let out a cry of agony. It was so shrill that it caused me to wince. When the witch removed her hands, the heart was gone. She waved her hands over Evangeline's stomach, and it began to swell and ripen before my eyes. Evangeline looked the way she had on that cold winter night when she gave birth.

Now I could see a black churning mass balling up and pushing against her skin from inside. Evangeline cried out as the mass grew more prominent, and her belly swelled to the point of bursting. Then her paralysis broke, and Evangeline was in the throes of childbirth. Teeth fully bared and gritting down hard, her neck bent so far forward that I thought it would snap. Seemingly racked with pain, Evangeline grabbed her knees and pushed with all she had. I could see the black mass rolling in her body. Evangeline grunted and screamed, and a spindly, jointed black leg burst through her stomach. Evangeline wailed as another leg poked through, and her flesh tore open. Having had the better part of a decade to process the madness, I will do my best to describe what I saw emerge from my wife's broken body.

With my eyes shut, I can still see it clear as day. Let me begin by saying that the creature most closely resembled the astacus, or crawfish as they were called by the peddlers in La Louisiane when Evangeline and I first arrived in this godforsaken country. But unlike the astacus, this creature was enormous. To pace the length of its body, I would have taken no less than five good strides. The body, black and slick with Evangeline's blood, was covered in spines like the alligator's. The length of the underbelly was covered in small stalks, like the legs of the centipede. Attached to its side were eight additional legs, much larger, segmented, and spindly like the spiders' legs. The head, silky and scaly but also lumpy like a walnut shell. It resembled that of an eel save for the fact that its mouth contained many rows of fanged teeth disappearing down into its gullet, giving the impression that, were one unfortunate enough to get one's arm caught inside, there would be no retrieving it. Lastly, the monster, for I know no better word to call it, had a pair of legs, like a man's legs only also covered in the same wrapping as the head.

Now that you have some understanding of what manner of creature my wife birthed, I will continue with the telling of the events as they occurred. Note here that the thing, intentionally or not, seemed to disembowel my wife as it dragged itself from her desiccated womb. Once free of her body, the monster ate not her body but did consume her intestines before burrowing itself into the soft mud along the riverbank.

Let me pause here once more to say that I know my descriptions and telling likely seem cold and callous. Believe me when I say that it was not always this way. Evangeline and I were very much in love. We left the comfort of our ancestral homeland because our families forbade us to marry. We chose the dangers of a sea voyage and life in a world we did not know over a life apart. In fact, I still love my wife very much, but my wife died the day the soldier killed our son. The thing that delivered that black demon into the world may have looked like Evangeline Reaume and may have even borne her name, but that was not my wife. Very well, you have my word that I will endeavor to minimize my asides from here out.

Continuing once again. When my paralysis broke. I believe it happened sometime during the emergence of the monster though I was frozen with fear. I crawled to Evangeline. She lay broken open and dead. Her once brilliant blue eyes, milky and sightless. I took what there was of her in my arms and wept. As I held her, I watched Evangeline's supple young skin pucker and furrow. Her hands curled into claws, and her alabaster skin turned the color of ash and fell from her bones. Then her bones turned to powder in my hands, and my Evangeline was no more.

I buried my face in the ground and trembled. Trembled at the thought of losing my world and trembled at the thought of the monster reemerging and dragging me down to Hell with it. Then the strangest thing happened. I heard a baby's cry. The sound pulled me from that place of fear and grief, and when I looked up, the old witch was gone. In her place stood Evangeline holding our son. I rubbed hard at my eyes, trying to make sense of what they beheld. My wife was dead. I saw her die, but there she was, standing right in front of me. She carried Ezra over on her hip and spoke to me. When she spoke, she spoke Evangeline's words with Evangeline's voice.

"I told you that we would be a family again," she said. "Would you like to hold your son?"

With this thing that I believed, though now I see it for the lunacy it was; to be my wife and our unnaturally conceived child in tow; we returned to our homestead.

13

Part 3 - The Unforgivable Act.

For months I walked around in a daze, not sure how or what to think. My mind waged war with itself over what I knew to have happened and what I saw before me. Because what I saw was a happy baby boy. Did it really matter how he came to be? And as for Evangeline, well, the new Evangeline. She was once again the carefree girl I knew back in Saint-Baudel. In fact, I dare say that I preferred the new Evangeline to the old, and seldom from that day forward did I bring up the incident in the woods. The few times when I tried, Evangeline would dismiss my memory or distract me with a trip to our marriage bed. And as previously mentioned, it had been some time since I had known the pleasure of Evangeline's body. Our love-making, which had always been routine, almost mechanical, had changed with the new Evangeline. It had become passionate and, at times, violent. I had even begun to take milk from Evangeline's breast. When she'd first suggested it, I found the idea vulgar, but I had acquiesced.

I found the taste to be fine, something akin to the flavor of cucumber, but there was something else that I found in her milk. I had always been a small, some would say, frail man, but within the first month of taking her milk, I found myself lifting 100-pound sacks of cotton. Understand that I had previously used hired men from the village to stack the heavy bails, but now I tossed them without effort. After two months, I was toting 200-pound sacks of salt as though they were filled with goose down. It seemed that the more I fed, the more robust I became. Soon, I, Jules Reaume, was one of the strongest men in the region. One of the strongest and the richest, and I was revered by all in the outpost. Even the captain of the guard, the one who insulted me, showed proper respect. All was going well. Then one day, when Ezra was about five years old, I returned home from a hunting expedition to find that my beautiful wife had begun to age rapidly.

"What happened to you?" I asked her.

"Jules, I am dying." Was her reply.

I collapsed to the ground. Just as my life seemed to have sorted itself out, and my mind made peace with my eyes, my world twisted at its core once again. Evangeline rushed to my side, caressed my cheek, and burdened me with the millstone that would drag me to the depths of Hell.

"I am dying, your son is dying, and only you can save us," she said.

I looked at Ezra. He, too, looked deathly ill. Evangeline told me that a settlement lay sixty miles southeast and that there I would find a young girl almost ready to give birth. She told me I was to bring her to the river. Evangeline said I should deliver her to the spot where I found her holding our dead son so many years ago. I asked her how I was to find this girl. She said that a red star would guide me. Giving all that I had seen, I had no reason to doubt her.

I left that night under cloud-covered skies heading southeast as best I could manage. Early the following day, the sky opened up the rain began to fall. It came down in sheets all day and hadn't stopped by nightfall. Feeling nearly dead from exhaustion, I decided to take shelter from the wind and rain in a small cave and get some rest. So hard was the rainfall that the cave itself was flooded. Sitting there sopping wet, it had occurred to me that nature itself was against me, against my mission. I hadn't seen the red star in two nights and was traveling on sheer instinct. Chilled and soaked to the bone, I moved to higher ground in the cave, and, much to my surprise, I found branches and twigs and managed to get a fire started. The heat felt good on my bare skin, and I was able to dry out my clothes. I woke around midday with the rain still falling and started off.

Hunger twisted like a living thing in my gut. I hadn't thought to bring food and rode with my eyes peeled for something, anything I might consume. I managed to find the remains of a small fur-covered creature. An old crow sat pecking the eye from its socket, so I knew it couldn't have been long dead. I can't give the manner of death with any certainty, but its head was crushed, leading me to the thought that it had been trampled by a horse. That thought only added to my troubles. If the animal had, in fact, been crushed, that meant that there were other riders on the trail, and those riders were undoubtedly savages or highwaymen. It mattered not which, as both would just as soon slit my throat and scalp me, as not. I used my blade to skin the small animal and ate it raw, not wanting to give myself away with fire or smoke. Just as the sun was setting on the second night, the rain stopped, and the clouds cleared. There, in the distance, hung the reddest star I'd ever seen, and I rode till I was directly beneath it. Ever so silently, I crept to a tree line, took cover beneath the boughs of a large Jack Pine, and studied the small cabin in the clearing ahead. As I sat and watched, thunder peeled in the west. Another storm was coming, but that didn't matter. I had found what I came for.

She waddled swayback from around the side of the small cabin carrying a pail of water. From behind her came a hulking form toating a bundle of wood. So large was the load that I would have needed a horse to carry even in my new state. Had the man not been burdened with the wood, I might have mistaken him for a bear. I hadn't foreseen this. I don't know why the thought of a spouse had eluded me but had I considered it, my imagination would have fallen short of the behemoth that lumbered along behind my quarry. I leaned back against the tree trunk and swallowed dry and hard. There was no way I could best this man. Perhaps I could wait for the two to separate. If the man were to leave to hunt or; or what? I knew what task lay before me. It would be murder. I would kill the man while he slept.

I waited hours past the dousing of the last oil lamp inside, and when I was confident that all in the cabin were sound asleep, I crossed the distance from the pine-grove to the front door. I moved through the darkness like a stalking predator, and I felt alive. Lightning flashed in the distance, and I dropped quickly to the ground where I laid my hand upon a rock. Perhaps I could just knock the man unconscious and not kill him. I collected the large rock and crossed the rest of the distance to the cabin. My heart throbbed in my ears and in my throat as I pushed on the door. It opened only an inch and stopped.

I froze. Maybe the man was standing on the other side of the door, armed with a rifle, but there was no push back and no sound of a rifle shot. Carefully, I ran my hand along the opening, feeling for a latch. I drew my blade and sliced effortlessly through the horsehair rope used to secure the door. Once inside, I slid like a serpent through the cabin. The rain had begun again, and it was my hope that the soft drone would mask any sound I made. I worked my way to the bed where the man and his wife lay sleeping and raised the rock to bash against the man's head. The woman brought herself up onto one elbow. In another flash of lightning, I saw the blueness of her eyes, and I was reminded of Evangeline.

As she drew in a breath to scream, I slammed the rock against her head and felt a strange sense of satisfaction. But it lasted only a fraction of a second. The husband shot up in bed and seized me by the throat. I buried my blade in the man's neck, and he released his grip. As he pulled back, the blade slid forward, slicing through his larynx and carotid artery. Blood sprayed from his neck like a fountain.

"I'm sorry." The words escaped my lips in a whisper.

Slinging the woman over my shoulder, I burst out the cabin door and ran for the cover of the pine grove. My heart raced, my skin slick with blood and rain, I tried to set the woman across my horse's withers, but the roundness of her belly made that all but impossible. I looked back at the house and spied a buckboard but decided it would be too slow. I removed my horse's saddle, and we rode double. I lashed her hands and secured the binding to a rope slung just behind my horse's front legs.

For the next hour, I rode as hard as my bareback skill would allow. Fueled by fear and adrenaline, I was finally able to put some distance between the blood-soaked cabin and myself. With the worst seemingly behind me, I took my first conscious breath. I am quite sure I'd been breathing the whole time but couldn't swear to it. Then the reality of it all began to set in. The scene that seemed only a split second at the time replayed itself slowly in my mind, and bile rose in my throat at the thought.

"What have I done?"

I'd never killed anyone before. I, Jules Reaume, was a good man, a hard-working man. I treated my customers fairly; I wasn't a drunkard or a philanderer. I attended Sunday mass.

But if all of that was true, who then was this man riding my horse? Who was this man who'd taken a pregnant woman from her bed? Taken her and murdered her husband. Rolling waves of nausea crashed through me, but I had no time for sickness. My shame and rage erupted in a cry that, even to my own ear, sounded other-worldly. I wanted to stop, to go back in time and undo this evil, but what was done was done.

At the sound of my cry, the woman awoke and began to scream. I pled with her to be silent, but that only served to ratchet her up. I pulled the woman down from the horse and clamped a hand over her mouth. She bit hard, drawing blood. I responded with the back of my hand, and the woman fell silent again. Needing a way to keep her quiet, I searched around and found a rock sufficient for the job. Blood flowed from her cracked teeth as I forced the stone into her mouth and secured it with a leather binding.

It must have been the pain of the cracked teeth that jolted the woman awake, and she smashed her head into my nose. Blood sprayed from my nostrils, and I seized her by the throat and began to squeeze. Her eyes were wide with fear. Oddly, excitement swelled in me as I watched her life begin to slip away.

Then I remembered Evangeline telling me that she wanted her alive. Like a petulant child, I screamed mockingly into the woman's face and released my grip. She sucked air in through her nose. Her nostrils flapped, making a honking sound that struck me as humorous. When I stopped laughing, we took up again and rode on into the dawn of the next day. We took shelter in the same small cave I had used on my way to collect her. I preferred to ride with my captive under the cover of darkness. The water in the cave had receded into a small basin near the cave entrance, and I drank good and long. When I had my fill, I offered water to the woman, but she refused. Blood had caked to her hair and scalp where I struck her with the rock only a day ago, though it seemed like another lifetime, so I tended to the wound as best I could, seeing as she clawed and kicked wildly at me when I came near her. I did my best to express my sorrow at her situation, but there were no words capable of soothing her. With the woman hogtied, I pulled her body close to mine, and we both succumbed to exhaustion.

That night I dreamt. In my dream, something pursued me. An equestrian as old as time itself rode on a horse with hooves that struck the earth with sparks and thunderous blows. Snarling brays seemed to come from all directions at once, but I saw just the one rider. He was faceless, and his form shifted every time I tried to look upon him. Who was this rider? I considered the woman's husband and thought I saw a resemblance, but just as one face seemed to be coming into focus, another would take its place. I was awoken by the crunch of gravel next to my head.

As I opened my eyes, a boot heel came down on my head, and stars exploded in my brain. The pain, sharp first and then lingering sobered me. I shook my head clear just as the boot was coming down again. My blade pierced the man's calf, and he fell to the ground. I was on him in an instant and buried my knife to the hilt in the man's side. I could hear the air escape his punctured lung.

The thought struck me as odd. Earlier, I had been feeling sick over having murdered someone. But there I sat, twisting the knife to free it from my attacker's rib cage, eager for my next kill. Was it simply that, like with many things, the first time is the hardest, or was it that the first man I killed did not deserve to die? Whatever the case, this time was certainly different, almost intoxicating. The power to watch as a man breathes his last at my own hand. The thought occurred in less time than it takes to blink one's eyes. Was my dream a premonition? Was the rider faceless because the rider was all men that I have ever or would ever kill? Then, just like that, it was gone as I lunged forward, shoving my blade into another attacker's eye. Warm spittle and blood splashed my face, and I breathed deep the coppery smell of freshly spilled blood.

Three more men encircled me now. My chest heaved as I, Jules Reaume, a shopkeeper turned killer, drew air into my lungs. I studied each of the remaining men, their eyes wide with fear as they shuffled side to side on nervous feet. I stretched the tendons in my neck, waiting for the slightest twitch that would determine my next victim. Then from behind them, there came a voice.

"My friend," the man said. His voice was thick with a Mexican accent. "There is no need for any more blood spilling. "We just want the woman. She is your property, no?"

He was a small man with brown skin and hair so black that it almost shined. Unlike his compatriots, this man looked calm and collected. I decided that he would be the next to die. Two of the little man's henchmen held hatchets, the other a much larger knife than mine.

The little man stepped forward empty-handed. "We will even pay you for the woman. Now how can you say no to that? We will give you money and let you keep your life. It's a generous offer, no?"

I exhaled hard. "What do you want with her?" I asked.

"Senior, what does every man want with a woman?"

"But she is with child," I said, drawing attention to her large stomach.

"It makes no difference, my friend. My men have needs."

I stood my ground and glanced from man to man. No one moved.

"Is she your woman, senior?"

The woman looked up at me, and I could read the pleading in her eyes. "She is mine, and she will remain mine. Now, which one of you wants to die next?" I gestured toward the two bodies on the floor with the tip of my blade. "I'll send you on to be with your friends."

"Why so hostile, my friend? After all, you are guests in our home, and you killed two of my men. It seems that we should be the hostile ones."

I watched as several other men filled in behind the little man.

"I'll kill her before I let you have her."

"That is okay too, though we would prefer killing her after we are done with her."

"You're Mexicans, right?"

"Yes, we are."

"What are you doing so far north?"

"Senior, have you made up your mind? Is today the day you die?"

I don't know if I was stalling; now, it certainly seems to have been a pointless question with time and distance. The woman looked up at me, pleading with her blue eyes. I decided to change my plans, just slightly. I sent my knife into the throat of one of the two hatchet men. As the first Mexican dropped to his knees, I took his hatchet and split the little man's head right across the bridge of his nose. The man with the machete swung in a high arc and hit the cave ceiling, sending a shower of sparks cascading down. Before he could adjust the angle of his attack, I took his leg at the knee with the razor-like edge of the hatchet. The second hatchet-wielding man tried to lunge past me to get to the woman, and I caught him across the back of his neck. The blade cut through bone in a loud splintering, and the man dropped sideways following the weight of his head as it hung only by a few tendons.

I retrieved the second hatchet and whirled like a dervish, hacking the remaining men to pieces. When the last man fell, I stood slathered in viscera and breathed deeply the smell of blood that permeated the cave. Then I turned to the woman. She was crying softly, and I cut the bindings from her hands to her feet, removed her gag, and helped her up.

She looked into my eyes. "What do you want with me?"

"It's not what I want. My wife sent me to get you."

The confusion on her face was unmistakable. "Your wife, who is your wife?"

"Evangeline Reaume," I answered.

"But I don't know her. What use could she have for me?"

"I couldn't say."

Confusion tightened into anger though her voice remained controlled. "You murdered my husband, didn't you?"

I stood there, dripping blood and sweat. "I'm sorry."

Tears began to stream down her cheeks, cutting rivers through the dirt and grime that had formed there. Her breath hitched once, and then she spoke again. "Joseph was a good man. You'll burn in the fires of Hell for what you have done."

I wiped my forearm across my face and mouth. "Of that, I have no doubt," I told her.

"My name is—"

I lunged toward her. I did not want to know her name. "Enough! Enough talking," I said, and moved to replace the gag. But before I could reach her. She spoke her name.

"Manette."

The name itself meant nothing to me, but simply by uttering it, she became real. I dropped to my knees and wept. Manette placed a hand atop my head and pulled me to her stomach. I placed my hands on either side of her large belly as I had done so many times with Evangeline, and I felt the tiny life within Manette moving about.

"If our baby is a boy, we are going to name him Joseph, and, I think Josephine if God gives us a girl."

A tiny ember began to grow in my gut. In a rage, I slammed my forearm into the side of her head. Manette fell to the ground, stunned but not unconscious.

"No more talking!" I screamed at her.

I shoved the rock back in her mouth and tied the leather thong so tight that it cut into the flesh of her cheeks. Then I mounted the horse, tied a rope around her neck, and dragged Manette stumbling behind.

I met Evangeline at the river's edge, just as she had instructed. She had changed much in the five days I had been away, bearing some resemblance to the old witch who vanished in the woods. I removed Manette from my horse. I had opted to walk and let her ride when she could walk no more. I did not want to ride holding her for fear that I might feel the unborn child kick again.

At the sight of Evangeline, Manette attempted to bury her face against my chest but I pushed her away. Evangeline, who now looked more like the witch than herself, approached and blew the paralyzing powder into

Manette's face. I turned away, not wanting to witness the rest of the ritual. I had seen it once before, and sadly, though I did not know it at the time, I would see it again and again.

But as it was slightly different from Evangeline's rebirth, I will describe what transpired. There was no crow and no dead child this time. Evangeline stripped the woman naked and laid her on her back. Then she dragged a hooked nail sideways across Manette's belly and cut her baby from her womb. It was a boy, and he emerged crying and fussing as had my own son. Evangeline held the child in the air by one foot, slit its throat, and drank the blood as it flowed from the dying child's body.

Manette was unable to move but cast her eyes in my direction as if hoping I would intervene. I have taken many women who were with child for Evangeline since, but Manette is the one who haunts my dreams.

As Evangeline drank freely from the dead infant, a stirring arose at the river's edge. The thing that had crawled from my wife's body some years before dragged itself out of the water and stood next to Manette. Her scream broke through her paralysis as the monster plunged its face into her body and feasted on her until there was nothing left but one single white bone. Evangeline picked up the bone and tossed baby Joseph's body to the monster that snapped it out of the air like a hound catching a piece of meat given by its master. Then Evangeline knelt before the monster with our Ezra by her side as the creature slipped back into the river.

* * *

Part 4 An Attempt to Right my Wrongs

As previously mentioned, Manette was only the first of the women that I had taken. I do not know the number because I have not let myself keep count or dwell on the memories. Suffice it to say that the number was great. So many that pickings had become slim, and I was forced to begin hunting closer to home. The homesteaders turned to the French for protection, but it was no use. My skills had surpassed those of the greatest hunters, and soon the expectant wives of French soldiers began to go missing. For a period, pregnant women were secured in a heavily patrolled guardhouse. That was when Evangeline struck upon a scheme. We would find a scapegoat, thereby calming the villager's fears and bringing our prey back into the open.

We would point the soldiers in the direction of the Mooka'am. After all, it was the Mooka'am who summoned the Inaki. I was forced to ride an even greater distance than when I took Manette, but with Evangeline's guidance, I was able to find a pregnant woman. When Evangeline and the Inaki had finished their ritual, The Inaki agreed to leave the woman's body, less her organs, to be used as bait. I hid the body in the same cave that Manette and I took shelter in and convinced a young Mooka'am brave that I had trapped the monster within. I told the brave that I needed his help to kill the beast taking women and the unborn children. Perhaps eager to show his prowess, the spirited young brave followed me deep into the cave, where I murdered him.

I returned with the dead Indian and the woman's hollowed-out corpse and told the French that I had caught an Indian in the act of consuming the woman's innards. I told the captain of the guard that, in an attempt to spare his own life, the brave admitted that the Mooka'am consorted with the devil. I told him that the Mooka'am sacrificed the women and their unborn children to a demon called the Inaki. The captain gathered his troops and began hunting down the Mooka'am. They killed a small number, but the Mooka'am nation scattered into the woods and vanished. After a while, life returned to normal until another pregnant woman disappeared from the village.

Convinced that the terror would not end until every last Mooka'am was captured and killed, the French ordered their best scout, Makadewa' Mahingan, the Black Wolf of the Aakwaadizi, in from the field. They told the Black Wolf the story I had imparted. The Black Wolf, along with several of his scouts, tracked the remaining Mooka'am and delivered them to the captain. Lacking a jail sufficient to hold the remaining Mooka'am, the soldiers herded them to the islet on the river. There they remained through the coldest part of the winter until every last man, woman, and child had starved or frozen to death. With the end of the Mooka'am, it became clear that I would no longer be able to procure what Evangeline needed. Evangeline took Ezra and left. With Evangeline gone and feeling that I had exacted my revenge on the Mooka'am for the destruction they had visited on my life, I summoned the Black Wolf to my bedside. Without Evangeline, my body began to fail. I confided all truth in the Black Wolf, and it is with his kind consideration that I have been allowed to complete this diary. He has also agreed not to bury my body on that accursed islet. For I am sure that the spirits of the Mooka'am will search that islet for me for all eternity, and I fear them more than the fires below. With that, I conclude this journal and prepare to begin my eternity in Hell.

With a sorrowful heart,

Jules Reaume

14

Nick closed the ancient manuscript and rested it on his lap. He shut his eyes for a moment, contemplating what he'd just read. Aside from Achak, Babe, and the river that passed silently by, he was the only person who knew. He'd spent years slogging through dusty books in dank libraries and dragging his tired eyes across an endless stream of microfiche, and in less than an hour with Reaume's diary, he may have found his answers. Gone were his concerns of fraud or prank, but Nick still wasn't ready to declare himself a believer.

"Holy shit," Nick said, breaking his silence. He dragged a hand over his face. "That's un-fucking-believable."

"But it is the truth, Nick."

"So, whatever happened to Evangeline and her son?"

"Black Wolf tracked her into the northern woods," Achak said. "He discovered her hiding in a cave, but the boy was nowhere to be found. Evangeline was brought back to face the tribunal. As it was the dead of winter, it had been presumed that the boy froze to death, though his body was never found."

"And Evangeline?" Nick asked excitedly, "What did they do with her?"

"The tribunal decided that it was not appropriate for a white woman to be buried with the Mooka'am, but they also did not want to bury her on their own land. They ordered Black Wolf to give her to the river, just as she had done with so many. So, Black Wolf and his brothers opened a hole in the ice. Black Wolf said that ice was as clear as glass, so clear that he could see the river bed below. Evangeline offered no resistance. She told Black Wolf that, without her son, she had no reason to live. She stepped willingly into the opening in the ice, and Black Wolf watched as her body, weighted with stones, sank down into her watery grave. Black Wolf said that she stared up at him, burning the image of her blue eyes into his soul. Then she closed her eyes, and the river bed pulsed and swallowed her. The men heard a loud crack as the ice began to fail. It was as thick as anyone had ever seen, but somehow it began to splinter. Black Wolf was the only one who made it back to shore. He watched as his brothers, six in all, thrashed and tried to cling to chunks of ice that rolled and tossed in the moving water. One by one, they were dragged down by their heavy winter clothing. When spring came, Black Wolf searched for their bodies, but neither they nor Evangeline were never found."

"Are you okay, Nick? You look a little pale," Babe said, placing the back of her hand against his cheek.

"Yeah, I'm fine. So, what happened to Jules?"

"Well, back then, my people believed that outside of war, the act of repaying killing with killing was wrong. Our system of law was geared more toward the restoration of balance rather than punishment. But for a fucking monster like Jules Reaume, exceptions were made. Still, no one wanted his blood on their hands, so it fell to Black Wolf. He decided to bury Reaume alive. Black Wolf kept his word and buried him not on the islet but rather headfirst, facing the islet just over there," Achak pointed across the river. "Do you see that twisted dead tree trunk?"

Nick craned his neck and nodded.

"Unlike his wife," Achak continued, "Reaume struggled and fought till his end. Black Wolf never spoke of the execution to anyone aside from the first-born sons of my bloodline. Now, you get to be a part of the history of the Inaki and the Mooka'am. Probably not what you were expecting when you came looking for answers."

"Not exactly. I can't believe you're breaking, I don't know, tradition, for me."

"I'm not breaking it for you!" Achak snapped. "I'm not breaking it at all. My family has been burdened with this secret for hundreds of years.

I'm telling you because Babe and I have tried to tell the world, and we have been mocked and ridiculed. Shit, you heard her; Babe got laughed out of the reporter's office when she went to the paper. Even the authorities have targeted us so much that I can't even walk down Main Street without fear of arrest. No, Nick, I'm telling you this because if Babe is right, your word, as a man of science, might provide the credibility we need to make people listen. We can't afford to let this town keep its secret."

It had been one hell of a day, to say the least, and Nick was still in a bit of a daze. But he had to get his head in the game. He stood up and began to pace. "And you believe the Inaki is still out there?"

"Yes, Nick, it has never stopped," said Achak.

"But how is that possible? If that many women were disappearing, it would be all over the news."

"It is all over the news, Nick," Babe said. "But do you think that a missing woman from Cairo, Illinois, is going to make the 10 o'clock news in Chicago or even Saint Louis? Hell no, besides, most of these cases are chalked up to domestic violence and closed out. Others are considered likely victims of serial killers. When a serial killer is caught, the cops try to tie as many unsolved murders or disappearances to them as possible to clear their caseloads."

"Then why haven't you reported this to the authorities? I don't mean the locals. I'm talking FBI."

"Nick," said Achak calmly. "Do you realize that right this very moment, there are upwards of 50 active serial killers running loose in the United States alone? Your *authorities,*" his tone tinged with disdain, "have their hands full searching for human monsters. They have no time or inclination to take on the paranormal world's killers. That's left to the lunatics, like Babe and me, and now you."

Nick closed his eyes and shook his head. "And you're telling me that this, this monster, is running around out there right now?" He said, gesturing toward the river.

"It is," Babe answered. "Just a little over a month ago, a woman from the town of Millbrook, just north of Chesapeake Station, went missing. Her name was Jessica Upshaw."

"Yeah," said Nick. "I saw the signs all over town, but that doesn't mean some monster climbed out of the river and snatched her."

"That's not how it works, Nick. The Inaki has a human counterpart. Someone like Evangeline Reaume."

"What does that have to do with Upshaw?"

Achak continued. "Jessica Upshaw was expecting the couple's first child."

Nick swallowed hard. "Still, that's a hell of a jump."

Achak pulled a folded-up newspaper article from his pocket and handed it to Nick.

Expectant Millbrook Mother Taken from Her Home
in Broad Daylight. Police Baffled.

"Nick, the police interviewed everyone, cooks, housekeepers, gardeners, even Jessica's live-in nurse. Jessica had been experiencing problems, and her doctor ordered bed rest. The nurse checked on her at 9 AM when she took her breakfast. No one saw her after that. At 10:30, the nurse and two housekeepers went to get Jessica out of bed to change her linens, but Jessica was gone.

Maids and gardeners?"

"The Upshaws are a very wealthy family, Nick. "As I said, the police interviewed everyone and felt confident that it was not an inside job."

"Then maybe it was a kidnapping," Nick said. "You know, for money."

Achak ignored him. "Within thirty minutes of Jessica's disappearance, the authorities began a search of the area. No expense was spared. Ground and air teams searched day and night. The Upshaws, Brian and his parents, stayed glued to the phone waiting for a call from the kidnappers, but it never came."

Nick said nothing. He just sat and listened and tried to take it all in.

"Police and volunteers searched the woods in all directions from the family home. The search went on for days. Then two more women went missing a couple of days apart. But unlike Jessica Upshaw, those women were not pregnant. About a week into the investigation, a hunter and his dog came upon the remains of several women. They were found in the woods about twenty miles north of Millbrook. Most of the remains were unidentifiable, but the authorities were able to match a piece of clothing to the nightgown Jessica Upshaw had been wearing the morning she was taken. The police closed all three cases."

"Well, there you go," Nick said emphatically.

"It was all too scripted, Nick. Someone leaked pictures to the press. There were pentagrams and upside-down crosses and literally everything you would expect to find in a 1970s devil worship cult classic. I believe it was all staged to draw attention away from the Upshaw case, and it worked."

"Nick," Babe said. "When you drove into the county, did you happen to notice the condition of our crops?"

"Crops? What do crops have to do with what we're talking about?"

"Did you, or didn't you?"

"Yeah, they looked like shit. What about it?"

"Just listen," she said. "This year, every county in the area with the single exception of Chesapeake Station experienced bumper crop growth. But most of the growers in Chesapeake Station didn't even bother planting. The few that did, the mom-and-pop holdouts, lost everything."

"What do you mean, *holdouts*?"

Babe didn't answer. "Our growers expected yields on par with the other counties, but as the farmers prepared to bring in their harvest, everything withered and died," she paused to make sure he understood. "I mean, they actually watched their crops age and rot before their eyes. We lost a few more mom-and-pops, but the huge operations that grew for SowMax and Agri-Grow avoided the losses by not planting. It was like they knew what was coming."

He was trying to follow but wasn't making the connection. "Are you saying that the big corporations somehow arranged for the small farm's crops to fail?"

"I wouldn't put it past them," Babe sneered. "But no, not in this case."

"Nick," Achak interrupted, "When the islet burned, the last thing anyone heard was a lone voice cry out 'Nibo gitigaan,' It means dead fields."

Babe locked her gaze on Nick, and he could feel it. "What?" He asked sharply.

"The Mooka'am cursed the land, Nick, and now the mayor and city council are in some kind of pact to keep the county's fields producing."

"That's what you think is going on?"

"Back in the 1800s," said Achak. "The railroad made Chesapeake Station the last stop before the Mississippi crossing, and a lot of wealthy families put down roots here. They bought up enormous plots of land. They bought out farms, displacing local families. Then in the early 1900s, in came SowMax and Agri-Grow. They sold off the livestock, tore down the family farms, erected huge storage sheds, and brought tractors by the trainload. Their investors made a fortune, Nick."

"Corporate buyout isn't anything new."

"No, it's not," Babe said. "But it was much more than that. Tax revenue filled the town's coffers and put Chesapeake Station on the map. Hell, presidents made it a point to stop here, and I'm not talking stumping. They actually stopped here. They got off their trains and busses and walked through town. They met with the town's mayors and aldermen and made backroom deals. Then suddenly, all that was in jeopardy, and no one knew why."

"No offense," Nick said. "But Chesapeake Station is a small town, like a hundred other small towns in Illinois. Why would a president give a shit about a small rural town in *fly-over-country?*"

"Chesapeake Station may be small," Babe countered. "But we are the Chesapeake County seat, and Chesapeake County is over 1500 square miles of farm country. It's the second-largest county in the state and the largest by far when it comes to farming acreage," Babe said sternly.

"Sorry, like I said, I didn't mean any offense."

"None taken. Anyway, twenty years ago, Chesapeake Station had a similar crop failing. At that time, a man named Pozerac Gemein came to town. He asked for a meeting with the newly appointed Mayor Steel and a few select aldermen and county board members. The following summer's crops came in, and for the next 8 years, all seemed normal. Then the crops failed again. Two years of bad crops, and then he came back. He called for another closed-door meeting and was gone. Eight more fertile years followed that visit."

"Wait," Nick stood up again. "How do you know all of this?" His tone was challenging rather than inquisitive.

"My father was one of the board members excluded from the meeting twenty years ago. And he was excluded during Gemein's last visit as well. He, along with several other board members and aldermen that were well-respected members of the community. And as if that wasn't insulting enough, SowMax and Agri-Grow had representatives come in for the meetings. Can you believe that shit? Outsiders, deciding what happens in our county while actual county board members are kept out. What kind of bullshit is that?" Babe was raising her voice.

"Babe, please," Achak said, reminding her to keep her voice down.

"Well," Nick said, "sounds like the big corporations hold more sway over your town than your town's people do. It's shitty, but not uncommon."

"Yeah? Well, it's bullshit."

"We're getting off-topic," Achak said. "Nick, this has been the second year of bad crops, and we, Babe and I, are sure Pozerac Gemein will be back."

"Who the hell is Pozerac Gemein, and what does he have to do with farming?" Nick asked.

"Forget about faring for a minute," Achak said, shot Babe a look that Nick read as; *careful, we're losing him.*

"Nick, we believe that Pozerac Gemein is connected to the Inaki. Remember when I told you that Black Wolf captured Evangeline and brought her back here?"

"Yeah."

"And how they assumed that her son a died, but they never found the body?"

"Wait, are you suggesting that the kid is still alive? That would make him...." Nick tumbled numbers around in his head, "over almost 300 years old!"

"I know it sounds crazy, Nick."

"It sounds crazy because it is crazy! No one could live that long."

"He could if he was never really alive, to begin with."

Nick threw his hands up. "Okay, this is where I get off. I thank you both for a pleasantly fucking bizarre evening," Nick said as he stood up and walked back toward the ladder.

"Please, Nick, just hear me out," Babe said, desperately grabbing a hold of Nick's arm. "Whoever he is, we think he is the one who had been taking the expectant women. Nick, we have checked back issues of newspapers across the Midwest over the past fifty years. Each time Gemein has come to Chesapeake Station, a woman has gone missing. In August of 1945, a woman expecting a child vanished from New Glarus, Wisconsin. In 1955, several women went missing from Chicago. One was a young woman expecting her first child. She lived in the Greater Grand Crossing neighborhood, and a missing black woman in a black neighborhood in the 50s would never have made the paper, except that her husband claimed to have fired a shot striking the white man that took his wife. He said he was no more than five feet away and knew he hit him, but the man jumped from the couple's second-floor window and ran off with her."

"Jumped from the...."

Achak pulled photostatic copies of each article as Babe summarized the stories.

"In 1965, a woman in her third trimester was taken from Hannibal, Missouri, right across the river." In 1975, an expectant mother was taken from her home in Clinton, Iowa. The husband was tried but not convicted; her body was never found."

Nick held his hands up, "Okay, I got the picture. You think it's Gemein. He's kidnapping these women and sacrificing their unborn children to the witch, and he's doing it with the blessing and protection of certain members of your city and county government. Am I missing anything?"

"Lots," said Babe. "But we don't have time to go over everything."

"It's so fucking hot up here. I gotta get outside."

Nick climbed down the ladder, followed by Babe and Achak, and the three regrouped outside. Nick ran his hand roughly over the top of his head, trying to stimulate brain activity. "Seriously, guys, this is a lot of shit to lay on someone the first time you meet them."

"We know," said Achak.

"I'm going to need some time here. This is a big ask, guys. It could end my career before it even gets started."

"Fair enough, Nick, but time is of the essence."

Nick walked back into the barn and began pulling the 100 pound bales away from his car.

"Let me give you a hand with that, Nick," said Achak.

"Thanks."

Nick climbed in and started the engine. "Can I give you a ride back to get your car?"

The sound of the engine firing up tore through the stillness of the night. A spotlight shot across the water, and a voice over a loudspeaker called out.

"Stay where you are. This is the Chesapeake County Sheriff. You are trespassing on Chesapeake County property, and you are under arrest. Do not move, or you will be charged with resisting along with trespassing."

"Fuck!" Nick said. "I don't need this shit."

Babe jumped into the back of the Bronco, and Achak climbed into the front seat.

"What the hell do you think you're doing? The police are coming."

One of the officers across the river fired a shot into the air to show he meant business.

"What the fuck!" Nick exclaimed. He had heard gunshots before, but they were never intended for him either as a means of death or warning.

"Punch it, Nick!" Babe called from the back seat.

The noise from the squad car's engines grew louder and Nick pinned the accelerator to the floor dodging trees as the headlights picked them up. The Bronco bucked and kicked, but they had finally made it out of the woods and burst from between the trees onto Lake Side Road. Nick had forgotten which way he'd turned in and took a left instead of the right that would have led him back to Black Horse Road and the Pleasant View Motor Lodge. They'd gotten about a half-mile down the road when one of the county patrol cars bounced onto the road ahead of them. Nick cut the wheel hard, and the compact SUV leaned hard to one side. The Bronco bucked as two of its wheels broke contact, momentarily with the ground. With his 180 completed, Nick slammed the accelerator down hard, and the Bronco jumped like its name's sake after a sharp spurring in the sides. The Bronco was built for power more than speed and was no match for the Police Interceptor's big V8. The squad was closing in fast when another patrol car emerged from the tree-line and blocked the road ahead.

"Hang on!" Nick yelled.

He cut the wheel, almost rolling the Bronco for the second time. All held tightly as they bounced through the culvert and into the field. The Bronco took the rough terrain like a champ. Asses were in the air, but the seatbelts kept the occupants from flying out. One of the squads tried to follow but quickly lost its battle with the unplowed field. As the squad shrunk in Nick's rearview mirror, another shot rang out, and the spare tire mounted to the tailgate hissed in response to being struck.

"Babe, are you okay?" Nick called.

"I'm fine, just drive this fucking thing!"

***

Sheriff Tucker knew better than to chase a four-wheel-drive vehicle through a field and decided to take the main roads and try to head it off when it came out on the other side. As he drove, he got on the radio.

"Abernathy, you dip-shit! If you can manage to get yourself unstuck, you get your ass out to Baseline Road and grab them if they head north!"

He watched the felling vehicle's headlights bounce across the field. He tried as best he could to drive parallel to it, but then suddenly, they were gone. He looked for brake lights, but no luck there either. Tucker slammed his meaty hands on the steering wheel. "Sum-bitch," and turned back toward the Pleasant View to wait for the mysterious visitor and his passengers to show up.

15

I t felt like an invisible hand grabbed a fist full of his guts and gave them a twist. Maybe he could sneak back into the house and back into bed. Then, if his father ever went looking for the binoculars, Levi could just play dumb. But even as the thought was forming in his head, he began to dismiss it. Levi Waters was no liar, not even by omission. He crawled to the edge of the deck. He would climb down, hold onto the wood, and reach under the water to see if he could feel for them. Levi peered over the edge looking for the best way to navigate the wooden supports, and could hardly believe his eyes. There, dangling just beyond his grasp, was the neck strap. The binoculars were half-submerged, but they weren't gone.

Levi hung his body out over the edge of the dock and reached and strained until his fingers hooked around the strap. Once he felt like he had a good hold, Levi tried to pull them up, but something had a hold of his pajama sleeve. He pulled hard and heard a rip. There was a tinge of pain as a nail sticking out of one of the supports tore his skin, but he didn't have time for pain. Levi pressed the glasses to his eyes to make sure they were okay. The right lens was perfect, but the left was not. It must have cracked when it hit the deck, and the crack allowed water into the prism housing.

"Fuck!"

He hadn't meant to say it out loud and looked around in a panic to make sure his mother hadn't wandered into the yard after discovering him missing from his bed. Thankfully the house was still dark. Levi sat there on the deck with his father's broken binoculars and his torn PJ shirt and considered the pickle he'd gotten himself into. Funny how self-preservation could trump a nightmare and a gash to the arm. He got to his feet and snuck back into the house. Levi pulled the flashlight from his PJ pants pocket and stuffed it back into the junk drawer, and hurried back to bed, slipping the binoculars beneath his pillow until he could figure out how to deal with them.

He slept the rest of the night without dreaming of crows or cold, wet hands, or even of how sore his ass was going to be after his father kicked it good and hard. The actual threat was, "Levi, you're gonna get my boot up your ass," but he was sure that was just a figure of speech.

In the morning, his mother whipped open the blinds in his room, but she still had to call him three times to wake him for church. When he finally got up, he tossed his PJs into the bottom of the hamper and covered them with dirty clothes. Levi washed his face and hands and brushed his teeth, and made it to the table just in time to down a piece of toast and swallow some orange juice, which tasted bitter.

It was almost 10 O'clock, church started at 10:30, and though it was only a twenty-minute drive, he figured he was still good to go for communion. The Waters family maintained a strict one-hour rule when it came to receiving the Eucharist. No food one hour before receiving the sacrament. Levi doubted the Lord cared about such things, but that's how his parents had been raised, and now it was his and Frankie's cross to bear.

Scott had to park two blocks away and complained the entire walk. The single white steeple of Saint Michael's Catholic Church reached high into the clear blue sky, and Connie commented on the picture-postcard beauty. Levi thought it looked like something you would see on a Christmas card, except that it was mid-September, hot as balls. Not to mention the belfry, besieged by huge black crows, the sight of which made Levi very uneasy.

The Waters family made their way up the steps and through the doors that stood like two open arms waiting to embrace the faithful. Inside, the smell of wood and wax hung in the thick humid air, and even though the church's stained-glass windows were all tilted open, there was no breeze to be felt. Two rows of pews across and about twenty deep, the family made their way up the middle aisle, looking for a place to sit. Scott opted for a bench on the right side near the back, which suited Levi just fine. Even the short walk up the aisle made him feel weird. Like everyone was staring holes through his back. Like they knew what he had done. Throwing rocks at defenseless birds, sneaking out in the middle of the night, stealing his father's binoculars, and then breaking them and hiding them, and let us not forget about the PJs. *Well,* he thought, *no better place to ask forgiveness.* His mom put the kneeler down, and the whole family knelt and joined the rest of the congregation in silent, meditative prayer, and Levi immediately went into negotiations.

"God, I know I messed up. I'm sorry, but if you can just give me a pass on this, I promise, no more," he paused, the thought catching in his mind. In the not too distant past, he'd discovered the art of self-manipulation, and he'd almost offered that as a bargaining chip but stopped himself. Now he was stuck, like a frozen computer monitor, the little wheel just spinning and spinning. He supposed he was expected to ask forgiveness for that too. His thought process was interrupted as lightning split the sky and thunder shook the small white church.

"That's odd; the Courier didn't mention rain today," Connie said, referring to Red Hook's local newspaper.

Scott grunted something that sounded like agreement as the rain fell in hissing sheets against the church's shingled roof. The hypnotic sound stole Levi's thoughts, from prayers of pardon to feelings of disappointment. The rain was going to ruin his day. Instead of spending the day outside—and getting to see Kaylin again, he would probably get stuck in the house doing stupid chores. As he sat silently grousing, Levi thought he heard something that sounded like a whisper between the heavy patter of the rain. He perked up his ears, thinking it was his imagination, but there it was again. Words— definitely words repeated in a sentence, only, it didn't make any sense. He strained to pick out one word at a time, like trying to learn the lyrics of a song. Nibaa, that was one of the words; wiin—nibaa. A chill ran up his spine. It was the same thing he'd heard in his dream: wiin *nibaa anaamibiig, wiin nibaa anaamibiig, wiin nibaa anaamibiig.* The words made no sense in his dream, and they made no sense now, but they grew louder and louder as the whisper turned into a murmur and then into a droning that overtook his conscious thoughts. He looked around, but no one else seemed to be noticing.

Levi shifted uncomfortably on his kneeler. He did his best to focus on his prayer, but it was no use. He felt hot; he was getting dizzier by the second, and if he couldn't quiet the voices, he thought he was going to run straight up a wall. Then, even more suddenly than it had started, the voices ceased. Levi exhaled in relief, but his respite was brief. The voices came crashing over him, and his eyes began to loll wildly before rolling back in his head. Levi knelt there, frozen in a dead white stare. He saw the crow standing right in front of him. With its head tilted to one side, the bird locked him with one larva encrusted eye that burrowed right into his soul. Levi's blood ran cold, and he began to shiver. Connie must have noticed her boy shaking because she took him by the shoulders and turned him to face her.

"Levi," she whispered harshly, but he didn't respond. "Scott—Scott, there's something wrong with Levi."

Connie was about to shout his name when the altar boy rang the chimes announcing Fr. Guerin, and all rose to greet him, all but the Waters family. The bells seemed to break the spell, and Levi was back.

"Are you okay?" Connie asked. "You look white as a sheet," she whispered and put her hand to his cold and clammy forehead. "I'm taking Levi outside for a minute," she told Scott as she led Levi out.

The priest, a young man, seemed to notice two of his flock slipping out the back. "Was it something I said?"

The congregation chuckled, and Scott replied. "Sorry, Father, my son is a little under the weather."

Father Guerin held up a forgiving hand and continued with the service.

Connie led Levi out into the vestibule and sat him down on a bench near the white marble baptismal fountain. Levi was feeling better, and he hated that she had made such a fuss. He tried to stand up, but Connie put her hand on his forearm. Levi rolled his eyes but sat back down without a word. He loved his mother, even though she was a worrywart. Constantly feeling foreheads and checking for swollen glands.

"I'm fine, mom, seriously," he said.

Connie shook her head, "I just wish it wasn't Sunday so that I could get you in to see a doctor."

"A doctor," Levi protested. "I don't need a doctor. I just need to go sit in the car and rest."

Like most mother's Connie Waters knew her boys. She knew that instead of paying attention to what was going on in the service, Frankie was thinking about how lucky Levi was because he got out of church. And she also knew that there was something wrong with Levi. Perhaps it was just a bug, but whatever it was, sitting in the car alone was out of the question.

"If you're well enough to sit in the car, you're well enough to sit in church."

Connie stood up and pointed toward the doors. Levi stood up, dropped his shoulders, and marched. He opened the massive wooden doors as slowly as he could, hoping to sneak back in unnoticed, but the creak sounded like a trumpet blast, and a sea of eyeballs turned and locked on him. Levi exhaled, his drooping shoulders drooped even further, and he proceeded to his pew. As he glanced around, he started seeing faces that he knew. Finn, Stan and McKenna, Stevie and Lonnie, and even Kaylin, *hail, hail the gangs all here*, he thought to himself as he plopped down next to Frankie.

"Wow, Levi, that was embarrassing," Frankie snickered.

"Shut up, Frankie."

The priest commented about lost sheep returning to the flock, which garnered laughs from the parishioners, and Levi slunk in his seat. He had already hated church; he thought it was a complete waste of a good Sunday morning, and Father Funny wasn't doing anything to change his mind.

"Hey, father, did you hear the one about the priest and the rabbi?" He wanted to say. He bet he could out-funny a priest any old Sunday, but he kept his mouth shut and began his Sunday calisthenics.

Kneel, stand, sit, stand, sit, kneel, sit, mumble some prayer, and he was right for another week. It wasn't that he didn't believe in God; on the contrary, Levi knew God was real. God answered his prayers when Frankie was six years old and needed surgery. His mother told him that Frankie needed his appendix taken out. Levi asked what he could do to help, and his mother told him to pray to God that Frankie would be okay. Levi prayed, and Frankie was okay. He prayed for his father when he was in a terrible crash on the Dan Ryan Expressway two summers ago. The accident landed Scott Waters in intensive care at Rush. Levi prayed, and God made his dad better. Levi absolutely believed in God, but he thought that God was cool. God didn't care if you went to a white building with a steeple on Sundays, and he sure didn't care if you wore jeans or dress slacks to Sunday morning calisthenics, kneel, stand, sit, stand, sit, kneel, sit. Levi believed that God wanted him to be a good person, and to help those less fortunate and that the rest would take care of itself.

The priest said something, the altar boy jingled the bells, and everyone knelt down. As he knelt there, between his mother and Frankie, Levi began to feel light-headed again. The rain picked up and sizzled on the roof of the church. And the whispers were back, wiin nibaa anaamibiig, win nibaa anaamibiig, wiin nibaa anaamibiig. Levi shook his head to clear the voices, but it did no good. Wiin nibaa anaamibiig, wiin nibaa anaamibiig, Wiin nibaa anaamibiig, and this time Leeeviiiii, the voices hissed. Levi's body shuddered, and Connie placed her hand on his forearm again.

Levi squeezed his eyes shut and prayed in his head. "Please, God, make it stop," and almost immediately, the rain stopped, and with that, the whispering voices were silenced.

"Hallelujah, someone's prayer has been answered," proclaimed Father Guerin. This time there was only a smattering of laughs followed by soft muttering. Apparently, some in the flock didn't think prayer jokes were as funny as sheep jokes.

Levi exhaled in relief and quickly decided to ask God to fix the broken binoculars. Fixing broken field-glasses had to be a piece of cake compared to *creating* the whole world.

In his sermon, Father Guerin read passages from Genesis and Second Kings. He talked about how, unlike Enoch and Elijah, everyone must face death, but how it need not be a fearful thing. How the gates to Heaven are open to those baptized in faith and repentant of their sins. Real snoozer stuff if you asked Levi. Then the priest admonished the non-believers. He read something from the book of Psalms. He said that God's people had rebelled against Him, and God turned the rivers to blood. That got Levi's attention. He forgot all about the whispers and the dizziness and even the broken binoculars. Frogs, locusts, lightning splitting stuff in two, and God sending His army of destroying angels in to kick the crap out of the ingrates. Oh yes, Levi Waters was now fully engaged in the sermon. Levi liked the *wrath of God* stuff, but he was still glad to hear the words he'd been waiting for.

"I bless you in the name of the Father, and of the Son, and of the Holy Spirit," Father Guerin said, as he held his hands out toward the church body. "Go now, to love and serve the Lord."

The Waters family stepped out of the church and into a sauna. The rain did nothing to cool things down. Instead, it just made it steamy. When they were back in Chicago, the Waters' ritual was to go to breakfast after Sunday Service unless it was football season. During the season, it was straight home after service to watch the Bears. But, as luck would have it, on this particular Sunday, the game didn't start till 3. They crossed the bridge on Endicott and turned left onto Main Street. They drove past Founders Park, already filling up with picnickers, and rolled right past Burton's.

"Remind me to stop there after breakfast; I'm making chicken cacciatore for dinner," Connie announced.

The Waters men rolled their eyes. They hated grocery shopping. Levi exhaled audibly; he hated chicken cacciatore even more than shopping. It was probably the only thing his mother made that he didn't like, and it seemed like they had it all the time. But, in his mom's defense, Levi had never told her that he didn't like it, and it was his father's favorite. Levi considered that maybe having his favorite meal might make his father's punishment a little less severe when he told him about the busted field glasses. They pulled into one of the diagonal spots about a block away from the No Finer Diner and walked.

"So, what did you think of the sermon today, boys?" Scott asked.

The brothers harrumphed but didn't offer their opinions.

"Just shows to go ya," Scott said. That was one of his favorite idioms, and it drove Levi crazy that he purposely said it wrong.

"You don't screw with your father," Scott finished.

"Scott!" Connie snapped.

"Sorry, babe, mess, you don't mess with your father."

"I don't think that was God's message at all," said Frankie. "I think God was mad because the people were greedy, and they were testing him."

"You're exactly right, honey," said Connie as she stroked the top of his head.

The diner was packed. It would be a good half hour before they would be seated.

"Levi, you come with me to Burton's; you can help carry the groceries back to the car. Scott, you and Frankie can wait for a table."

Levi was more than happy to go with his mom. Every moment he spent with his father made him feel guilty. He knew he had to tell him what he'd done, and the longer he waited, the harder it would be. Levi considered telling him right then and there. His dad couldn't come unglued right in the middle of a crowded restaurant, or could he? No, it was better to wait. As he walked, he whispered a little prayer to God for help.

He hadn't realized it, but the answer to his prayer was walking down the sidewalk headed right for him. Levi burst out laughing when he saw him. Stanley Howard, walking around in broad daylight wearing a bow tie.

"Jeez, Stan, did ya lose a bet?"

"Never mind, Levi, you look very handsome, Stanley," said Connie.

"Thanks, Mrs. Waters. I just wanted to look nice for church," replied Stanley.

"Oh, in a pig's eye, I had to argue with him for an hour before he put it on."

Elizabeth Howard was an attractive woman who looked like she tried too hard. She wore a dress, it *was* Sunday Service after all, but the dress was bright blue and cinched tight at the waist. The hemline ended just above the knee, and she looked like she was wearing nylons; either that or the woman had perfectly tanned legs. And still, all of that would have been fine, but she capped it all off with black high heels with red soles.

Connie swallowed hard. "Are those Christian Louboutins?"

The overdressed woman extended a hand. "Hi, you must be the family who bought the Ryan's place. I'm Beth, Stan, Finn, and McKenna's mom."

"Pleased to meet you; I'm Connie, Connie Waters," she said, still staring at the shoes.

Beth held a hand to the side of her mouth and whispered, "They're knock-offs, shh don't tell anyone," and smiled warmly.

"Well, you could never tell," Connie said, tugging uneasily at her simple sundress.

Levi rolled his eyes.

"And you must be Levi," Beth said, having to look up to make eye contact. "Stanley said you were a big kid."

"Yes," Connie said, "sorry. This is Levi. My husband Scott is waiting in the diner with Frankie."

"Well, that's where we're headed," Beth said with a smile.

"Is your husband parking the car?" Connie asked.

"No dear, he was killed five years ago. He was a Lineman for the power company. He was out cutting power to the old girl's school when a power line blew into the boom on his bucket truck. He had a hand on the controls, and, well, they said he didn't suffer."

Connie gasped, and her hand flew to her mouth. "Oh, my God! I am so sorry, I didn't know."

"It's okay, dear, really it is. We've come to terms, haven't we?" She said, addressing her children, who all nodded.

"Jeez, guys, I'm sorry," offered Levi.

"It's okay, man," Stan said. "It was pretty hard for a while, but I think we're all okay, and I'm sorry about making fun of you the other day," he added under his breath.

"Dude, it's okay," Levi said, and the two shoved one another playfully.

Connie and Beth struck up a conversation and seemed to forget all about grocery shopping, which was fine with Levi.

"Hey, what are you and Frankie doing tonight?" Finn asked. The kids gathered for their own conversation.

"Nothing; I have a feeling I'm going to be grounded till Christmas."

"Why?" Asked Stan.

"I broke my father's binoculars," Levi glanced over his shoulder to make sure his mother hadn't heard him. "He's gonna kill me."

"Maybe he won't," said Stan.

"What do you mean, maybe he won't? He has a strict rule about not touching them, and not only did I touch them, I broke them. The next time you see me, I'm going to have a boot up my ass."

McKenna looked at him queerly.

"It's an expression," Levi said.

"Bring them over tonight, and I'll see if I can fix them," Stan said.

"You know how to fix binoculars?"

"Stan can fix anything," McKenna said.

Down the block from in front of the diner, Scott called to Connie, "We got a table, babe, chop-chop!"

The Howards walked with Connie and Levi as Scott stood waving them in like a coach waving a player home from third.

"Relax, we're coming," called Connie.

"Do you not know what chop-chop means, woman?" Scott asked as he held the door, and they all filed in.

"Scott, this is Beth Howard and her children Stan, Finn, and McKenna."

"Pleased to meet you," he said. "Connie, I got us a table."

"Can we squeeze the Howards in with us?" She asked.

"Oh no, please, we can wait," said Beth.

Scott looked around and saw some chairs stacked over in a corner.

"Come on, the more, the merrier," said Scott. "Levi, give me a hand."

Scott and Levi grabbed two chairs apiece, and they all crammed around the four-top. They hadn't finished their first cup of coffee before they were all carrying on like they'd know each other for years. After breakfast, Scott paid the bill, and they all stepped out into the heat of the day. The sun felt good, the AC in the diner was set a little high, and Levi was glad to be back outside. He watched as his father patted his belly and let out an airy burp, then Levi copied him.

"Mr. Waters."

"Please, call me, Scott."

"Well, Scott, thank you for breakfast. That was very kind," Beth said.

"You are more than welcome," said Connie. "Maybe we can have you and the kids over for dinner—crap, Scott. We never did make it into the BGS."

"That's okay, mom; I don't really like chicken cacciatore anyway." There, he'd said.

"Levi Waters, since when don't you like my chicken cacciatore?"

"Mister Waters, can Levi and Frankie come over? We just live about six houses up the river from you," begged Stan. "Maybe they can eat with us, can they, mom?"

Beth Howard looked uncomfortable. "Well, I don't know, it seems like Mrs. Waters was...."

"Oh no, it's fine with us if it's okay with you," said Connie, with a whisp of sarcasm that only her family would catch.

"Wonderful! Beth exclaimed. I'll make burgers for dinner. Do you boys like burgers?"

"We sure do!" Frankie's eyes lit up.

"And what do you say to brownies for dessert?"

"Oh, boy!" Frankie was giddy with excitement.

"Maybe we can do it another day," Levi said, catching the look of disappointment in his mother's eyes.

Connie hugged her son and kissed his cheek; the days of kissing the top of his head were long gone. Levi had been taller than his mother since last summer. "It's fine, sweetie; you guys can head over after you do a few things for me around the house."

"Awesome! We can watch a movie," said Stan.

"Yeah, we got a huge rear projector TV," said Finn.

"Projection TV dummy," corrected Stan.

"Stanley Howard, you tell your brother you're sorry," Beth Howard scolded, but Stan was busy whispering something to Levi.

"Don't forget to bring the binoculars."

16

Nick parked the Bronco to the rear of a bar called Dad's Mustache and hopped out to look at his spare. The bullet entered near the top of the tire, but he couldn't find an exit hole. A good thing because it would have exited right into Babe's back if it had. Babe stood on the back seat and reached out a hand. Nick took it and helped her down.

"I don't suppose Chesapeake Station has a tire shop."

"We aren't in Chesapeake Station, Nick. We're in Whitehead County, Millbrook, to be exact."

"Millbrook, you mean Jessica Upshaw's...?"

"The very same."

Why did you pick this place to stop?"

"My father was good friends with Mike, the original owner of the Stash. Mike's son TJ runs it now, and he'll help us out."

"Does he sell tires? Because unless he sells tires, I got no use for the guy."

"No, but..."

"Then I suggest we get back in the car and head to Chicago. We need to put some distance between that psycho sheriff and us."

"We can't leave, Nick," said Achak.

"The hell we can't! That lunatic just shot at us for trespassing in an old barn! He could have fucking killed Babe!"

"The sheriff doesn't know who he shot at Nick," Babe said.

"Is that supposed to make me feel better?"

"Doesn't it?" Asked Babe.

"No, Babe, it most certainly does not."

"Well, what about your stuff at the hotel? You can't just leave it there."

"The hell I can't," Nick challenged, "and if you guys aren't smart enough to come with me, then I'm sure you can find a ride back to town." Nick massaged his forehead and paced nervously. "And if you're coming, we better get going before the local PD shows up. I'm sure your sheriff put out an APB on us."

"APB?" Asked Achak.

"All points bulletin, it means all-points bulletin," Nick snapped.

"I know what it means. Look who sounds paranoid now."

"All points bulletin on what?" Asked Babe, "On an unknown make and model vehicle that might have a bullet hole in it? A bullet which, as you pointed out, was fired at subjects suspected of trespassing. I'm sure even Tucker couldn't get away with that."

"So, what do you suggest we do, Babe?"

She was already walking toward the bar. "I don't know about you, but I could use a drink."

Achak shrugged his shoulders and started after Babe. Nick kicked at the ground, shook his head, and followed reluctantly. The Stash was dark and loud, and spirits of many-a-spilled drink wafted up from the booze-soaked floor. The smell reminded Nick of the County Cork back in Red Hook. Only God knew how many times he'd had to drag his old man home from that place. Tim Ryan had never been a bar-guy. He remembered his mother teasing him about being more of a homebody than she was. But after the incident at the Ironweiler place, he stopped coming home after work. Eventually, his father, the guy he once thought of as Indiana Jones and Bruce Springsteen, rolled into one, quit work altogether, and locked himself away in the room above the garage.

In his temporary daze, Nick bumped into a small fat man in a leather biker vest and knocked the man's drink out of his hand.

"What the fuck, buddy?" The fat little man clamped his hands-on Nick's T-shirt, pulling out a clump of chest hair. As he drew back to send a pudgy fist into Nick's button nose, Achak stepped into view and looked down at the biker.

"You got a problem with my friend, Dead-eye?"

Nick was surprised he hadn't noticed sooner. The little guy's right eyeball was missing. In its place was a puckered piece of flesh that looked, to Nick, like an asshole.

"Problem, what problem?" The biker laughed nervously and smoothed the front of Nick's T-shirt. "I was just making sure I didn't spill my beer on him; that's all, Achak. You know me, I'm a lover, not a fighter."

Achak put a hand on Nick's shoulder and directed him toward the bar.

"I could have kicked that guy's ass, Achak," Nick said.

"I have no doubt, but his friends would have beat the living shit out of you."

Nick glanced back over his shoulder and noticed that the biker's buddies held pool cues fat end up like fine cudgels. As he turned back in the direction Achak was leading him, he saw Babe standing behind the bar. She drew a beer and tapped the bartender on the shoulder.

"That's TJ, said Achak.

TJ took Babe in his arms and lifted her off the ground in a long embrace. She whispered something into his ear and pointed at Achak and Nick. The bartender waved at Achak, and Achak waved back. Then he nodded toward a guy shooting pool at a table in the back of the bar, and Achak changed course.

"So that was TJ?" Asked Nick.

"That was TJ," replied Babe, who had met them near the pool table.

"He got a thing for you?"

"Boys always want what they can't have," Babe said. "Hey, Jimmy."

"Hey, Babe."

Jimmy was a skinny young man with the herky-jerky movement of a speed freak and the crooked yellow teeth of an English smoker. He wore a sleeveless flannel shirt and a ball cap that read *KEEP ON TRUCKIN*, over the brim. The human embodiment of everything the average northern elitist believed about southern boys.

"I need a tire."

"Damn, you're looking fine tonight, Babe." Jimmy leaned over the table, lined up his shot, and pocketed the 8-ball. "That's game. Who's next?"

A guy, almost as big as Achak, slammed ten bucks on the felt, grabbed his beer off the rail, and walked away.

"I'm closed, Babe," he said, but for you," he reached clumsily toward her, and Babe grabbed two of his fingers and twisted them backward, causing Jimmy to wince—air whistled through his teeth. "Ow, what the fuck Babe, why you gotta be like that?"

"Come on, Jimmy," she said. "Do you want to sell tires or not?

"You're shit out of luck, especially with that fucking attitude," he said as he shook his fingers out. "Come on, who wants to give me their money?" Jimmy called to the crowded bar.

"Jimmy, I wouldn't ask if it weren't important," said Babe.

"Babe, I got a good buzz going, and I'm cleaning up on the table," he paused and then shouted to make sure everyone in the bar could hear him. "Because no one in this place is good enough to rack my balls," Jimmy said, and slid his pool cue between his legs and flicked his tongue Gene Simmons style at the guy he'd just hustled.

"Fuck you, Jimmy," the big guy said.

Jimmy flipped the guy the bird and grabbed his crotch with his free hand. Then he turned back toward Babe. "So, unless you want to play, or um, you know," he glanced down at his hand still clutching the front of his pants. "Let me get back to my table. Ya hear that bitches? My Table!" He turned to search the bar to see if anyone was taking the bait.

"Jimmy, it's like an emergency."

Jimmy spun back at Babe. "Look, bitch, I said...."

Achak was reaching for Jimmy's neck when Nick stepped between them.

"Jimmy, is it?" He asked rhetorically. "I'll play you, but not for this ten-dollar bullshit. I'll play you for the cost of a Goodyear 225/75R15."

Jimmy dropped his voice and shot a nervous glance at the bar. "Dude, that's like a hundred bucks."

"You wanna shoot pool or," Nick glanced down and grabbed his own crotch.

Jimmy stammered and sputtered out a couple of *buts* and *wells,* and his face lost its rosy glow despite the heat and alcohol. Nick knew he had him, so he turned the screws.

"Hell, you're the king of the table, right?" Nick made sure everyone could hear the challenge. "So, let's make it four tires. I'll be a sport and let you swap one of my old tires for the spare."

Jimmy swallowed hard. He was beating a bunch of drunks for chump change. Guys who couldn't walk a straight line, let alone decide which of the three balls they were aiming for, was the real one. His eyes darted around the bar wildly as he looked to see who was watching. By now, a large group of regulars gathered to see if loud-mouthed Jimmy had the balls to back up his talk. Nick leaned to his ear.

"Sell me my tire, and I'll let you beat me. Cross me, and we'll go double or nothing."

Jimmy nodded and regained a little of his composure. "Rack 'em, ch-ch-chump."

Nick gave Jimmy a, *watch your ass* look. "How about you rack and I break. That way, you can't say I rigged the rack."

Jimmy racked em, and Nick broke, sinking 2 solids. He followed that with three more solids and missed on the fourth. Nick was a decent pool player, but no one was more surprised than he was by his fast start. Jimmy went to work and dropped three balls of his own. Nick sank another, but it was all Jimmy from then out. Nick had played the best game of his life, but Jimmy beat him. Nick made a big show of the loss and even threw in a bow for good measure.

"You're really good, Jimmy," he said loud enough for the on-lookers to hear and then leaned in again, "but you would have lost your ass."

Jimmy whispered back, "Yeah, I thought you changed your mind there for a minute."

"A deal's a deal, Jimmy," and then again for all to hear. "I'm going to need to go to an ATM to get the cash. Why don't you come with me?"

Jimmy agreed and left the bar through a gauntlet of back pats and cheers. One guy even offered to buy him a beer when he got back. Once outside, Jimmy told Nick, Babe, and Achak to follow him to his shop. Nick could see that Babe and Achak were confused. Jimmy drove a tiny truck on gigantic tires with a Tire King stenciled on both doors.

"Why are we going to his shop? You lost," said Babe.

"Jimmy and I had a deal. I would let him beat me if he agreed to sell me a tire. If not, I would have taken him for a whole set. His ego couldn't let me trash talk him, and his bank account couldn't swing a whole set of Goodyears."

"Oh, so you let him win?" Babe asked.

"No, I tried like hell to beat him. That guy is actually a pretty good pool player," Nick said with a smile.

"You were bluffing?"

"Let's say I was testing a theory."

They arrived at the Tire King, and Jimmy went in and opened the overhead garage door. Lickety-split, he swapped out the spare for a new non-ventilated tire and thanked Nick for not embarrassing him. Nick paid him for the tire and parted company, with Jimmy being none the wiser for having been played.

"Head back to the Stash," Babe said.

"Why? I got the tire."

"TJ is going to let Achak hide out there for the night."

They drove back to the Stash, dropped Achak off, and started for the Pleasant View Motor Lodge.

"What's the plan, Babe? I mean, I just came here to do some research to write a paper, and you've got the cops shooting at me."

"Nick, if this goes the way I hope it does, you'll have enough information to write a book, and it will be a bestseller."

"I'm not writing a book; I'm writing a doctoral dissertation and no offense Babe, but I need more than one old diary to source. If I went back with what I had, even *if* Achak let me take the diary, Doctor Bondiani would laugh me right out of the anthropology department."

"You want more proof; I'll get you more proof. You just have to trust me, just a little longer," Babe said, almost pleading.

"Look, you seem like a nice—um,"—*girl, lady*, Nick wasn't sure which way to go here, "person, you seem like a nice person, but I hardly know you."

Babe's shoulders slumped, and the hopeful pleading turned to a look of sadness. Nick closed his eyes and shook his head.

"I can't believe I'm asking this, but what are we talking about here?"

"Well, you're not going to like it."

"I don't doubt that," Nick said.

Babe cleared her throat. "We're going to have to break into the mayor's office and find a key."

Nick snapped his head in her direction, taking his eyes completely off the road. "Are you fucking crazy? You're right, I don't like it. You have to be insane if you think I'm adding breaking and entering to my list of crimes".

"Don't forget gambling and grifting," Babe said with a smile.

"This isn't funny, Babe. This may be normal stuff for you, but I don't do stuff like this."

"Oh, get off your high horse," she said. "We're not stealing money from a church, we're gathering evidence of decades of murders and corruption, and it's all connected to the Mooka'am. And isn't that what you came here to learn about? Or do you only want the information if it's easy to get?"

"Easy is one thing, felony breaking and entering is another."

"Then drop me off and go back and tell your doctor guy...."

"She's a girl," Nick interrupted.

"Who's a girl?"

"Doctor Bondiani, she's a girl, not a guy. Well, a woman, but you know what I mean."

"You mean a person," she said with a slight sneer.

"I didn't mean—"

"Nick, I really don't care what you meant. What I care about are these poor women and their unborn babies! So, if that doesn't matter to you more than some fucking paper, leave now, and Achak and I will figure this out without you."

What started out as a roar trailed off toward the end to something that

Nick might have heard his mother say to his father toward the end. Babe did need him. Even with the giant Achak by her side, she couldn't do it without him. And Nick wasn't going to let her down.

"What's it going to be, Nick?" Babe asked, sounding like she was prepared to be disappointed. "Are you going to help, or are you going to tell her that you quit when it got too hard?"

Nick pictured Jinan sitting at her desk with a smug look on her beautiful face. He stopped his train of thought. When had he decided that she was beautiful? *I mean, she is*, the train started up again. *Big brown eyes, full lips, long brown hair, and olive-colored skin, hell yes, she was beautiful.* And here he was with a chance to impress the ever-living shit out of her, and he was considering passing on it? "Hell no!" Nick said out loud.

"Hell no, you're in, or hell no, you're out?" Asked Babe.

"I'm in," he said with newfound grit and determination. "But how are we going to do it?

"Just leave that to me," said Babe. "Achak and I have been planning this for a while. It's a two-man job, and we just couldn't risk him being seen. But now you're here…"

As they pulled onto Black Horse Road and neared the motor lodge, they saw a Chesapeake County Sheriff's squad parked in the lot.

"Shit," said Nick. "I thought you said they didn't know who they were shooting at.

"Relax, said Babe, swallowing a little harder than she meant to. "He's probably just here visiting Margie and Phil, and even if he's looking for us, and I don't see how that's"—she was going to say, possible, but stopped mid-sentence. "That bitch! I bet Margie saw us leave together," she said and placed her hand on his thigh, dangerously close to his twig and berries.

"Not the time Babe!" Nick said.

"Wrong, exactly the time. Now just picture your doctor and act like we've been on a date."

"Doctor Bondiani? I don't…."

"The hell you don't. But right now, you are into me, got it?"

She rested her head on his shoulder and ran her fingers up and down his leg as they pulled into the lot, making sure Sheriff Tucker was watching. The Bronco slid to a stop in front of number 11, and they got out. They started for the door, arm in arm when Tucker called out.

"Just a minute, you two."

"Us?" Asked Babe?

"Yeah, you, and don't play dumb."

Nick stopped but didn't immediately turn toward the sheriff.

"What's your name, boy?"

"You already got his name from that busy bitch in the office."

The sheriff was standing closer to them now and raised the back of his hand. "You watch your tongue, so help me. If you were my daughter, I'd slap that mouth of yours."

"If I were your daughter, I would hang myself from a tree in the middle of town!" Babe fired back.

Nick, always the peacemaker, intervened. "Hey, come on. There's no need for this. My name is Nick Ryan. I'm from Chicago, and...."

"That supposed to impress me, boy?" Snapped Tucker.

"Impress you? No, sir, I was just answering your question."

"I don't remember asking you where you were from."

"No, sir, I just...."

"You just what? Thought you would intimidate the hick sheriff with your address?"

"You leave him alone. He hasn't done anything wrong—yet," she smirked.

"She's right Sheriff, we just went for a drive."

"Yeah? Where to?"

"That's none of your damn business," Babe snapped.

"Well, I'm making it my business. Seems we had some trespassers over to the Cavanaugh's barn."

"That shit-hole? That's for teenagers. I have my own place, and Nick here has this nice little cottage that we can mess around in, ain't that right, sweetie?" She threw her arms around his neck and kissed his cheek.

Tucker regarded her with a look of disgust. "Margie tells me you've been gone about five hours. You been driving around that whole time?"

"Margie should mind her own fucking business," she said, turning toward the office and shouting. Then Babe reached into her tight pocket, leaning forward, giving Sheriff Tucker a little look at her décolletage. The sheriff grunted as he started to say something, but the view threw him.

Babe produced a wrinkled receipt from Dad's Mustache. "Here, Here's our receipt from The Stash." It was stamped with the date and time, 8 PM, according to the receipt. "What time did you get the call for your trespassers?"

Tucker walked around toward the back of the Bronco. "The O-fenders," he said it just like that, o-fenders, "fled the scene in a pickup or a Jeep or something," he said as he shined the light around the back of the Bronco. He flipped his flashlight in his hand and whacked it against the spare, which responded with a ringing thud.

"Well, Sheriff, um, sir," said Nick. "I'm not from around here, but I haven't been to a barn."

"There were three people in the vehicle," he put the accent on the 'hicle. "You two out with a third party tonight?"

Babe pressed her body against Nick's. "Does it look like there's room for a third in this party?"

Tucker snorted through his bulbous nose, rubbed his chin, and shot a look toward the office.

"This is a respectable town, and you'll conduct yourselves accordingly while you're in *my* town. Is that clear?" Tucker held the butt of his flashlight about an inch from Nick's nose.

"Pffff," Babe made the sound as loud as she could.

"Mind yourself, young lady," Tucker snapped, redirecting the heavy D-cell at her. "How long you staying here, boy?"

"The name is Nick, and I'll be staying as long as I want."

Babe smirked. "Well, look at who found his balls."

Nick smiled nervously, and Babe reached down and patted his package. Nick's face flushed.

"You make me sick," Tucker said as he turned and walked away.

Babe hurried Nick into his little cabin, slammed the door closed behind them, and drew the shade. Nick reached for the light switch.

"No," Babe said. "Leave the light off."

"Why, what are you...."

He joined Babe near the window and peered around the side of the shade. The sheriff shined his light into the passenger compartment and opened the glove box.

"That fat son-of-a-bitch," Nick said. "That's an illegal search!"

He could see the wad of yellow parking tickets in Tucker's pudgy hand. Tucker studied the tickets and then tossed them onto the floorboard. Seemingly satisfied that he would find no incriminating evidence of trespassing, Sheriff Tucker turned and walked toward the motor lodge's office.

"That was close," said Babe as she burst out laughing and rested her head against Nick's chest.

17

Levi wrapped the binoculars in his torn pajama top, stuffed them in his backpack, and he and Frankie rode their bikes to the Howard's house. When they arrived, Finn, who was standing in the driveway, waved them in. Levi rolled to a stop and set his kickstand. Frankie came in on a skid, a recently acquired skill, and laid his bike on its side.

"Cool, Frankie," Finn said. "Come on in, my mom got ice cream to go on top of the brownies," his eyes glowed with a ravenous glare.

The smell of the brownies made Frankie's mouth water.

"The burgers are almost ready, boys," called Bethany Howard from the kitchen.

Stan met them in the hallway, and they all hurried through the kitchen toward the back door.

"Where do you think you're going?" Bethany asked.

"The garage; I want to show Levi something."

"But Stan, dinner is almost ready. Your sister and I have been working very hard on making a nice meal for your boyfriends."

"No, *we haven't*," said McKenna with the accent on *we*.

"Friends, mom, not boyfriends! Jesus!"

"Stanley Howard, you say an 'Our Father' and ask for forgiveness before you go anywhere!"

Stan rolled his eyes, made a quick sign-of-the-cross, and trotted off to the garage with Levi and Frankie following behind. Stan unlocked the padlock, pushed open the door, and hit the switch. The fluorescent lights flickered and bathed the room in a clinical light. Hammers and screwdrivers sat on a cluttered workbench alongside a doll with a wick protruding from its forehead. Above the bench, glass jars, some containing nuts and bolts and others holding such oddities as eyeballs, presumably plucked from McKenna's old toys, filled a shelf. Scattered across the floor was a menagerie of things most people would have thrown away. To Levi, it looked like a cross between a working garage and a mad scientist's lab.

"Welcome to the Stan-cave. This is where I do all of my important work."

"What's that?" Frankie asked and pointing to the doll.

"Oh, that's baby-go-boom. She was one of McKenna's stupid dolls. I took it and fixed it up." He grabbed one of the jars from the shelf. It was full of what looked like black sand. "See this?"

Levi and Frankie nodded.

"It's gunpowder."

Both Levi and Frankie's eyes widened.

"Where'd ya get it?" Asked Levi.

"Been collecting it for like the last five 4th of Julys. I find all the dud firecrackers and break them open," he pantomimed the act with his hands. "Then I dump the gunpowder in here," he said, shaking the jar. "Next 4th of July, I'm lighting her off. Boom!"

"Cool," said Frankie.

"Now, let me see what you broke." Stan held out his hand.

Levi slipped off his backpack, carefully unwrapped his father's binoculars, and handed them to Stan. "Be careful!"

"Relax, butterfingers, I'm not the one who broke 'em," Stan said, turning the binoculars over in his hands. "Tasco model 118; good field glasses."

"Wow, you know a lot about binoculars," said Frankie.

"Sure do," Stan said, sounding cocky. "And besides, it's written right here," he pointed to the branding on the binoculars and laughed.

"Stan, sometimes you can be a real jackass," said Finn.

"Shut up, ya big baby, Frankie knows I was kidding, right, Frankie?"

"Yeah, sure, I guess."

"See, the kid can take a joke," he said dismissively as he rummaged through one of the many boxes he had in the Stan-cave. "Yep, here it is, the answer to your problems." Stan held up a pair of Tasco binoculars and began unscrewing the housing over the lens and then set it carefully on the work table. He did the same thing with Levi's dad's binoculars, stuck a rag down inside and wiped the moisture away, and then carefully threaded the housing back in place. He held the glasses up to his eyes and then handed them to Levi. "There ya go, good as new."

"Get the hell out of here!" Levi put the binoculars to his eyes and looked through them. "You did it! You freakin' did it!"

Stan blew on his fingernails and polished them against his shirt. "Told ya, don't panic when old Stanley Howard is around. I get my friends out of jams all the time."

"Thanks, man, I owe you one."

"Stan, mom wants you guys in the house now."

Levi turned and saw McKenna standing in the doorway. She was wearing a floral print shirt and tight jeans, and as she turned to head back to the house, Levi read the tag on the waistband.

"Bongo, man, I'd like to bongo that." The words were out before he realized he was talking out loud.

"Watch it, dickhead, that's my sister," Stan said, delivering his most stern look.

"Dude, I, I, I'm sorry," stuttered Levi. "I didn't mean anything; I don't know what the hell is wrong with me lately!"

Stan laughed and snorted. "Don't have a cow man, I'm just messing with you."

Levi blew out a hard breath. "Good, dude, cause...."

"But she's still my sister," said Stan, cutting him off mid excuse.

***

The movie choices were between *some stupid movie about a princess and a movie about two idiots trying to return a briefcase to some girl in another state. Even though Kaylin showed up and cast her vote with McKenna and* Mrs. Howard, the princess movie lost. Connie Howard walked into the living room carrying a tray of hamburgers and took a headcount for ice cream and no-ice-cream brownies. Then she popped the VHS tape into the VCR and bounced happily back into the kitchen. After dinner and the movie, Levi and Frankie thanked Mrs. Howard, flipped on the headlights on their bikes, and rode for home. Levi peddled, feeling relieved. Stan had saved his bacon. The binoculars were fixed, and he could probably stitch up the pajama top. Yes, all was right with Levi Waters. There were only a few streetlights on Sugar Maple Lane, and the fullness of the trees blocked out most of the moonlight. So, it was no wonder Levi didn't notice the large black crow watching them from the tree at the end of their driveway until it let out a loud raspy caw.

"Mrs. Howard phoned that you were on your way," called Connie Waters from the doorway. "Park your bikes in the garage and get in the house. We have to sort through your school things. Classes start in less than a week."

A new school meant new kids and new jerks to deal with. But at least he had Stanley and the other guys. The boys hopped off their bikes and walked them into the garage. Levi pulled the binoculars from his backpack and returned them to the box marked *Scott's Stuff*. As they walked back toward the house, Levi looked at the tree where the crow had been sitting, but it was gone. He rubbed the back of his neck and had just turned back toward the house when a giant black bird swooped at him. Levi punched at the air, and he and Frankie ran into the house.

"What the heck was that?" Asked Frankie.

"What was what, sweetie?" Their mom asked.

"Nothing, mom, just a bird," Levi said, catching his breath.

Pens, pencils, notebooks, binders bursting with loose leaf paper, and even boxes of crayons were scattered across the living room floor.

Levi sifted through the school supplies. "Mom, I'm in high school now; I don't need crayons."

Frankie sat on the floor with his nose in the crayon box. "I'll take his mom. That way, I can have a box for home and a box for school."

"Well, if your brother is sure he doesn't want them," she left it hanging like a question.

Levi didn't answer. He'd gone over to the window and was looking at the tree.

"Levi, did you hear me?"

Hearing his name caught his attention. He turned and looked at his mother.

"Well?" She asked.

"Well, what?"

"The crayons, are you sure you don't want them?"

"Oh, sorry. No, Frankie can have them."

"What's wrong with you, Levi? You seem a million miles away."

"Nothing, mom," answered Frankie. "He just saw his girlfriend tonight."

Levi gave his little brother a look. Connie walked over to her oldest son, put her arm over his shoulder, got up on her toes, and kissed his cheek.

"You never mind about girls. School is starting in a few days. You'll have enough to keep you occupied without girls on your mind."

Levi rolled his eyes, sorted through the school supplies, thanked his mom, and carried them to his room. He dumped the load on his bed, opened his backpack, and shoved the torn pajama top back into the bottom of his hamper. He felt stupid for hiding it. Over the years, Levi had torn lots of clothes. What was one pajama top in the grand scheme of things? He knew the answer. It wasn't the tear, it was the story he would have to make up about how they got torn, and Levi didn't feel much better about a lie of omission than a regular lie. That night, Levi tossed and turned and slept a dreamless sleep.

The morning sun flooded his room and woke him. Levi sat up and swung his feet over the side of his bed. He felt a little nauseous but chalked it up to getting up to fast. He stood up, took a step, and fell down hard. Frankie bolted upright in bed.

"Are you okay?" The younger Waters brother asked.

"Yeah," said Levi, rubbing the back of his head. "Why is the floor wet?" He asked, sitting in a puddle of water on the floor next to his bed.

18

Nick awoke hot and sweaty. Even with the blinds shut, the morning sun heated the little cabin to an uncomfortable temperature. He sat up and realized that he was alone. Babe left sometime during the night but hadn't woken him to say goodbye. She had, however, gone through the bother of making the second bed. Nick shambled over to the tiny bathroom and regarded himself in the mirror.

"You, my man, look like a bucket of shit."

Nick's stomach growled. The last meal he'd had was the day before at the Triumph, and he was starving. He ran a hand over the sandpaper stubble on his chin and decided that before he could worry about breakfast, he would have to do something about his face. He had one of those patchy beards, the kind that required daily shaving lest he look like a guy on a three-day bender. He gave his armpits a quick whiff and drew back from the smell. A hot shower and shave were in order. As soon as that was out of the way, he would see to quieting the beast in his belly. Nick turned the faucet and pulled the stopper to send the water up and out of the shower-head. There was no shampoo or conditioner, and like an idiot, Nick had forgotten to pack any. He unwrapped the tiny bar of Ivory soap supplied by the Pleasant View Motor Lodge's management and lathered up.

Nick considered everything that had happened to him since arriving in Chesapeake Station. First, he'd had the; what was the right word; unique experience of meeting Babe. That would have been more than enough excitement for one day, but it didn't stop there. Next, he'd driven out to the middle of nowhere to a dilapidated old barn where he listened to a giant

Indian tell crazy ghost stories, only to be driven from there by a town sheriff taking pot-shots at him. After running from the cops, Nick found himself hustling pool in a towny bar and then capped off the night by letting the crazy waitress crash in his cabin for the night. Nick shook his head and finished rinsing off. The motel towels were almost as rough as his beard, but they did their job, and after running his razor over his face, Nick got dressed, locked up the cabin, and climbed into the Bronco.

He checked his watch, 9 AM, and already his seat and the steering wheel were almost too hot to touch. Nick drove straight down Black Horse Road without turning his radio on. He wanted some peace and quiet before he saw hurricane Babe again. He stopped at the first stop sign, the one that, had he taken a left, would have seen him safely to the Country Dumplin', well clear of Babe Adams. Nick decided that maybe there was something to fate. Perhaps it was real, and it hated him. He pulled into the same spot he'd parked in the day before, checked himself quickly in the rearview mirror, and walked into the Triumph. Babe gave him a nod and then flicked her eyes toward a table in the back corner of the restaurant.

"Sit anywhere, Nick. I'll be right with you."

Nick caught her drift and grabbed a table in the back, though he wondered what difference it made where he sat. It was just after 9 AM, still well within most people's usual breakfast time parameters, but the restaurant was empty. *How does this place stay open*, he wondered to himself? Babe, who had just finished what looked like a proper chewing out of the other waitress, walked out from behind the counter toward Nick. The other waitress, Nick, guessed she was in high school, scowled at him the way only a teenage girl could, and stomped off into the kitchen.

"What was that about?" Asked Nick.

"Oh, that's nothing," she said with a dismissive wave of her hand. "I just told her she had to cover my afternoon shift. Some night we had, eh sweetie?"

Nick smiled. "The most adventurous night of my life. Why didn't you wake me?"

"You looked like you needed your sleep."

"Yeah, I guess I did," Nick said. "But why did you make the bed? I mean, it was nice, but I'm paying for that to be done."

Babe's nose crinkled when she smiled. "I didn't do it to be nice; I did it to screw with Margie."

Nick raised a wondering brow.

"The thought of us defiling her little cabin will drive Margie crazy," she said, her smile growing wider.

"Haha, very funny, now I'm going to be getting dirty looks."

"All that woman has are dirty looks," she said.

"We need to talk, Babe."

"We need to do more than talk, sweetie, but this isn't the time or place. So, what are you feeling like this morning?

"How's your French toast?"

"Fine, how's yours?"

Oddly, or maybe not oddly at all, "I'll *French toast you*" popped into his head. Nick snickered. "Kind of your thing, huh?"

"What, the French toast?"

"Never mind, I'll have the French toast, crispy bacon, and coffee, black."

"As you wish, big fella," she said with a glance toward his crotch.

Nick's face turned bright red.

The French toast was even better than the stuff his mother used to make. *Was that nutmeg and vanilla he was tasting?* Nick wondered why a man who possessed such culinary skill worked in a crappy little diner in the middle of nowhere. He could easily work in some crappy diner in the middle of a large city. Nick sopped up the last of the syrup with his last piece of French toast and finished his coffee.

"You ready, sweetie?"

"Ready for what?" Nick asked.

"We have a busy day ahead of us," Babe said, clutching her purse and heading for the door.

The heat of the morning sun was stifling, and Nick regretted not trying to squeeze an AC repair out of the Tire King. But, on second thought, he doubted they did that kind of work at a tire shop. One thing was for sure, he would have it fixed before next summer. Nick shielded his eyes from the glare as he crossed the sidewalk from the diner to his Bronco. Babe pushed past him and hopped in the driver's seat.

"Uh uh, no way. You slide your ass into the passenger's seat. Nobody drives Gus but me."

She stuck out a pouty lower lip. "Please? I've always wanted to drive one."

"You said you always wanted to ride in one."

"Well, I've done that. It's time for a new dream!"

Nick knew Babe had probably always managed to get her way, and she probably had a deep and wide stubborn streak, but this was one fight Babe was going to lose. He folded his arms in resolute certainty, the body language equivalent of an ultimatum when he noticed that the already short skirt had hitched itself up onto her hip. She followed his eyes down to the lump in his throat as he swallowed hard.

"Please, Nick?" She locked him with a grin that let him know that she caught him staring.

Busted, Nick cleared his throat. "Fine! But we are putting the top up!"

She batted her eyes. "Please, can we keep it down?"

Nick threw his hands up. "Screw it," he said and tossed her his keys.

She started the Bronco and instinctively reached for the radio knob. Nick reached out and grabbed her hand, and Babe's eyes widened. Nick had the feeling that she'd been handled roughly before.

"I'm sorry, but I can't let you emasculate me completely," he said.

Babe let her hand fall to the gear shifter and smiled back. "No, I'm the one who should apologize. I know I can come on a little strong."

"A little strong?" Nick said incredulously. "The Crimson Tide could take a lesson from you! You grabbed my twig and berries in front of the sheriff," he said.

"More like a branch, big boy."

Babe pressed her lips together, but the laugh would not be stifled. Nick tried to hold onto his grimace, but as the saying goes, laughter is contagious, and Nick caught the bug. The laugh turned to a roar, and Nick knew instantly that he'd made a friend, a forever-friend, the kind you could not talk with for five years and then pick up right where you left off. He couldn't quite put his finger on why, but he knew that he and Babe would always be connected, one to the other. Babe reached for the knob again, and Nick just leaned back in his seat and enjoyed the ride. Before long, they were in the parking lot for the Stash. There were no other cars in the lot, not even the cars belonging to the over-served who opted to take rides from less drunken chauffeurs. Babe walked around back.

"That's strange; TJ's car is gone," she said as she began pounding on the back door.

"What are you banging for? If his car isn't here, who is supposed to answer the door? "

"Achak is probably asleep in the upstairs room," she said, pointing above at the running air-conditioner, and resumed pounding and added some yelling.

Nick held his hands against his ears. "Babe, stop! There's no one in there! Shit, you're gonna get the cops called on us."

"Well, what's your suggestion?" Babe asked, crossing her arms in frustration.

"I don't know; we could wait in the truck for TJ to show up. Unless you know where he lives."

She exhaled hard through her nose and jutted a thumb up at the air-conditioner.

"He lives in the bar?" Nick asked.

"Yeah," replied Babe. "His apartments on the second floor."

"Well, if Achak is asleep up there, all the banging in the world isn't going to wake him over the sound of that friggin thing," he said, pointing at the buzzing, whirring window unit.

"I guess," she said and chewed her lower lip. "Boost me up; I'm going to try and push the window open."

"We are not breaking and entering!"

"It's not breaking and entering, more like opening and entering. I don't plan on breaking anything."

"Well, I don't plan on boosting you up, so you aren't going to be doing any kind of entering.”

“You’re the one with the paper to write and the girlfriend to impress.”

“Girlfriend? What? I don’t have a—”

“Save it; just get over here and give me a boost, but no looking up my skirt, you pervert.”

Nick shook his head, “Babe 2, Nick 0,” he said.

“That’s right, you sweet little thang, Babe, always gets her way.”

“He cupped his hands, and she put a foot in the webbing of his fingers. She was about to jump up when she cocked her head and gave him a look.

“Yeah, yeah, I know. No peeking.”

She gave him a wink and launched herself up to the window ledge. She pushed, and the window slid open. “See, nothing to it.”

Babe, who was surprisingly strong for her size, probably from carrying trays of food all day, had never developed the muscles needed for chin-ups.

“Um, Nick.”

“Yeah?”

“Boost me.”

“What?”

“Boost me.”

He looked up, caught a flash of her electric blue silk panties, and looked away as quickly as possible.

“How am I supposed to do that?”

“Put your hand on my ass and shove so I can get in the window.”

“I don’t know....”

“Jeez, you’d swear you’ve never seen a girl’s panties before.”

“You told me not to look!”

“You don’t have to look; just shove.”

Nick reached up, careful to make sure her skirt was between his hand and her butt, and gave a shove. Babe slipped up and into the window knocking pots and pans onto the floor. A second later, she was standing in the doorway.

“Well, if that didn’t wake Achak, maybe he ain’t here.”

“Good, then let’s get out of here before the cops show up.”

Maybe she didn't hear him, or she heard him and was just ignoring him, but she left the door standing open and turned back into the bar. Nick stepped into the door-jam keeping his ass and heels just the right side of legal.

"Babe," he said, somewhere between a whisper and a full-throated yell. "Get your ass out here. I don't feel like going to jail."

But Babe had already made it up to the second floor and had begun pounding on the door and screaming Achak's name. Nick let out a frustrated growl, glanced around, and stormed in after her. The stairway was barely wide enough to accommodate the width of his shoulders, and he had a hard time imagining Achak making it up the stairs without getting stuck. Nick called out to Babe as he came up behind her.

"Babe, stop!"

She turned and looked at him. Worry lines creased her brow.

"He's not here, and if he were, do you think he could have made it up these stairs?"

Nick turned width-wise, his shoulders touching either wall. Babe turned and sat on the top step.

"Then, where is he?"

"I don't know," Nick said. Maybe he went to breakfast with TJ."

"Achak would never go out in public like that."

"What are you talking about? He was out with us last night," Nick said.

"He was here with us last night. This is a safe place. That's why we came here."

"Well, he's not here now," Nick said as he turned back down the stairs.

He hadn't gone a step when the two barrels of a 12-gauge side-by-side swept up and filled his field of vision. Nick threw his hands in the air.

"Who the fuck are you?" The voice seemed to come from deep inside the barrels.

"Nick! Nick Ryan!" The words flew from his lips with the force and urgency of projectile vomit.

The black circles grew more prominent, the barrels now mere inches from his face. Nick wasn't sure which he'd feel first, the left barrel, the right barrel, or the warm sensation of piss running down his leg.

"I don't know any, Nick Ryan."

"TJ, it's me."

TJ leaned to his right to see Babe peering out from behind the stranger.

"Babe? What the hell are you doing here?"

"Where's Achak?"

"Achak? He's not here."

"I can see that, TJ," Babe said, not bothering to hide her irritation.

TJ lowered the shotgun and turned back down the stairs.

"You knocked my shit all over the place Babe," he said.

"TJ, where is Achak?"

"Man, you dented my stockpot," TJ said as he began picking up the mess Babe made when she climbed through the window.

"TJ!" Babe yelled.

"He left just before closing time." TJ picked up the handle from a broken beer mug and then let it fall. "And you broke about a dozen beer glasses Babe, Jeez!"

"Nick opened his wallet and pulled out a twenty-dollar bill and extended it toward TJ."

TJ shoved his hand aside. "Get the fuck out of here. I don't even know you, man."

Nick stepped back, a little shocked at TJ's response. "Sorry, man, I just wanted to—"

"You just wanted to what? Did you break my glasses?"

It was apparent to anyone present that Babe was the only one who could have fit through the narrow window opening.

"No," Nick said. "I just, I just thought."

"You just, you just thought what?" He said, mimicking Nick's awkward stutter. "Twenty bucks would cover a hundred dollars' worth of glasses?"

Nick opened his wallet and looked inside. He was well shy of 100. "I could go to an ATM."

Babe had heard enough. "Nick, put your wallet away, TJ; shut up about the fucking glasses. The only reason you have this place is because my father bailed your ass out when your dad hadn't paid taxes for two years, so if I want to break a glass," she pushed a glass off the counter, smashing it onto the floor, "I'll break a fucking glass. Now, did Achak say where he was going when he left?"

TJ huffed and puffed in exasperated defeat. "I don't know, Babe; like I said, he left just before we closed last night. He was pretty hammered."

"What do you mean 'hammered'?" Babe asked. "Achak doesn't drink."

"The guys were buying him Captain and Cokes, easy on the Captain heavy on the Coke, at first anyway. By the end of the night, he was sucking Captain right out of the bottle."

"And you let him leave?" Babe balled up her fist and punched TJ in the chest.

TJ winced and rubbed the spot where she'd punched him. "Shit, Babe, that hurt." He sucked air through his teeth. "I didn't let him *leave*, he chose to leave, and I chose to live. Besides, he didn't walk; Billy Pennington gave him a ride."

"Gave him a ride where?"

"I don't know; into town, I guess. He said he was going home. He said that he missed his wife and kids, and then he said—,"

"Said what?" Babe asked.

TJ looked hesitant.

"Said what, TJ?" Babe's tone turned from simple questioning to interrogation.

TJ exhaled hard. "He said, 'fuck that white bitch,' I figured he was talking about you," TJ flinched, likely expecting another punch.

Babe pushed open the swinging door to the bar and grabbed the phone off the counter. She punched in a phone number and spoke quietly. Nick and TJ exchanged uneasy glances. Nick opened his mouth to say something, but before he could, TJ fired off a quick, "fuck you," followed by, "So, what did you guys spend the night together?"

Nick grinned. "You bet your ass we did."

Babe set the phone back down and started for the door. "Nick, we gotta go."

"Don't worry about all the broken glass," TJ called as Babe and Nick cleared the back door for the parking lot. "I'll take care of it — asshole."

Babe jumped into the driver's seat, and Nick hopped in shotgun without so much as a word. She put the Bronco in gear, flew out of the parking lot, and sped down County Line Road.

"Where can he be, Nick?"

"I don't know, maybe he went home like your asshole friend said."

"He didn't go home, Nick, I called his wife, and she hasn't heard from him or seen him since he left home for Chesapeake Station last week. We have to find him, Nick."

Nick thought for a minute. "Does he know where you live?"

Babe cut the wheel hard onto SowMax Boulevard. "Oh my god, I don't know where my head is. Of course, that's where he went. Remind me to kiss you later."

Nick could see all the tension leave Babe's body. Her shoulders dropped; she exhaled loud and long and changed the subject.

"This road used to be called Union Street, but SowMax bought up all the small family-owned farms from here to the interstate. So, now I live on fucking SowMax Boulevard, and I have to drive past this monstrosity every day."

As the Bronco sped past the SowMax guard station, Babe beeped the horn and flipped off the security guard stationed there. Nick sunk into his seat, but the guard didn't seem to take notice.

"You hate SowMax because they bought up all the family farms?"

"They didn't just knock on their doors and offer them tons of cash, Nick. They squeezed these people out. They drove up the cost of seed, feed, and supplies by creating artificial demand and then slashed their prices so low that the small farms couldn't afford to stay in business. Then SowMax waited for the property to go into foreclosure and bought the land for pennies on the dollar, so yeah, Nick; I fucking hate SowMax."

"What happened to the families?" Nick asked.

"Some stayed and went to work for SowMax or Agri-Grow. Most of them moved into the trailer parks in town. Some left the area for who knows where. My father told me that some of the farmers killed themselves so their families could collect on their life insurance."

"Fuck," Nick said and shook his head.

He knew plenty of farm families growing up in Red Hook and spent most of his summers working on their farms during middle school and high school. Babe cut the wheel and turned onto a dirt road that led back to a small single-story house, not much bigger than his motel cabin. The place was isolated, a good ¼ mile from the Plahutniks, her nearest neighbors. She flew out of the Bronco and made a bee-line for her house. Nick hurried behind her as she burst through the front door, tossed his car keys on the kitchen table, probably her regular routine, and called out for her friend.

"Achak! Achak, you here?"

Nick scooped his keys off the table and shoved them in his pocket. Babe ran through each room, which took no time.

"He's not here, Nick." Where could he be?" Babe's face clouded over, and she was breathing heavily, and then the tears began to fall.

"If anything has happened to him—"

Nick walked over to Babe and wrapped her in his arms. She tried to push him away, but it was a half-hearted attempt, and Nick refused to let go. Babe sobbed in his arms. Worry for her friend, frustration with all that had been going on, the lack of sleep, all of it seemed to boil up. Babe would have collapsed to the floor if Nick hadn't been holding her so tightly. Her body racked as she sobbed. When the racking finally slowed to small shudders, Nick held her at arm's length, swept her hair from her face.

"So, where to next?" He asked, wanting to draw her out of her current state.

A knock at Babe's door answered that question.

19

Frankie said something about Levi wetting his bed and snickered but stopped when he noticed his big brother wasn't laughing or even yelling at him to shut up. Instead, Levi's eyes were fixed on several smaller puddles leading out of their room. Levi stood up and followed the diminishing pools to their back door, where they disappeared altogether. Levi stood looking out the back porch door toward the river when somewhere outside, a crow cawed, sending a shiver up his spine.

"Hey, wait up for me," Frankie said, running to catch up with his brother.

"Did you go out to the river last night?" Levi asked.

"No, did you?"

Levi shook his head.

"Who made those puddles, Levi?"

"I don't know Frankie, maybe it was a—." But he had nothing.

"Come on, Levi, you're just messing with me. I know you did it."

Levi could hear the fear in Frankie's quivering voice, and it hurt him. He'd always been Frankie's protector. Levi forced a smile onto his face. "Man, I sure got you ya little turd."

"You dumb idiot!" Frankie yelled, and pounded a tiny fist into his big brother's shoulder.

Connie just stepped through the door. "Frankie, we don't call people names," she said and then gasped. "And why is the floor all wet?"

"Sorry, mom. Levi was trying to scare me," said Frankie.

"Well, I'm going to scare both of you if that water damages my beautiful hardwood floors. Now get some towels and wipe it up, or I'll wipe you up."

Levi and Frankie ran to the linen closet to grab towels hurried back to dry the floor while their mom stood with her hands on her hips and supervised.

"And you had better hope the floor isn't damaged, Levi Waters," she said as she turned and walked out of the room. "Then get your butts in the kitchen and eat your breakfast. We have to do some shopping for school clothes."

Levi exhaled hard and rolled his eyes.

"And don't you roll your eyes at me, Levi Francis Waters."

"How did she know?" Levi asked Frankie. "She was already in the other room."

Frankie shrugged his shoulders, and the brothers finished drying the floor.

***

After breakfast, Levi and Frankie went out back to toss the football around while their mom got ready. The Waters men, Scott included, hated shopping of any kind, but clothes shopping topped the list. Still, they knew they'd get nowhere arguing. Scott had always told them that when there was a shit job that had to be done, it was best to dive in at the deep end and get it over with.

"Get the ball, Frankie. It's in the garage," Levi said, making a slow windmill motion to loosen up his arm.

"Okay!" Frankie ran to the garage and stepped inside. "Hey, Levi," Frankie called.

"It's on the box right next to the door!"

"Dad doesn't smoke, right?"

"No, stupid, now get the ball!"

"I smell cigarettes, Levi."

"Maybe it's the ghost," Levi taunted.

Frankie felt a slight chill but shook it off. The ball was sitting on the floor near the steps to the upper room, and Frankie walked over and picked it up. He was just about to turn and leave when he got the feeling that he was being watched. Frankie's eyes went up the stairs to the open door on the landing above, just as then the door slammed shut. Frankie staggered backward, almost falling on his ass.

"Dad, are you up there?" Frankie inched closer. "Hey, dad!"

No response. "Maybe I imagined it," Frankie said to himself.

"Frankie!" Levi bellowed. "What are you doing, making the friggin thing?"

"Be right there," he replied and ran out to the yard.

"Throw it here and go deep," called Levi.

Frankie reared back and threw with all of his might. The football wobbled but made it all the way to his brother. Frankie pumped his fist. "Yes!"

"Nice throw, dork," Levi said. He pump-faked, dropped back, and threw. The football spiraled beautifully through the morning sky and landed softly in Frankie's breadbasket. Frankie spiked the ball and then chased it down and pitched it back to his brother.

"I'm gonna drop this one over your right shoulder."

Frankie ran hard toward the house. Again, a beautiful tight spiral flew through the clear blue sky and fell into Frankie's outstretched hands. Frankie turned around and spiked the ball again and added his version of the Ickey shuffle. Levi raised his arms in a triumphant V.

"Just like Montana and Rice, baby!"

Frankie stopped dancing and stared dumbly at a point above and beyond Levi's head.

"What's wrong, Frankie?"

Levi turned and watched as one crow after another flew smack into the window on the widow's walk above the garage. Thump, flop, thump, flop, thump, flop again and again. Now ten, now eleven crows, a murder of dead crows.

"Dad!" Frankie yelled at the top of his lungs.

Scott came running out of the house, holding a hammer that he'd been using to put up a shelf. Frankie stood in the yard, staring at the second floor of the garage with a look of horror on his face.

"What are you screaming about?" He asked his youngest son.

Frankie's hand rose and pointed at the widow's walk. Levi stood slack-jawed next to his brother, his eyes fixed on the same point. Scott shot a glance at the second level of the garage but saw nothing.

"The birds, dad, the birds."

"Crows," Levi corrected, neither brother breaking their gaze.

Scott looked again. "What crows? I don't see anything."

"They crashed into the windows, dad," Frankie turned, eyes pooling with tears.

"I think they broke their necks on the glass," Levi said, his eyes still fixed to the widow's walk.

"We have to help them, dad," said a pleading Frankie.

"They're already dead," Levi said, still not turning away. "Why would they do that?"

Scott glared at Levi, "I'm sure they're okay, Frankie, but we can't get up there. We have to wait for Mr. Merlyn to make us a key to open the door."

"The door's already open, dad," said Frankie.

"What do you mean open?" Levi asked.

"Tell him, Dad," urged Frankie.

"Tell him what, son?"

"Wasn't that you up there?" Frankie's voice quivered.

"I was in the house, Frankie. What's going on?"

"When I went into the garage to get the football, I saw the door open. I called you, but you slammed it shut."

"Frankie, I was in the house the whole time." Scott walked toward the garage and gestured for his boys to stay put, but they followed anyway.

Scott walked up the stairs. The door was closed, and when Scott pulled on the knob, it wouldn't budge. "See, tight as a drum. I'm not sure what you think you saw, son, but that door is locked up tighter than a nun's—" Scott Waters trailed off, not finishing his statement.

"A nun's what, dad?" Levi asked, daring him to finish the remark.

Frankie didn't care about the ending. "Get a ladder, dad; we have to help them."

"They're already dead stupid," Levi said dismissively.

Scott locked angry eyes on Levi but spoke softly to Frankie.

"We don't have a ladder, son. We never needed one in Chicago."

"Well, we need one now," Frankie said, fighting back the tears.

Scott looked around at their new home. He looked at the gutters at the shingles, and he looked at the second floor of the garage. "I suppose we do," he said.

Connie Waters walked across the yard toward the garage, her fingers crawling across the bottom of her purse in search of her car keys, and she hadn't noticed the looks on the faces of her boys until she spoke to them.

"Ready, boys?" She said, her face aglow with satisfaction as she fished the key-ring from her bag.

"What's wrong, guys?

Scott fixed the boys with a stare and delivered a quick but meaningful head shake. The message was clear. Not a word of this to your mother.

"Hey babe, nothing's wrong, just having a father-son moment," he said behind a placid smile.

"Right, boys?"

"Aw, mom, do we have to?" Frankie whined.

"Yeah, mom, we still have our stuff from last year. I don't see why we need new crap," Levi added.

"Don't say crap, Levi," she corrected.

The last thing Levi and Frankie wanted to do on a beautiful summer day was to shop with their mom. And this was the worst kind of shopping, clothes shopping.

"Don't argue with your mother, or I'll crap the both of you," Scott said.

Frankie and Levi began snickering. "Then we'd be your little turds," Frankie said, through snorts of laughter.

"Huddle up, boys," Scott called.

Connie huffed and rolled her eyes.

"Listen, you guys go with mom, and I'll call over to the hardware store in town and get them to deliver a ladder. Then I'll go up and check on the birds."

"Crows," Levi corrected.

"Right, crows, and your mom will be none the wiser."

"Why can't we tell her?" Frankie asked.

"Because stupid, you know how mom gets if we even kill a spider," Levi said.

"Don't call your brother stupid, you moron," Scott said. But the moron's right, buddy. We just don't want to upset her if we don't have to. You guys got it?"

The boys nodded again.

"Good," said Scott. "Hands in." Levi and Frankie each placed a hand on top of their father's. "Waters on two! One, two!" All three yelled "Waters" and broke the huddle.

"You guys are idiots," said Connie.

"What?" Scott protested. "I just told the boys that they better behave and not aggravate you."

"I'm sure that's what you told them," Connie said and then walked over to kiss her husband on his cheek. "Try not to break anything before I get back."

Connie turned for the Wagoneer, and Scott gave her a playful smack on the ass. The boys were already in the car. Levi in the front, Frankie alone in the back, both doing their best not to let the backs of their legs make contact with the hot vinyl seats.

"Mom, can we go? It's like an oven in here," complained Levi.

Connie climbed in, fired up the engine, and backed toward the road. Levi turned on the radio and cranked the volume.

"Levi, please, let me get out of the driveway before you blast it," Connie said.

"Sorry, mom." Levi turned the radio down but kept his hand on the knob. As soon as she put the car in drive, he turned the volume up again.

Connie's face soured. "What is that?"

"It's Dam the River, by Alice In Chains," said Levi.

"Who is Alison Chains?"

Frankie laughed, though he could hardly be heard over the radio.

"Not Alison Chains," Levi corrected. "Alice In Chains."

"Well, whoever she is, turn it down. It's too distracting."

"Fine," Levi turned the volume down to a dull roar. "And it's the name of the band. They're all guys."

"Alice Cooper is a guy," Connie said. She smiled like she'd gotten off a good one.

"Oh, nice one, mom," Frankie chimed in.

Connie scrolled the dial, and as luck would have it, Schools Out was just starting on another station. From the opening guitar riff, the boys were hooked. Once the chorus started, the Waters boys were all in. Connie turned it up and basked in the glory of being a cool parent.

***

The delivery truck from the Red Hook Hardware Store pulled up in front of the house, and a young man in overalls hopped out.

"You, Mr. Waters?" He asked, shielding his eyes from the sun.

"That's right, Scott Waters."

"I got your ladder, Mr. Waters," he said as he lifted a shiny aluminum ladder out of the truck-bed.

Biceps the size of softballs, skin tanned golden bronze, Scott made a mental note not to let Connie order anything from Red Hook Hardware.

"Where do you want it, sir?"

Scott pointed toward the widow's walk and started for the house to get his checkbook. "Just set it over there; I'll be right with you."

He walked back out to the driveway and asked, "Who do I make this out to?"

The delivery boy didn't answer.

"Buddy, who do I—" Scott looked up and saw what had captured the young man's attention. The entire railing around the walkout was covered with crows. "What the hell."

"You have a crow problem, sir."

"I can see that. Any suggestions?"

"Cats," offered the young man.

"Funny," Scott said. "You think you can steady the ladder for me while I climb up there and shoo them away?"

The kid glanced at his watch and shrugged his shoulders. "Sure," he said and leaned the ladder against the handrail on the widow's walk, causing the birds to light off the rail. "Well, that was easy," Scott said as he climbed up the ladder and stepped over the railing.

"Holy shit,"

"What's the problem, Mr. Waters?"

The kid climbed to the top of the ladder and stopped.

"Holy shit," he said.

"That's what I said. Have you ever seen anything like this?" Scott asked the kid.

"No, sir, never."

"Think you could give me a hand cleaning this up?"

The kid looked hesitatingly at the carpet of dead and broken birds. "I don't know, sir—I—I— really should be heading back."

"What's your name, son?" Scott asked.

Wilford Ambers, sir, but I go by Will."

Well, Will, there's ten bucks in it for you," Scott said in an attempt to sway the young man.

Wilford Ambers' eyes widened.

"There are some garbage bags on the shelf in the garage, and grab the shovel. It's on a hook on the opposite wall."

The young man descended the ladder and disappeared into the garage.

"Sir," he called from below.

"Yeah?"

"You know there's a door up to the second level in here, right?"

"Yeah, it's locked, and I don't have a key," Scott called down. "Just grab the bag and shovel, Will.

"On it, sir." Will was back up the ladder in a flash. "All I could find was this old snow shovel."

"Yeah, that's all I have. It will do the trick."

The two set about removing the carcasses from the widow's walk as dozens of crows watched from nearby trees. Scott scooped, and Will held the bag open, filled it with dead birds, and tossed it over the side.

"Hey, what if that bag broke?"

"Sorry, sir. Hey, Mr. Waters," said Will, raising his voice at the end to suggest a question was coming, as he opened a second bag.

"What is it, Will?"

"I wasn't being nosy or anything, but I didn't see a tractor in your garage."

"That's because I don't own one."

"Well, it's just that we have a sale going on lawn tractors this week."

"I was planning on buying a lawnmower," Scott replied, still focused on crow removal.

"With a lawn this size, you're really going to want a tractor, Mr. Waters."

"I have two strong boys; I'm sure they can manage."

"Yeah, but it's not just the lawn, sir. You're going to have to plow this driveway in the winter, and that shovel isn't going to do the job."

"What are you saying; I should mow the snow?"

Will laughed. "No, Mr. Waters, but they sell snow-blades and even blowers that you can attach to the front of the tractor."

Scott was still working his way through the clean-up and not paying much mind to what Will was saying.

"Anyway, sir, like I said, there's this big sale this week, and—well, if you mention my name, I could get a pretty nice commission on the sale. It's like a twenty-five-dollar bonus, and I'm saving for college—and."

Scott finally stopped shoveling and turned to look at Will. "Tell you what, Will. If I have time,

I'll stop in and take a look."

"Right, and if you could—"

"Mention your name; you got it. Now, how about you open another bag? That one is about full."

"I'll have to run back down; I only brought two."

As Scott waited, he leaned on his shovel and looked out toward the river.

"Hey, Will," he said.

"Yeah, Mr. Waters?" Will called from the garage.

"Is that the Ironweiler house?

It was his first look at the place. He hadn't been able to see it from the ground.

"Yep," he called up. "It's haunted."

Will climbed back up the ladder and opened another empty garbage bag. "You are probably going to want to buy some contractor bags, sir."

"What are contractor bags?"

"They're really big garbage bags."

"You must be Red Hook's number one salesperson," Scott said as he noticed the enormous, black bird in the gable window. "Ready when you are, sir," Will said, holding the bag open.

20

Shopping took the better part of the morning, and the accompanying boredom allowed thoughts of crows and mysterious puddles to crawl back into his mind and fester. He tried to think of other things. He ran football plays in his head and even tried praying, but it was no use. Seeming to notice something was bothering her oldest son, Connie turned to the heavy-metal station to bring him out of his funk.

"Come of Levi, do you really hate shopping that much?"

Levi just shrugged.

"Well, it's over now, and I promise that you won't have to shop for clothes again till next year."

Slowly, a smile worked its way onto his face, and Connie beamed.

"See, all better."

But it wasn't his mother's promise of a shopping reprieve that made him smile. Kaylin Vaughn, her hair dancing on the breeze, the sun kissing her already tanned skin, leaned against her bike and plucked the butter-yellow petals from a dandelion. Seeing Kaylin swept all thoughts of crows and puddles out of his head.

"Hi Mrs. Waters," Stan said, in his best Eddie Haskell voice. "Can Levi and Frankie go to Memorial Park with us?"

The voice surprised Levi. He hadn't even noticed the rest of the gang.

"They have to put their new school outfits away."

Levi rolled his eyes. She has to be doing this on purpose.

"Then they can go out and play."

He shot a quick look at Kaylin, who smiled and looked down at her feet.

Levi harrumphed and stomped into the house with his bags.

"Put my outfits away? Go out and play?" Levi said to himself, once safely out of earshot. "I'm not a little kid, mom," again out loud and indignant, but careful not to be heard. He knew what she was doing. She was trying to embarrass him. Probably because Frankie said something about him liking a girl. Levi dumped the bags on his bed. He considered leaving them where they fell to display his displeasure at being treated like a child but reconsidered. Instead, he hung them carefully in his closet and then joined his friends back outside.

"What are we doing at the park?" Levi asked Stan.

"We ain't going to the park."

"Well, where are we going?"

"You'll see," Stan said, wearing a shit-eating grin.

Hooking a hard right onto Main Street, they rode out to Peace Road. The sun felt hot and Levi could smell the asphalt. It reminded him of the city, but that was the only thing that reminded him of his old home. He hated to admit it, but the old man really nailed it. He glanced over at Kaylin and smiled. She smiled back and Levi knew he never wanted to leave Red Hook. After riding for over half an hour, they arrived at Route 6, where it met up with Square Barn Road.

"Well," said Stan. "There it is."

"I don't get it. It's a gas station," Levi said.

"I get it," Kaylin said. "Stanley Howard, don't you even think about it."

"Oh, it's more than a gas station, Levi," Stan said as he dismounted and set his kickstand.

Levi took a closer look. "Yeah, you're right. It's a closed gas station."

Kaylin rolled her eyes, "Jeez, Stan, you can be so stupid. A family was killed here, Levi."

Stan glared at her, his cheeks flushed red. "Not just a family."

Levi's mouth fell open with an audible gasp.

Stan smiled. "Weren't expecting that, were you?"

"No, Stan, who would? You must have a screw loose, man."

"What? Why?" Stan asked, seeming genuinely perplexed.

"What's with your fascination with death? And what's with this town and all the killings?"

"What are you talking about?" Stan said defensively.

"We've been here all of three days, and you've told us about two murders. I don't know Stan; it seems like a lot."

"The murders at the house across the river was like 10 years ago. Other than this, it's been pretty quiet. Besides, I heard the guy that killed these people was from Chicago. Your hometown."

"No, he wasn't, you imbecile," said Kaylin. "He was some weirdo who lived in the woods in Wisconsin."

"Bullshit," Stan fired back. "Besides, how would you know?"

"Christopher Vecchio is my uncle, ya ding-dong."

"Who's that? Asked Levi.

"He's the chief of police," said Lonnie.

"B F D," Stan said. "It's not like he knows everything."

The consensus, it seemed, was that Kaylin had Stan in checkmate, and he made no additional arguments to the contrary.

"Whatever, the point is, there was a mass murder here, and the cops just took down all the crime scene tape, so now we can take a look without worrying about getting busted. Far as I know, no one else has been in there yet, not even the seniors."

Stan started walking, but no one followed. They hadn't even gotten off their bikes. Instead, they all sat looking at one another. Stan stopped and turned back toward them.

"Bunch of fucking babies!"

"I'm telling mom. You think because you start high school in two days, you're some kind of big shot. We'll see how big you are when mom beats your ass!" The red that started on McKenna's neck began creeping up onto her face.

"You said ass! I'm telling on you!"

"What you said was way worse than ass," McKenna fired back.

"Would you two shut up?" Finn said. "No one is telling mom anything.

She doesn't need the aggravation. Stan, if you want to go look, then go ahead. Anyone else who wants to look can go right ahead. If you don't want to, that's fine, but you rode a long way for nothing." Finn let his bike drop and started toward the Never Close.

"Well," Kaylin said with a sharp nod of her head. "Okay then," and hopped off of her bike.

"Wow," Lonnie said, "What's with Finn?"

"Right?" Stevie said in agreement.

The Johnson brothers were next off their bikes, followed by Levi, Frankie, and Finally McKenna. Each kid found a spot on the glass and cupped their hands around their eyes. But the posters for milk, bread, and various cigarette brands cast the little store in shadow, and no matter how hard they squinted, they really couldn't see anything.

"Should we go in?" Lonnie asked.

Stevie grabbed the door handle and pulled, probably not expecting it to open. Startled, he let go of the handle, and the door closed again. Now the group had another choice to make. Even Stan, who, for a little guy, had big brass balls, was hesitant.

"I—I don't know," Stan said. "Maybe we should—"

"Fuck it," Lonnie said, and pulled the door wide open.

Stevie was hot on his brother's heels as they stepped inside.

There were a lot of shoulder shrugs, but the rest joined them inside the Never Close. Dust floated on the thick shaft of sunlight that broke across the threshold and vanished as the poster-covered door swung shut. Stan reached back and gave the door a push to make sure it didn't lock behind them. For a moment, they all stood mute in the stillness, seeming to sense the need for reverence, and then Kaylin spoke up.

"It's so quiet," she whispered. It's kind of eerie."

"What's eerie, Levi?" Frankie whispered to his brother.

"It means creepy."

"It sure is eerie," Frankie agreed.

"Yeah," McKenna said. "I've never been in here when the radio wasn't on."

"Anyone bring a flashlight?"

"It's the middle of the day Lonnie, I'm sure no one thought to bring a flashlight," said Stevie.

A display on the counter held C cell flashlights. Stan walked over and helped himself to one.

"You're not stealing a flashlight Stanley Howard," McKenna said.

"Relax," said Stan. "I'll put it back after I have a look around."

He thumbed the light on and swept it around the room. Candy, lighters, and a few magazines lay scattered around the floor, and a shelf behind the counter was knocked over. Clearly, there had been a terrible fight in the store.

"Dude," said Stevie. "Looks like somebody robbed the place, but it sure doesn't look like anyone was killed here."

"See," Lonnie said. "All those rumors were bullshit."

"No, I bet the cops just cleaned everything up," Stan said, offering an explanation for the lack of blood and gore.

McKenna exhaled. "Well, I'm glad they cleaned up."

A click and a whirring sound came from the back of the store, and they all jumped.

"What the hell was that?" Finn asked.

"Stan, the next time you get a stupid idea like this, you can leave Kaylin and me out!"

"Nobody twisted your arm McKenna, or yours either, Kaylin. Why don't you both just leave?"

"Easy does it, guys," said Levi. "We're all just a little nervous. I think that was just a compressor for the air-conditioning or something."

"Levi's right. It's hot as balls outside, but it's pretty nice in here," Finn said. "The air has to be on. Let's just check it out and get out of here. I bet no one is going to be able to top this story at school."

"Yeah," Stevie agreed. "What I did on my summer vacation, by Stephen R. Johnson. I went fucking ghost hunting! What did you jerk-offs do?"

Lonnie roared with laughter, and Finn joined him.

"Okay, calm down. We need to be able to hear."

"Hear what?" Lonnie asked.

"I don't know," Stan said, his voice quivering. "Maybe the cops?"

They walked behind Stan, who was the only one to pick up a flashlight.

"Shine it over there," Stevie said, pointing toward the refrigerated cooler at the back of the store.

"No, point it over here," Finn said, standing near the magazine rack.

"Go back and get your own damn light or shut the hell up," Stan snapped.

He passed the light over a display rack near the back of the store and saw another flashlight sitting on a shelf.

"There, someone grab that one."

McKenna grabbed it and clicked the switch, but instead of white light, the flashlight gave off a purple glow. "What the hell kind of light is this?" She said as she moved it around the store.

"I don't know, but if you don't like it, go back to the front and get another one of these," said Stan, waving his light around.

"This light is creepier than the dark Stan, just come back to the front with us...please?"

"Jeez, I guess I'm never going to finish exploring this place if I don't," he said and began moving back toward the front of the store.

Stan pointed the light at the floor so they could all see where they were walking. McKenna didn't bother turning the purple light off and followed behind. As her purple light passed over the floor near the front of the store, splotches of a luminous crystal blue color appeared all over. She moved the light and found more of the blue color spattered on the wall. Closer inspection revealed two holes in the wall. Kaylin, who hadn't left McKenna's side since they walked into the store, gripped her friend's arm.

"Oh my god, that's blood... that's blood," Kaylin said in a loud whisper.

McKenna turned toward Stan, her light following her eyes, and screamed as he was about to put his hand on the counter.

"Stan, no!" She yelled, freezing Stan in his tracks.

They all looked down and saw the blue light emanating from the counter.

"What the hell is that?" Levi asked.

"It's blood," Kaylin replied.

"Blood is red dummy," Lonnie said, with a snort of superiority.

"No, sometimes it's blue," said Stevie. "Just look at your veins; some-times, you can see it."

"You're both wrong," said Kaylin. McKenna's light is a black-light."

"Cool," said Stevie, "like for a black-light poster?"

"I guess, but my uncle showed me how the cops use this stuff called luminol to show where blood was, even if someone tried to clean it up. The luminol reacts with something in the blood and makes it glow blue. All this blue stuff is leftover traces of blood."

McKenna slowly moved the light around the store.

"See!" Stan said triumphantly. "I told you, mass-fucking-murder!"

"Who died here?" Asked Frankie.

"A whole family. The Thortons," said McKenna.

"And Jessie! Don't forget Jessie," said Stevie.

"Man, she was so hot," added Lonnie.

Kaylin punched Lonnie in the arm. "You pig!"

"Sorry, but she was," he said, rubbing his shoulder.

"Yeah, she was," Stevie offered in support.

"Not everyone died," Finn corrected. I heard that Ronnie lived. I heard the cops sent him to live with his aunt and uncle somewhere."

"No, Ronnie died," said Stan. "He would have been in your grade. Eddie, he's our age. He's the one who survived.

"I heard that Mr. Parker went crazy," said Kaylin. "His daughter Mary Jane is in our grade, McKenna."

McKenna didn't acknowledge her; she was busy with her black-light. There was blue light everywhere. On the floor, the counter, the walls, and the ceiling. Even the flashlight in Stan's hand had glowing blue specks on it. A guttural noise rose up from Stan's diaphragm, and he dropped the light on the floor.

From the back of the store, the part cloaked in darkness, came a loud bang. In the beam of Stan's dropped flashlight, a can of ravioli came rolling into view. The gang bolted for the door. Stan hit the door with his shoulder, but it didn't budge. The rest of the group hurried to help. They pushed and pulled on the door, but it wouldn't open, and they all began to scream, all except for Frankie. Frankie walked to the other side of the double door and pushed.

"We came in this door, guys."

They careened out the door banging into one another and didn't stop running till they were back at their bikes. That was when McKenna realized she was still holding the black-light.

"Shit, I still have this thing. We gotta put it back."

"You got a mouse in your pocket?" Stan asked.

"Don't be a jerk, Stan, we have to put this thing back, or they'll know someone was in there."

"Screw that. I'm not going back in there."

"He's right, McKenna," Lonnie said, and Stevie agreed.

"Then what am I supposed to do with it?"

"I'll take it," said Stevie. "Then when I get a black-light poster, I'll already have the light."

Stan's face lit up. "We're going to take it to the house across the river. We're going to see just how much blood is still in that place."

"Hell no," Levi protested. "No way in hell, Frankie, or I am going back there."

"Don't be a baby," said Stan.

"Stan, you do what you want, but me and Frankie are out."

Levi got on his bike. "Let's go, Frankie; we shouldn't be here anyway. We told mom we were going to the park."

Frankie got on his bike, and the Waters brothers started riding off. Stan grabbed his bike and hopped on it from a running start, and the rest followed.

"Wait up, guys!" Stan called, but Levi and Frankie just kept riding.

"Come on! I'm sorry! You don't have to go!" Stan peddled hard and caught up. Out of breath, he said, "Levi, I'm sorry, man, I know you're not a baby. Just wait up a minute."

Levi stopped and looked at Stan. "You think everything is a joke. Do you think it's cool being sneaky and lying to your mom? Cause I don't."

"I said I was sorry," he fired back.

"What are you even sorry for?"

Stan looked perplexed.

"You don't even know what you've done," Levi said, and set his foot on the pedal.

"So, tell me, what did I do?"

Levi shook his head but didn't answer him. "Come on, Frankie."

"Where are you guys going?" McKenna asked.

"Leave them alone; Levi's got his panties in a bunch about something," Stan said.

"You really are an ass, Stan," said Kaylin.

"Jeez, Kaylin, what, do you like him or something?"

Levi stood up on his pedal, ready to take off when he heard the question, and squeezed his handbrakes a little harder.

"So, what if I do? I've known him for three days, and I like him better than you," Kaylin said.

Levi turned his head to make sure none of the gang could see the huge smile on his face and released the hand brake. Frankie called after him to wait up and took off after his brother.

21

Levi and Frankie rode their bikes into the garage. Levi was about to let his bike drop but decided to park it against the wall so their dad would have room for his car. Naturally, Frankie followed suit. It was a big two-and-a-half car garage, but Levi still felt a little guilty and figured he'd grease the wheels on the karma train with a bit of voluntary good behavior.

"Remember, Frankie, don't say a word to mom about where we went," Levi said, speaking quietly to his little brother.

Frankie nodded but looked worried.

"You okay, buddy?"

Frankie shrugged his shoulders. "I guess. Hey, Levi, do you think Stan is a nice kid?"

Levi thought about the question. He thought about Stan fixing the broken binoculars and figured that had to count for something. "Yeah, I think he's probably okay. I just don't think he's afraid of anything. Dad says people who aren't smart enough to be afraid are reckless, but I don't think that makes them bad."

"I'm glad you said we aren't going back to the house across the river. That place gave me the eeries."

Levi smiled. "Me too, buddy."

"Levi, were you scared?"

"Heck yeah, I was scared," Levi answered.

"But you went anyway?"

"Being scared doesn't mean you don't do something; it just means you do it a little more carefully. Sometimes it's good to face your fears," he said, and knelt down to tie Frankie's shoe.

Frankie's face scrunched up. "Really, like when?"

Levi paused and stroked his chin the way he'd seen his father do it when he had to give a thoughtful answer. "Like Uncle Terry."

"Uncle Terry's a cop; he's not afraid of anything. He told me so." Frankie said.

"He's full of crap. I'm sure he's been scared lots of times! But he's brave, and that's what makes him so cool. He faces his fears and does what he needs to do."

The confusion lifted from Frankie's face. "You think he'll come for Thanksgiving?"

Levi stood up and gave Frankie a light tap on the back of the head. "Yeah, I'm sure he will, and I bet he'll tell us some good stories. Now come on, I'll race you to the house."

"Scott?" Connie called from the kitchen.

"No, mom," answered Levi. "It's just us."

"Well, go wash up for dinner; we're having meatloaf. I sent your dad into town for more butter. I used the last of it in the mashed potatoes."

As if on cue, the Wagoneer rolled into the driveway. Levi heard the tailgate open with a screech and then slam shut. A few seconds later and the screen door banged.

"Levi, make yourself useful," Scott said, thrusting a couple of bags at his son.

"I only sent you for butter."

"I know, but I picked up some beer and munchies."

Levi set the bags on the kitchen table and fished around inside. "Hell yeah!"

"Levi, watch your mouth!"

"Sorry, mom," Levi said sheepishly. "Frankie, dad got Oke-Do-Ke!"

Frankie came running and slid to a stop. The boys loved the delicious cheese popcorn, but their mother hated the stains it left when they wiped the orange cheese dust on their clothes.

"Hey, Dad! Did you get the birds down?"

"Crows!" Levi corrected, still rummaging through the bags. "And didn't you hear what I said? Oke-Do-Ke!".

"Last I checked, crows were still birds," Connie said, adding her two cents as she stirred more butter into the mashed potatoes. "And you leave that junk food alone; dinner is almost ready."

"Yeah, champ, there were no crows or birds," he said, raising his voice for Levi's benefit. "Not even any feathers, so I guess they just flew away."

"What are you guys talking about?" Connie asked.

"Nothing, babe, the boys thought some crows flew into the glass door up on the walkout above the garage, but there was nothing there." No one had to know that Scott had paid the kid an extra five bucks to take bags of dead birds to the dump.

"How did you get up there?" Connie asked. I thought the door was locked."

Scott thought of the young stud from the hardware store. "The guy from the hardware store delivered the ladder. I ordered it the other day," Scott said and tossed the boys a look.

"What do we need with a ladder?" Connie asked.

"We got gutters, babe; those things don't clean themselves."

Levi cast a wary glance at his father, but it wasn't about the lie he had just told. The crows smashed into the glass loud enough to hear. Levi thought he'd even heard some bones snap, but he didn't let the thought germinate.

"Dinner in five, out at the picnic table. Bring your own drinks," Connie said as she bumped the back door open with her hip and slipped outside.

The Waters family sat outside and dined under the stars, and there was no more talk of crows or birds of any kind. As they laughed and ate, something dragged itself out of the water on the river's east bank and clawed its way into the Ironweiler house.

***

After dinner, Scott let the boys watch some of the Dolphins vs Steelers game on Monday Night Football. By halftime, Dan Marino had the Dolphins up 14-03, and halftime meant bedtime for the two youngest members of the

Waters family. Levi argued the point, but it was no use. Besides, Scott always recorded the games. Then he and Levi would watch the tapes and go over the plays.

Connie curled up next to Scott on the couch and rested her head on his shoulder. Scott put an arm around his wife and squeezed her tight. The central air had just kicked off, and the television was turned down low while a commercial for the new 1995 Lincoln Town Car ran.

"We could do it easily in that back seat," Scott said.

Connie looked at him and wrinkled her nose. "Easier than in the back of the Wagoneer?"

"Only one way to find out," Scott said playfully.

"You want to buy a new car just to fool around in the back seat?" She didn't exactly call him a moron, but her tone suggested it.

"What? Hell no! We can't afford a new car, not on a vice principal's salary, but we can run a test in the Wagoneer," he said with a grin.

"We're adults, Scott. We aren't screwing in the car. Besides, we always managed in that piece of shit Nova of yours, and those were pretty tight quarters."

"Okay, first off, my '78 Nova SS was one bad ass ride."

Connie waited a moment; "And second?"

"Second?"

"You said first off, so what's your second off?"

"Scott smiled and laughed softly, "My second off is, I will take you anywhere I can get you, Mrs. Waters." Scott leaned in, kissed her tenderly, and both let out satisfied exhalations as they sunk deeper into the couch.

"Did you ever imagine we would live in a place this peaceful?" Connie asked.

The house was still. Even in the quietest moments, their place in Chicago was never this serene. There was always noise. Traffic, the trundling clank of a passing EL-Train, or the upstairs neighbors who always sounded like they hopped from place to place rather than walked, there was always noise.

"It's like camping with indoor plumbing," Scott said, drawing a laugh from both of them.

"Seems like the boys have made some nice friends," Connie said.

"Who, that Mrs. Howard's kids?"

"Yeah, and the other ones too," said Connie.

"Yeah, they seem like nice kids," Scott replied.

"Frankie says Levi is interested in one of the girls in the group," Connie added.

"That's good," he muttered. The game had resumed, and his attention was waning.

"I don't know," she said hesitantly. "He needs to focus on schoolwork."

"That's good. Do we have any of that pie left?"

Connie baked an apple pie with apples she picked from the tree in their own yard. It was a little tart, the apples could have done with a few more weeks to ripen, but it was still delicious.

"Are you even listening to me?"

"What? Sure," said Scott, "the boys made some friends."

Connie gave him a playful punch in the arm. "Ass."

"What?"

"I was talking about Levi and that girl."

"What, girl?" It was the first he'd heard of it.

"The one Frankie said he likes. I just think he should forget about girls and focus on school."

"Bullshit, you just don't want him to grow up. Well, I got news for you. Sister Ann called me at the end of last school year. He was passing notes with Rosalina Tecorri." Scott shook his hand as if he'd just touched an open flame and made a *foof* sound. "Hot stuff."

She punched him again. "You really are an ass," she paused. "What did it say?"

"Hey, I can't break the bond of trust I've established with my son."

Connie cocked her fist, and Scott threw up his hands in defense.

"Okay, easy, Rocky. It was just the typical names in hearts and 'Mrs. Rosalina Waters' and 'let's make a baby,' you know, typical."

She really let him have it. "Scott Waters, you are an asshole." And she fell on top of him, and they kissed a good long while. Then Scott scooped

Connie up in his arms.

"Scott, the TV."

"Screw the TV," said Scott, and he carried her off to their bedroom.

***

With all but Frankie sound asleep, the little house on Sugar Maple Lane was peaceful and quiet, except for the soft hissing static and gray glow from the living-room television. Frankie Waters sat up, shivering in bed. It felt like the middle of winter with the windows open. As he pulled his covers up tighter around himself, his bedroom door swung open slowly and silently on well-oiled hinges, and the room filled with spillover from the television. Frankie rubbed the sleep from his eyes, and he could feel icy fingers wrap around his heart. Standing next to his brother's bed, a little boy, maybe six years old, turned to face him. The boy was sopping wet and looked like he'd just gone for a swim in the river. Even through all the water, there was so much that it seemed to be coming out of the boy; Frankie could tell he was crying.

The boy looked terrified, and Frankie felt the icy fingers release for a moment. Frankie danced somewhere between terror and compassion, but in an instant, the pity was gone, and the grip tightened again. The boy's eyes turned a milky gray, and his mouth fell open in a wide yawn. Water poured from the black maw, and the boy flew at Frankie. Arms outstretched, hands groping and grabbing. Francis Scott Waters pulled his covers over his head and pushed himself hard against the wall. Frankie could see his breath coming out in rapid puffs of vapor in the gray light from the television that penetrated his thin sheets. He was petrified. He wanted to call out, to yell for Levi, his protector, but in that horrible moment, Frankie hoped the *thing* would turn back toward his brother and forget about him. Frankie pressed his eyes shut and held his breath. He tried to pray but couldn't remember the words to the Lord's Prayer. All he could manage was *Our Father, who art in Heaven*, which he repeated in a loop.

After a few moments, he opened his eyes again and tried to slow his breathing. Nothing had happened. The boy, or whatever it was, didn't grab him. Frankie's mind raced. Was he standing next to his bed, just waiting for Frankie to pull the covers down? Frankie tried not to move, he wanted to listen for any sign that it was still out there, but between his breathing and the uncontrollable shaking of his body, he couldn't make anything out.

What was it that Levi told him? Frankie knew it had something to do with being scared. Something about fear being a good thing. No, that wasn't it. He closed his eyes tightly and focused. Levi told him to face his fear; that's what it was. He told him that even Uncle Terry got scared and had to face his fears. He said that was what made Uncle Terry so cool. Frankie took a deep breath, braced himself, and ripped the covers off. The boy thing was gone, and the room felt warm again. Frankie exhaled hard.

That was when he realized he was wet. In his terror, he had pissed his pajama pants. He was almost a teenager, and he pissed himself. He was so ashamed; He felt his stomach drop. He had to get up and change and hide his wet PJs at the bottom of his hamper before Levi found out. Frankie tried to get up, but his fears came creeping back up. What if he put a foot down and that thing was under his bed? It would drag him under, and that would be it. Frankie knew that things hid under beds, at least they did in movies. Last Halloween, his dad rented the movie Poltergeist from the Blockbuster store, and Frankie knew that monsters hid under beds.

Frankie decided that he'd done enough fear-facing for one night. He pulled the pillowcase off his pillow and laid it down as a barrier to keep the pee from soaking into his mattress. He laid there all night in his pee-soaked PJs, too afraid to get up and too scared to fall asleep. As the morning sun came up and splashed against the wall in his room, Frankie climbed out of bed, stripped naked, and put on clean, dry underwear and fresh pajamas.

"What are you doing?" Levi asked in a whisper.

"Nothing, I, I," he stammered. "I had to go pee."

"Well, get back in bed and be quiet. I'm not waking up early on the last day of summer vacation."

Frankie kicked his wet clothes under the bed and crawled back under the covers. He could smell the ammonia of his piss-soaked pajama bottoms and underwear wafting up from under the bed, and he wanted more than anything to get rid of the evidence before Levi smelled it. If he could just sneak over to the hamper. Then, later, he could throw it all in the washing machine before anyone knew what happened. He'd never done laundry before, but how hard could it be? And sure, his mom would probably wonder what he was up to, but maybe the shock of someone wanting to do something *for* her instead of always wanting something *from* her would disrupt her mom-radar long enough for her curiosity to pass.

Once he was sure Levi was back asleep, Frankie slid quietly out from under his covers and knelt down next to his bed. The sunlight that slipped between the blinds reached the floor near the beds. Still, the space beneath remained in shadows. Another thing that Frankie learned from movies was that monsters didn't come out in the daylight. Still, he was hesitant as he groped around in the dark for his wet things. Frankie fished his hand around in the inky blackness under his bed until it landed on the cold, damp pile. Seizing it, Frankie suddenly had the feeling that something was watching him, and had he not already let go of his bladder, he would have pissed himself again.

Moving his head very slowly and keeping his body perfectly still, Frankie turned to find Levi, up on one elbow, watching in wonder at what his little brother was doing. Frankie exhaled.

"What are you doing?" Asked Levi.

Frankie sat on his bed and dropped his wet clothes, plop on the floor at his feet.

"Promise you won't ever tell anyone." It was a demand, not a request.

"Tell anyone what? What is that?"

"Promise Levi."

"Okay, I promise," he said, eager to hear the secret.

"I had an accident."

"What do you mean, you had an accident?"

Frankie didn't answer; he just looked crestfallen at his big brother.

"You mean you wet the bed?" Levi's voice dripped with disgust; at least, that was the way Frankie heard it.

Frankie let his head fall.

"Holy shit! Dude, you're twelve years old."

"I know Levi," he said as tears welled up in his eyes.

"I'm sorry, Frankie," Levi said. "What happened?"

"I saw him."

Frankie's face blanched white, and his stomach lurched and tumbled.

"You look like you want to puke. Are you okay?"

Frankie placed a hand over his mouth to steady himself. "No, Levi, I saw him."

"Saw who, Frankie?"

"I think it was the little boy from the house across the river."

"The dead kid?" Levi's face went pale. "That's crazy."

Frankie pointed at the floor next to Levi's bed. He looked down where Frankie was pointing and saw that the floor was wet. Like the morning before, there was a puddle and smaller pools, like footprints, leading to the door.

"Wha... what did it look like?" Levi stammered.

"It was bad, Levi, really bad. I think he's still out there in the river. I don't know why, but I don't think he wants to hurt us. He looked so sad. I think he wants our help."

The morning sun heated up the room and brought the pee smell back.

"Okay, we can talk about this later. Right now, we have to deal with your pajamas. Grab them and toss them in the hamper. I'll grab a towel from the hall closet and dry the floor."

The boys hopped to action and were in the laundry room with the door closed. They dumped the hamper into the washing machine, and Levi's torn pajama shirt came tumbling out. There was blood where the tear was, and Frankie asked Levi what happened. Just as Levi was going to tell him, the door to the laundry room flew open.

"What are you two up to?" Connie asked.

"Morning, mom," said Levi.

"Yeah, morning, mom," Frankie parroted.

"We just thought we would help out and do our laundry," Levi said with the sappiest sweet smile he could conjure.

Connie looked skeptically at her oldest son and then at Frankie, who tried to match the sappiness.

"You're up to something, but for now, I'll just take the help," she said as she turned and walked toward the kitchen. "Cereal or eggs for breakfast?"

The brothers shared a look of surprise. They had pulled it off.

"Just cereal, mom," called Levi.

"Yeah, me too, mom," said Frankie.

The boys ran back into their room to get dressed, but Frankie stopped.

"I think I better take a shower first."

"Good call," agreed Levi. "Then we'll take our cereal and eat it on the boxes in the garage. We need to talk."

After Frankie's quick shower, the boys ran into the kitchen, filled their bowls, and turned to leave.

"And where do you think you're going?" As she turned, she saw Frankie. His hair was wet, and his face looked freshly scrubbed. "Frankie, did you take a bath?"

"No, mom, a shower," he said, "girls take baths."

Connie's mouth fell open as he and Levi hurried out before their mother could query them further. It was another hot morning. The heat hadn't let up since early June, and it seemed no change was on the horizon. Levi didn't care; he loved the warmth and took in a deep breath of fresh summer air and frowned.

"You smell that, Frankie?"

Frankie sniffed at the air. "Smell what?"

"Cigarettes, do you smell cigarette smoke?"

Frankie sniffed again, "no, but remember, I told you I smelled yesterday?"

Levi followed the smell toward the garage.

"It's coming from the garage," Levi said.

The boys entered the garage and froze in their tracks. The mysterious, locked door leading to the upstairs room was standing open about six inches.

"See, Levi, I told you."

22

Cindy Plahutnik stood bent over with her hands on her knees, trying to catch her breath. Babe had known Cindy, and the rest of her family, for nearly six years. And while they were always friendly, hello, goodbye, and such, Babe couldn't recall a single other time that she'd found Cindy on her doorstep.

"You okay, Cindy?"

Cindy let out a loud *woo* sound and straightened herself out. "Doc says I gotta do more walking," she answered.

"Um-hm, so what brings you by?"

"That big Injun fella that's been staying with you?" It sounded like a question.

Babe rolled her eyes. "Yeah, Cindy. What about him?"

The large woman in the colorful moomoo placed her hands on her hips, arched her back, sucked in air, and blew out hard. "Hate to say it, but I think doc's right."

Babe restrained herself from physically grabbing the woman replying instead with a terse smile.

"Anyway, like I was saying, that fat fuck Tucker snatched him up last night. Said he was breaking into your house."

Babe's eyes widened.

"I tried to stop him. I told Tucker that the Injun's been staying with you, but he told me I was full of shit. Said I should smoke some-more crack and mind my own business — son-of-a-bitch is lucky Jimmy wasn't home, he'd have knocked him on his fat ass."

Babe started to close the door in Cindy Plahutnik's face and then offered a quick "thanks, Cindy," right before it clicked shut.

"Well, how do you like that shit? I walk all the way over here, and…" her voice faded.

Babe grabbed up a few things and shoved them into a large shoulder bag that, to Nick, looked like the hemp bags the *hippie chicks*, their vernacular not his, carried on campus. She stopped at the table and began rummaging through weeks or perhaps months of bills and magazines, and God knew what all.

Nick pulled his keys from his pocket, held them high over his head, and gave them a jingle.

"Lose something?"

Babe lunged for the keys, and Nick extended his arm, keeping them just beyond her reach.

"Give me the keys, Nick. This isn't funny."

"It's not supposed to be funny. Babe, ever since you knocked on my motel door, I have felt like I'm being dragged behind a runaway horse, and I'm tired of it. I'm tired of feeling out of control."

Babe stopped reaching and dropped her head.

"I'm sorry, Nick."

"Look, if the Sheriff's got Achak, we know where he is. Right: so, suppose you slow down and help me get my head around this? I mean hell—," he paused, hands on his hips; he darted the tip of his tongue out to moisten his lips and began pacing. "Murders, witches, curses, and some sinister cabal kidnapping expectant mothers?" Even you have to admit this all sounds nuts."

"But you read the—"

"I know what I read!" Nick pulled out a chair and sat down hard. "Fuck!"

Babe jerked back, startled, and Nick saw the same fragility that he saw when he grabbed her wrist as she went for the radio. "I'm sorry, Babe, I guess It's been building up."

"Don't apologize, Nick; you're right. We threw a lot at you. Honestly, I'm surprised you didn't leave back at the barn."

"I almost did." Nick stared blankly.

"What stopped you, the diary?"

"That and... I don't know something about duty and courage in the field. Seems stupid to say it out loud, but it made sense in my head."

"It's not stupid; you took a big chance driving to the middle of nowhere with a woman you really didn't know."

Nick smiled, "I thought I was going to shit when I saw Achak."

She chuffed air through her nostrils and smiled. "I'm glad you decided to stay, Nick," she said, and placed her hand on his.

The touch made him uncomfortable, and he bolted to his feet. Babe looked at him with an expression that he read as confusion. She had been hanging on him back at the motel, but that was all for show. This was different, this felt intimate, and Nick Ryan didn't do intimate. His normal default defense against such things was humor, but he wasn't feeling particularly humorous at that moment. He began pacing again.

"I'm glad too, but this still sounds crazy. I mean, the diary," Nick's hand flew to his forehead. "You don't think the sheriff took it, do you?"

"I don't know," she answered.

"Shit, I really need that thing. That's the only documentation I have for any of this."

Babe stood up and walked over to her fridge, and grabbed hold of it.

"You gonna help me with this?"

He walked over and grabbed the other side of the appliance. "What are we doing with it?"

"Help me slide it."

The old avocado green refrigerator screeched as they shoved it aside to reveal a small safe built into the kitchen floor. Babe spun the dial forward, backward, and forward again, and the locking mechanism retracted with a hard, metallic clank. She was down on all fours, and Nick adjusted his position to avoid any accidental or not so accidental peeks up her skirt. Babe strained as she lifted the steel door and then reached into the safe and removed a box. The box was completely black except for what looked like a crimson-colored harpoon with a single wicked fluke piercing two hearts, one large and one small, carved into the lid. His mind whirled. It was the same design branded on Achak's arm. The same unsettlingly familiar image.

"Here, take this."

Nick reached for the box and then drew his hand back, though he wasn't sure why.

"It's not going to bite you."

Apprehensively, Nick took the box and set the box on the table, and then offered Babe a hand up.

"What is it?"

"We, Achak and me, we believe it's the answer to all our questions and with the diary, maybe the proof we need to stop all of this."

"That's the thing Achak had branded on his forearm."

"Yes, that's what drew him and me together. Achak got that brand in the twelfth grade. We all thought it was weird, but he just said that it was some tribal ritual, and that was the end of it. At least it was until I saw this box for the first time. I ran into him at the Stash on the night I got this damned thing," she gestured toward the box. "I was getting pretty hammered. I had the box sitting on the bar. Can you fucking believe it? On the fucking bar." She shook her head. "Achak was bouncing that night, and he came up to the bar for a Pepsi. His eyes locked on the box; mine locked on his arm. He grabbed the box and me and told TJ to have someone else bounce, and neither of us had been back there till last night."

"What's in it?"

"We don't know for sure; we can't open it."

Babe turned the box over. In the bottom of the box, dead set in the center was a keyhole. Nick's neck and head throbbed once. The ballistic muscle response to a sudden shock. "The keyhole," Nick said, the words coming out in a harsh whisper.

"Yeah," Babe picked up a canister marked FLOUR and dumped a pile of skeleton keys on the table. "We've tried all of these, and none of them work."

Nick pushed through the pile, searching. "That's because you don't have the right kind of key."

All of the keys in the pile were standard skeleton keys.

"No shit, that's why we have to break into the mayor's office."

"You need a key with four heads."

"Well, I don't suppose you have one," she said.

"As a matter of fact, I do."

Her eyes widened. "Let me see it!"

"I don't have it on me; it was my father's key."

"What do you mean, your father's key? Why would he have a key for this box?" Babe's eyes widened, and she clutched the box to her chest.

"It wasn't for the box; it was for his office. He had the key, and the lock made specially to keep anyone from breaking in, and believe me, it worked. You're going to have to destroy that box if you want to get it open without the right kind of key."

"Do you think it will open it?" Her eyes flashed with excitement.

"I don't know it might."

"Well, where is it? We have to try."

"It's back home."

The hope in her eyes faded. "Shit, then I guess we're back to breaking into the mayor's office."

Nick wasn't ready to follow her on that adventure. "Here me out. What if we go get Achak? You can tell the Sheriff that you're the homeowner and that Achak had your permission to be here. Without charges, they'll have to let him go. Then we all head to Red Hook, get my key, and see if it works."

Babe frowned, "And if it doesn't?"

"Then we take the box to a man that I know. The man who made the key for my father's door."

"Okay," she said.

Nick sighed in relief. "Where did you get the box anyway?" He asked.

Babe got up and walked over to the floor safe. "A man named Benjamin Shippen gave it to my father. Old Ben Shippen was one of the few county board members allowed into the meetings with Pozerac Gemein. Shippen told my father two things when he gave him this box. Number one was that the key would come for the box."

"What's that supposed to mean?"

"I'm not sure," said Babe.

"And what was the second thing?"

"That they wouldn't know the box was gone until Gemein returned."

"Then the key isn't in the mayor's office. It's with this Gemein guy."

"I don't know, maybe."

"And you think Gemein is coming back?"

"I do, Nick. The letter my father got with the box said that he would know Gemein was coming. He said that the crops would die and something about the feeling in the air, I can't remember exactly."

"What does that mean, feeling in the air?"

"Beats me, but we are in the second season of our crops dying, so we're pretty sure he's about to make an appearance. That's why we have to move fast," explained Babe.

"And the connection to the mayor's office?"

That's where the box was kept, and according to Shippen."

"Where is Shippen now?"

"He died six years ago, lung cancer. He told my father that he wanted to do one good thing before he died. That's why he gave my father the box. He knew my father would do the right thing. But daddy followed him to the grave, not even a month later. The box and the letter my father wrote were left in his safe deposit box at the bank. He handed me the key on his deathbed."

"So, no one else could have read the letter?" Nick asked.

"No, I don't see how."

"Where's the letter now?"

She knelt down at the safe and pulled out a couple of letters bound together with twine, and walked back over to take a seat at the table. Babe pulled the string, undoing the knot with the tenderness of a mother untying her baby's shoe. She picked up the first envelope marked: To My Beautiful Babe with a Heavy Heart. She removed the letter from inside, unfolded it, and handed it to Nick.

9th August 1989

Dearest Daughter, I am so very sorry to leave you. You were the light of my life. It was your love and your inner strength that carried me after your mother passed. You were the life raft that saved me from a sea of despair. And as sorry as I am to leave you behind in this cursed place, I am doubly sorry to leave you with my burden.

Nick glanced, confused at Babe, who motioned for him to continue.

As you know, Ben Shippen and I have known one another since we were boys. We served together on the town council, and you once asked me why he and I never spoke outside of the meeting hall. You asked why we always looked so sad when we saw one another. I believe I told you that it was because war does horrible things to a man's spirit. While that was true, especially in our case, it wasn't entirely true. Ben and I served during the Korean War. And, where so many other, more deserving men died, Ben and I survived.

When we came home to Chesapeake Station, Ben and I parted ways. Never hostile and never with any hard feelings, but we never spoke outside of council meetings. What you sensed in Ben and me wasn't sadness; it was shame. Seeing each other reminded us of what we'd done.

Babe, I have never told anyone about this, not even your mother, whom I loved more than life itself, and I suspect old Ben, having never married, took it to his grave. But as I pass this box and these letters on to you, I owe you a full explanation. To understand the redemption I am seeking, you first need to understand the sin, my sin.

It was the Battle of Chosin in the mountains of North Korea, the place where Hell froze over. I'd never been so damned cold in all my life, Babe. You asked me once why I always wore shoes, even in the house. It was because I lost three toes on my left foot and two on my right to frostbite. And I was lucky. Men lost limbs and lives to the cold.

Me and Ben, we lied on our forms. We were only turning seventeen when we signed up. Babe, I never saw such evil in all my life. Not until returning home anyway. But like I was saying, Chosin was Hell on earth, and we were just kids. All through the day and into the night, good men were torn to pieces by Gook machine guns, snipers, and bombs. On the third day of battle, there was a sort of pause in the fighting. We were all exhausted. Now that's no excuse for what we'd done, but maybe, just maybe, if you can understand what we were going through, you might find it in your heart to not think poorly of your old dad.

We were pinned down in a place called Yudam-Ni, and the fighting had stopped for a short time, not the shooting that never stopped, just the swarming, the hand-to-hand slaughtering. We decided it was a good time to get some rest, but we had to have guys standing watch. Well, Ben and me, we took the second watch. The two fellas coming off the first watch woke us and then bedded down. Now we couldn't smoke, and they didn't even want us talking because our company commander said, 'if you're talking, you ain't listening.' Well, we didn't last more than fifteen minutes before we were fast asleep. I'll tell you, the few seconds before I fell asleep was the only time I ever felt warm when I was there, but it didn't last. We woke to the sound of gunfire and screams coming from all around us. Those lousy Gook bastards made us pay for those few seconds of warmth. We fell asleep, Babe, and our brothers died. But that wasn't the worst part.

It pains me deeply to tell you, but I have confessed to Almighty God, and now I confess to you. You see, the fellas who were supposed to relieve us were killed in that attack, and me and Ben, we put the blame on them. So, help me, I could taste the ash in my throat as I spoke those words, and I wished right there and then that I had been killed instead of them. I wished it right up until the day you were born, Babe. Your mother had you, and I had a reason to live again.

I can tell you honestly that until I got the letter from Ben, the one I have included here with mine, I had no idea what was going on in Chesapeake Station. I will leave it at that. I want you to take the second letter and this damned box and go across the river. Don't read the letter, and for God's sake, don't try to open the box. Take them both to the authorities, and get the hell out of this god-forsaken town. Don't trust no one around here, Babe. This is an evil place.

I have enclosed Mr. Rasmuson's card with this letter. He's a financial advisor, and he is holding a trust in your name for four million dollars. You and your mama were the best things in my life, and I loved you both more than anything in this world, even baseball.

All of my love,

Dad

Nick stopped reading and looked up. Babe reached for the letter and took great care as she folded it and placed it back in the envelope. She pulled the second letter from the envelope and handed it to him. Nick unfolded the letter and began reading.

16th July 1987

To my friend Abraham,

Even as I write this letter, I can feel death in the room. He stands silent in the shadows in the corner. He has stalked me from the Chosin Reservoir, where my debt should have been paid, and I tell you, Abraham, I wish it had. I wish the angel of death would have wrapped its black wings around me then and there. If it had, I might still find a home in Heaven. I know that you think we have avoided one another over the years because we felt guilty about what happened in Chosin. And while for you, I am sure that is true, for me, it turns out that was only youthful indiscretion. My true sins are so great that I fear even the blood of Christ is insufficient to wash them away.

This town, our town, is an evil place, more evil than Chosin. From a time before the first tracks were laid, this land has been an unholy place. A place with a ravenous, gluttonous hunger that must be fed. If it's not, the town will die. I realize that none of what I'm saying makes sense, but if you'll bear with me and continue reading, I believe it will. What I offer in this letter is a chance at redemption. You have always been a better man than I, and I have never been more aware of that fact than now. Because the redemption I am offering is more for myself than for you. And I ask that you consider that as you proceed. I am sure you have ruminated and even fumed over the goings-on in the closed-door meetings. From the first days, the days that preceded us, preceded our fathers and their fathers, this land has been cursed. Cursed by the actions of one grief-stricken young mother at the loss of her child.

"Evangeline," Nick whispered, the name slipping from his lips, and he read on.

To my knowledge, what I am about to tell you has been said outside our group only once. It happened a few years back, not long after our last closed-door meeting. There was a man named Mark Ironweiler, one of the SowMax representatives."

Nick's stomach lurched. The letter slipped from his hands onto the table.

"Nick, are you okay?" Babe touched him, but he gave no response, just sat stone still. She shook him by the shoulder. "Nick, you're scaring me."

Slowly, like a man awaking from anesthesia, Nick blinked his eyes and tried to speak. Only a raspy croak at first. "I...I knew the man in this letter. Mark Ironweiler, he killed himself about ten years ago. The same night my father tried to save a little boy named Josh Ironweiler from the river." Nick's eyes darted around like he was looking for something.

"Maybe it was a different Mark Ironweiler. There has to be more than one Mark Ironweiler, right?"

Babe wrapped her arms around herself as if trying to fend off a sudden chill. Nick picked up the letter and continued reading.

Mark and his wife Sadie were found dead in their home up north. According to police reports, he hung Sadie in their garage, and he died of a self-inflicted gunshot wound to the head. They had a little boy, but they never found the boy's body. The police wrote it off as a murder-suicide, but I knew the truth. Three of our higher-ranking members, yours truly being in the select group, received letters scratched across parchment in a troublesome plumb color. It came about a week before the event and was written by a hand that coursed with fury. The letter reminded us of the penalty of violating our blood oath and instructed us to watch for news from the north. That was all the letter said. That was all it needed to say.

Abraham, I urge you again to consider what I have told you to this point before you continue reading. I have left my entire estate to you, old friend, and it is yours, regardless of your decision. As for my place on the board, I have named you as my successor. That is our way, and it is the only way you will be able to get close enough to Pozerac Gemein to kill him. Plunge a knife into his heart, and release our town of his curse. It is my selfish hope that killing him at my behest will also free my soul. You'll know when he is coming. Our crops will fail with no explanation, and the skies will grow heavy, Abraham.

Now you know everything that I know, old friend. My estate is yours; sell it. It will bring just under four million dollars. Refuse the seat on the council, and leave this place. That is my advice. My hope, however, is that you will accept the seat and kill Pozerac Gemein. Just remember, you must pierce his heart.

Kill him and free an old friend's soul.

Yours,

Ben

Nick set the letter down on the table with trembling hands and pinched the bridge of his nose between his fingers, giving the area a good rub.

"Can I ask you something, Babe?"

"Anything," she said.

"Why did you read the letter? Your father told you to turn it over to the authorities. Why the hell did you read it?"

"I honestly don't know."

"There's still time to turn the letter over."

"I can't turn my back on this, Nick," she said.

"Aren't you afraid?"

"I'm fucking terrified. I don't think I can kill anyone, not even a monster like Pozerac Gemein."

"Well, maybe that's exactly why your father wanted you to go to the police."

"And what if they don't believe me, or worse, think I'm insane and lock me away in an asylum?"

"They wouldn't think—." Nick was about to say; *you're crazy*, but thoughts of his father clawed their way into his head.

23

The garage felt suddenly cold and damp, and a wave of nausea washed over Levi as something drew him up the stairs toward the darkness beyond the threshold of the mysterious door. Whatever that force in the darkened room above was, Levi knew that it, not he controlled his movement. Levi wanted to stop, but his legs plodded up, up, up the stairs. There was a noise, like the static on a dead radio-frequency. It may have been coming from the room, or perhaps it originated in the center of Levi's mind; he couldn't be sure, but where ever it came from, it grew louder with each step. Amidst his climb and the deafening static, Levi was vaguely aware of another sound. It was the sound of a little boy's voice, maybe Frankie's voice, but it was thin and distant, and Levi couldn't make it out.

Reaching the landing. Levi watched as his hand moved toward the knob. Levi's vision narrowed to a pinprick. The buzzing static faded, replaced by the sound of his blood whooshing through his body. Levi pushed the door open and began to step across the threshold, but he could not break the plane.

At some point during Levi's ascension, Frankie had clamped his arms around Levi's waist, interlocking his fingers like a human seatbelt.

"Levi, no, you can't go in there!"

Levi's eyes fluttered. It seemed that the room had rejected him.

"What's wrong with you, Levi?"

"What?" He was coming out of his stupor. "Nothing, nothing's wrong with me. What are you talking about?" Levi blinked a few times, bringing the world back into focus.

"Why are you acting so weird?"

Levi looked down at his little brother, clinging to his waist. "Get off of me!" Levi pushed Frankie, who had to grab hold of the banister so as not to tumble down the stairs, and spun back toward the door. Levi grabbed the knob and tried to twist it, but the door was locked. Nostrils flared, eyes red with rage, Levi turned back toward Frankie. "Why did you close the door?" He snapped.

Frankie flinched. "I didn't close it; it closed by its self."

"Bullshit!"

"What's wrong with you, Levi?"

Levi grabbed the doorknob again, but it still wouldn't turn. "Shit!" He glared at his little brother.

"Nice going, asshole."

The concern that clouded Frankie's face fell away, replaced by hurt and sadness. Frankie's eyes pooled with tears, and he turned and ran down the stairs and out of the garage. Levi stood alone on the landing.

"Shit, I'm sorry, Frankie," he said to himself and sighed.

With his head hung low, Levi started down the stairs. He stood in the doorway and watched his little brother as he crossed the yard toward the river.

"Frankie, wait up," he called, but Frankie just kept walking.

Levi walked back to the base of the stairs and bent down to pick up the spilled cereal bowls. He'd never unloaded on Frankie like that before, and he had no idea why he had just then. Levi drew in and then exhaled a long slow breath. "I have to go apologize," he said to himself. Levi stacked the bowls and set them on the bottom stair. He had just turned to leave when an enormous black crow appeared in the doorway. It was the crow from the Ironweiler's gable. Larger than any bird he'd ever seen in the city, even bigger than the condor he had once seen at the Lincoln Park Zoo, the crow's body looked like it was covered in black hair rather than feathers. Its wings resembled those of a giant bat, veiny and leathery. The bird cocked its head and jerked its body toward Levi. Levi stepped back and glanced around quickly for something to use as a weapon. He lunged for the snow shovel that had been left resting against the stair railing, but before he could reach it, the bird struck, cutting a large gash in Levi's right hand. Levi winced and pulled his hand back, pinning it against his chest. He looked down, saw the clean white bone, and watched as blood pooled in the open wound. Levi stumbled backward and sat down hard on the stair. The crow launched itself at him, and Levi kicked hard with both legs connecting with nothing but air. The bird was gone, and so was the gash on the back of his hand.

"What's happening to me?"

Levi got to his feet and trying to gather his wits when he heard something creak behind him. Levi turned, expecting to see the crow, but instead, he watched as the strange door began to swing open. The static returned, and he could feel his limbs stiffening, the way they had just before he had been drawn up the stairs, moments ago. Levi Waters pushed every thought from his head, but Frankie's hurt face and forced himself to turn away from the door. He grabbed the banister with both hands, pulled his body off the stairs, and forced his legs to carry him outside. The warmth of the sun wrapped itself around him, and Levi was back in control of his body, senses, and emotions. He had to find Frankie and apologize, but even more than that, he had to get away from that fucking door.

Levi walked toward the river feeling stronger with each step. He reached the dock and saw Frankie sitting there. His arms were wrapped around his legs, and his face was pushed into his knees. Levi forgot all about the crow for the moment. He walked down the dock and sat next to his brother.

"Hey Frankie, I'm really sorry, buddy."

"F you Levi, you're not my brother anymore, so why don't you F off?"

Levi smiled; rage looked ridiculous on Frankie. "I don't know what happened; I kind of lost it back there."

Frankie kept his face buried in his knees. Levi looked at his little brother and then out at the water.

"Something happened to me in that garage, Frankie. That wasn't me."

Frankie shuddered, and Levi could tell that he was crying.

"After you left, the door opened again."

Frankie's breath hitched, and he fixed his tear-soaked eyes on his brother. "What?"

"It opened again, and the only thing that kept me from going up those stairs was you. Or at least the thought of you. I focused on you, and that gave me the strength to get out of there."

"No, fooling?"

Levi shook his head, "No, no fooling."

Frankie threw his arms around his big brother's neck. "We're brothers Levi, we always look out for each other."

"Well, this makes my heart smile," said Connie. "Nothing makes a mother happier than knowing her sons love each other."

The boys pushed each other away.

"Eww, mom, don't say weird stuff like that!"

"Yeah, mom, jeez," Frankie agreed.

She brushed Frankie's bangs away from his face with her fingertips and smiled at her little boy.

"Anyway, Stan called and asked if you guys could come over for a play-date.

"Seriously, mom," Levi said, "you have to stop saying things like that! We hang out; we do not have play dates!"

"Fine, he wants to know if you guys want to hang," Connie stopped mid-sentence.

"Frankie, what's wrong? Were you crying?"

"He got something in his eye, mom; he's okay now."

"Maybe you should come inside and let me look at that eye, Frankie."

"It's fine, mom," Frankie said as he pushed himself to his feet to follow Levi toward the garage to grab their bikes.

A place of mystery and possibility, just minutes ago, had now become a place as scary as any spook-house the boys had ever visited.

"Our bikes are in there, Levi."

"I know," Levi said apprehensively. "It's only a few blocks. Wanna walk?"

Frankie swallowed hard and nodded, and they started walking. At the end of the block, the hedge apple tree was already dropping its lumpy green fruit, and Frankie bent to pick one up.

"What is this?" He held it out to Levi.

"Don't touch that!" Levi yelled. Frankie pulled his hands away, letting the thing fall to the ground with a thud.

"That's a monkey's brain!"

"No, it's not, liar."

Frankie kicked the ball-shaped fruit toward Levi, and Levi kicked it back, and they went along that way down the road. They heard screams and laughter as they approached the Howard's place and ran for the backyard.

"Hey, guys!" Levi called from the fence.

They all turned their attention toward Levi and fired a barrage of water balloons, soaking Levi from head to toe. Levi picked Frankie up and used him as a shield as he ran for the big washtub filled with wobbly water balloons. He set Frankie down and filled his arms. Stan got Frankie in his sights and let fly. Frankie was small, but he was fast. He was a boy possessed with the lightning reflexes of a small animal that had spent its life surviving large animals. The water bomb burst on the grass; not a drop landed on Frankie. Even the snipers, Stevie and Lonnie, who were perched up in the tree branches, missed their target. Stan reacquired his target, cocked his arm, and caught an ear full of water courtesy of big brother Levi's cannon arm. Not to be outdone, McKenna slammed an orange water balloon down two-handed on the back of Levi's neck. And so, it went until every last balloon was spent. The combatants lay sprawled on the wet grass like the fallen soldiers of some jolly war reenactment when the battle was over.

Laying there, sopping wet in the hot sun with his little brother and his new best friends, Levi quickly forgot all about the events of the morning.

"Hey," said Stan. "Any of you guys want to ride the river down to Gert's?"

"We don't have any money," said Stevie, cramming his hands into his sopping wet empty pockets.

Stan stood up and pulled a wad of wet bills out of his pocket.

"My treat, my mom let me and Finn turn in all the empties."

"Hey," McKenna protested. "A third of that money is mine; I helped collect the bottles, remember?"

Stan rolled his eyes. "So, we going or what?"

Levi and Frankie looked at one another. "What's Gert's?"

"What's Gert's?" Stevie asked incredulously. "Where you been, under a rock?"

Stan waved a dismissive hand at Stevie Johnson. "Don't listen to him. Gert's is an ice cream place on the river. It's got this huge dock on the back. On weekends we can't get near the dock. All the jagoffs with the power-boats park there and don't move."

"Yeah," said Lonnie. "They think they own the fuckin' place."

"Well, it sounds cool, but we are just gonna head home, guys," said Levi. "Stop by our house on the way back."

Frankie's shoulders drooped.

Levi squeezed the water out of his shirt. "Come on, Frankie."

"No way, we're all going," said Stan. "School starts tomorrow. It's the official end of the summer ice cream run!"

The gang cheered.

"We can't all fit in the rafts, Stan," said Levi. The truth was, he didn't want to go back out on the water. "How about if we head home and ride our bikes to Gert's."

"Yeah," said Finn. "Hey, we can raft down to your house, and you guys can ride along next to us on the path."

The idea sounded perfect to Levi. "But how are you going to get the rafts back to your house?"

"My mom will drive down, and we'll throw the rafts on top of the wagon," said Stan.

"We do it all the time. You guys get started walking. We'll meet up with you at your house."

Levi and Frankie started jogging, but Frankie quickly ran out of gas, slowing to a walk.

"I really like those guys, Levi," Frankie huffed and puffed but trudged along.

"Me too, Frankie."

"Especially Kaylin," Frankie said and shoved his brother.

"Shut up, Frankie, I do not."

"Oh, come on, you get all stupid around her," Frankie replied. "But I don't know what you see in her. McKenna is way hotter."

"Do you want to see how hard I can punch you?" Levi drew his arm back, and Frankie laughed and ran ahead, his arms flopping at his sides.

The river was running slow, and the walkers beat the rafters back to their house.

Connie Waters was busy planting perennials near the mailbox when Levi and Frankie came up the block. "Are you boys back already?"

"Yeah, mom, we are grabbing our bikes and meeting the guys at the ice cream shop in town," Levi said.

"And Kaylin," jibed Frankie.

Levi took a swipe at the back of Frankie's head, but the nimble younger brother ducked.

"Well, you boys, be careful."

"We will, mom," he assured her.

Levi and Frankie walked to the garage, and Levi stopped Frankie. "You wait out here. I'll run in and grab the bikes."

Levi's legs went wobbly, and his hands were shaking. He swiped at his forehead with the back of his wrist, giving his hand a quick check for the gaping wound.

"Okay, Frankie, here I go."

"Hey! Hey Levi, Frankie!" Stan was tying off his raft down at the dock. "Hurry up, you gotta see this."

Levi, glad for the reprieve from the garage, turned and ran for the dock. As he neared the water, it became clear what Stan was yelling about. The Gypsy Soul was back and tied to their dock. Levi's mouth hung open in stunned silence.

"Let's take the boat Levi, I don't want you to go back in that garage."

Levi glanced at the garage and then back at the boat. He pasted on the best carefree smile he could muster and walked toward the little rowboat.

"You okay, Levi? You look kinda sick," said McKenna.

"He's fine," said Stan. "He's just nervous about his first date with Kaylin."

They all laughed, all except for Levi and Kaylin, who smiled a shy smile at Levi.

Frankie saw that his brother wasn't laughing or smiling. Levi was scared. He pulled on Levi's shirt, getting him to stop. "I can tell them I don't feel good," Frankie whispered. "Then you don't have to go."

Levi barely heard Frankie. He was too busy trying to discern the apprehensive smile on Kaylin's face. "What? No, I'm fine; let's go."

They climbed aboard the rowboat and shoved off from the dock. Levi steered the Gypsy Soul toward the center of the waterway, and Frankie watched the riverbed drop away down, down, down through the cold, clear water.

"Hook me up!" Finn called, extending an oar to Levi.

"What?"

Finn stared back at Levi, looking perplexed. "The oar, grab the oar dummy."

Levi grabbed the oar, and Finn pulled their raft alongside the Gypsy Soul, lashing a short rope from oarlock to oarlock.

Lonnie and Stevie dug into the water with their oars, pulled along the opposite side of Levi and Frankie, and hooked up, creating a decent-sized float. Once the boats were secured one to the other, Lonnie Johnson hit play on his boombox, and Possum King blared out of the speakers shattering the hot stillness of the peaceful Red Hook River Valley. They whooped and hollered and sang along, "I'm not gonna lie, I'll not be a gentleman behind the boathouse...." Finn stood up to pee in the river, and McKenna walloped him in the head with one of the plastic oars.

"What the fuck, McKenna?"

"Hey stupid, don't piss in the river, and mom told you to stop using that word."

"Well, she's not here, so you can suck it!"

"You suck it!" McKenna fired back.

"Knock it off, you two," said Stan. "She's right, don't piss where we're going to swim and watch your fuckin' mouth."

The boys roared with laughter. McKenna shook her head and shared a, *boys are so stupid*, glance with Kaylin.

"When are you idiots going to grow up?" McKenna scolded.

"Relax ya virgin," called Lonnie from his raft and followed it with a paddle slap, spraying the Howard's raft with cold river water. "I now baptize you, En el Nombre del Padre' del Hijo y de Espírito Santo."

"Don't blaspheme, asshole," Stevie scolded.

"Sorry, Father Stevie," he replied and spun the oar to use it as a guitar to rock out with the Toadies.

They all splashed and slapped water at one another, a welcomed relief from the punishing sun that shined hot and unfiltered from the cloudless sky above. Levi watched as Kaylin pulled off her t-shirt and slipped her jean shorts down, revealing the other half of the bright yellow bikini.

"Dude, you got it bad," Frankie said as he jumped off the back of the boat, splashing Levi.

"Man overboard!" Stevie Johnson yelled, and the rest of the gang followed, their t-shirts flying into the sky as they all cannon-balled into the Red Hook. Everyone but Levi, who sat uncomfortably aware that he was the odd-man-out. The exuberance of being with his new friends, the rush of…, well, he wasn't exactly sure what was rushing, but Kaylin's smile at the mention of their first date made something rush through him. All of it faded, replaced by self-consciousness.

"Come on in, Levi," Kaylin called. "It's not deep here. See? My feet are touching."

Levi opened his mouth to speak, but nothing came out.

"No way," Stan protested. "Your boyfriend was too slow, so he has to stay with the boats!"

Levi exhaled and did his best to look disappointed. He held up his hands in a '*what are you going to do*' gesture and caught Kaylin's smile again. It was turning out to be a beautiful afternoon.

The swimmers climbed back into their boats, shivering from the breeze on their wet skin, and Levi made his move. He pulled his warm, dry t-shirt up over his head, tanned skin stretched tight over muscle, and tossed it to Kaylin. She slipped it over her wet body. It hung on her like a too-short dress, and Levi felt that rush again. He was ready for the comments from the p-nut gallery. Stevie, Stan, and Finn piped up but were quickly shut down by Lonnie, who took on a somber tone.

"Hey dickheads, shut up. I gotta tell you something."

The laughing and singing stopped, and Lonnie turned the radio down.

"Come in closer; I don't want to have to yell."

They all scrunched in closer to the middle of their makeshift raft.

"So, check this out," said Lonnie. "Donnie Lazzara told me that there's a guy who lives somewhere on the river, and this guy snatches kids and drowns them."

"Bullshit," challenged Stan. "We'd have heard about that if it was true. Besides, Donnie's a jock; why would he talk to a stoner like you?"

"Hey, I heard the same thing," said Finn. "The guys were talking about it at two-a-days last week."

"What are two-a-days?" Asked Kaylin.

"Football practice for the jock-itchers like my stupid brother," answered Stan.

"Has anyone else ever heard of that?" Asked McKenna.

"Jock itch or two-a-days?" Stevie said. His comment got them all laughing again.

"No, dipshit, you know what I meant."

No one spoke up.

"See idiots? No one else has heard your BS story."

"That's because they don't tell little kids about it, you ret—," Finn stopped himself, seeing McKenna raising the paddle again. "Don't do it, McKenna. I'm not kidding."

Finn shut his mouth and raised his middle finger at his sister.

"They just don't tell you guys cause they know you can't handle shit like that," said Lonnie.

"Like you're so big and bad," challenged Stevie.

Kaylin, who'd been quiet for the most part, chimed in. "Guys, I remember hearing something like that last summer when I was out at the Never Close getting pop for my dad. Two high school kids were talking about it."

"They say it happens like around Thanksgiving," Lonnie said.

"Shit, I bet that's what happened to the kid across from your guys' house," said Stan.

"I heard that kid killed himself because of what he saw his dad do to his mom," Stevie said as he began unlashing his raft from the Gypsy Soul.

"I bet the boy did it because he wanted to be with his parents in Heaven."

"You don't go to Heaven if you kill yourself, Frankie; everyone knows that," said Lonnie.

"Well, maybe, he didn't."

"Go to Heaven or know that?" Stevie asked.

"I don't know. Maybe both."

The kids sat silently as the water lapped the sides of their rafts, and the warm summer breeze took on a noticeable chill. Levi Waters had had enough of the river and wanted to beach the boats and walk the rest of the way, but he kept his mouth shut. They finished untying the boats and began paddling again, their mood dampened by the thought of the dead boy.

24

Thick gray clouds rolled in low from the north as Pozerac Gemein strolled into town dragging misery and affliction, like squabbling children in his wake. Gout exploded in the aching bones of the arthritic, unseen hands reached into the chests of asthmatics and squeezed hard on their lungs, fresh pain echoed through time to revisit old wounds and tighten old scars, and a bone-rattling cold fell upon Chesapeake Station.

Gemein arrived at the steps to City Hall and paused to regard an elderly woman across the street, and in doing, sent the cancerous cells in her body into full bloom. Evelyn Crenshaw, head of the Kramer Island Bridge Committee and president of the Senior's Jazzercize and Recreation Club, hadn't even been diagnosed with cancer. Yet her autopsy would show that her body was riddled with malignant tumors. As Gemein turned and ascended the stairs, Evelyn fell to the ground, where she convulsed for a moment before expiring. A bemused smirk wormed its way across Gemein's lips as he stepped into the marble-floored vestibule. Inside, a short fat man in a blue pinstriped suit greeted the town's patriarch beneath a truly gaudy chandelier.

Richard Steel bowed as deep as his paunch would allow. As town mayor, it was his job to greet all dignitaries who visited his town.

"Mr. Gemein, please come in. We have all been eagerly awaiting your arrival."

Gemein stepped past him and entered the board room without a word. He crossed the highly polished white marble floor to the Mayor's high leather wingback and took a seat. Behind him, like a rectangular bronze halo, hung a magnificent bronze relief of the town's first locomotive, the John Henry. Steel raised a hand and drew in a breath as if to protest Gemein having taken his seat but said nothing and scurried weasel-like to the closest unoccupied chair.

Tucker chortled at the slight, and Mayor Steel responded with a contemptuous sneer before addressing the council. "Mr. Gemein, Sheriff Tucker," It sounded as if he'd spat the name, "aldermen and councilmen, we gather once again to present our tribute to Mr. Pozerac Gemein, the savior of Chesapeake Station."

The room came alive with reverberations of knuckles rapping on the chamber table under a chorus of *hear-hear*.

Sheriff Tucker rose to his feet. "If I may, Mr. Gemein, I wanted to be here to welcome you back to our town, but now I have to beg your pardon, sir. You see, I have a surprise for you, and I must tend to it."

Gemein smiled. It was a look he did not wear well, and several councilmen slunk in their seats.

Mayor Steel, outraged, sprung to his feet. "Cyrus Tucker, are you attempting to usurp my authority here? I called this meeting to order, and I will gladly allow you to leave once our business is concluded. Is that clear?"

Gemein turned his head very deliberately toward Steel, who swallowed hard as if forcing down a lump that had risen in his throat. Pozerac Gemein slammed his palm on the table with a deafening crack.

"Your authority?" They were the first words he had spoken since he arrived, and they hissed from his throat like the air escaping a sarcophagus unsealed after millennia. "There is no authority here but mine and none in my absence that I have not bestowed."

"Now, Mr. Gemein, no one was suggesting," began Mayor Steel, with a noticeable quiver in his voice.

Pozerac Gemein bolted up out of the seat, and Steel collapsed back into his chair.

The room fell silent as a grave. "Do not presume to explain to me the way I should take meaning!"

"No, sir, never. I was just."

"You were just about to retrieve my box. Now bring it to me," he snarled.

With the fear paralysis subsiding, Richard Steel rose on unsteady legs, walked over to the bronze relief, and went to work. Sheriff Tucker got to his feet and raised a hand, like a patron signaling for the bill in a restaurant. Gemein waved dismissively, and Tucker slipped out of the room.

The massive frame of the John Henry relief was mounted to a rail system, which upon releasing the catch mechanism, allowed Steel to slide the 700 pound work effortlessly out of the way. Behind the relief, sunken into the wall like some blasphemous tabernacle, sat a black steel door. The Mayor spun the dial, first left, then right, and then left again. Grasping the handle firmly, turning it, and feeling the bolts slide, the Mayor exhaled. With a smile only a little less sickening than Gemein's, Richard Steel pulled the door open, and the crotch of his pants grew warm and dark.

The safe stood empty for all to see, and the air left the room. Gemein lifted the Mayor's considerable wingback and hurled it through the air, smashing it against the far wall. Pozerac Gemein flew into a rage, and Steel fell to the floor, squeezing his eyes shut and covering his ears like a frightened child. Long black talons grew out from Gemein's fingertips, and he seized the Mayor through the stomach. The talons ripped through Steel's belly like sharpened spears and latched tight to his spine.

Holding the egg-shaped man aloft, Gemein roared. "Where is my box?" Spit flew from his lips, splattering against Steel's bloodless white face.

Gemein slammed Steel's body onto the chamber table, cracking the wood and shattering the vertebrae in Steel's body. Gemein dropped him to the floor, his head breaking open with a sickening crack as blood pooled across the fine white marble.

"You," growled Gemein, pointing a finger that dripped with blood.

Terry Peterson, the newest member of the council, was unaware he was being addressed. The young, by council standards, SowMax representative sat transfixed on the viscus, crimson stain that spread symmetrically from beneath the broken table. Peterson had come to Chesapeake Station ten years earlier, after the untimely demise of his predecessor, and had never taken part in a meeting with Gemein. Steel explained the process over drinks, not a week prior, but with the box missing and Steel's blood spilling from his body, all the preparation was out the window. Gemein vanished in a puff of ash that fell to the floor and then, just as quickly, reappeared with his face next to Peterson's right ear.

"Is this the ear that's giving you problems?"

Peterson smelled and felt his hot, sour breath before his mind made sense of the words, but it was too late. The pain was white-hot and blinding. Peterson leaped from his chair and pressed his hand to the side of his head. A warm, pulpy hole occupied the place where his ear used to be.

"What the fuck!" Peterson stood 6'4" and weighed 300 pounds, but unlike Tucker, who was made mostly of fat, Terry Peterson was layered in muscle, earned in the executive's gym at SowMax.

"I asked you a question," Gemein hissed.

"Fuck, fuck, fuck! What question? You bit my fucking ear off!"

"I believe a man with one ear must pay closer attention for fear he might miss something—important." The words were slow and deliberate. "Where is my box?"

"I don't know, Mr. Gemein."

"There, you see?"

The sharp pain had dulled to a slow, aching throb, and Peterson was surprised to find clarity of mind between the pulses. "But I have a thought on how we might find out." His mind was functioning on a level higher than he'd ever know. Peterson was aware of the fight or flight response in the face of danger, but now he thought that maybe there was a third response. Reason, or in his case, scheme, and, to his mind, scheming was reasoning at a slightly higher level.

"I'm listening," said Gemein, that same sour smell wafting up from deep inside his body.

Peterson did his best not to react to the putrid odor. "Sheriff Tucker told me earlier that he and Deputy Abernathy chased someone away from the old barn out by Consumption Lake yesterday. He said that a stranger had come to town and started snooping around. Tucker said they had to take a couple of shots at the trespasser to drive him away."

Peterson didn't know if it had anything to do with the missing box, more likely just a lawman in a sleepy town trying to create the mystique of danger, but either way, it would serve its purpose. The plan was simple. Peterson would summon Deputy Abernathy to the council chambers. There, in front of Gemein, he would demand an explanation regarding the mysterious subject alluded to by Tucker. If Abernathy failed to provide a satisfactory response, Gemein would likely get the urge to do more gutting, and Abernathy would be the gut-tee. It was a bold move, but if he played his cards right, Perhaps Terry Peterson could set himself up for the vacated mayoral seat.

His peers and underlings at SowMax would probably think he was crazy to even entertain the job if it were to be offered to him. Peterson was a high six-figure man, and everyone knows the position of mayor in most towns the size of Chesapeake Station was merely a job of ceremony. Lots of baby-kissing, handshaking, and ribbon cutting for what amounted to a very meager salary. Most small-town mayors had to work 9 to 5s just to make ends meet. But Chesapeake Station was no ordinary small town. In Chesapeake Station, the Mayor wielded great power, and no one knew that better than Peterson's bosses. The SowMax bigwigs, the guys whose asses he had to kiss, would be the ones puckering up from now on. The corners of Peterson's eyes crinkled, and an involuntary smirk forced its way across his lips. Joe Murphy, appointed to the council at the passing of his father, twenty years prior, was the only one who seemed to notice Peterson's power-play. Murphy narrowed his gaze ever so slightly, but Peterson caught it, and it was like waving a red flag at a bull.

"Joe, grab a radio," he ordered.

"What?" Murphy stammered like a kid caught sleeping in class.

"We need Abernathy front and center. Now get him on the radio and tell him to get his ass in here."

Joe Murphy didn't move; he just stared dopily at him.

"Move your ass, Joe!" Terry yelled. "And once you get that done, take Grover Horn and head out to the Kramer Cabin. Make sure nothing has been disturbed, and Joe, don't fuck this up!"

It was another bold move. Grover Horn was Peterson's counterpart from the Agri-Grow corporation, the only two men in the company, aside from their bosses who understood the true value of their investments in Chesapeake Station. If he could get the town council and Horn to fall into line, Gemein would be sure to see that he was a natural fit for the job of Mayor.

"The rest of you, clean this mess up," he paused to make sure Pozerac Gemein took notice. "If there is a problem, report to me immediately!

No one moved.

"Damn-it! Mr. Gemein has traveled," he realized he had no idea where Gemein came from, "what I assume is a long way to be here, and we owe him our best effort! Now go!"

It was a risky move, but Terry Peterson knew it was better to be considered a *get shit done guy* when the head man came in swinging the ax. Besides, he was sure this kind of bullshit would never happen again, not under his watch. The only thing Steel had to do was to guard Gemein's stupid fucking box. How hard could that be? But Steel, bloated, pretentious ass that he was, had become complacent in his duties, and he allowed a thief to enter and pillage his master's shrine. The penalty for the careless execution of his duties was death. Pretty harsh, but it was a risk Peterson was willing to take.

"We'll get to the bottom of this, Mr. Gemein, I assure you."

***

If he heard a word, Peterson said, Pozerac Gemein didn't respond. Instead, he lamented over the four-headed key that he wore suspended by a leather strap around his neck. The key he twirled between his fingers was a forgery, a brilliant forgery, but a forgery nonetheless. He'd lost the original to an Aakwaadizin assassin, and with it, its supernatural connection to the box. If he'd only had the original key, it would lead him, like a homing beacon, right to his beloved box. Now he feared, he may never find it. And, unlike the key, a replacement could not be forged. Nor could the precious cargo it contained. It was a jagged pill to swallow indeed. Jagged and bitter all at once. *How was it,* he wondered, *that an insignificant worm-like Steel could throw a god's life into turmoil?* And not even by an act of defiance, but rather careless stupidity.

Gemein understood, even respected the Aakwaadizin. The assassin had spent his life tracking him. From town to town, camp to camp, from as far north as the sparsely populated town of Park Rapids, Minnesota, to as far south as the congested streets of New Orleans. From Cape Girardeau, Missouri, where the great flood of 1927 was his saving grace, to the tiny house just outside Albany, Illinois, nearly 300 miles north.

It was there that the Indian stole his precious key. Gemein woke to a blade at his throat. He felt the cold steel as it slid in at the jugular notch just above his sternum and sunk deeper and deeper until it met the resistance of his spinal column. Gemein watched in horror as the Aakwaadizin put his weight into the knife and forced it down with a sickening crack. In his memory, Gemein could still hear the Aakwaadizin's victory cry as it echoed through the valley.

Gemein placed a hand atop his head as he remembered the assassin grabbing hold of his hair and dragging his paralyzed body down to the east bank of the Mississippi River. As Gemein lay on the shoreline, unable to move, the Aakwaadizin wrapped his fingers around the leather strap and ripped the key from his neck. Gemein watched as the Indian set the key on a rock and removed an ancient weapon from his belt. A tomahawk fashioned from the jawbone of a buffalo. Gemein hadn't seen it in over a hundred years. It was the very same weapon wielded by another assassin who had come for him. The Aakwaadizin brought the archaic tool down onto the metal key and divided it into sections. Then, one by one, he threw the pieces into the rushing water. The Aakwaadizin then laid the razor-sharp blade against Gemein's neck. Gemein looked into the Indian's eyes and saw both sadness and joy as the tomahawk reached the apex of its swing and froze there. Gemein mouthed the words *Bashkwegin Oningwiigan*, Leather Wing, as his guardian appeared behind the Aakwaadizin and split the top of his skull with its beak. The Aakwaadizin fell dead to the floor, and Leather Wing pecked and tore at his flesh and ate his fill before seeing to his master.

"Mr. Gemein, Mr. Gemein, sir, I have things under control here, sir."

Pozerac Gemein stopped twirling the key and regarded Peterson with a glare, quieting him instantly.

Gemein, still deep in thought, considered the stranger that Tucker had mentioned to Peterson, and a chill ran through him. Could it be that a descendant of the Aakwaadizin had come to steal the box? Gemein's mind whirled. Perhaps the thief would seek out a craftsman to have a key made. After all, the box could never be opened without the key, and Gemein knew of only one man in the region skilled enough to make such a key. Gemein admired the work of gifted artisans. It was the only reason he left the clock maker alive. Gemein walked out of the chambers into the darkening day and vanished into the dense fog.

25

B abe whipped a U-turn into the vacant spot marked, No Parking - Authorized Vehicles Only, and hopped out of the Bronco. The other spot, occupied by a dirt-covered, cream and dog-shit brown Chesapeake County cruiser, caused Nick to pause.

"Hey, Babe, you think that's one of the cars that chased us last night?"

Babe answered with a dismissive wave of her hand and was already pushing open the Chesapeake County Sheriff's Department door before Nick was even out of the truck.

Nick stood in front of the one-story, gray slat board building with CHESAPEAKE STATION SHERIFF'S DEPT. mounted over the door in what Nick presumed were once white porcelain letters, but now looked more the color of a smoker's teeth, and wondered if he should just jump back in the Bronco and leave town. As quickly as the thought came to him, so did the realization that Babe still had his keys. Nick hustled up the stairs after Babe and caught up to her in the small lobby. The deputy stationed behind the counter was doing the work of three men as he tried his best to keep up with the jangling of multiple phone lines.

"Chesapeake Station Sheriff's Depart— yes ma'am, it did turn cold awful fast — no ma'am, there is no one I can send over to light your furnace, no ma'am, please hold ma'am," the young deputy clicked over to another line. "Chesapeake Station — yes, sir, this is the sheriff's department," the deputy cast a wary eye toward the two people who just walked into his little slice of hell and held up a finger indicating that it would be a minute. Paying the finger no mind, Babe walked up to the counter and thumbed down the cradle, hanging up on the caller.

"Hey, you can't just—."

"Shut up Jimmy, I'm here to bail out Achak." She'd known Jimmy Hain since middle school, and Jimmy knew her.

"You can't."

"The hell I can't. What's his bail?" She asked.

"Ain't none," he answered.

The phone lines kept ringing, ratcheting up the stress level in the young deputy, but Babe wouldn't let her thumb off the cradle. "What do you mean; 'there ain't none?"

"Achak attacked Sheriff Tucker on their way in last night and then absconded. Sum-bitch was trying to break into some woman's house out on Sow-Max Boulevard. Probably gonna rape her."

"You mean he got away?"

"What the hell you think absconded means?"

"I know what it means asshole, I just wanted to be sure you did."

"Yeah, well, you better sit your cute little ass down there," he said, nodding toward a wooden chair next to a sea foam green coffee vending machine. "Sheriff's gonna want to talk to you. We been looking for that sum-bitch for six months. Fucking Indians won't let us on the rez to pick him up."

Babe let her thumb off the cradle of the ringing phone, grabbed Nick, and walked out the door. Deputy Hain called after, "Hey! You get your ass back—no, no ma'am, I wasn't talking to you—yes, it is cold, ma'am."

Babe and Nick hopped back into the Bronco and tore off down the road.

"Holy shit, babe, I can't believe he attacked the Sheriff!"

"At least he got away. Thank God for that," Babe replied.

"Babe, he's a fugitive, that's a felony, and we are helping him, that's called aiding and abetting, and guess what? That's a felony too!"

Babe fired a worried look at Nick and pressed harder on the accelerator.

"Where could he be, Nick?" She asked, chewing the side of her lower lip.

"I don't know," he answered. "Maybe the barn? Are you listening to me?"

"Not likely, seeing as we just got chased out of there, but we can give it a shot."

"Babe; aiding and,"

"Yeah, I heard you. But he didn't do anything wrong. He wasn't breaking in."

"That doesn't matter, Babe! Right now, I'm sure there's a warrant being issued for resisting arrest and battery to a police officer."

"Tucker ain't a police officer; he's a pig."

"That may be, but that badge on his chest makes him one powerful fucking pig, and I—"

"Fuck-sake Nick. Would you shut up and let me drive?"

"Fine," he said, throwing his hands up.

Nick didn't know what he was getting himself into, but he knew he would see it through. He had to. He felt he owed it to the tiny, ferociously loyal woman sitting next to him, and he owed it to himself. He had to prove to himself that he could keep going when the going got tough. He knew he had a paper to write. A paper, that when he submitted it, was going to make some heads explode. His advisors would probably bury it in some hole-in-the-wall journal of Native American folklore, but it would be honest work, and, perhaps most importantly, it would be published.

Babe drove the back roads that led to the bridge to the west side of the river and the little cabin they saw from across the lake in the old weather-beaten barn.

"What are we doing?"

"I want to check the cabin, Nick."

The Bronco slid to a stop, and Babe hopped out. No sooner did her foot hit the ground than she spun on her heels and slammed her hands down on her hemp bag that contained the mysterious locked box. Startled by Babe's quick movement, Nick threw his hands up. Slowly, Babe pulled her hands away from the bag,

"I'm sorry, Nick," said Babe. "I didn't mean to...."

"It's okay, Babe, don't worry about it," he reassured her.

"No, Nick, I have to worry about it. You and Achak are the only people in the whole world that I can trust. And you, sticking with me through this;

well, I could never thank you enough. If I lived to be a hundred years old, Nick, I just ....”

She didn't finish the sentence, but she didn't need to. Her eyes conveyed her feelings far better than her words ever could.

“It's okay, Babe.”

She smiled sadly. “Will you watch my bag?” It was a small but meaningful gesture.

“Of course,” said Nick.

She left the bag and turned for the cabin. Nick watched her go to the door and try the knob. She moved from window to window, trying to force them open. She ran off, her feet slipping out from under her in her growing panic, and disappeared around the corner. Nick could hear her rapping on the glass at the river-facing side of the house. Nick began thinking about the next step they would need to take and, perhaps selfishly, began formulating a plan for his paper when she popped up around the other side of the cabin.

“He's not here; let's try the barn.”

As they made their way toward the bridge just north of the Kramer property. Babe spotted two Chesapeake Station cruisers across the river, parked next to the old Cavanaugh barn. She turned off the motor and let the Bronco roll into the cover of some low-hanging branches of a willow tree. They both got out, and Nick pulled a pair of binoculars out of his glove box.

“Creepy,” said Babe as she took the binoculars from him.

Since leaving Babe's place, the temperature had gone from sweltering to freezing and back to sweltering. Sweat beaded on Babe's forehead, and she wiped at it with the back of her hand.

“Nick, I think Gemein is here, or at least he will be,” she said. “This is where it's going to happen.”

Nick took the binoculars from her and picked up some movement near the barn.

“What's going to happen?”

“I'm not exactly sure, but we have to get that box open.”

She took the field glasses back. “Tuckers leaving, and he's leaving that little shit Abernathy behind,” she lowered the glasses and turned toward

Nick. "If he's leaving Abernathy there, it must mean they haven't found Achak yet." She chewed ferociously on her lip. "I hate to leave without finding Achak, but maybe we should go see about the key."

"Okay," agreed Nick, but first, I need to find a phone."

***

They pulled off the road beneath the glowing orange globe of a Union 76 Station just outside Millbrook. Babe hoped out and started pumping while Nick ran into the service station to break a couple bucks for the payphone.

"Does this look like a bank, mister?"

"Fine, Nick said and grabbed a couple packs of Wrigley's Doublemint from the rack. He tossed them on the counter along with three one-dollar bills. The attendant took one of the bills and a couple of pennies from the leave-a-penny-take-a-penny tray and rang the register. Nick stared in disbelief as the attendant slid his gum, two dollars, and two quarters back across the counter.

"Are you shitting me?"

"What," the attendant said, clearly playing dumb, "The gum is twenty-five cents a pack," and smiled a half-wit's smile.

Nick was about to light into the boy when Babe walked in. Nick saw the boy swallow hard and stepped aside.

"What's taking so long? I thought you were just coming in for change?"

The boy's eyes raced up and down Babe's body with the frenzied fervor one would expect from a young man approaching his sexual prime and locked on her breasts.

"Goober here doesn't seem to know how to make change for a dollar unless the cash register tells him."

The kid didn't take offense at the insult. Perhaps it failed to register, or maybe his name really was Goober? But Nick thought it was more likely that the little turd was caught in the tractor beams of Babe's perfect tits.

"Is that right?" Babe asked.

"Wha—what?"

"Is what my brother said true?"

"Brother?" Nick rolled his eyes. The kid was a novice and no match for a woman like Babe. There was no need for her to break out her feminine wiles, but who was he to deny her a little fun?

"Is it true that you don't know how to make change?"

"N-n-n-no, it's just a rule," he answered, not once making eye contact. "No change without purchase." He pointed in the general direction of the sign above his head.

"So, you do know how?"

Nick thought that she sounded genuinely interested. *"Holy shit, she's laying it on thick."*

The boy swallowed hard again and nodded, eyes still locked on their target.

Babe leaned in, and the boy's eyes turned to half-moon hubcaps, like the wolf in the old MGM Red Hot Riding Hood cartoon. The boy's fingers found the button that released the drawer on the register, and he pulled out a hand full of quarters and plopped them, jangling on the counter. Nick reached over and grabbed eight quarters. Babe dropped her hand on the pile and grabbed the two bucks plus a couple of dollars in quarters herself.

"I knew you could do it, sweetie," she said and turned, tossing in a wiggle for good measure.

As fixated as the boy was on Babe, Nick couldn't help but regard him with equal amazement.

"We going, honey?" Babe said.

The boy looked like he was about to pass out.

"Relax, Goober, she was talking to me. Nick turned and followed her out of the service station.

"Holy shit, I hope I was never that pathetic."

"Oh, I bet you were worse," Babe said with a laugh and followed him over to the payphone.

Nick shielded his eyes from the glare coming off the silver payphone enclosure. The sun was burning the shit out of everything it touched. Nick grabbed the receiver and tossed it hand to hand like a game of hot potato until it cooled. Then he plunked in a handful of quarters and punched in the number to Jinan Bondiani's office from memory. The phone rang several times and was answered by an answering machine.

Hello, you have reached the office of Doctor Jinan Bondiani. My office hours are 8 AM to 6 PM Monday through Friday, but I am available on weekends by appointment only. If you have reached this answering machine during regular office hours, I have either stepped away for a moment, or I am on the lecture circuit. Leave a message, and I will return your call.

"Hello, Jinan? I mean Dr. Bondiani, this is Nick, Nick Ryan. I know I should be doing this myself, but I need a favor. I've dug up some unbelievable information about the Mooka'am, and I was hoping you could run a Lexis Nexis search on a couple of names. The first is Pozerac Gemein. It might be an anagram or something, I'm not sure…."

Jinan picked up, interrupting the message. "Nick, this is Dr. Bondiani."

"Dr. Bondiani, I'm so glad I got you." He was talking a mile a minute.

"Nick, slow down," she said.

"Sorry, but time is important."

"Just take a breath and tell me what you need."

"I need you to run a couple of names through…."

"Yes," she interrupted. "Lexis Nexis, I heard. Give me the names."

"The first is Pozerac Gemein. It should be pretty easy. I can't imagine there are many Pozerac Gemeins in the world."

"I wouldn't know," said Jinan, "but we shall see. Anything, in particular, I should be looking for with this gentleman?"

"Anything and everything you can find on the guy."

"And who is he?"

"I don't have time to explain, but I'll tell you this. He may be the key to unlocking the mystery of the Mooka'am."

"Do you have a birthday for Mr. Gemein?"

Nick considered her question. "Hard to say, some time during the mid–1700s, I'm guessing."

"Mid 17—Nick, Lexis Nexis won't have information on someone that has been dead for over 200 years."

"He's not dead," replied Nick.

"Excuse me?"

"At least I don't think he's—"

"Nick, are you okay? You're not making sense."

"I'll explain it all when I see you. Now, the other name is Benjamin A Shippen. Up until about… six," he looked over at Babe, who had joined him under the glow of the gas station sign. Babe responded with a waggle of her hand that Nick took to mean, close enough. "Yeah, about six years ago, he lived in the town of Chesapeake Station in Chesapeake County, Illinois."

"Got it," said Jinan. "And where does he live now?"

"He's dead, but we believe he has ties to Gemein."

"Right," said Jinan. And was he also born in the 1700s?"

"No, probably around 1934, he fought in the Korean Conflict."

"Of course, and he's somehow tied to the disappearance of the Mooka'am?"

"We think so."

"We? Who are we?"

"The people helping me with research."

"Well, make sure you grab their *particulars* for citing in your work."

"Will do, and I need one more favor, a huge favor."

"I'm listening," she said, sounding cautious.

Would you please go to my apartment? It's number 910 in the Sheridan Building. In my nightstand, there is a box, and in the box is a four-headed skeleton key. Please grab it and bring it to 289 Sugar Maple Lane in Red Hook, Illinois."

"Nick, I hardly think.…"

"Please, Jinan, I wouldn't ask if it weren't detrimental to *our* work," Nick chose the word *'our'* very carefully, hoping it would give her a sense of ownership.

"And there's no one else you can ask?"

"Humph," he grunted, suddenly aware that he'd lived in the city for almost eight years, and there really was no one else that he could ask. "There really isn't."

"Very well, but you are going to owe me."

"Thank you so much! I'll meet you in Red Hook in a couple of hours. I'll fill you in on the rest when we speak."

"Very well."

"Thanks, Jinan," he said and hung the receiver back in its cradle. He looked at Babe. "You ready?"

She smiled and nodded.

"Next stop Red Hook," he said.

Babe threw her arms around his neck. "Thank you, Nick, thank you for doing all of this," she said and kissed his cheek. They walked arm-in-arm back to the Bronco. Nick laughed when he looked over and saw the attendant with his nose pressed up against the glass and let his hand drop a little lower onto Babe's hip.

Babe glanced quickly down toward Nick's hand and then back toward the service station. "You're so mean," she laughed.

Nick hopped into the driver's seat. He could feel the heat coming off the fake leather and the steering wheel. Babe just slid onto the passenger's seat and let out a high-pitched squeal. She pressed hard against the seat-back separating the hot seat from the tender flesh on the back of her thighs as she tugged ineffectively at her too-short skirt. Nick reached back, grabbed an old T-shirt from the floor, and shoved it under her butt.

"Thanks," she said and settled in as the Bronco pulled out of the gas station and back onto the road.

Above them, the brilliant sun hung in the serene blue sky, and all of the colors of the world popped in perfect contrast. Babe turned down the radio so they could talk.

"So, you never told me. What did you find in your dad's office?"

"Nothing, I never went up there."

"Are you kidding? Weren't you curious?"

"Very, but—.

Babe paused, perhaps sensing that she'd hit a nerve.

Nick scratched roughly at his head.

"I've never really talked about this with anyone before."

"About what?" She asked.

"About my dad."

"Oh, well, if you'd rather not—"

"No, it's okay. It might be good to talk about it," Nick paused and cleared his throat. "When I was a kid, my father had a room above the garage. Mom and I called it his office only because we didn't know what else to call it. No one, not even my mother, was allowed in there. To make sure no one got in, my dad had Merlyn; he's this guy that has a clock shop in Red Hook, a genius with anything mechanical. Anyway, my dad had Merlyn make him a lock that no one could pick. See, skeleton key locks are easy to pick. Two small screwdrivers, and you're in—" he snapped his fingers, "like that. The keyhole on my dad's door looked like the one on the box your father left for you. They're impossible to pick because picking one mechanism would lock the next one, and so on."

"Are you saying that you think the clock maker made the lock on Gemein's box too?"

"I don't know; I doubt it. Far as I know, the guy has never left Red Hook. But my father's key is the only other key that I have ever seen made for a lock like this."

"Then we should try it," Babe agreed and then paused before asking. "So, you really never went up there?"

"No, my dad died when I was eighteen, and even then, I just never felt right about disobeying him."

"I'm sorry, Nick. Pneumonia is a terrible thing."

Nick shifted uncomfortably in his seat. "He was a great man, my dad. He was a good father and a good husband."

Babe placed a hand on his forearm.

"There was an incident—a little boy drowned in the river behind our house. My father tried to save him, but he drowned."

Softly, Babe asked, "and that was how he caught pneumonia?"

"Probably, I don't know. But I don't really think it was pneumonia that killed him." Nick paused again. "The truth is—my father died in a mental institution."

Nick kept his eyes on the road, but he could imagine the shock on her face, and he couldn't blame her. He continued.

"That night, the night the boy drowned, my father started talking about some creature at the bottom of the river. When the cops and firemen pulled him out of the water, he said that this—this thing pulled the little boy under and wouldn't let him go. The paramedic told my mom that my dad was in shock and that it would pass, but it never did. When he came home, he started spending more and more time in his office. This thing, this imaginary monster, had become his life's calling. He lost his job with O'Kray's."

"What's that?" She asked.

"It's a construction company back home. When he stopped showing up for jobs, Mr. O'Kray had to let him go. Our family had to rely on the church for handouts. My mom took a job in town, and I helped out as best as I could, and we made it work. My dad got sicker and sicker. My mom tried to get him to go to the doctor, but he said that we couldn't afford it. He said that he would be fine. When he got really sick, too sick to argue, we put him in the hospital. That's when everything went to shit. He started talking to the doctors about the river monster, they tried to ignore his rantings, but when he started getting violent, they sent him for observation." Nick made air quotes around the word observations. "They let him die in the fucking nuthouse."

"Oh my god, Nick, I am so sorry."

They rode in silence the rest of the way. Eventually, Babe put her head on Nick's shoulder and fell asleep. As they neared Red Hook, the weather turned quickly. Nick woke Babe, pulled onto the shoulder, got the top up, and continued on.

"There's the sign for Red Hook," Babe said.

Nick signaled right and pulled off I-39 at the Grove Road exit. As they reached Square Barn Road, the hairs on Nick's neck stood up. The old Welcome to Red Hook sign stood right where it had for as long as he or probably anyone else could remember. The American flag flying proudly on one side and the crimson red hook on a navy-blue field of the Red Hook Township flag on the other.

<h1 style="text-align:center">26</h1>

After a while, the somber mood broke, and they were all laughing again, all but Levi. Levi was busy, struggling to make the Gypsy Soul travel in a straight line and worrying about the swirling black clouds closing in fast over Red Hook. The bow of the Gypsy Soul rubbed up against the Howard's raft. "Hey, who taught you how to row a boat, dip-shit?" Stan jibed, but Levi did not respond.

"What's his problem?"

Kaylin followed Levi's stare up toward the churning black above. "Guys, I think we better get off the river fast."

Stan followed her gaze. "Holy shit! Kaylin's right, guys. We better find a place to portage."

With the intense heat and lack of any significant rainfall since spring, the Red Hook River's water level had dropped, leaving them walled in by high ground on either bank. The sense of urgency seemed to have spread throughout the group as they all searched frantically for a low spot to disembark. As they paddled hard for a clearing on the eastern bank, the Red Hook picked up speed, pushing their boats like toys along a gutter in heavy rain. The warning buoys for the boil bobbed on whitecaps about 300 feet ahead as the boaters sped toward the dam. The Gypsy Soul listed hard to port on a small wave, and Frankie fell went overboard. Levi lunged for him and let go of the oars, sending them speeding off down the river.

"Frankie!" Levi screamed.

"We got him!" Stevie yelled back.

The rafters dug their oars wrist deep into the now freezing water and pulled hard for shore. Frankie struggled against Stevie's grip.

"Levi's not stopping!" He screamed.

The rafters made it to shore a mere fifty feet from the dam and watched in horror as the Gypsy Soul went over with Levi clinging to her rails. They broke into a sprint, running toward the dam. Kaylin beat them all, even Finn, who had always been the fastest in the group. The sky opened up, and the rain began falling in sheets. Kaylin shielded her eyes and peered into the churning water. Several large tree limbs that had fallen and been swept down to the dam by spring storms made it difficult to see but also harbored hope that Levi might be clinging to one of the downed giants.

"Do you see him?" Stan asked, arriving winded next to Kaylin.

"No," she said. "I don't see anything, not even the boat."

"Finn!" Called Stan, "go call for help."

***

Finn turned to run, but Kaylin was already clearing the grass to the parking lot up the river bank. With burning lungs and her heart pounding in her ears, Kaylin tore across the bridge and headed for the bait and tackle shop just as the first drops of rain began to fall. She grabbed the screen door handle and ripped it open, slamming the wooden frame against the outside wall.

"What the hell, Kaylin?" Said Anthony, the young man behind the counter. "You trying to rip the damned door off?"

"9-1-1! Call 9-1-1!" She demanded.

"What?'

"9-1-1! Call 9-1-1! Levi's in the boil!"

"Who's Levi?" The confused young man asked.

"Anthony, so help me, God, if you don't start dialing, I'm gonna...."

Anthony grabbed the phone and punched in the numbers. "Yeah, Tammy? It's Anthony. Listen, Vecchio's niece just came in. She said there's a kid in the boil. Yeah, hang on." For whatever reason, Anthony covered the mouthpiece on the receiver. "Hey, Kaylin, where'd he go in?"

Kaylin Vaughn hopped in place like a little kid who had to pee. "Right around the middle, he lost his oar—" "She said he went in around the middle.

I'm heading out there right now. Get the guys started!" Anthony slammed the receiver down, grabbed a rope and two life vests from behind the counter. Grabbing Kaylin by the hand, he dragged her to his truck. "Get in!" Anthony tossed the rope and life jackets on the seat between them and hopped into the cab. The F-250 roared to life and spit gravel as he pinned the accelerator to the floor.

The rain hung in the air like a good soaking mist, and the F-250's wipers worked in a hypnotic rhythm, trying to keep the windshield clear. The big engine had worked its way up into third gear by the time he skidded onto Water Street, the short half-block that led to the parking lot on the western bank of the river.

"Not today mother-fucker, not today," he said, challenging the pitiless boil. He looked up. Black storm clouds so thick that it seemed like night had fallen, churned like the waters of the boil. "What the fuck were you guys doing out there in this weather?"

The sharpness in his tone made Kaylin jump, but she didn't answer. She just stared straight ahead, lost in the beams of the truck's lights that pierced deep into the misty darkness. Anthony flung his door open and pulled on one of the life vests. He slung his arm through the armhole in the other and grabbed the rope.

"Stay put!" He ordered. Kaylin didn't respond.

Anthony ran to the railing and tied off. He fastened the other end around his waist and launched himself over the railing into the river. The water was only about two and a half feet deep at the outwash, but the river was running fast, and he had to lean into the rushing water to keep from being swept away. He fought his way out toward the middle of the river, searching and calling out to Levi as he went. Across the river, Frankie, Stan, McKenna, and the Johnsons sat huddled together against the cold, drenching mist.

***

The emergency tones blared through the firehouse as the dispatcher's voice came over the speaker. "Red Hook Fire, general alarm, river rescue, 0 McKinley Avenue, a subject in the boil. Engine 208, Engine 201, squad

206 and 207, truck 205, and medic 251 all due to respond.”

The huge doors in all three bays opened, and the trucks' sirens howled like banshees into the storm. The engine companies, geared up, headsets on, heard their Chief's mic crackle to life.

“2-1-1 on scene and going in, east bank, twenty-five feet below the dam. Not assuming command.”

“10-04, 2-1-1, going in, east bank, twenty-five feet below the dam. Not assuming command,” the dispatcher said, repeating the Chief's radio traffic.

***

Chief Tony Carlini had been out running an errand when the call came over his radio, and he made it to the river's edge just as the Gypsy Soul came crashing through the water's surface before getting dragged back below by the backwash of the boil. He looked across the river and saw his son's big red F-250 with its headlights and Baja lights shining out at the water, and his heart sank. Carlini knew his son wouldn't have waited for help to arrive.

“Fuck!” He shouted. It wasn't bad enough that he had a kid to rescue. Now he had to worry about his own kid going all cowboy and putting himself in danger as well. The Chief ran down the hill to the river's edge and saw his son wading out. Securing his own line, Tony went in.

“What the fuck is wrong with you?” He yelled as he reached his boy. Anthony pulled the spare jacket off his arm and handed it to his father.

“I knew you'd come, dad.”

The elder Carlini strapped into the jacket dug his heels into the river bed and took hold of the rope.

“Okay, I got you!” He said as he eased the line out, allowing his son to get closer to the dangerous boil.

“His arm, dad! I see his arm,” Anthony cried as he lunged for the boy and lost his footing. In an instant, the young firefighter was sucked beneath the water.

“Anthony!” The rope tore across the Chief's hands, burning and drawing blood, but the old Chief only tightened his grip. He anchored his feet and wrapped the line around his arms, despite every water rescue drill he'd ever participated in.

"You mother-fucker! You're not taking my son!"

The Chief pulled like a bull until he'd dragged his son from the boil. Anthony came up, coughing cold black water and gasping for air.

"Dad," he said, harsh rasping coughs disrupting his words, "I was so close!"

Anthony turned to try again, but the Chief took up the slack and grabbed his son by the shoulders.

"Listen!" He yelled into his son's face and pointed into the sky. "Do you hear that?"

Through the cacophony of wind and the thundering river, the wail of sirens grew louder. Squads and engines poured onto the scene flooding the river and the boil with all manner of light as afternoon skies continued to darken under the heavy storm clouds above.

Chief Carlini's radio crackled. "D.C. Ballazhi is on the scene, east side of the river, assuming command."

"The cavalry is here, son," he said and wrapped his arms around his boy. "Let's get out of this fucking river."

As the rescue boat was backed into the water at the east bank's launch. The Chief and his son, exhausted from their efforts, turned for shore. But the river had other plans.

***

About an hour outside of Red Hook, near the town of Meridian, Nick pulled onto the side of the road. The air had taken on a sudden chill, and Nick looked up at the thick bank of clouds that hung heavy in the sky far off to their north, the direction they were heading. He fished an old jean jacket out of the back seat and handed it to Babe, who threw it over herself like a blanket.

"How much farther?" She asked.

Nick glanced left and right and pulled back onto the roadway. "About an hour, maybe a little less. You doing okay?"

"Okay, as I can be, I guess," she pulled her knees to her chest so that she could cover her legs with Nick's jean jacket.

"Stupid heater, the thing worked great last summer."

"Your blower motor is shot," said Babe, through chattering teeth.

"Are you sure?" Nick raised an eyebrow.

"Sure, I'm sure. You have the fan turned all the way up, and no air is coming out of your vent, dummy."

"Humph," Nick grunted as he ratcheted the fan switch back and forth. "I hadn't noticed."

"Haven't you used your air?"

"No, that's not working either."

Babe leaned over and looked at the sticker on the windshield.

"What are you doing?" Nick asked.

"Checking to see when you did your last oil change."

Nick checked the sticker and then glanced at his odometer.

"I was planning on doing it when I got back home." He ripped the sticker off the windshield and let it fly off with the wind.

Babe shook her head. "You have to do upkeep, Nick; if you don't, the little problems turn into big problems."

It sounded like something Nick's father would have said.

***

Something beneath the water snagged Anthony's foot and dragged him under. The Chief felt his son slip from his grasp and clawed wildly at the water, trying to grab hold of the biting rope still fastened around his son's waist. Anthony cartwheeled and spun madly in the backwash, unable to get his bearings and unable to dodge the logs and other debris that bobbed and crashed in and out of the boil. Something smashed into the back of his neck and sent flashing bolts of pain through his brain. Then all went black.

Above, two police officers, who had arrived on the scene just before the fire department, were already making their way toward the fire chief, clinging to his tie-off line. The Chief was transfixed on the churning water of the drowning machine and didn't hear them calling out to him. As the officers neared him, Tony drew in a deep breath and lunged forward. Officers Jensen and Fisher grabbed hold of his vest and pulled him back. The Chief spun and took a swing at his rescuers but was too close to land a good shot.

"Chief! We got this! Head in!" Jensen yelled.

"I can't; it's Anthony; he's in there!" He said, wrestling free of their grasp.

Carlini turned back toward the boil just in time to see his son's arm breach the surface. He latched onto Anthony's wrist with one hand and the safety line with the other and pulled, but the boil would not let go. The Chief let go of the rope and wrapped a second hand around Anthony's wrist. The boil spun Anthony's body violently, causing his shoulder to dislocate. Tony felt the thud that passed through his son's arm like the vibration from a taught snapped rubber band but refused to let him go. Fisher wrapped an arm around the safety line and grabbed onto the drag-strap on the back of Jensen's vest, and Jensen did likewise with the strap on the Fire Chief's vest. All three pulled hard against the raging water, but the boil would not give up the body.

***

The bubbles around him went from blue and red to black, blue and red to black, over and over as the turbulent water spun Levi's body. He broke the surface a few times where he gulped frantically at the air and clawed at the water, trying to keep from being dragged back under, but it was hopeless. In a split second, he was sucked back down to tumble and slam against the rocks and debris, again and again. And then it all stopped. Like an astronaut in deep space, he hung weightless beneath the black water, and Levi understood with absolute certainty that he was dead. Levi let his breath go and breathed in the cold black water, and felt soothing coolness enter his burning in his lungs. As he floated there, motionless in the turbulent water, Levi could feel the weight of the water pressing in on him as colorful bubbles began to fade.

He looked around and realized that he was alone; perhaps he would always be alone. The thought crushed his soul. To be alone, utterly and forever alone. He felt like he wanted to cry, but he couldn't. He hung there in the dark, pitying himself, and then noticed a commotion near the surface. There was another body in the boil. Levi moved, effortlessly, eel-like, toward the surface, a master of his new domain. His first thought was that Frankie hadn't made it into the Howard's boat but quickly noticed that the body was much bigger than Frankie, much bigger than anyone in his group. Suddenly, Levi found himself whipping and spinning around the boy's body and wrapping his arms like tentacles around the boy's body. Some part of Levi knew that what he was doing was wrong, but he couldn't bear the thought of being alone. But something was working against him to free the boy from the boil. Levi wrapped tighter around the boy's legs and was joined by more, just like himself. Wretched, watery specters, mostly boys, but a few girls, and all young, certainly none older than he was, rose up out of the riverbed. Levi could sense that they were coming to help, and he released his grip and let the boy go as he began to sink into the riverbed.

***

Fisher helped Carlini drag his son's body to shore while Jensen, joined by other rescuers, stayed in the water looking for the missing boy. The Chief laid his son's body on the ground and began CPR.

Farther up the hill, McKenna, holding Frankie tightly in her arms, lost her grip as he launched himself to his feet.

"Is that him?" He asked excitedly.

It was immediately clear to her that the boy was much bigger than Levi. "No, but they're going to find him, Frankie. He's going to be okay," she said, though she knew that was a lie.

The Red Hook claimed one or two lives a year and rarely let anyone leave her boil. Through the hazy glow of searchlights and the warbling red and blue of the emergency lights, she watched the rescue teams at work. Brave men and women risking their lives in the hopes of, and that was just it. In the hopes of what, rescuing a battered corps? An image that she was sure would haunt her for the rest of her days popped into her head. Two summers ago, she and Kaylin found the body of a kayaker who'd gone over the dam. It was a mile up the river past Gert's. He was naked, and his skin was shredded. The rocks and tree limbs in the backwash had torn his clothes and flesh to ribbons. His arms and legs twisted and broken at unnatural angles. White shards of bleached bones, poking through fish-belly-white flesh. She would prefer to remember Levi the way she had known him, strong, kind, and fearless. As she sat deep in thought, one of the paramedics knelt down in front of McKenna.

"Are you okay? Do either of you need medical attention? Miss?"

"That's my sister. She's okay," Stan said.

"What's her name?"

"McKenna," replied Stan, and the man jotted her name on his pad. "McKenna, can you hear me?

Is this your little brother?" The medic placed a hand on her back and waved something under her nose. The strong ammonia smell made her snap her head back, and she pushed the medic's hand away from her face.

"Do you need medical attention?" The paramedic asked again.

"No! "Get that away from me!"

"What about your little brother?"

"Frankie? Frankie's not my brother. He's Levi's brother," she answered, barely realizing what she was saying.

"Who's Levi?" The medic asked, looking down at his pad where he'd written the names of all the kids he'd spoken with. There was no Levi on his pad.

Without a word, Frankie raised his arm and pointed at the dam.

"Oh shit, I'm sorry, kid," said the medic. "Can you come with me?"

But Frankie didn't move; he just clung tighter to McKenna and her to him.

"Please, we need some information. We need to reach your parents."

Frankie, wide-eyed and mute to that point, began to shake and cry, and McKenna hugged him tighter.

27

Emergency service workers with high-powered binoculars scoured the river for any sign of the missing boy while the first responders took turns wading in and out of the water, trying to snag the body with hook-poles. It had been 40 minutes since Levi went into the boil and, although no one had made it official, everyone there knew that the mission had gone from a rescue to a recovery. The scene commander sent an additional team far south of the dam to search the banks for the boy's body. As bad as it was to lose someone, it always seemed worse when there wasn't a body to bury. The protocol was for the recovery team to work all through the night and well into the next day before calling it quits. Then, a couple of days later, they would search the shoreline downriver to the edge of town, with agencies to the south doing the same. It wasn't uncommon for it to take a few days for the body of a drowning victim to wash up on shore, sometimes three or four towns down river depending on the depth and flow of the Red Hook.

A paramedic was busy setting Anthony's arm in a sling as he sat on the back of the ambulance wrapped in a blanket. When Tony was sure his son was in good hands, he went up the hill to the command vehicle to meet with Chief Vecchio. Christopher Vecchio was his counterpart from the Red Hook Police Department and a lifelong friend.

"Hey, T."

Tony acknowledged his friend with a nod.

"Have we identified the victim?" Vecchio asked somberly.

"One of my guys is with the brother, a kid named Frankie Waters. Our victim is Levi Waters. I don't recognize the name; you?"

Vecchio shook his head. "No, maybe they're from out of town."

"Maybe, but the little boy is hanging with the Howard kids.

"Sometimes I really fucking hate my job," Vecchio said.

"Me too, brother." Both men had been on the job for years and had seen more than enough tragedy to last a lifetime.

"Well, I suppose we have to find out where Frankie's parents are and make notification."

Carlini looked over at his own son, the young man he loved more than life itself, and then up at the falling rain, grateful for the camouflage it offered. "I'll make the notification with you, Chris."

"I'd really appreciate that, T."

"Ballazhi, you good?"

"Yeah, Chief, I got it."

"I'm going to make notification with Chief Vecchio."

Ballazhi didn't say a word because there were no words to say to a man going to tell a family that they have lost a child. The two chiefs walked over to the ambulance, where Anthony was resting.

"Your father tells me you're a dumbass," Vecchio said.

"Oh, hey, Chief. Yeah, I know. I should have waited for backup."

Vecchio leaned over and whispered in his ear. "Your old man would have done the same thing," then standing back up and in a normal tone, "glad you're okay, son."

"Thanks, Chief, but I wouldn't have been if it weren't for my old man," he said, looking at his father. His dad looked tired, not just weary but worn out. The day had taken a lot out of him.

"Anything I can do to help dad?" He asked.

Tony placed a hand on his son's shoulder. "You've done more than enough, son."

Anthony winced a little, and his father pulled his hand back. "Sorry," he said.

"It's cool, and dad, thanks for pulling my ass out of the river."

"Had to; you're one of my men. And besides, your mother would have made me sleep on the couch if I hadn't."

The father and son smiled at one another, and Tony turned to follow Christopher Vecchio over to the pavilion where one of the firefighters sat with the kids.

Vecchio looked at the wet, sad faces recognizing all but one. "You must be Frankie Waters."

Frankie looked up, momentarily hopeful. "Did you find my brother?"

Vecchio's heart sank. "No, son, I'm sorry."

"Frankie, I'm Chief Carlini with the fire department; that's Chief Vecchio. He's the police chief; we would like to take you home to your parents now if you're feeling up to it."

Frankie's eyes widened. "I, I can't. I can't leave! If I leave, it means I'm giving up."

Vecchio knelt down in front of Frankie. "No, son, it's not giving up. See all of those brave men and women," he pointed toward the firefighters and police officers. "They're going to stay here and keep searching."

Frankie turned toward McKenna. "Will you come with me?"

McKenna swallowed hard, "umm, I don't know if…, I mean."

Vecchio offered a suggestion. "How about if we take Stan and Finn with us, then we can drop you guys at home. We'll get another car to take Stevie and Lonnie home. You guys can sit in the car while we speak with Frankie's parents."

The kids agreed, but McKenna stopped. "Where's Kaylin?"

"Kaylin? She was out here with you guys?" Vecchio asked, with no attempt to hide the panic in his voice.

"Yeah," said McKenna, she's the one who called 9-1-1."

Vecchio keyed up on his mic. "Anyone have a 20 on my niece Kaylin?"

All was silent for a moment, and then a small voice crackled over the radio. "I'm here, Uncle Chris."

"Where's here?"

"In Anthony's truck."

Vecchio let out a sigh of relief. "Stay there. I'll be right over." Then, bending back down, closer to the children, he said, "What do you say we get going, guys?"

The kids piled into the back of Vecchio's unmarked squad. Vecchio drove over the McKinley Avenue Bridge and parked in the grass. Tony's truck was parked farther down near the river with its headlights and Baja lights directed at the water. Vecchio hopped out of the car and ran to the pick-up. He pulled Kaylin out of the truck and wrapped his arms around her.

"Are you okay?" He asked.

"No, I don't think I'll ever be okay again," she said and burst into tears.

He held his niece for a moment, doing what he could to comfort her, and then guided her to his squad. Seeing her friend, McKenna flew from the backseat and took Kaylin into her arms. The girls cried and clung to one another until Vecchio told them it was time to go.

"Can we fit another one in the back?" Asked Tony.

"No, but I'm sure they'll make it work rather than be separated."

The carload worked its way up Sugar Maple Lane to the Waters' house. Vecchio parked on the street under a big oak and got out.

"Frankie, would you mind introducing Chief Carlini and me to your parents?"

Frankie looked at McKenna, who nodded her approval and got out of the car. He led the two men to the front door, and Vecchio rang the bell.

"Just a minute," came a soft voice from inside.

"That's my mom," said Frankie, looking up at the men.

The door swung open, and Connie Waters went white.

"Mrs. Waters, I'm Christopher Vecchio, and this is Anthony Carlini."

She looked at Frankie, who burst into tears and ran into his mother, grabbing her around the waist and sobbing."

"What did you do? Where's your brother?"

Frankie cried harder.

"That's why we're here, Mrs. Waters," said Vecchio. "Levi went into the boil. Our men are searching for his body."

"No, no, no no no," she said, shaking her head.

"I'm so very sorry, Ma'am."

"No, no, no," she screamed.

Scott came running from the back of the house. "What's going on?" He looked at Frankie and then at his wife. "Where's Levi?"

"Levi went over the dam into the boil about an hour ago, sir," said a somber Christopher Vecchio.

"What? How? This must be some kind of mistake. They rode their bikes to the ice cream shop. Frankie, where's your brother?"

But Frankie didn't answer. He just buried his face in his mother and wept.

Stan walked up behind Vecchio and stepped into the light from the house.

"It's true, Mr. and Mrs. Waters," he said.

"You're Stanley Howard, right?" Asked Scott.

"Yes, sir," Stan replied. "We saw it happen, but there was nothing we could do."

"How could you?" demanded Connie. "You knew he couldn't swim. How could you take him on the water in a flimsy raft?

"I didn't, Mrs. Waters. They took your boat."

"We don't have a boat," she snapped.

"Yes, we do, mom," Frankie said timidly.

Connie shot daggers at Scott. "God help you if you bought a boat, Scott Waters."

Scott looked perplexed. "What are you talking about? We don't have a boat."

"Yeah, we do, dad," said Frankie. "The Gypsy Soul."

Vecchio and Carlini shared a confused glance.

"Son, we don't have a boat," said Scott.

"Well, it was tied to our dock, and me and Levi took it to go down the river for ice cream."

"Was this your idea?" Connie asked Stan.

"Yes, ma'am, it was." Tears fell from Stan's eyes as he stood straight as a toy soldier.

Connie raised a hand, and Vecchio pulled Stan back.

"No, mom! It wasn't his idea. It was mine," said Frankie. "I wanted to take the boat because I was afraid to go in the garage. It's not Stan's fault. He saved my life. The water got super choppy, and I fell out of the boat, and

Stan and Finn saved me. They tried to save Levi, but the boat went over."

"Take me to him," demanded Connie. "Let's go, Scott."

Scott was already out the door, but Connie wasn't following. Frankie clung to her. "I don't want to go back there," cried Frankie.

Connie looked helplessly at Scott.

"We can stay with him here if you want," offered Stan.

Behind Stan stood Finn, McKenna, and Kaylin.

"You're the little girl who was so kind to Levi earlier today," she said to Kaylin.

"Yes, ma'am, I'm Kaylin."

"Hold on a minute," Vecchio said. "There's no reason to go anywhere just yet."

"I don't understand. You said that your people are searching for him," Connie said.

"That's right, ma'am."

"So, you haven't found him?"

"No, ma'am, not just yet."

"Then how do you know he's dead?"

"Ma'am," said Carlini. "He's been in the water for over an hour."

"But you don't have a body." It was a statement, not a question.

"No, ma'am."

"Stan, will you guys stay with Frankie? Mr. Waters and I are going with these men."

"Of course, Mrs. Waters, whatever you need."

Connie placed her hand on Stan's cheek. "Thank you for saving Frankie."

Stan didn't speak.

"Right this way, Mr. and Mrs. Waters," said Vecchio.

"We'll take our own car, officer."

"As you wish," said Vecchio.

***

Scott and Connie Waters got into the Wagoneer and followed Vecchio's Crown Vic back down Sugar Maple Lane.

"First thing in the morning, this fucking place goes back on the market,"

Connie said, staring straight out the window.

Scott didn't say a word. The Crown Vic turned onto McKinley Avenue, and Scott followed it over the bridge and into the parking lot on the river's east bank. It looked like half the town had turned out to watch the goings on. Connie was the first one out of the car. She ran to the river and would have run right into the water had one of the firemen not grabbed her.

"Let me go! My son is in there!" She screamed as she rained blows down on the fireman.

Scott ran down and grabbed his wife from behind holding her tightly as she continued to thrash. Vecchio and Carlini stood by, having nothing to offer. Slowly, Connie's flailing subsided. The rain had slowed to a fine, soaking mist that wobbled drunkenly in the glare from emergency vehicles' overheads.

28

Storm clouds, black as pitch, churned in the skies above Red Hook, casting the town in total darkness. As it was only half-past twelve in the afternoon, none of the streetlights were on. To most of the town, at least to anyone born after 1936, when the REA brought electricity to rural America, it must have seemed that Red Hook had never been darker. Below the threatening sky, rescue workers battled the turbulent dam as they searched for the body of young Levi Waters.

Across the McKinley Avenue Bridge and down Main Street, the little bell above the door at Merlyn's Clock Shop jingled, and a small man in a black suit stepped inside. Pozerac Gemein walked up the aisle toward the proprietor and dragged a sharp yellow fingernail across an antique table, sending ribbons of wood spiraling to the floor. Merlyn, who sat hunched over a project, looked up at the sound of the bell and pulled a hand rag over his work.

"Mr. Gemein, what brings you in?"

"My dear Mr. Merlyn. It's been over thirty years; how is it that you remember me?"

"What can I say? I have a mind like a steel trap. And it's Merlyn, just Merlyn. Besides, you haven't aged a bit."

"Merlyn, you flatter me."

Merlyn sat still as Gemein gave him the 'once-over.'

"The years haven't been as kind to you, I'm afraid."

"Well, I'm still on this side of the dirt, so that's something."

"I suppose it is, I suppose it is," Gemein said and sniffed at the air.

"Is there something I can do for you?" Merlyn asked as he watched Gemein's face cloud over.

"It's not here," Gemein said, sounding surprised.

Merlyn sniffed once and then asked, "What's not here?"

"Merlyn, I am looking for my box. You do remember my box. Don't you?"

"Sure, I made a key for it. I remember you sat here the whole time and then didn't even let me check to see if it worked."

"Yes, well, your work was satisfactory, I assure you. You haven't been commissioned to make another, have you?" Gemein moved a hooked nail toward the shop towel on Merlyn's work table.

Merlyn casually placed a hand on the towel drew it a little closer to himself. "Is that why you're here? You need another key made?"

"Not exactly." Gemein drew his hand back slowly and fixed his eyes on Merlyn's.

"Well, I'm busy, man Gemein. What is it that you need?"

Gemein gave another quick sniff. "It really isn't here," he said, the disbelief seeming to settle into fact. Gemein focused his glare on Merlyn.

"I don't have time for your spooky nonsense Gemein. You took that—box," he knew *box* wasn't really the right word for it, "when you left, and I haven't seen it since."

Gemein stepped closer and slammed his hand on top of Merlyn's, and grabbed hold. Slowly, Gemein increased the force of his grip until his nails sunk into Merlyn's flesh, causing the shopkeeper to wince. Gemein lifted his hand off the rag and released him. Merlyn clutched his hand to his chest, blood dripped onto his shirt. Gemein picked up the rag revealing the key. He took the key from the table and held it for inspection. Reaching into his shirt collar, he pulled the key he wore suspended by a leather strap from around his neck and held it up for comparison.

"A bit shoddy, by your standards, wouldn't you say?"

There were notable differences in the cuts made to each key.

"That's not for your box. After I worked on your key, I started building locks like the one on your box," Merlyn said, still gripping his bleeding hand. "That's for another customer."

Gemein rolled the replica in his fingers and snapped it in two with his thumb. Merlyn stared in disbelief. He'd made the key from iron.

"Who asked you to make this key?"

Merlyn stared defiantly, not answering the question. "Get out of my shop before I throw you out."

"No, I don't suppose you would tell me," Gemein said and began twirling his key between his fingers. "Pity, this could have been such a nice reunion."

He twirled the key faster and faster until it turned into a whirling blur. At once, the hands of all the clocks in the shop began to spin, coming to rest on twelve o'clock. The small shop erupted in sound as the clocks simultaneously chimed the hours, joined by a deep thrumming ring that seemed to come up from the center of the earth. Merlyn dropped his tools and clamped his hands over his ears, but it did no good. The cacophony grew louder and louder until it reached its peak, exploding the windows out of the tiny shop. Merlyn felt a trickle of blood from his nose and wiped at it with a handkerchief he'd pulled from his back pocket. The trickle turned to a flood and was joined by discharge from his ears. Merlyn collapsed on the floor, and the clocks ceased their booming. Pozerac Gemein gripped his cuffs, adjusted his shirtsleeves with quick snaps, and exited the store to the jingle of the little bell over the door.

***

Jinan pulled into the driveway at 289 Sugar Maple Lane, parked her car, and walked up to the door. After double-checking the address, Jinan rang the bell and waited. A young girl with bloodshot eyes and tear-streaked cheeks opened the door and stared blankly at her.

"Are you okay?" She asked.

"Who are you?" The young girl responded.

"My name is Jinan Bondiani; I'm a doctor of anthropology at…" even to her, it sounded pretentious.

"What do you want?" The girl interrupted.

"I'm looking for Nick Ryan. Do you know him?"

"He doesn't live here anymore; I think his parents used to own this place or something," she said and began closing the door.

"Excuse me, little girl, are your parents home?"

"My name is Kaylin, not, little girl."

"I'm sorry, Kaylin. But I have driven a long way, and…."

Frankie came to the door. "Who are you?"

"Her name is doctor Bondi or something," said Kaylin.

"It's Bondiani, Jinan Bondiani, and I'm looking for Nick Ryan."

"He doesn't live here, ma'am."

Frankie's eyes were even more red and puffy than Kaylin's.

"Is this your home?" She asked, double-checking the address.

"Yes, ma'am."

"Are your parents home?" Jinan asked.

"No, they're down at the river. My brother Levi drowned and," his breath hitched, "and they're down there."

Jinan gasped at the news, and the strange key she had been holding fell from her hand. Frankie stared at the key for a moment and then bent to pick it up. He twirled the key between his fingers and studied it. "Where did you get this?"

Jinan was about to answer when a pair of headlights back lit her. Nick and Babe hopped out of the Bronco and ran to the door.

"Jinan!" He called. "Thank you for coming."

"Who are you, people?" Kaylin asked.

"You must be one of the Waters boys," Nick said, completely ignoring Kaylin.

"I'm the only Waters boy," said Frankie.

"Oh, I'm sorry, I thought the Realtor said there were two boys."

Jinan put a hand on Nick's forearm. "Nick," she whispered. "His brother drowned, just today, I think."

Nick's knees almost buckled, but he caught himself. His mind went screaming back to the night so long ago when Josh Ironweiler drowned. The night that started, his father on on the road to Bull Run State Mental Hospital.

"When did it happen?" Nick demanded.

"Nick!" Jinan chided.

"About an hour ago," said Stan, who came walking up with Finn and McKenna. "Who are you?"

"Nick Ryan, I used to live here. Are your folks home?"

"They're still down at the river," said Jinan.

Nick saw the key in Frankie's hand.

"You brought the key."

"Yes, you said it was important."

Frankie held the key out for Nick to take it. Nick reached out, but his hand stopped short of touching it.

"Go on, mister, it's your key," said an exhausted Frankie Waters.

"Babe, do you have the box?"

Babe patted the handbag that she held clutched to her chest. "Right here, Nick."

"Frankie, would it be okay for us to come in?" Nick asked.

Frankie looked at the others for direction and was met with shoulder shrugs. "I guess so."

Nick stepped into his old house and felt a flood of emotion and memories pour over him. When he'd sold the place, he thought that he would never see it again. The connection was strong and immediate, and he proceeded through the house like he still lived there.

"Hey, slow down, pal," said Stan. Frankie said you could come in. He didn't say to make yourself at home."

Nick ignored Stan and proceeded into the kitchen.

"Are you ready?"

Babe nodded, pulled the box from the bag, set it on the table, and stepped back. Nick took the key, fitted it into the keyhole, and paused for a moment. "Here goes nothing." He licked his lips and tried to turn the key, but it wouldn't budge.

"Shit! I was hoping it might work."

"Do you mean to tell me that you had me drive two hours for that?"

Nick looked up, but not at Jinan. "Do you smell that?" He asked?

"Smell what?" Asked Babe.

"I smell it," said Frankie.

Everyone else sniffed the air but seemed to have no idea what they were smelling.

"It smells like cigarettes," Frankie said.

"Not just cigarettes, Frankie. Those are Camel Cigarettes, my father's brand. Come on." Nick hurried out the back door and around the side of the house toward the garage. "It's stronger in here. Come on!"

"Nick," Jinan shouted. "What are you doing?"

Nick flipped the light switch on and was about to tear up the stairs when Frankie shouted at him to stop.

"No! You can't go in there; I don't think it's safe!"

"Look, kid," said Nick.

"His name is Frankie, not kid, and you can't just run around here like you own the place. This is Frankie's house, and if he says you can't go up there, you can't go up there."

It's always the little guys who have the big mouths, Nick thought. He wanted to tell the kid to pound sand, but a quick glance from Jinan and Babe settled him down.

"You're right, kid."

"It's Stan, and this is my brother Finn, my sister McKenna and our friend Kaylin, and Frankie is our friend, and we're not going to let you push him around."

"No, of course not. Look, I'm Nick, this is Babe, and this is.

"Doctor Bon Jovi, yeah, we know, she told us," said Stan.

"Bondiani," said Jinan quietly, seeming to realize it wasn't important.

"Frankie, I'm really sorry about what happened to your brother."

Frankie had to crane his neck to look Nick in the eye. "Not as sorry as I am, mister."

Nick could hear the loss and loneliness in Frankie's voice, and he remembered feeling that way when each of his parents died. It was like a part of himself died with them.

"I know it hurts, Frankie, and I wish I could tell you that it will stop hurting soon, but that would be a lie."

"I just keep remembering the look on his face before he went over the dam. He looked sad. That's crazy, right? I mean, he should have looked scared, but he looked sad."

"I—I don't know, kid," Nick said.

"Levi told me everyone gets scared, even our uncle Dan, and he's a policeman. But Levi said that sometimes it was good to face your fears," a slight smile crept onto his face and then faded. "So maybe he was facing his fears," as quickly as the smile rose, it had vanished. "He just looked so sad."

"Maybe your brother was sad because he was leaving you, and that was more important to him than the fear," said Babe. "So, you helped him not to be scared."

Frankie tried to take a deep breath, but his body shuddered. He looked up the stairs. "Levi said that something was trying to pull him into that room, and I saved him. I just wish I could have saved him from the river. I wish I was stronger. I could have jumped in and saved him."

Nick knelt down. "Frankie, listen to me. No matter how strong you are, if you had jumped in, your parents would be mourning two sons tonight."

"Maybe, but I just wish it had been me instead of him."

"Don't say that," Nicks snapped. "Don't ever say that. Your mom and dad are going to need you to be strong. I'm sorry to have to tell you this, Frankie, but the hurt you're feeling is going to be with you for a long while. But eventually, the sad memories will fade, and you'll start to replace them with happy memories. That's when the hurt starts to fade too."

"Really?"

"Really. I'm not saying it will ever stop hurting completely, but it will hurt a lot less, and instead of crying and feeling sad when you think about Levi, you'll smile."

"Did you ever lose a brother, mister?"

"No, Frankie, but I lost people that I loved. You'll see, one day, you will be thinking about Levi and feeling sad, and then, out of nowhere, a good memory will start pushing its way into your head. That will be Levi, trying to take some of the hurt away."

"I sure hope so, mister."

"You can call me Nick."

"My parents don't allow us—I mean me, they don't allow me to call grown-ups by their first names."

"Well, I'm not much of a grown-up."

"No, he's not!" Jinan added.

Nick smiled, and Frankie smiled too. "See, what did I tell you? But if your parents don't allow it, then you just call me whatever you think is best."

"Okay, mister."

"You good with me calling you, Frankie?"

"Sure, that's my name."

Well, Frankie, I think there might be a way to stop some of these drownings, and the answer may just be in that room," he said, pointing up the stairs.

Frankie glanced hesitantly back up the stairs. "I don't think we should go up there."

The smell of Camel Cigarettes still hung in the air. Nick inhaled deeply.

"You smell that, don't you?"

"Yeah," said Frankie, breathing in."

The others stared, looking confused.

"That's my dad. He's trying to tell us something. And whatever he wants us to see is in there." Nick pointed to the door.

"Then, I'll unlock it." Frankie looked determined, even more determined than sad. "My brother wanted to see what was in that room more than almost anything, so I should be the one to open it."

Nick, still on a knee, handed Frankie the key and stood up.

Frankie took the key and braced himself for the climb. "Will you come with me, mister?"

"Of course, I will."

Frankie started the climb. By the time he reached the landing, his whole body was shaking. He looked back down the stairs at his friends, his face blanched white, his eyes deep and pleading.

"You want us up there with you?" Asked Stan.

Frankie nodded, and some of the color returned to his face. Without a word, Stan, Finn, McKenna, and Kaylin bolted up the stairs. Frankie managed to put the key in the lock, though he would have lost if he were playing Operation. One quick turn, and the lock clicked. Frankie turned the knob, and the door creaked open on old neglected hinges. The group moved forward.

"Hang on, guys, I think I have to do this part myself."

"Are you sure?" Asked Kaylin. "Because we'll go with you if you want."

"Thanks, but I'm sure." But just before Frankie stepped across the threshold, he took hold of Nick's hand. "Maybe I'm not so sure. Will you come with me, mister?" He said, giving Nick a tug.

The room was dark but not pitch-black. Through the bank of windows that made up the east wall, lightning from the approaching storm flashed silver in the night sky. Frankie slid his free hand on the wall to the right of the doorway, looking for a light switch.

"Is there a light in here, mister?"

"I don't know, Frankie; I've never been up here before." Nick fished in his pocket and pulled out a Zippo, and sparked it to life.

"That's a cool lighter."

"It was my father's."

The orange glow was just bright enough for Nick to find the switch. A single naked bulb flared and bathed the room in a clinical white light and turned the glass into a giant mirror. Outside, a soft thudding, like the sound of eggs hitting the side of a house, started against the window panes.

"Well, it's a really cool lighter."

"You like it?"

Frankie's eyes widened. "I sure do."

Nick regarded the keepsake and tossed it to Frankie. "It's all yours, kid."

Frankie's mouth dropped open in surprise. "Really, you really mean it; it's mine to keep?"

"Sure, just don't burn the house down."

Frankie clutched the lighter to his chest and then studied it. Now it was Nick's turn to be surprised. He stood like Frankie, mouth agape, eyes unblinking, as he took in the room. Before him, on every wall and piled on tables, was the work that drove his father mad.

"Mister, are you okay?"

Nick finally blinked. "What, kid?"

"His name is Frankie," came a voice from the doorway.

"Shut up, Stan. He can call me kid if he wants." Frankie paused and regarded Nick with soulful eyes. "So, are you?"

"Yeah, I'm okay. It's just a lot to take in."

Jinan, who had followed the kids up the stairs with Babe, placed a hand on Stan's shoulder.

"Shh, just give them a minute Stanley."

"Only my mom calls me Stanley."

Jinan gave his shoulder a squeeze, probably just like his mother had cause to do on many occasions, and Stanley Howard shut his yap. Frankie walked deeper into the room and then turned back toward the door. A boy's picture was pinned on the wall above the light switch with a red thumbtack. Now it was Frankie who was struck dumb.

"What's wrong, Frankie?"

"That boy," his hand rose, and his finger unrolled. "Who is that?"

Nick pulled the newspaper clipping off the wall and studied it. "That's Josh."

Then, in a whisper, only Nick could hear, "That's the boy who came to my room, mine and Levi's."

Nick knelt down and whispered back. "Are you sure?"

"I'm sure, mister. Only he looked different—bad."

"Frankie, that's Josh Ironweiler, the little boy who drowned in the Red Hook ten years ago."

"Well, I've seen him," said Frankie. "He's been in my room, and he leaves puddles to the back door."

Nick felt a chill run up his spine. "Frankie, I have never told this to another living soul, but he used to come into my room too."

"No, fooling?"

"No fooling, kid. I never told anyone because I didn't want them to think

I was crazy like my old man."

Slowly the rest filed into the room.

Jinan, ever the scientist, let out an audible gasp. Maps, drawings, and newspaper clippings covered the walls. It was like opening a time capsule, and that seemed to speak to her.

"Nick, we have to collect and file all of these documents. There could be something significant among all of these papers."

"Frankie, this house, this garage, even this room. It's all yours, but the stuff in this room belonged to my father. Do you understand?"

"And now it belongs to you. Yes, I understand."

"Thanks, kid." Nick smiled and tousled Frankie's hair. "There's a message in all of this," he said, addressing Jinan and Babe. "We just have to find it."

Jinan took in the room, studying the items covering the walls. As she moved closer, she noticed something behind the hundreds of pieces of paper that had been pinned up.

"Nick, we have to remove some of this stuff."

"Would you guys mind helping us?" Nick asked Frankie and his friends.

"You can count on us," Frankie said enthusiastically.

"Babe, you and I will pull it down. Jinan, would you tell the kids where to stack it?"

"Of course."

They all went to work. Nick and Babe removed clippings, notes, maps, and scribblings from the wall and handed them to the kids. Jinan directed the piling's, and slowly something emerged from behind the papers.

29

Written repeatedly across the walls, like the scrawling of a madman who spoke another language, were words wiin nibaa anaamibiig and the name Skadegamutc. Jinan studied the words. "I didn't know your father spoke the languages of the First Nation."

Nick shook his head. "He didn't."

"Well, this writing," she pointed to the first set of words. "This seems to be Ojibwe. And this," she said, pointing to the second word. "Skadegamutc is the name of the ghost witch of the Wabanaki."

Nick caught Babe's eye, remembering that Achak mentioned the Wabanaki back in the hayloft.

"Wiin nibaa anaamibiig, translates roughly to, he lies sleeping beneath the water," Jinan said, watching the color fade from Nick's face. "Nick, are you okay? You look white as a sheet."

Nick felt light-headed. The room, the picture of Josh, the strange writing on the walls; it all just came crashing down on him. The mechanism that drove his father insane stared him in the face, and Nick could feel himself beginning to lose traction. There was something there, something in the writing. But it wasn't the words, or at least not their meaning. It was something else. Nick felt like a person expected to build a puzzle without the benefit of the picture on the box. The pieces were all there, but he had no idea what he was looking at. He walked forward and placed a hand on the wall.

There were several desks in the room, and each was covered with books, maps, and the newspaper clippings they'd just peeled off the walls. Jinan walked over to one of the desks, picked up an old leather-covered book titled *Native American Folklore and Findings*, and thumbed through it.

"Look at these books. This one is a first edition. Nick, do you have any idea how rare this book is?"

But Nick didn't answer. He ran his hand over the hurried brushstrokes on the walls. His father had been a meticulous man. The Tim Ryan he knew would have painted so slowly, so deliberately, that you would have sworn that the letters had been stenciled on the wall. This, this looked like it was done by a hyperactive preschooler. He followed the words and sentences that branched off like veins across the walls.

"Nick, Nick!" Jinan raised her voice to get his attention. "I'm speaking to you."

"What? I'm sorry."

"This book, where did your father get it?"

"What book?"

"Are you okay, Nick?" Babe asked.

"I'm fine."

Jinan pushed through the pile of books and picked up another one. "All first editions, Nick." She was beaming. "Look at this," she said, handing one of the books to Nick. "This belongs in our library, not hidden away in an attic."

Nick took the book on folklore from Jinan and turned it carefully in his hand, like a child who discovered the gun his parents had hidden in the house for protection.

"Nick, sweetie, are you okay?" Babe stopped sorting papers and put a hand on his neck.

"I said I'm fine," Nick snapped.

"The hell you are," Babe said and took his face in her hands. "Talk to me. What's going on?"

"I don't know; it's just being here, with all of his," Nick waved a hand around the room. "All of this shit. This is what drove my dad insane, and I'll be damned if I'm going to let that happen to me."

"I'm sorry, Nick. I didn't know your father suffered from mental illness,"

Jinan said softly.

"He didn't suffer," Nick said, raising his voice. "We did, my mother and me." Nick exhaled long and slow. "After Josh drowned, my dad quit work and started drinking. I mean, he always drank, but he started drinking heavily, ya know? Like it wasn't a beer with dinner anymore, it was a bottle of whiskey, and then two." Nick rubbed his forehead. "Thanksgiving, 1985. That's when it all started. I was helping my mother with the dishes; my dad went out to have a smoke down by the river. I heard him yelling about something, so I ran out back. By the time I got out there, he was in Gypsy Soul, halfway across the Red Hook."

"Gypsy Soul?" Jinan asked. "What's that?"

Nick opened his mouth, but Frankie spoke. "It's a rowboat."

Nick looked quizzically at him. "How did you know that?"

The rest of the kids stared wide-eyed at Nick.

"Levi, and me, we were in the Gypsy Soul. I fell out, and Finn saved me, but it took Levi over the dam, and he —."

That's impossible," Nick said. as he began rubbing the pad of his thumbs in small circles against the pads of his middle fingers. "The Gypsy Soul got smashed to pieces that night. My dad jumped out of the boat to save Josh, and the current carried the boat downriver."

"He's right, Mr. Ryan," McKenna said.

"We all saw it," offered Kaylin.

Finn and Stan nodded in agreement. "Yeah, we did. It was an old beat-up rowboat," added Stan.

Nick's mind raced as he rubbed his fingers together faster and harder, the sound catching both Frankie and Jinan's attention.

Jinan raised a hand to her heart, perhaps too conscious of Nick's feelings to call out the nervous tick. Being young and less attuned to social mores, Frankie said, "What are you doing with your fingers?"

Nick glanced down, totally unaware that he'd been doing anything. "I— nothing." Nick stopped the rubbing.

"My brother did the same thing. Back when we were in the house."

"What house, my house?" Nick said, catching but not caring about the disapproving look on Stan's face.

"No, the house across the river," Frankie said, his hand gesturing in the general direction.

"What the hell were you doing in the Ironweiler house?"

"We, we were exploring."

"You were trespassing! That place is dangerous!"

"We're sorry," Frankie said. The others nodded their agreement.

Nick's eyes scanned the floor like he was looking for something. "I'm sorry too, Frankie. I shouldn't have yelled."

"It's okay, Mr.," Frankie spoke for the group.

"Please, Nick, go on with your story," Jinan urged.

"My dad said that Josh was drowning or something," Nick scrunched his face trying to remember. "He yelled for me to call 9-1-1, so I turned and bolted for the house. I'd made it halfway to the house when a—a crow," Nick raised a hand to the small scar on his cheek. "A crow swooped on me and gashed me just under the eye."

"I thought you said you got that in a bar fight," Babe said.

"No," Nick corrected her. "You said I got it in a bar fight; I just didn't bother correcting you.

Anyway, the cops had to pull my dad out of the river. The paramedics took him to the hospital, but he was fighting with them, and he had to be handcuffed to the stretcher," Nick said. The words coming faster. "He was saying something about something being in the river, and whatever it was, it took Josh. He was yelling so loud; we could hear him clear across the Red Hook." Nick's eyes took on a vacant look as his mind replayed that horrible night.

Babe took the book from Nick, set it on the desk next to him, and took his hands in hers. It seemed to calm him, and his words came at a less frantic pace.

"He was in the hospital for almost a whole week. After he came home, my mom and I tried talking about that night with him. We tried a few times, but he would just start babbling some bullshit about Josh and a monster that lived in the river and then start crying." The soft edges of Nick's face turned hard. "Drunk crying. Have you ever seen a drunk on a crying jag?" Nick's face soured. "It's fucking pathetic."

"Nick, the children," Jinan said.

"Hell, lady," Stan said. "We've heard worse."

McKenna rolled her eyes.

"We told him to get some help," Nick continued. "He had a family to take care of. I mean, Josh drowned, not us. His problems were over. But us, after a couple of months with him not working and with his binge drinking, well, our money was running out. We were living paycheck to paycheck back then. And as kind, as his boss was, he couldn't support his family and ours. He sent us checks, a hundred here and hundred there, but after a couple of months the pity-checks, that's what my mother called them, 'pity-checks,' they stopped. Mr. Burton, at the general store, let us run a tab for a while, and between that, the pity-checks, and handouts from our church, we were able to survive. But my dad, he didn't care that we had to live like beggars."

Nick paused and looked around the room. All eyes were glued on him, and he felt suddenly like an object on display in some museum for hard-luck stories. "You guys don't want to hear anymore. Let's just—"

"Yes, we do," insisted Jinan. Perhaps she thought she might gain some insight into what made her strange pupil tick.

He drew in a breath and continued. "That Christmas, we were supposed to go to my aunt's house, but my dad was in no shape for a family gathering. The church gave us a small ham, and my mom made mashed potatoes and carrots and set a beautiful table," a smile slipped across Nick's face and then faded just as quickly. "My dad was shitfaced before dinner and kept drinking during dinner; he got into it with my mom and ended up smacking her around. I tried

to help her, but he knocked the shit out of me too. Thank God for Mr. Haring. His wife, Michelle, baked us a pie and sent him over to deliver it. He heard the commotion and let himself in. He got my dad in a bear hug and held him till the police came. After that, my mom started locking him out of the house. We just assumed he was passed out drunk up here." Nick looked around the room. "Well, I just had no idea."

Babe leaned forward and placed her forehead against his. "I'm so sorry, Nick. I'm sorry that I dragged you into all of this."

Nick swept his thumb across her cheek, wiping away the tear that had settled there, and then placed his hand on the back of her neck and gave a gentle squeeze. Clearing his throat and standing tall, he continued.

"My dad was a great man, but that great man died on November 28th, 1985. "As for where he got money to buy all these books, I really couldn't say."

Jinan seized the moment to redirect the energy in the room away from emotion and back toward work. She would have been the first to admit that she was uncomfortable with public displays of feelings.

"Let's take a look at your work, Kaylin."

Kaylin had arranged newspaper clippings into two separate piles.

Jinan thumbed through to the stacks. "These clippings all seem to be about missing women and children."

Babe and Nick looked at one another.

"This one," Kaylin pointed at the smaller pile. "Has articles about women and children who have been recovered. And these," she hefted a stack of clippings the size of the Sears catalog, "are about women and children still missing," she said, with a satisfied smile.

"Or at least they were when your father collected them. Nick!" Jinan sounded horrified. "You don't think that your father—."

Nick knew exactly what she was driving at. "What? No!"

"Nick," Babe said, staring at the words on the walls and totally disregarding Jinan's idiotic statement. "There's something about this writing."

Stan, oblivious to anyone or anything else, made a bee-line for a rifle that sat undisturbed for a decade, next to a telescope in the corner of the room.

"Freeze! Don't you dare touch the rifle, Stanley Howard," McKenna scolded.

"Shut up, McKenna; I don't have to listen to you."

Nick, his attention pulled away by the raised voices, turned in time to see Stan reach for the weapon."

"Hey, jackass. Get away from there."

Stan turned on a dime. "Who are you calling a jackass? This ain't your house anymore, so this ain't your rifle." Stan sneered, filled at least momentarily with false bravado.

"Listen, you little shit, you touch that rifle, and I'll drop-kick your ass down the stairs. Are we clear?" Nick rushed toward Stan and snatched the rifle up. All of the color faded from Stan's face, along with his swagger.

"I told you," McKenna sneered.

"Whatever," Stan said, trying to sound cool despite the noticeable quiver in his voice.

"Nick, look at this." Babe held up Gemein's terrible box.

The image on the box of the two hearts impaled on the harpoon was represented in the scribblings beneath the papers that had hung on the wall. There was no way for Nick to deny the connection.

"May I take a closer look at that box?" Jinan asked.

Babe checked Nick for guidance. It was clear that there was some apprehension.

"I'm sorry, Nick didn't bother to properly introduce us. I'm Jinan Bondiani, I am a professor of anthropology, and Nick is one of my students. I take it, you're his girlfriend?"

Babe stared at Jinan for a moment and then spoke. "You're his teacher? You can't be much older than Nick," she said.

Jinan leaned in and whispered loud enough for Nick to hear. "I'm not; I'm just much smarter," she said with a smile. "And you're his girlfriend?"

"Oh, we're not dating. Nick's not exactly my type," Babe said.

"I see," replied Jinan. "I just assumed; I mean, he keeps calling you Babe."

"Yeah, Babe. That's my name, Babe Adams. My father was a huge baseball fan."

"I'm sorry, I don't get the connection," said Jinan.

"Babe Ruth." McKenna stared in disbelief. "Are you telling me you've never heard of Babe Ruth?"

"I'm sorry, no."

Slack-jawed, Babe, handed the box to Jinan, who rubbed her thumb hard around the rim of the lid and then touched her fingertip to her tongue.

"Frankie, do your parents have rubbing alcohol and Turmeric?"

Frankie stared dumbly. "Turmer..."

"What about Worcestershire sauce? Do they have Worcestershire sauce?"

"That stuff in the brown bottle? I think so."

"Good, and what about rubbing alcohol?"

"Yes!" He said excitedly. "It's in the bathroom."

"Would you mind getting it?"

"I'm on it," Finn said as he tore down the stairs, taking them two at a time.

"And bring a dish towel and a bowl," she called after him.

Wait, what are we doing?" Nick hadn't been able to tear his eyes away from the image on the wall.

"You'll see. If this is what I think it is, my little experiment should provide some insight into its origins."

"And what do you think it is?" Nick asked.

"I think it is ojichaaqwan dasoozh, a spirit trap."

"What's that?" Stan's voice trembled.

"Just what it sounds like stupid," McKenna said, "I mean, probably, right?"

"Yes," said Jinan, "and if I'm right, there will be a hidden message on this box."

Finn was back in a flash. "Here you go, lady. What are you going to do with it?"

Jinan poured the Worcestershire sauce and rubbing alcohol into the bowl and dabbed the dishrag into the mixture. Holding the box firmly on her lap, she scrubbed at it with the concoction.

"Native American's used water and soda ash to make invisible ink for secret messages. Then the recipient would use a mixture made of alcohol and red cabbage or the like, and voila."

Before their eyes, words in an unknown text, unknown to all but Jinan, revealed themselves.

"How did you know it was there?" Babe asked. "I've had it for years and never thought to clean it off."

"Thank God you didn't. If you had, you might have washed away the secret of the box."

"But how did you know?" Nick asked.

"I could feel the indentations of the carvings in the wood, and when I touched my finger to my tongue, I could taste the tart alkali of the soda ash on my finger."

"Holy shit, you really are smarter than me."

Jinan rolled her eyes.

"Can you read it?" Nick asked excitedly.

Jinan ran her fingers over the box like a blind person reading braille and studied each line and curve. "I can make out some of the words, but this is a very old box. We're lucky any of the writing has remained. She pointed at some of the markings on the box. "See this? This is the word *gawaji*; it means to freeze. Specifically, to freeze to death."

Babe let out an audible gasp.

"Does that mean something to you?" Jinan asked.

"Please, keep reading," Nick insisted.

"Well, this," she pointed at another, "*gidaanawe*, that means to devour, to eat everything. And you see this here?" She pointed to what looked to Nick to be Egyptian hieroglyphics on the other side of the box. His eyes darted back and forth from the box to the wall.

"This says *the food of the gods*. That is usually a reference to human souls. And this," she looked at several jagged lines. "These are symbols for water, and when combined with this, it means river." She pulled a small pair of reading glasses from her pocket. The years of pouring over text late at night under dim light had taken a toll on her warm brown eyes. "It's a history of the owner of the box."

Jinan, who had stood up in her excitement as she explained the box, sat back down hard onto the stool. "I've heard of ojichaaqwan dasoozh, but I have never seen one. I don't think anyone has," she said excitedly. "What I do know is that they were never meant to be opened once sealed, but this one has a key lock for some reason. Perhaps it is still being filled."

She paused. "Nick, this is an unbelievable find. We have to get this back to the university to thoroughly study it."

"Nick," Babe said, her voice sharp as a razor. "You're not taking my box."

"Nick, listen to me," Jinan said. "This is as big as discovering why the Mooka'am vanished; bigger even."

"The Mooka'am *vanished*," she made air quotes, "because of the Inaki, and it's still out there. Nick, we have to stop it."

"The what?"

"The Inaki," Nick said. It's a soul reaper. Achak, our friend, he tried to tell me, and I told him he was crazy."

"I don't understand," Jinan said.

"It's a long story," Babe said. You can read about it in Nick's book. "Nick, sweetie, we have to get this thing open."

"No!" Cried Jinan. "That must be opened in the most sterile of conditions. There's no telling what secrets it might hold. Nick, please. You're a scientist, you must see the—"

Nick cut her off. "Babe's right," he answered, still reeling a bit. "It's her box, so it's her call."

"I'm sorry, Nick, but this box belongs to the scientific community," said Jinan.

"The hell it does; it was left to me by my father. That makes it mine." Babe squared herself, prepared for a fight.

"You must understand," Jinan began.

"No! You need to understand. Women are dying, and my town is cursed by this damn thing. So, fuck you and fuck your scientific community." Babe snatched the box away from Jinan and turned toward Nick. "We gotta get this thing open."

Across the room, Stan, who seemed to have lost interest in the grownup's conversation, if he ever had any, to begin with, asked, "Would it be okay if I looked through the telescope?"

Nick waved him off with a dismissive hand.

Stan shrugged his shoulders and put his eye to the telescope lens and then stepped back, disappointed. "I think it's broken," and then, throwing his hands up. "I didn't do anything, I swear!"

"Did you take the cap off, dummy?" McKenna mocked.

"Of course, I did," Stan snapped and then looked around at the front of the telescope to make sure he had.

"It's not broken Stan, it's just too bright in here. See how we can see our own reflections in the windows? The darkness outside makes the glass act as a mirror?" Kaylin pointed at their images reflected dimly in the windows and large glass door. "Can we turn off the light for a minute?" She asked.

No one answered. Finn must have taken the lack of a response as permission and flipped the switch. For a moment, the adults stopped arguing, and the room went silent. The soft thudding against the glass, a sound to which all had grown accustomed, slowed and then stopped.

"Guys, you should see this," Stan whispered.

They all gathered near the windows. As their eyes adjusted to the darkness of the room, the source of the noise from outside became clear. Dozens, perhaps hundreds of crows, their feathers shimmering in the flashes of lightning, lay broken and piled up on the widow's walk.

"I don't understand," said Babe. "How did they not break the glass?"

Nick rapped his knuckles against the window. And turned to answer Babe's question but fell mute. The words that covered the wall vanished in the darkness of the room. In their place, something else appeared—an image in phosphorescent paint.

"Maybe we should get out of here before those things get in," Stan said excitedly. The utterance snapping Nick out of his momentary daze.

"Relax; the glass is at least an inch thick. There's no way they're getting through it." Then, addressing Babe, "Are you seeing this?"

"It's the rivers," she said. "They're all connected."

"We have to get over to the clock shop and see if Merlyn can make us a key for this box. Will you kids be okay on your own?" Nick asked.

"We'll be fine," Frankie said, answering for the group.

"Okay," Nick said. "Say, Frankie, would you mind doing something for me?"

"Sure," said Frankie, his chest puffing up with pride. No one ever asked him for help, especially not grownups. If something needed to be done, people always asked Levi.

"I saw some boxes stacked in the garage."

"Yeah, my dad hasn't gotten around to burning them yet."

"Well, that's good because we need all of this stuff packed up. Do you think you guys can do that for me?"

"We sure can," Frankie said eagerly. It wasn't a big job, but it was still a job that a grownup asked him to handle.

Nick patted Frankie on the shoulder, "Thanks, Frank."

"It's Frankie."

"Frankie is a little kid's name; you seem more like a Frank to me."

Frankie beamed as Nick turned for the door and then stopped and pointed at Stan. "I'll be back for my dad's gun. You touch it, and you'll be digging my size 10 out of your ass. Are we clear?"

Stan nodded his understanding. "Yes, yes, sir."

"We'll be back as soon as we can, Frank; you tell your parents that I was here, okay?"

"Okay," said Frankie.

"I'm so sorry about your brother," said Babe.

"As am, I." Jinan placed a hand softly on the boy's cheek.

They made their way out to the driveway, and Nick turned to Jinan. "Thank you so much for bringing the key, Jinan."

"You're very welcome, but if you think you're ditching me that easy, you have another thing coming. I'm going wherever that box goes. Now, which one of us is driving?"

"Please," exclaimed Babe, let her drive. I can't go another mile in that hunk of shit."

"Gus? Gus is battle-hardened and more dependable than that Euro-trash," Nick said, nodding toward Jinan's Audi.

"The only thing battle-hardened are the callouses on my ass from riding in that thing. What do you say, Jinan, do you mind?"

"Not at all."

"Good," said Babe, "I got shotgun."

30

Jinan's Audi S6 turned left off of Sugar Maple Lane and right into the roadblock. The wiper blades swiped at the mist as the patrolman in his rain slicker approached, an orange coned flashlight waving in the air.

"Road's closed, folks, you'll have to go...."

Nick lowered his window. "Donnie? Donnie Marshall?"

"Nick! I thought you left us for the bright lights, you jerk-off."

"Sort of, but home is where the heart is, right?" Nick said.

"So, they say," replied Patrolman Marshall, the wind and the rain hitting his yellow slicker.

"I heard about the boy who drowned. Have you guys recovered the body yet?"

"Not yet; there's no sign of him. Hell, we can't even find the rowboat he went over in, and you know that stuff usually pops up pretty quick."

Nick felt his stomach roll.

"You okay, buddy? You look like you're gonna barf."

"Yeah," Nick said, dragging a hand over his face. "Fucking river."

"We almost made it a whole year," Donnie said.

"Say, how's Patrick? I heard he's with the Staties."

"Yeah, West Central Region 4. Mom and dad wanted him in 1, but he's running a task force, and he's not about to give that up."

"Where's the west-central region?"

"It's where the name says it is dip-shit. The western area of Central Illinois. How much did you pay for that fancy college education of yours anyway?"

"Too much."

"No shit, I never went to college, and I'm doing just fine. A waste of money, if you ask me."

"Yeah, anyway, do you think you could give me Pat's number? I'm doing some work down that way, and I might want to look him up."

Donnie pulled out a notepad and scribbled some numbers, and tore out a sheet. "Here you go buddy, I'm sure he'd love to hear from you."

"Thanks, say, any chance we can cross? I'm trying to get to Mr. Greer's shop."

"What the hell for? You in the market for an old clock?"

"No, my friend up there," he motioned toward Babe. "She's Merlyn's niece. They ain't seen each other in years."

Donnie Marshall ducked his head on a routine inspection, and his eyes locked onto Babe's short skirt. Nick cleared his throat, and Donnie bolted ramrod straight. "Go slow, and uh, stay in the center lane."

"Thanks, Donnie; say hi to your folks, and be careful; that kind of thing could blind you."

Donnie gave Nick a one-fingered salute. "Take care, Nick."

"You too, Donnie, be safe."

They turned onto Main Street and made their way to the clock shop.

"You are such a liar," Babe said.

"If anyone in the world can figure out how to unlock this box, Merlyn can. And if a little white lie gets us there, what's the harm? Besides, I didn't see you pulling your skirt down."

Jinan looked over, "What, what are you...."

"Just working with what God gave me," Babe said.

Jinan stopped in front of the clock shop. They got out of the car, and Nick noticed the broken glass on the sidewalk. He rushed into the store, almost knocking the bell off its hanger.

"Merlyn! Mr. Greer, where are you?" He yelled as he hurried through the shop.

Merlyn lay crumpled and unconscious on the floor behind his workbench. His head was cocked at a strange angle, having struck the wall on his way down. Dried blood caked the right side of his face from the nose down and collected in a small jellied pool on the floor.

"Oh my god," Nick gasped. "We need paramedics."

Merlyn began to wake. "Don't... need a medic," the words came out like they were being dragged over tree bark.

"What the hell happened? Someone rob you?" asked Nick.

"No, nothing like that," he said, the words coming a little more easily. "Just an unhappy customer."

"You want me to call the cops?" Nick asked.

"No, this is a matter for a higher authority, son. Besides, all the policemen are busy tonight with more important matters." Merlyn reached out his hand. "Give me a lift, would ya?"

"I don't think you should move him, Nick," cautioned Jinan.

Merlyn started lifting himself on one elbow. "Looks like he's getting up either way," Nick said as he locked an arm under Merlyn's and helped him into an old wooden chair next to a roll-top desk. "Thank you... Nick? Nick Ryan?"

"Yes, sir," he said and offered a warm smile.

Merlyn returned the smile. "What brings you back home, son? I heard you sold your folk's place. Seller's remorse?"

"Not exactly," Nick said, not wanting to get bogged down with small talk. "I need your help with something," he said and reached his hand toward Babe. Babe pulled the box from her bag and gave it to Nick. Merlyn's warm smile faded into something dark.

"Where did you get that?" His tone was harsh and accusatory. A trickle of blood ran from Merlyn's nose.

"Merlyn, you're nose; it's bleeding," Nick said, his concern genuine.

"Fuck my nose; I asked you a question." Merlyn pulled himself up out of the chair and squared to Nick. Nick stood there dumbfounded; he'd never known Merlyn to get angry, and it was beyond unsettling. Merlyn locked his pale blue eyes on Nick. "Don't make me ask you again, boy," he snarled.

Nick had four inches, fifty pounds, and the advantage of youth on his side, but still shrank in the old man's glare. There was something intimidating about men from Merlyn's generation. Men who had faced the brutal machinery of war returned home, not with tales of bravery but heads full of memories. Memories of death, either dealt by them or visited upon their friends. Merlyn exhaled hard, and blood spattered on the floor at Nick's feet.

"I got it from my father," Babe said urgently.

Merlyn spun and faced her. "Your father?" His voice boomed. "Who is your father?"

"My father was Abraham Adams." Unlike Nick, Babe showed no sign of fear. "He left me this box, and you look like you know something about it," she snapped.

Merlyn pulled hard at his goatee, once white with age now stained pink by his blood. "On the table, please," he said, nodding toward his workbench.

Babe looked at Nick, seeming to want him to make a decision. "I don't know what his connection is to the box, Babe, but I know we can trust him. He's a good man," Nick said. That seemed to be all she needed to hear as she placed the box on the table and stepped back.

"I haven't seen this box in thirty years," Merlyn said.

"What do you know about it?" Babe asked. "Can you tell us what's in it?"

"I know that it's evil, just like its rightful owner," Merlyn said, glancing around at the damage done to his shop.

"Gemein did this?" Babe said.

Merlyn's eyes widened with surprise. "You know him?"

"No, but I'm gonna kill him."

Merlyn's eyes narrowed, and Nick stepped in. "She doesn't mean that literally," he said, trying to fix her with a stare.

"The hell I don't!"

"Sir," said Jinan, her voice soft and disarming. "We believe this was box may be the key to understanding what happened to the Mooka'am. It is my belief that this box may have been used in a soul trapping ritual several hundred years ago."

"More recently than that, I bet," Babe said.

"A soul trapper," the words slipped in a whisper over Merlyn's lips. "Yes, that makes sense."

Nick's throat clicked. He tried to swallow, but his mouth had gone dry. "Do you think you could make a key to open it?"

"Open it; why the hell would you want to open it? If I were you, I would drop that thing into the deepest darkest hole I could find and forget all about it," Merlyn said and backed away from the box.

"We can't do that," said Babe. "We need to know what's in it," Babe said.

"No. You *want* to know what's in it. Believe me when I tell you; whatever is in that box is darker than Pozerac Gemein himself, and you need to stay away from him."

"Wait," said Jinan. "Is that the same Pozerac Gemein that you asked me to look into, Nick?"

"The very same," Nick said resolutely.

"Then there has to be some mistake." She put on her reading glasses, dug into the messenger bag she had been carrying, and pulled a file. "The only Pozerac Gemein I could find," she flipped some pages and found what she was looking for. "Yes, here it is. According to the records I could dig up, and mind you, they were the *only* records of anyone being named Pozerac Gemein, though he hadn't been given that name yet, say that he was a ward of the federal government. He was delivered by fur traders in 1739 to an orphanage in Natchez, Mississippi. We can assume that he was white because the orphanage only accepted the children of European parents. Some were the children of settlers killed by indigenous people, some were the product of rape, others orphaned by highwaymen."

"Please, Jinan, save the history lesson," Nick urged.

"Of course. As I was saying, the child was there for several years before being adopted by a wealthy German couple, Dubist and Ottilie Gemein. They named him Pozerac, and he obviously took their surname. Pozerac remained with the Gemeins for several years but was remanded back to the orphanage after the couple perished when their home burned. From there, he bounced from family to family but always ended up back in the orphanage. The last entry I was able to find was from 1749 when he was put out from the orphanage to fend for himself. So, as you can see, Mr. Gemein is long dead."

"He's not dead," Merlyn said.

"I'm sorry to be difficult, sir, but he would be over 250 years old. He is most certainly dead."

"I can assure you, he is very much alive," Merlyn said, not taking his eyes off the box. "Just take a look around my shop." Jinan studied the ruins. "All courtesy of Pozerac Gemein," said Merlyn.

"But that's impossible," Jinan challenged.

"My father always said anything is possible," Nick said, staring vacantly at the box. "I gotta tell you, I'm starting to think he was right."

"Well, call me a doubting Thomas, but I'm going to have to touch him to believe he's real. As for the other guy," Jinan flipped several more pages in the file. "Benjamin Shippen was a wealthy landowner. He lived his whole life in a town called Chesapeake Station, and, as you said, Nick, he served in the Korean Conflict. He made a fortune in farming and land dealings and left his millions to," she paused and looked at Babe, "Abraham Adams."

"That was my father," said Babe.

"You're rich?" Asked Jinan.

"I don't know, I guess," answered Babe dismissively. "Nick, we have to get this damned thing open and get back to Chesapeake Station and find Achak."

"That means spirit," offered Jinan.

"What means spirit?" Babe asked.

"Achak, it's Algonquin. It means spirit."

Babe smiled. "Well, Spirit's life is in danger. If Sheriff Tucker finds him, he's as good as dead."

"Whoa," said Jinan. "Slow down; why is he hiding from the sheriff?" She looked at the box. "Is that thing stolen? Because I can't be getting involved in any — and Nick, you shouldn't be either. Stealing antiquities; Nick, this isn't Indiana Jones; you could be in serious trouble."

"Calm down, it's not what you think — well, it's a little like what you think, but please, hear me out."

Jinan folded her arms and cocked her head. "You have one minute."

"Fair enough," said Nick. "According to Achak, his people, the Aakwaadizi, had been ordered to hunt down the last of the Mooka'am."

"Ordered, ordered by whom?"

"The French. The Mooka'am had been found guilty of devil worship and were said to have been responsible for unleashing an evil spirit called the Inaki on the world."

"That's utter nonsense," said Jinan. "Let's say they were a Satanic tribe. There were lots of tribes that worshiped gods other than the Christian god. I'm sure some tribes worshiped tree frogs. Why would that make the Mooka'am so hated?"

"Because," said Nick, but Babe finished his thought. "The Inaki harvests babies from their mother's wombs for ritualistic sacrifice."

Nick could feel the hairs on his neck stand up. "Merlyn, we have to get this box open. Can you do it?"

Merlyn turned to an old metal file cabinet and began rifling through folders toward the back.

"Yes, yes, here it is."

"What is it?" Asked Nick.

"These are the sketches I used the first time I made a key for this box. Gemein came into my shop with that very same box. I had no idea what it was. Had I known..."

"Can you make another?" Babe interrupted.

"Sure, but it's going to take some time."

"We don't have time," Babe said.

"Then you don't have a key," Merlyn replied sternly and then softened his tone. "Look, why don't you all go over to the No Finer and grab dinner while I work on this? I promise I will get it done as quickly as I can."

"What do you say, Babe?" Nick asked.

"I guess I could eat."

"So could I," said Jinan. "I rushed out here and hadn't stopped for dinner."

"I don't know," Babe said, "I feel funny about leaving the box with a stranger, and then quickly added, "No offense."

"None taken," Merlyn smiled. "How about you two go get food and bring it back here? Nick can stay and keep me company."

"Yeah," agreed Babe. "I guess that's fine. I mean, I can't just stand around here doing nothing. Besides, we really should have something in our stomachs besides pop and gas station candy."

"Leave it to Nick Ryan to know how to show a girl a good time," Jinan teased.

"You have no idea," Babe said. "Is that okay with you, Nick?"

"Sure," Nick replied.

"Oh, just one other thing." Babe patted her hips.

Nick rolled his eyes, dug his wallet out of his back pocket, and tossed it to her. "Don't go ordering steaks," he said smiled. "How about we do burgers all around?"

"I don't eat meat, but I'll find something," Jinan said as she and Babe turned to leave a small man in a black suit appeared in the doorway.

<h1 style="text-align:center">31</h1>

The council members filed back into the chamber, absent the leadership of Mayor Steel. In times past, Steel would remove his diminutive master's box and present it with a deep bow. A short, sacrilegious ceremony would follow. A gruesome mockery of the last supper, wherein Steel would place a wafer of baked human flesh on the tongue of each in attendance. Then he would raise a glass to Gemein. Again, each in attendance, save Gemein, would drink from a cup containing a deep-red port wine spiked with human blood. Once the ritual was complete, each member would meet privately with Pozerac Gemein to pay personal tribute.

At nightfall, all would gather at Consumption River for the final act of desecration. But the recent disemboweling of the town's mayor had left Chesapeake Station rudderless and her wealthy and powerful somewhat impotent.

All except for Terry Peterson, who found himself presented with an opportunity that, if he were totally honest with himself, he wasn't entirely sure he was ready for. But ready or not, the pieces were falling into place, and Terry was confident that Pozerac Gemein would install him as the new mayor of Chesapeake Station. As a matter of course, there would be an election, but, if named by Gemein, Peterson would run unopposed.

He would have the council's full support, and should a contender rise up out of the masses, Sheriff Tucker would see to the smearing of their good name. Terry Peterson would be moving from Easy Street to Lavish Lane, provided he could prove himself useful. Peterson knew he couldn't secure the return of the stolen box; he wouldn't even know where to begin looking.

But he could offer a fresh, new start with a robust and young administration that he would handpick—an administration that would make protecting Gemein's interests' job one. But first things first. Terry Peterson would have to find a scapegoat, someone he could blame for having been asleep at the switch when the crime occurred. Then, as a gesture, sure to curry favor with Gemein, Terry would kill them and deliver the body to Gemein. He would say that the person confessed, and he beat them to death in his rage at their failure to guard such a precious treasure. He knew he was capable, physically anyway, of beating any member of the council to death. The question was who. Who among them posed the greatest threat to his take-over?

The answer was obvious. Sheriff Tucker was the only other person who held any kind of sway over Chesapeake Station. People feared that fat bastard, and come to think of it, so did he. Beating one of the old dusters on the council to death would be a cakewalk, but Tucker, fat as he was, was a force to be reckoned with. Perhaps he could just frame the Sheriff and let Gemein disembowel him as he had Steel. Either way, it had to be Tucker, and step one in framing him was to haul Abernathy front and center before the council and Gemein.

"Murphy, where the hell is Abernathy?"

Half of Joe Murphy's face contorted into a look of pure contempt while the other maintained its usual doughy, servile half-smile. It was a look manageable by only schizophrenics and career politicians, but somehow, Murphy managed to pull it off.

"He said he was tending to a call and that he'd be right in. He asked if Tucker was somehow indisposed."

"And what did you tell him?" Peterson flared.

"Relax, Terry," Murphy squared his shoulders. "I told him not to worry about what Sheriff Tucker was doing and that we wanted to see him." His tone was less amiable, and all of the doughiness had left his face.

Peterson sensed a challenge to his authority. One that might encourage other council members to stir if not properly managed.

"Thank you very much, Joe. We're all going to have to pull together to get through this. I know I speak for the whole council when I say that it's great to have a man like you in our ranks," Peterson said and smiled approvingly.

Murphy's face turned beet red, and Terry Peterson knew he'd struck a direct hit. The SS Murphy was taking on water, and none of the other council members answered his distress call, seemingly content to let Terry Peterson claim the mantle of leadership. Peterson's smile went from approving to smug as Pozerac Gemein appeared in the council chambers' doorway.

"Have you worthless maggots located my box?"

Peterson's stomach dropped, and his bowels loosened as all eyes in the room fell to him for answers. *Where the hell was Abernathy*, he thought to himself. Gemein looked around the room and addressed Peterson directly.

"Seems the larva has appointed you as their leader. What say you?"

Peterson's mouth went dry, and it felt as if his tongue had swollen to the size of a beer can. He tried to swallow and was sure everyone heard the dry click. Then, as if by divine intervention, or at least that was the thought that popped into Peterson's head, Abernathy stepped into the chamber.

"You wanted to see me, Terry?"

He'd always been on a first-name basis with the deputy, but the man in charge couldn't have his underlings addressing by his first name.

"It's Mr. Peterson," he said in a scolding tone. "And, where the hell have you been?"

Deputy Abernathy's face contorted as he drew in a breath to speak, but Gemein held up a silencing hand and then whispered something into Abernathy's ear. Andrew Abernathy's eyes rolled back in his head and turned black. It was only for a moment, but Peterson caught it. Then Abernathy's eyes returned to normal, and he regarded Peterson with a ravenous look that made Terry Peterson think that he might have actually shit himself.

"Terry, you are addressing Chesapeake Station's new undersheriff, a position recently vacated by the late mayor," said Gemein.

"Um, well I," Peterson sputtered. "I just wanted to ask Deputy Abernathy,"

"Are you dense? It's Undersheriff Abernathy, dipshit, didn't you hear Mr.—"

"Gemein, son, Pozerac Gemein," said the little man.

Now it was Peterson who turned red, "I hardly think name-calling is needed in this situation," Peterson gently corrected.

"No, you're right. What's needed is a council who can do the one simple job Mr.," Abernathy paused, careful to get the name right. "Mr. Gemein has given you!"

"Well now, Andy, to be fair, it really is more complicated than that. You see, we have more than one job...." Beatrice Kibling was the council's oldest member, but that didn't seem to impress Abernathy.

"Beatrice, shut the fuck up. It is one job. And that job is to protect Mr. Gemein's interests in this town. If you can't do that, what fucking good are any of you?" The veins on Abernathy's neck stood out in cords.

"Oh," Gemein purred through a crooked smile. "It seems I have picked the right man for the job. Wouldn't you all agree?"

The chamber remained tomb still.

"One fucking job, people!" Peterson parotid. A pitiful attempt at mattering, and he knew it, but he was in it now. "If you can't do one job, what good are any of you?"

The faces in the room could only be read as embarrassed. Not for the piss-poor job they had done but embarrassed for Peterson.

Terry Peterson was in danger of being rendered obsolete, so he chose his next words carefully.

"Mr. Gemein, you have made a wonderful choice. Abernathy will make a perfectly wonderful undersheriff. Only...,"

"Only what?" Gemein asked, tenting his fingers.

Peterson hadn't forgotten that fat ass Tucker had something planned to curry favor with Gemein, and Peterson had to do something to let some of the air out of that big balloon if his plan were to have any hope of succeeding.

"Well, he has been under the tutelage of the man in charge when your box was stolen." He paused, concerned that he might have insulted Gemein with his choice of words. But with no response from the dark little man and Abernathy not raising an eye at the insinuation made against Tucker, Peterson continued. "I am quite sure young Abernathy will perform admirably as the Under Sheriff to Sheriff Tucker and continue to dispense justice with a firm hand. But, as for the office of mayor, I should think you might want a more nuanced approach in dealing with the public," he finished his statement with a slight bow of the head.

"What I want, Mr. Peterson is a competent worm. Perhaps a man like you."

"Like me?" Peterson said, feigning surprise. "Why I would be honored, sir."

But Gemein went no further, leaving the council members, and especially Peterson, in anticipation.

"Clear the room. I want to speak with the newly appointed Undersheriff of Chesapeake Station," Gemein said and waved a dismissive hand.

Everyone got up and left, but Grover Horn, the Agri-Grow representative, stopped just outside the chamber door. Horn was slower on the draw than Peterson, but he wasn't one to leave his cheese out in the wind.

"Horn, let's go, you heard Mr. Gemein." Peterson stood, arms folded and impatient.

"In a minute Terrence." Horn cleared his phlegmy throat. "Mr. Gemein, if you're taking names to consider for mayor of Chesapeake Station, I would like to throw my hat in the ring. I believe you would find me quite useful."

***

Gemein waved his hand again, and the door slammed shut in Grover Horn's face. "Son-of-a-bitch, my nose! He broke my fucking nose!" Horn screamed on the other side of the door.

"Do you think that pejorative was directed at me?" Gemein asked earnestly."

"No, Mr. Gemein, I'm sure it was directed at the universe as a whole, sir."

"Andrew, may I call you Andrew?"

"Of course, Mr. Gemein," Andrew Abernathy replied, not sounding the least bit sycophantic.

"Good," hissed the old phantom. "I see big things in your future, son. Oh, I'm sure I will appoint Peterson mayor, but the true power will rest in you and Sheriff Tucker. And on the subject of the latter, Peterson, bootlicker that he is, makes a valid point. What of his role in the disappearance of my box?"

"I wouldn't presume to know, sir."

Gemein smiled. "There, my boy, you see? You are loyal and wise. Wise enough to know what you don't know. Perhaps you would be better suited for Tucker's job than he is," Gemein rubbed his chin in contemplation.

Andrew Abernathy grinned ear to ear like an idiot, seemingly unable to help himself.

"I see that pleases you," Gemein said rhetorically. "How old are you, my boy?"

"I'm twenty-six, sir," he replied, still smiling.

"Ha!" The laugh escaped Gemein, surprising himself and the young undersheriff. "That is wonderful. Here is my offer." Pozerac Gemein waved a hand over a chair. "Please, sit."

Abernathy sat down, and Gemein walked behind him and placed his hands on Andrew's shoulders. "My offer to you, young man, is riches and power beyond your wildest dreams, so long as you continue to... how did you put it? Oh yes, protect my interests in this town. Now how does that sound?"

"I'm your man, sir," again, not sounding the least bit obsequious.

"Gemein clapped his hand together. "Oh, that is wonderful. Of course, the first order of business is locating my stolen box. Can I count on you?" He asked.

With steely determination in his eyes, Andrew Abernathy replied. "Mr. Gemein, I don't have the slightest idea where to even begin looking, but rest assured, if the box is on this planet, I will find it."

"Oh, yes!" Gemein exclaimed and clapped his hands together again. "That is wonderful. I have certainly made the right choice in you, Andrew."

"I won't let you down, sir."

"What do you say we call the others back in and put them in their proper places?"

"I'm on it, Mr. Gemein." Abernathy got up and went to the door. "Get your asses back in here." He ordered.

The council members grumbled but entered the room and returned to their seats, all except for Peterson, who stopped to confront the young lawman.

"Just who the hell do you think you are, you little piss ant?"

Andrew Abernathy drew his baton with lightning speed and jabbed the butt end into Peterson's gut, driving the big man to his knees. Peterson made raspy, squeaky sounds as he struggled to draw breath.

"Bravo, Andrew!" Cheered Gemein. "Bravo indeed, but we mustn't disable our new mayor. Not unless he gives us a reason," he said dryly.

"Thank you, Mr. Gemein," croaked Peterson. "I won't let you down, sir."

Unlike Abernathy, Peterson was a true boot licker, and his cloying sentiment dripped with unfettered devotion.

"Gentlemen, and my dear Beatrice Kibling. This has been a truly disappointing day. The one bright spot it seems is the appointment of our new Under-Sheriff," he said, giving Abernathy an acknowledging nod. "Andrew, I trust you will inform Sheriff Tucker?"

"You can count on me, sir."

"Oh, I know I can," Gemein beamed like a proud father and then turned with a sneer toward Terry Peterson. "You will be mayor in name, but you will run the town as it pertains to my interests, with council from Sheriff Tucker and Under-Sheriff Abernathy. Do what you will with the rest of the town's business." Gemein stood up and waved at the chamber doors, which flew open. "Now, leave me. We will gather later along the Consumption River and see if we cannot salvage this visit."

32

The man in the black suit tipped his Red Hook Rivermen ball cap at Jinan and Babe. "Afternoon, ladies." Hank Storgul was Merlyn's oldest friend. Hardly a day went by that he didn't stop in to chew the fat with the clock maker.

"Good afternoon," replied Babe. Jinan was still sizing him up as he walked past them into the shop.

"Merlyn! Your shop is wrecked."

"You don't say," called Merlyn from back near the counter.

"What the hell happened here?"

Merlyn ignored the question and went about smoothing out the drawings on his work table. "Say, Hank, look who came to pay us a visit!"

"Nick, what brings you home?"

Nick extended a hand, and Hank clamped down and shook it with vigor. "Mr. Storgul, it's so nice to see you."

"I'm sure it is, boyo, but you didn't answer my question."

"Well, me and the ladies," he pointed to the door, but Babe and Jinan were gone. "Anyway, we came to see if Mr. Greer could open this box for us."

"What's in it?" Hank jabbed at it, making a thudding sound with his cane.

"Won't know that until we get it open," Nick replied.

Hank's eyes flared. "So, it's a mystery—sure do love a good mystery. Not many of them left when you get to be my age, well other than how many times I'm going to get up at night to piss." He laughed at his own joke; Merlyn just rolled his eyes.

"What say we meet up at the No Finer in about an hour? I have to get this done for the kids.”

“Good a plan as any,” said the old codger. “I’m gonna walk over to the newsstand and grab the Courier. Let me know what you find in there.”

“Will do,” said Merlyn.

Hank waved back over his head. “Your windows are broken too!” He called back over his shoulder.

“I’m aware, Hank, thank you.”

Merlyn picked up the pieces of the broken key. “I’ve been working on this one to let the new people up into your father’s room, but,” he held a piece in each hand. “I ran into a snag.”

Nick pulled his key from his pocket. “That won’t be necessary; this is the key to my dad’s room.”

Merlyn reached out and took it. “I remember making this and the matching lock for your old man,” sadness washed over Merlyn’s face. “Well,” he said, perking up. “That’s going to save us some time.”

Merlyn slid open a drawer on the metal file cabinet under his work table and ran a finger over the files. “Here it is!”

He held the folded blueprint triumphantly overhead and then spread it out on his workbench. Old key blanks hung on a pegboard. Before Tom and Kim Ahern opened the Ace Hardware in town, Merlyn managed a reasonably steady key-cutting business. The work was tedious; he had to make each cut using hand tools better suited for working on clocks, and he was glad to lose the extra business to the Aherns. Merlyn pulled four skeleton blanks off the board, set the first key in the vise, and removed the head. He repeated the process four times, leaving the last bow and stem in the vise as the new key’s body. After cutting each head to match his drawings, he welded the heads to the pin and carefully ran a file over the welds, cleaning them up. Merlyn finished up just as the girls walked back into the shop with dinner. He held the key out to Nick. Nick took hold of it, but the clock maker’s grip was as firm as his vise.

“Are you sure you want to know what’s inside that box?”

“I think so,” Nick said as he took the key.

“You think so; what?” Babe asked.

"Merlyn finished the key," he said and held it out to show Babe.

"We're sure we want to do this, right? Once we turn this key, there's no going back," he held Babe's gaze. "We have to deal with whatever is inside this box."

Babe chewed her lower lip. "I have been so focused on opening this damned thing that I never considered the reasons not to open it."

"Well," said Merlyn, "I can give you one reason, and it's a damned good one. Pozerac Gemein. He's an evil man, and you want to stay off his radar. Left me for dead, and I'm pretty sure he liked me. I can't imagine what he would do to the person who stole his box. Now, I don't know either of you ladies, but I would sure hate to see you come to harm. Nick, I've known you your whole life. Son, you have been through a lot, and you're stronger than most; I know that, but you don't know what you're up against. Evil took your father and dragged him down a deep dark hole. Don't let it do the same to you."

Nick smiled. "I appreciate your concern, and I appreciate the friendship you shared with my father, but I think this is something we have to do." Looking at Babe, Nick said, "It's your call. Like I said, I'm with you till the end."

"We have to do it; if there's a way to stop this guy, we have to try."

"I think you should be the one to turn the key," said Nick.

"No, wait," said Jinan. "You can't open it!"

"The hell I can't. I already told you...."

Jinan held her hands up, showing that she posed no threat. "No, I simply meant that you can't open it here."

"What do you mean 'not here'?" Nick asked.

"It has to be opened where the person died. Otherwise, according to folklore anyway, their spirit will be left to roam the earth looking for its resting place."

"Chesapeake Station, the islet," said Babe. "Then we have to get back there now.

Nick reached into his pocket and fished out the piece of paper Donnie Marshall had given him.

"Merlyn, mind if I use your phone?"

"Help yourself. It's right over there," Merlyn jutted a thumb toward the desk as he disappeared into the back room of his shop.

Nick dialed State Trooper Patrick Marshall's number. He answered on the second ring.

"Pat, it's Nick—Nick Ryan—yeah, I'm good, listen, I need your help—" Nick filled him in on the details as they pertained to a possible satanic cult and Jessica Upshaw, choosing to leave out all of the supernatural. He thanked him profusely and had just hung up when Merlyn reappeared from the back room.

"Here it is, my Colt M1911. I used it to kill those damned Gooks, and now I'll use it to kill Gemein, that son-of-a-bitch."

"Merlyn," said Nick. "We're actually going to need you to do something."

"Name it, son."

"After you board your windows up, can you please get over to my—I mean, the Waters' place and keep an eye on the kids there? The older boy—"

"Levi," said Merlyn. "That's right," Nick continued. "Levi drowned today."

Merlyn slumped back against the wall. "God, no. I just spoke with him."

"You knew the Waters boys?"

Merlyn dragged his hand down his face and tugged at his goatee. "I only just met them."

Nick could see the far-away look in the old man's eyes. "I'm sorry, Merlyn."

Merlyn didn't speak: she just held up a hand in acknowledgment.

"Merlyn, I think Frankie and the other kids may be in real danger."

"What other kids?"

"I don't know, just some neighborhood kids, I think. They were at the house with him," Nick paused. "His parents are down at the river, probably identifying their son's body."

Merlyn picked up the phone and dialed. "Just let me call over to the No Finer—hello, Rhonda? Merlyn—no, I'm fine, the store just got a little busted up—right, well, that's kind of why I'm calling. Would you be a doll and ask Hank if he could swing over and board up my windows? I got some plywood and a hammer and nails in the back of my shop, stuff I use for shipping—right; thank you, darlin."

Merlyn hung up the phone. "Okay, I'm ready.

"Thank you, Merlyn, Me, and Babe; we have to get back to Chesapeake Station."

"I'm coming with you, Nick," said Jinan.

"Are you sure?"

"I'm sure."

Nick smiled a soft, sad smile. Fearless, beautiful Jinan, ready to jump into the fray without the slightest hesitation.

"You can count on me, Nick," Merlyn said. "I'm going to right my wrong."

"Merlyn, you did nothing wrong," Nick assured him.

"I made a key for that damned box."

"You didn't know what the box was for, Mr. Merlyn," said Babe, placing a hand on his forearm. And then, through clenched teeth, "But if Gemein shows up there and tries to hurt those kids, you put a bullet in his fucking brain."

"And one through his heart, for good measure," added Merlyn, following them out of the store.

Nick, Babe, and Jinan all piled back into her Volvo, and Merlyn followed them over the Main Street Bridge where Donnie Marshall, still on duty, waved them through. At the bottom of the bridge, where Main Street intersected with Sugar Maple Lane, Merlyn signaled right and turned his Olds 442 toward the Waters' house.

33

A s soon as the grownups left, Stan told Finn to kill the lights. Slowly their eyes adjusted to the darkness. Stan licked his lips, picked up the rifle and looked out across the river toward the Ironweiler's house. "Guys, check this out. It's that crow again."

"Stan! Mr. Ryan told you not to touch that thing!" McKenna stomped a foot and clutched her hands at her sides like an angry little girl in a newspaper comic.

"What crow? Let me see." Finn grabbed the rifle from his brother.

"Hey! Slow down jerk, you don't just grab a rifle from somebody. That's how accidents happen!"

Finn swept the rifle up and looked through the scope. "Holy crap, he's right."

The mottled old bird sat in the gable window, craning its neck to fix one unblinking black eye back across the river on the upper room's windows. Finn turned rifle in hand and addressed the room. "It's the same crow Levi nailed with the river rock."

The barrel of the rifle was pointed right at Frankie. Stan grabbed the barrel of the gun and thrust it up toward the ceiling.

"What the fuck, Finn! You could have blown Frankie away!"

"Oh my god! Put that thing down, you idiot!" Kaylin screamed.

Finn blinked vacantly, "I'm—I'm sorry, Frankie—I."

But if Frankie heard him, he didn't respond. Frankie had his eye pressed up against the telescope's eyepiece as he peered across the river.

"Sorry, that's all you have to say?" McKenna was fuming.

"Relax, nothing happened," Stan said.

"Nothing happened? Are you insane?"

"Guys, forget about that!" Frankie said.

"McKenna, you can be a real—," Stan was going to say bitch but the sight of his sister, standing a good three inches taller than him, with her fist drawn back, caused him to sputter after the - b.

"So help me, Stanley Howard, if you say bitch, I'm going to split your lip." McKenna clenched her jaw and pulled her fist back a little further.

Stan recoiled ever so slightly and looked around uncomfortably to see if anyone had noticed the flinch, but Kaylin had drawn the group's attention.

"Guys, guys! There's something wrong with Frankie."

McKenna pushed past her brother and flew to Frankie's side. He sat on the floor next to the telescope and panted heavily. He retched a couple of times but had nothing in his stomach to throw up.

"Oh my God, Frankie. What's wrong?"

Stupid Finn almost blew his head off! That's what's wrong," Stan said, hoping to take the spotlight off of himself.

"Shut up, Stan! I said I was sorry."

"Both of you shut up," McKenna ordered as she knelt next to Frankie. "Is that what's wrong, Frankie?" She asked tenderly."

Frankie shook his head. "Then what?" McKenna stroked his hair. "Take your time; tell us when you're ready."

"We have to kill that bird," he whispered.

"Why, Frankie?" McKenna asked.

Frankie suddenly felt like he needed to swallow but seemed to have forgotten how. He tried to work the muscles in his throat, but they only seemed to tighten, cutting off his airway. Frankie's mouth fell open and worked to stretch itself wider in a desperate attempt to draw air. His eyes blinked wide, filled with terror.

"Move!" Finn dropped to his knees and shoved McKenna aside. "I know what to do!" He slammed the heel of his hand between Frankie's shoulder blades causing Frankie to lunge forward and suck in a long raspy breath of air. "There, see," Finn smiled. "Good as new."

McKenna scrambled up off of her ass and pushed her brother aside. "Frankie, oh my God, Frankie!" She pulled him to herself and hugged him fiercely. "You scared the shit out of me!"

"Jeez, you sound like his mother," Finn said.

McKenna didn't respond; she didn't have to. "Shut up, asshole," Kaylin said. "She's just worried about him, and you should be too. We all should be. He's been through a lot today."

"I'm sorry," Finn said.

"You're always sorry," Kaylin snapped. "Maybe try thinking before you do shit. Then you might not have to apologize so often."

Finn opened his mouth to say something, but nothing came out.

"Why do we have to kill that bird, Frankie?" McKenna asked softly.

Frankie closed his eyes and shivered; he could still see the old crow staring back at him. Pale yellow larva pulsing in the folds of skin surrounding a deep black hole that seemed to fill the telescope's eyepiece. Down in that blackness, flashes of dark crimson, and though he couldn't explain it, he knew that one of those flashes was Levi. Trapped forever in that pit.

"I think he needs some sleep," Kaylin said.

Frankie opened his eyes. "I don't need sleep; I need to kill that fucking bird."

The group seemed stunned at the use of the expletive. Not because they hadn't heard the word before, but because it came out of Frankie.

"Why, Frankie, why do you have to kill the bird?"

"Remember how Father Guerin was talking about how our souls go to Heaven? He said that only those two guys—the really old guys. They didn't have to die."

"Enoch and Elijah," Finn offered.

"Look at the big Bible brain on Finn," Stan said mockingly.

"Shut up, Stan."

"Yeah, them," Frankie continued. "They were the only people who got to go to Heaven without dying. Father said that the rest of us have to die, but that when we die, our souls go to Heaven, and when Jesus comes back, they're renited—"

"Reunited," Kaylin corrected.

"Yeah, reunited," Frankie continued. "Reunited with our bodies. Well, if there was something that could keep someone's soul, I don't know, like trap it, like in a bottle or something and keep it from going to Heaven—then it couldn't be re-u—"

"Reunited," McKenna said again.

"Yeah, reunited— with their bodies, and then they could never go to Heaven."

"I don't understand; what does that have to do with—"

"Jeez, don't be so dense. Frankie is saying that the old crow across the river trapped Levi's soul." As soon as the words were out of his mouth, Stan's face twisted into pained confusion. "Wait, is that what you're saying?"

"Not just Levi. I think it has that other kid too."

"What kid?" McKenna asked.

Frankie drew in a deep breath. "Remember when we went to that house," Frankie started.

"The murder house?" Finn asked.

"Of course, the murder house, dummy. What other house would he be talking about?"

"Shut up, Stan, and let him talk," Kaylin sounded annoyed.

"It started that night, and it happened again last night too." Frankie swallowed hard. "There's a little boy; I think it's the boy who lived in that house, the boy who Mr. Ryan said drowned. He came into our room and stood next to Levi's bed. Both times Levi was sleeping, and he didn't see him, but the boy was dripping wet like he just came out of the water. He was leaning over Levi and whispering something to him while he was asleep."

"No, shit?"

"No shit, Finn. Then the boy turned toward me. I dunno; maybe he realized I was watching him. Anyway, he held out his hands like he needed help, and then he opened his mouth, and water came pouring out," Frankie paused.

"Then what happened?" Finn asked.

Frankie looked at his feet. "I just pulled my covers over my head and hid. I hid like a scared little kid," he said and then slowly raised his eyes to face the gang. "But I'm not scared anymore." His sad eyes had taken on a hardness. "And I know what you guys are thinking. Maybe it was just a bad dream, but it wasn't. Dreams don't leave puddles on the floor. I think he's a ghost, and he lives in the river, and his soul is trapped in that bird. I think if we can kill that bird, the little boy's soul will be freed, and it can go to Heaven like it was supposed to. And Levi too."

"Holy crap, guys, a dead kid living in the river? That's a better story than sneaking into the Never Close!"

"Stan! You are such an asshole!"

The rest of the group shook their heads disapprovingly. It seemed everyone shared Kaylin's sentiment.

"I—I'm sorry, Frankie; guys, I'm really sorry. I guess I just keep expecting to see Levi come walking into the room." He sat down on the window ledge and shook his head. "None of this shit seems real."

"It's okay Stan, I know you didn't mean anything by it."

"No, Frankie, it's not okay," McKenna said. "My brother is an asshole, and he always gets a pass. I'm sick of it!"

Stan sat silent, looking gut-punched.

"It *is* okay, McKenna. All that matters right now is killing that crow and freeing Levi. Then we can worry about that little kid and whoever else might be trapped because of that thing."

"Let's shoot it," Finn said.

Stan's eyes widened. "I'll do it!"

"Bullshit, it was my idea!"

"Are you two, nuts or something?" McKenna scolded.

"Come on, guys, she's right. We can't shoot a gun. What if we miss it? Where's the bullet going to go?" Kaylin said, attempting to reason with a couple of stupid boys.

"You got a better idea?" Finn challenged.

"Shut up, and let me think." Stan's eyes narrowed. "Okay, here's what we gotta do. Frankie, you McKenna and Kaylin find stuff you can use as weapons."

"What kind of stuff?" Kaylin asked.

"Stuff like baseball-bats, and, and... I don't know, just stuff to kill that crow. Me and Finn are going back to our house to get supplies. Finn, while I'm getting stuff together, you run and get Stevie and Lonnie. Tell Lonnie that we need to borrow his old man's boat. He'll know what to do. Then we'll all meet down on the dock.

***

Finn took off running, and it wasn't long before Stan lost sight of him. Stan was a lean kid, and he had good wind, but there was no way he could keep up with Finn. He'd never seen anyone who could run as fast as his brother, at least not until he saw Kaylin bolt up the hill from the riverbank to go for help. As he reached his house, he could feel his heart pounding in his chest. He burst through the front door and shot up the stairs to his bedroom.

"Is that you, kids?" His mother sounded worried.

"It's me, mom," he called down.

"Oh, thank almighty God, I heard there was another drowning in the river," then, with the fear back in her voice. "Where are your brother and sister?"

"They're at Frankie's house," he yelled from his room as he dumped the contents of his new bookbag on his bed and ran back down the stairs.

"It's a school night. Where do you think you're going?"

Stan stopped, set his bookbag down, walked over to his mother, and hugged her. She hugged him back, and Stanley Howard broke down.

"What is it, sweetheart?"

Stan calmed himself enough to speak. "It was Levi, mom; we were going to Gerts, and the storm blew in, and Levi went over the dam. We were able to save Frankie, but—," he buried his face in his mother's bosom and began sobbing again.

"My poor angels, oh, and that poor Mrs. Waters! How could God let this happen?" Get yourself together, and I'll drive you back there. We have to *do* for that family."

"Mr. and Mrs. Waters went down to the dam. She asked us to stay with

Frankie till she got back."

"Then, I'll drop you there," she said as she grabbed her keys off the key hook.

"Do you think you could just head to the dam? I need a few minutes, and I want to walk back, so they don't know I was crying."

"Stanley Howard, crying is nothing to be ashamed of. You're a good boy, and you should be crying. It's perfectly natural."

"Thanks, mom, I just need a few minutes, and I'll be okay."

"Well, if you're sure."

"I am, mom."

Beth Howard kissed her son's cheek. "You take all the time you need. I'm going to see to Mr. and Mrs. Waters."

Stan watched his mother walk out the front door with her purse in the crook of her arm and her keys jingling merrily in her hand. Once he composed himself, Stan ran out to the Stan-cave, tossed his backpack on his workbench, and began gathering supplies. He grabbed two handfuls of flares, remembering how their flashlights failed in that house. Next, Stan spooled up about fifty feet of rope and shoved that into his pack. There were a few other odds and ends, and then, he grabbed Baby-go-boom. He looked at the stupid doll and checked the wick sticking out of it. Stan tugged lightly on the wick and found that the wax was still holding it in place. He picked up a box of wooden matches and gave it a shake. *Almost full from the sound of it*, he thought. As he crammed the last items into his bag, he heard the sound of a boat motor growing louder, and he hurried out to meet it.

"Did you have any trouble getting the boat?"

"No," said Lonnie. "Our mom and dad are down at the dam.

Stan tossed his overstuffed backpack into the boat and climbed aboard. Lonnie gave it the gas, and the boat tore downriver toward the Waters' place.

"Did you guys find weapons?" Stan asked.

"Yeah," said Lonnie as he held up a hatchet. Stevie waved a claw hammer in the air.

Lonnie brought the boat to a soft landing against the Waters' dock and waited as Frankie, McKenna, and Kaylin boarded.

"Did you guys find weapons?" Stan asked.

"Yeah," said Frankie, holding up a tennis racket.

"What the hell are you going to do with a tennis racket?"

"I don't know, Stan; I've never gone after a crow before."

McKenna rested an old Louisville Slugger Fence Buster over her shoulder, and Kaylin held a pair of hedge shears with worn wooden handles.

"What about you, Stan? What did you get?" Stevie asked.

Stan reached into his bag and pulled out Baby-go-boom. "If we can't beat it, chop it or racket it to death, I'm going to blow the shit out of it."

The small company aboard the boat let out a cheer, and Stan's heart lifted. Lonnie had to cut the wheel hard to port and give her the gas to make headway against the strong current, even with the big engine. Above them, the crows continued their attack against the unbreakable glass that made up the strange room's river-facing wall above Frankie Waters' garage. Lonnie steered the boat alongside what was left of the Ironweiler's dock and throttled back hard against the rushing water to hold her steady while Finn and Stevie tied her off.

"I hate this stupid river," said Frankie, as he jumped out of the boat and started for the house.

"Hang on," said Lonnie. "Someone should probably stay with my dad's boat."

"You can stay with the boat; I got a bird to kill."

Frankie tightened his grip on the tennis racket and started for the house. The rest of the group exchanged glances and took off after Frankie.

"Wait up, Frankie!" Lonnie called and ran to catch up with the group.

As soon as they reached the tree line, all went black. Weak, flashes of lightning fell in hazy shafts through the canopy of trees above them but didn't quite make it to the ground.

"Did anyone bring a flashlight?" Asked Lonnie.

"I grabbed one," said Kaylin, "but I don't think it's gonna work once we get in the house. Remember?"

"Well, it should work out here," said Stan. "I brought something else for the house."

Kaylin clicked the flashlight on and shined it around. The branches and ground cover wrapped in and out of itself, looking like a spider's web made of vegetation. She redirected the light, passed the beam over the group, and let out a stunted scream dropping the light as it passed over Frankie.

"What the hell was that all about?" Asked Lonnie.

Kaylin scrambled for the flashlight and directed it at Frankie, "I thought I saw something, but whatever it was, it's gone."

"What did you see? Asked Finn, with a tremble in his voice.

"Nothing," she said. "Sorry."

Kaylin pointed the light overhead, where black objects streamed endlessly toward the room above the garage.

"Guys," she said. "They're still coming."

As they all looked up, several birds broke rank and dove for the source of the light. The canopy of branches and leaves above them seemed to weave together in a vast tangle, but several red-eyed crows made it through. Stan dove onto the ground as one of the birds slashed at the back of his head. Stevie swung the hatchet in a horizontal arc, missing the bird completely. Lonnie pushed his brother aside and swung his hammer, catching nothing but air.

"Move, guys!" Frankie delivered a solid forehand and cracked the bird good and hard with his tennis racket. Another bird hovered, looking for a point of attack, as Kaylin snapped her hedge trimmer at the bird and managed to hold it at bay. Frankie caught it with a backhand, sending the bird careening to the ground. The final bird came diving at McKenna, who smashed the thing with her Fence Buster.

"Is everyone okay?" Frankie asked.

They all checked themselves and each other for any signs of injury. "I think we're all good, Frankie," said Kaylin.

The group's attention was called upward again as beaks and claws snapped and scratched at the snarled branch canopy overhead. Glowing red eyes peered down through every tiny gap in the entanglement.

Stan felt something hit his cheek.

"Kaylin, shine that light over here," he said.

She turned toward Stan, who held his finger to the light and saw that it was blood.

"Guys," he held his finger out to show the group, but it wasn't necessary. A shower of feathers and droplets of blood began to rain down from above.

"Kaylin, turn it off!" Stan shouted. "They're attracted to the light!"

She turned the light off, and they all stood silently and waited. Slowly, the commotion subsided.

"Here," said Stevie, handing Kaylin a red Holsum Bread bag and a rubber band. "Pull that over the light and rubber-band it."

"What's this supposed to do?" Asked Kaylin.

"That's what we do when we go worming with our dad. I guess worms can't see the red light."

"That's great," said McKenna, "but we're not hiding from worms."

"Shit, I don't know. Maybe it won't work, but it's worth a try," Stevie said.

"It's a good idea, "said Stan.

"Where'd you get it?" Finn asked. "You always carry a Holsum bread bag and rubber band with you?"

"Ha, ha, very funny. I got it at my house. I just dumped the bread on the counter. My mom is gonna be pissed."

"Nice going, dipshit," said Lonnie. "Now our bread is going to get all hard."

"Guys, can we forget about the bread?" Asked Frankie.

With the red lens covering the light, the crows didn't seem to notice them.

"Here," said Stevie, offering his hatchet to Frankie. "Wanna trade?"

Frankie smirked, "What do you think?"

They carefully made their way up the path, with Frankie and Kaylin leading the way, and reached the clearing. The house stood just ahead. Stan knew that houses weren't living things, but that didn't stop this one from looking dead. Even in the rain, the gray slat-boards looked like dried bones. The windows on the second floor, free of their glass — targeted over the years by disrespectful children with rocks — stared like dead, vacant, and sightless eyes into the night. And above the second floor, in the gable window, stood the weathered, leathery sentinel.

As they neared the path to the back door, the guardian of the Ironweiler's death house cocked its head and turned its unblinking black eye on its unwelcome visitors. A flash of lightning that spiderwebbed across the sky allowed anyone watching to see the crow step, not jump or hop or even fly, but step back into the darkness, and a chill ran down Stan's spine.

34

Merlyn pulled into the Waters' driveway right behind Nick's old Bronco and killed the engine. He sat there a moment, remembering the lovely young man he'd just met, and was sad to think that he was gone. He remembered the conversation he'd had with Levi. All about how it didn't matter that he didn't know how to swim. Merlyn wished he could have that conversation again. He would tell him how he was wrong. How it did matter, especially if you were going to live next to a fucking river. He opened his door and proceeded up the walkway to the front door. He tried knocking softly first, knowing how jarring an unexpected doorbell could be. When that failed to get a response, he knocked harder, but still, there was no answer. Hesitantly, Merlyn placed his thumb on the doorbell and pressed. The chimes rang out in the Waters' house, and Merlyn was sure it was heard by all inside. After waiting a full minute, he rang the bell again and added a firm knock for good measure. Still, no answer, and Merlyn felt his stomach drop. He tried the knob, and the door opened wide.

"Frankie? It's Mr. Greer, from the clock shop. Where are you, son?"

He walked through the house and stopped at what he presumed was the boys' room, but there was no sign of him. Kitchen, living room, family room, and even Scott and Connie's room, but there was no sign of Frankie or the other kids. Merlyn walked out into the backyard. About halfway down to the water, he clamped a hand to his forehead.

"Merlyn, you old fool. The kids probably took Frankie over to one of their houses."

He turned and started walking toward his car when he smelled cigarette smoke. Merlyn sniffed at the air. "Couldn't blame the kid," he said and followed the smell to the garage.

"Frankie? You in there, Frankie?" He called from the door, and just like the house, there was no response.

The smell was definitely coming from inside the garage. Merlyn poked his head in and hit the light switch. A quick flash and snap from the light and all fell back into darkness. Merlyn pulled a small penlight out of his pocket and shined it around the garage, looking for a breaker box. He found the panel next to the stairs that went up to the loft. He checked the breakers, but none seemed to be popped. He flicked the switch a few more times. Clicks, but no light. *Power outage?* He thought, but when he looked back at the main house, the lights were still on. He shined his light up the stairs and saw that the door was open. *Maybe they're hiding.* He could still smell the cigarette smoke.

"Frankie, are you up there?" And again, there was no response. "Frankie, I don't care about the smoking, son. I just want to make sure you're okay. Frankie?"

He reached the landing and pointed his penlight into the room, but the damned thing went out.

"Frankie, it's Mr. Merlyn, the clock guy. Remember? I showed you and—Levi," the name caught in his throat, "how to wind the clock."

He pushed the door open wide enough to fit through and instinctively felt along the wall for the light switch, forgetting that there was no power.

"Frankie, if you're in here, please say something, son. I just want to make sure you're okay."

He was suddenly aware of a soft thumping, not unlike an arrhythmic heartbeat, coming from across the room. Several small flashes of lightning lit the outside, and Merlyn discovered the source of the thumping sounds.

"Well, I'll be." He watched as dozens of black crows flew themselves into the windows of the second-floor overlook. "In all my days."

Noticing the telescope, he was drawn like a boy of twelve to want to look through it. Merlyn pressed his eye to the eyepiece and looked out into the darkness.

"Crap, it's too dark to see anything," he said and was about to back away when a second and much brighter flash of lightning lit the entire Red Hook River Valley.

A huge black crow sitting in the gable's window on the Ironweiler's house filled his view. Merlyn could see that the bird was fixed on something below. He tilted the barrel down where a beam of light bounced along the ground. As he watched the bouncing light, another flash brightened the night.

"Oh my God."

The Howard kids, the Johnson boys, Kaylin Vaughn and Frankie Waters, were all walking from the boat dock toward the Ironweiler's house.

Merlyn ran for the glass door to try and shout over the river to get their attention. As his hand reached the handle, the garage's lights flickered to life and turned the glass into a giant mirror. Merlyn pushed against the carpet of dead crows, but he couldn't budge the door. Merlyn charged down the stairs, through the rain, and to the dock. He'd hoped to find a boat, but there was nothing there. Merlyn ran back to his car, slipping on the wet grass and stumbling over a rock, but he made it. The 442 growled to life at the turn of the key, and Merlyn took off hell-bent for the Ironweiler place. He fishtailed off of Sugar Maple Lane onto McKinley Avenue and corrected as he headed for the bridge. There, waiting to delay his effort, was Donnie Marshall, waving his red coned flashlight in the air like some maniacal marshaller on an aircraft carrier.

"Mr. Greer! What do you think you're" — "Shut up, Donnie, and get in the car."

"What?" Asked Donnie Marshall, obviously taken aback.

"I'll explain on the way. Now get in!" Ordered Merlyn.

"Slow down, Mr. Greer, now suppose you tell me what's going on."

"It's the kids; they're at the Ironweiler place!"

"What, kids?" Donnie asked.

"Frankie, the Howards, the Johnsons, and your boss's niece!"

"Kaylin? What about Kaylin?"

"Dammit, Donnie, get your ass in the car!"

Donnie ran around the front of the car and jumped in. "I can't just leave my post Merlyn," said a nervous Donnie Marshall.

But it was too late. Merlyn had the 442 in second as he cut a hard left on Main Street before making a second left onto Sumac Road, where the river bent west.

"Get on the blower and tell your boss that his niece is in the Ironweiler house. Hell, he'll probably give you a medal."

"The blower?"

"Your walkie-talkie," Merlyn jabbed a finger at Donnie's portable radio.

"Right!" Donnie Marshall keyed his radio. "Chief, from Marshall, come in Chief."

Donnie's radio crackled. "Go ahead, Donnie."

Chief, it's Kaylin, well, her and some other kids."

"What are you talking about, Donnie?" Barked Vecchio.

Merlyn ripped the radio out of Donnie's hand, "give me that damned thing." He keyed up. "Christopher, it's Merlyn. Your niece and her friends are going to the Ironweiler house.

"What the hell are they doing there?"

"No time to talk, Chief. You need to get over there ASAP."

"10-04, Merlyn. Thanks for the heads up."

The 442's headlights cut through the rain as it flew down Sumac Road.

***

Frankie pushed the door open with his shoulder, needing both hands to grip his tennis racket. Inside, the house was as black as a sealed tomb. Kaylin crossed the threshold, and the flashlight flickered brightly, giving the group a little hope, but then pulsed and faded to black, plunging them all back into darkness. Frankie tried to breathe, but the air felt thick. He tried again, but his lungs would not expand.

It's the house making me feel this way. It's not real, he thought to himself, but it didn't seem to help.

"What the hell is that sound?" Stevie asked.

"It sounds like the guy who used to call the pizzeria, right, Kaylin?" McKenna asked. The girls both worked at Pizza Italia, the local pizzeria, taking phone orders on Friday nights.

"Yeah, it does." Kaylin shook the flashlight and banged it with the palm of her hand. "We need some light."

"Hang on," said Stan.

There was a quick pop, and the flare bathed the room in red light.

"Holy shit, it's Frankie!" Stevie said.

Frankie was doubled over, gasping for breath.

"He's hyperescalating!" Lonnie said.

"Hyperventilating, not hyper — whatever you said," McKenna corrected. "Kaylin, give me the bag."

Kaylin pulled the bag off of the light and handed it to McKenna. She placed it over Frankie's mouth and nose."

"I don't think you're supposed to use a plastic bag for that."

"It's all we have, Stan," McKenna said as she peeled one of Frankie's hands off the tennis racket and placed it on her chest so he could feel it rise and fall. "Frankie, slow your breathing. Try to match mine," she said, breathing slowly and deliberately.

Frankie nodded and concentrated as they all stood silently, hoping for the spell to pass. It took several minutes, but it seemed to work.

"I think I'm okay now," Frankie said, pulling his hand back nervously. "Thanks, McKenna."

"It's okay, Frankie, but we're not going to make this a regular thing," she said and smiled.

They all knelt down around Frankie. "You okay?" Stan asked.

"Yeah, I think so."

"Good." Stan dug in his bag and passed out the flares. "Don't burn them all up at once, guys," he said as he got to his feet. "Let's go, we got a bird to kill, and we ain't gonna do it sitting here on our asses."

Lonnie popped up next, gripping his hammer. "Stan's right. Let's kill that friggin bird and get the hell out of here."

The rest got to their feet, dusted off their backsides, and walked to the base of the staircase. From above, in the darkness, came a loud crash that froze them in their tracks.

"What the hell was that?" Stevie asked.

"Probably that bird," answered Frankie, placing a foot on the first step. "Whatever it is, I'm here to kill it for Levi, and I ain't turning back."

Another step — another crash from above. Again, the noise startled Frankie, but it didn't stop him. A third step, followed by another crash. "Be brave, face your fears, be brave, face your fears," he whispered to himself as he climbed.

Frankie popped his flare, raised his tennis racket over his head, and charged up the stairs disappearing into the darkness. One more loud crash from the blackness above, and all went quiet.

"Shit! Frankie! — Frankie! Should we go up?" Lonnie asked.

"Hell no," Stevie said, and Stan and Finn didn't argue.

"Screw you guys, I'm going up there," McKenna said, stepping onto the old wooden stair that creaked under her foot. Then, as-if-in response, there came another crash from above.

"Come on, guys! Let's go help him!" Kaylin said and charged up the stairs behind McKenna.

"Shit, shit, shit," Stan said, pumping his fists and sounding like a skipping record. "My sister's up there guys, let's go." He ran up the stairs with Finn, Stevie, and Lonnie hot on his heels.

Pale moonlight spilled onto the second floor through broken windows and one large hole through the ceiling and the roof above. It was still dark but not pitch-black like the first floor, and they could make out shapes if not actual features. It seemed that the storm was beginning to break.

"Frankie," Kaylin called out in something akin to a loud whisper.

"In here, guys."

Frankie stood in what used to be Josh Ironweiler's room. Yellowing wallpaper depicting faceless athletes playing various sports clung faded to the walls. Red Hook Rivermen pennants, their bright blues and reds scraped to dull gray and pink by over 3000 suns that had passed over the broken bedroom window, still hung where his parents pinned them. The thumbtacks bleeding trails of rust in their corners. But what had Frankie's attention was a puddle of water that grew from under the bed.

"I think he's under there."

"The bird?" Stevie asked as he reared back with the hatchet raised overhead.

"No, Josh, the little boy from the river."

They stared at one another in the bright red glow of the flare.

"Josh? Is that you?" Frankie called out.

"Don't call him out, stupid!" Stevie took another step back.

"I think he's afraid of us, Stevie." Frankie squatted down and held his flare out. "We aren't going to hurt you, Josh. I think we're here to help you. You and my brother."

A hand, black with rot, shot out from under the bed, sending the group back a few feet pinning them against a wall. The second arm appeared, followed immediately by the rest of the shimmering apparition. A boy, about half Frankie's age, with black holes the size and shape of small fists where his eyes should have been, stood next to the bed. Its mouth hung open, crooked, and water poured out as it worked lazily up and down as if he were trying to speak.

"Are you trapped here?" Frankie asked.

The Josh-thing tilted its head back, the mouth falling open wider than its jaw should have allowed. It let out a gurgling cry, then it snapped its head forward. The head jerked spasmodically, inquisitively, from face to face before fixing its black sockets on Frankie.

McKenna gripped the back of Frankie's shirt in one hand and reached the Fence Buster around in front of him. "We should get out of here, Frankie," she said and gave a tug. Stan, Finn, Stevie, and Lonnie had already backed out of the room into the doorway.

"Josh, I know that's who you are. We're here to kill the crow and set you free."

The Josh-thing tilted its head sideways, and water began pouring from its right eye socket. It was impossible for something so frightening to look sad, Frankie knew that, but somehow it did. Slowly Frankie reached a hand out toward the Josh-thing. It drew back, froze for a moment before it screamed, spraying water into Frankie's face and splashing McKenna and Kaylin, both of whom were holding onto Frankie. The Josh-thing flew forward, startling Frankie. Frankie stepped back and went sprawling to the floor dragging the girls with him. He swiped at the putrid-smelling water and looked around, realizing that the Josh-thing was gone.

"What the fuck was that?" Lonnie yelled, raising his claw-hammer in the air and darting his eyes around in the darkness in case the thing returned.

Frankie got to his feet, helped McKenna and Kaylin up, and retrieved his flare and racket from where he'd dropped them in his panic.

"Believe me now, guys? I told you there was a boy that has been coming to my room.

"Maybe we have to kill him too," said Stan.

"We aren't killing a little boy Stan!"

"Frankie's right," said Kaylin. "Remember when the birds attacked, and the trees closed up overhead?"

"Yeah," said Stan, not peeling his eyes off of Frankie. "What about it?"

"Well, I saw that same boy-thing right before the trees closed up over us. He was looking up and moving that weird mouth of his."

"What are you saying, Kaylin? You think he's trying to help us?" McKenna asked.

"Then why did he try to attack Frankie just now?" Stevie interrupted.

"I don't think he was trying to attack me; I think he's trying to warn us. To scare us away."

"Then maybe we should listen," said Finn.

"It's okay if you guys want to go," said Frankie. "But I have to kill that bird. I can't let that thing have Levi."

35

The green glow of the mercury vapor lights crawled on fragile tendrils of fog across the Whitehead County Sheriff Department's parking lot. At the far end of the lot, three black, unmarked Illinois State Police Crown Vics sat idling with their headlights, illuminating Patrick Marshall. Behind him, a small whiteboard had been set up with a rough outline of the Consumption River area described to him during his phone call with Nick Ryan. In the upper left corner were the team assignments. Four two-man teams would converge on the river. Two teams would come in from the south, one from the north, and the fourth, the sniper team, would find high ground to provide additional cover. As Marshall checked the radios, the rest of the troopers sorted their gear and made ready.

The Tactical Response Unit, TRU for short, looked more like a small militia than law enforcement. Faces covered with green and black greasepaint, dark-colored BDUs cinched tight at the ankles, black combat boots, and an array of ferocious-looking assault rifles, all selected with deadly purpose to accomplish their mission.

Marshall called out the teams. "Bill Saunders, you're with Mike Day, Arriaga, you're with —"

"Arriaga's not here," said Tom Speed, who was to be partnered with Marshall.

"Well, where the hell is he?" Marshall asked.

"He called and said he was running late boss," said Trooper Joseph Lightfoot, as a tricked-out Toyota pick-up bounced into the parking lot and skidded to a stop.

A strikingly handsome Hispanic kid of average height, with a soccer or lacrosse midfielder's lean muscular body, hopped out of the cab. Arriaga was the Don Juan of the force. His was the face on the recruiting posters gracing the walls of colleges and state-run facilities. Gone was the harsh-looking, square-jawed marine type with the high-and-tight haircut. Today's Trooper was young, a softer kind of handsome, and, perhaps most importantly, not pasty white.

"Sorry, guys, my girl wouldn't let me leave."

"Get your shit together, Arriaga. You're with Lightfoot," barked Marshall.

Lightfoot and Arriaga high-fived, and Lightfoot offered congratulatory barks, a staple of the recently canceled Arsenio Hall show. Marshall fixed them with a hard stare and continued.

"Lightfoot and Arriaga, you're on overwatch. Reading, you're with Hann, Kenders, you're with Gates, Tom, you're with me."

The men exchanged high-fives as Marshall continued. "Okay, guys, listen up. Just over an hour ago, I received a lead that I just can't ignore. I've been given information on a possible dumping-ground used by a serial killer."

The mood among the men hardened.

"A what?" Arriaga asked.

Marshall didn't repeat himself. "My source, a man that I have known most of my life, says that he has reason to believe that a serial killer and his acolytes are operating in the area."

"Acolytes?" Tom Speed asked. "Are you talking about a cult?"

"He didn't use that word, but we aren't ruling it out."

"Why are *we* doing this instead of the locals?" Kenders asked.

"My friend, Nick Ryan, has reason to believe that the sheriff and his men in Chesapeake Station are in on it."

Saunders threw his hands in the air. "Oh, for fuck's sake. And what exactly makes him think that?"

"Nick said that Sheriff Tucker tried to kill him and his friends while they were conducting research in the area."

"And he can prove this?" Arriaga asked.

"I don't know what he can prove, but I know this guy. He's a serious man, as solid as they come, and I trust him. Now, if we're done playing, *question the boss*; I'll get on with the briefing."

Gently rebuked, the troopers all sat silent.

"According to Nick, the area to the south," he pointed at the map he had taped up on the whiteboard, "is pretty heavily wooded and should provide concealment. We are going to fan out wide and work toward this point." Marshall pointed at the map again, but this time, directed his troopers' attention to a clearing on the west side of the river. Lightfoot and Arriaga, you'll approach from the east. My guy says there's a barn right about here," another quick reference to the map. "He says he's been up there, and it provides an unobstructed view of the clearing. The area in and around the clearing should be considered hot so keep your heads on a swivel. This is rural Illinois, folks; everyone has guns. We have to protect the scene, but not at the risk of our own safety," Marshall paused. "And here's the bitch of it all. Ryan says we may be interrupting a gathering, so we need to hit this thing fast. I don't have to remind you that Jessica Upshaw is still missing, so saddle up. We have work to do.

***

Jinan pulled the A6 off the road behind a line of evergreen trees. They were still a reasonable distance from the river, but it was far too dark to drive with the headlights off, and they couldn't risk being seen. With Babe leading the way, they picked their way through the growth and finally reached the path that led to the barn. As they entered, Nick called out softly. Patrick Marshall ordered him to stay clear of the area, and he didn't want to risk being shot by accident. With no answer, the three made their way inside and up to the loft. High in the night sky, the moon cast its glow on everything except for the water.

Jinan looked at the flat black surface of the water. "That's strange."

"What's strange?" Nick asked.

"Why doesn't the moon reflect off the water?"

"I don't know," answered Babe. "It just doesn't; never has."

"That is strange," Nick said. "Maybe it has something to do with refraction, the way the light bends when it hits the surface of the water, or maybe the river has a high algae content."

"Who gives a shit?" Babe said, elbowing Nick and directing his attention to the flicker of torchlights dancing in the misty air across the river.

"We have to get going," she said. "Achak may be there."

The three climbed down out of the loft and started quickly over tangles of exposed roots and fallen trees.

From across the river came the sound of chanting. "Do you guys hear that?" Asked Jinan.

A low droning sound rose and fell in a chant that Nick couldn't quite make out.

"Hang on a minute, Babe," Nick said. He'd assumed the troopers would be there waiting and take over the operation, but they were alone, and he wasn't sure how to proceed. "I don't know where Pat and his guys are."

"Nick, we can't wait for them; we have to go."

Babe took off running. Jinan and Nick followed after, but Nick simply could not keep up, and after a few minutes, he'd lost sight of them. Without Babe to lead the way, Nick had to slow down or risk falling and injuring himself. He stopped and listened for the sounds of chanting to lead his way. Once he got his bearings, he continued on as quickly as he dared, pausing every once-in-a-while to make sure he was going the right way. The last time he stopped, he heard something over the chanting. Several screams cut through the din and sent a chill up his spine. Nick took off running through the snares in the thicket of trees and found himself on his ass more than once. Finally, he reached the opening to the clearing near the cabin. As he stepped out of the tree line, Nick found himself facing the deep black sockets of a side-by-side shotgun. He glanced down to see Jinan on her knees with her hands clasped behind her head, and Babe sprawled unconscious on the ground, and that was all he saw. The gunman spun the shotgun in his hands and delivered a smash, breaking Nick's nose and sending him off to dreamland.

***

Three blacked out SUVs stopped at different locations south of the clearing, and their occupants slid out into the night.

***

Cold, swampy water splashed Nick in the face and drenched his shirt. The foul-smelling water made his stomach lurch and stung his broken and bleeding nose. His head hurt, his nose hurt, his ears were ringing, and he could taste the blood running down the back of his throat, but none of that mattered. Nick saw two forms through the flickering light of the oil lanterns that hung in a semi-circle on shepherd's crooks around the clearing. One of the shapes knelt, swaying dreamily from side to side. The other was lying dead still, sprawled face down in the gravel near the water. He blinked a few more times to clear his vision and recognized the jean-jacket on the crumpled form.

"Babe! You mother-fuckers!" Nick gritted his teeth, bore down, and forced himself to get to his feet. He tried to lunge toward Babe but staggered sideways and fell over like a drunk.

Laughter rolled through the air, but Nick, his head still spinning from the blow, couldn't pinpoint the source. The failed attempt at standing coupled with the musty, sulfur smell caused his stomach to lurch again and brought bile up into Nick's throat. The bile sloshed into his sinuses and burned like hell.

"Nick."

The voice was barely audible in the subsiding laughter, but Nick recognized it. It was Babe's voice. She was still alive, and his heart lifted. In the light of the lanterns, Nick could see about thirty men and women gathered in the clearing. But the harder he tried to focus, the more aware of the tremendous pain in his head and the scorching lava in his sinuses he became. He blew hard through his nose to stop the burning, and bloody snot flew from his nostrils. That seemed to help. He considered his chastising of Babe and Achak about making a mountain out of a ghost story, and he felt embarrassed, but none of that mattered now. He had to think of a way out of the mess they were in. Nick only had a moment to contemplate escape.

"You sum-bitch, you got bloody snot on my shoe," said a gruff voice from above him.

The cult member reared back and kicked Nick square in the ribcage, but there was no laughter this time. Nick collapsed onto his side and saw the river begin to churn and roll.

"Bind their hands and bring them here to the water's edge. Mother is coming," said a slight man in a black suit.

36

D o you hear that?"

"Hear what? I don't hear anything," said Arriaga.

"Exactly," whispered Lightfoot. Let's get off the gravel."

"Roger that," Arriaga acknowledged and moved onto the quiet of the grass.

Thirty yards down the road, Arriaga held his hand up and made a fist. Lightfoot halted.

"Yeah," answered Lightfoot, cocking an ear. "I hear *that*. Sounds like chanting." Arriaga turned his head slowly to gauge the direction. "It's coming from that way," he said, pointing farther up and to the west.

They moved toward the sound, and the chanting grew louder.

"It sounds Indian," said Arriaga. "Come on, Lightfoot, you're supposed to be an Indian; what are they saying?"

The comment drew a stern look from Lightfoot.

"Sorry — Native American."

"First of all," said Lightfoot. "I'm not Native American; I'm an American, just like you."

"Hey man, I'm a Mexican American," said Arriaga.

"Then I'm a Canadian American. Both of my parents are from Canada, and so were their parents."

"Well, both of my parents are third-generation Mexican American," said Arriaga. "So I guess I'm more American than you! But, still, you're —" he paused and then said it. "Indian, right?"

"Dammit, Arriaga!"

"Sorry, bro! I mean, we never really talked about it before," he said, throwing his hands up in a 'mea culpa' gesture.

"My parents are Saulteaux, First Nation Canadian."

"What's that supposed to mean?"

"Canada's indigenous people are called the people of the first nation. My mom and dad are First Nation, Saulteaux."

"Thanks for the history lesson." Now, what are they saying?"

"It's not history; it's anthropology, dip shit," Lightfoot said.

"Potato, tomato, what are they saying?"

"You're a dick."

"Agreed," said Arriaga dismissively. And he raised his eyebrows to show that he was still waiting for an answer.

"And just because I have First Nation blood and speak a couple of languages, that doesn't mean I know what they're saying. There are over 150 indigenous languages in North America."

Arriaga clamped a palm to his forehead and rubbed vigorously. "Hijo de puta! Do you know what they're saying or not?"

The chanting continued. Wiin nibaa anaamibiig — goshkozi, wiin nibaa anaamibiig — goshkozi, wiin nibaa anaamibiig — goshkozi.

"Yeah," Lightfoot said, sounding somewhat defeated. Arriaga had him in checkmate. "But it doesn't make sense. They're saying; she who sleeps below the water — awaken."

"What the hell does that mean?"

Lightfoot threw up his hands and shrugged his shoulders. "How the hell should I know? Right now, we have to find that barn and check the sightlines." Lightfoot pulled out the tactical map provided by Marshall. "Let's try there," he said, pointing ahead. "I think the barn is up ahead."

"Good, because I don't feel like climbing no fucking trees."

They hurried their steps but still managed to move quietly. They came through a small grove of trees and were immediately assaulted by the smells of swamp gas and musty earth.

Arriaga blew out a puff of air. "Smells like your mama's feet," he said, waving a hand past his nose.

"Shut up, dick head," Lightfoot said. "There's the barn. Let's get ready to move."

They held up and listened for a moment, but all they could hear was the damned chanting. They moved swiftly into the barn, weapons up and ready, sweeping left and right, but there was no one inside. Lightfoot splayed his fingers over the lens of his flashlight to control the amount of light it gave off and swept the beam around the barn. Straw, a short stool, probably a milking stool, beer cans, crumpled-up cigarette packs, and a soiled mattress.

"Not much imagination needed to know what that has been used for," Arriaga said.

"How could anyone get a hard-on with this smell?" Said Lightfoot.

"Where there's a will, there's a way, brother," Arriaga answered.

"What the fuck is wrong with you?"

Spotting the ladder to the hayloft, Arriaga hustled over. "Cover me."

Lightfoot trained his rifle up at the opening. Once Arriaga was up, he followed. The large hay doors hung open and provided a perfect vantage point. They could see people with torches across the river, but they were too far to make out much else with the naked eye.

Lightfoot held his binoculars to his eyes and keyed his radio. "Marshall from Lightfoot."

"Go ahead, Lightfoot."

"Hey boss, you guys better get to humpin; there's some shit going down north of your position."

"What kind of shit?"

Through the binoculars, the images became clear. "I can see three people tied up near the water and a bunch of scary-looking fuckers with torches and a shit load of rifles. I shit you not. It looks like something out of a horror movie, boss."

"Roger that, we are moving as fast as we can. Saunders and Day, you copy?"

"Roger that boss," answered Bill Saunders.

"Kenders and Gates?"

"10-04, boss, we're high-speed, low-drag."

***

Nick, Babe, and Jinan knelt at the water's edge with their hands tied behind their backs. The chanting grew louder, and some in the group, men and women alike removed their shirts and engaged in acts of self-flagellation with switches they had cut from the trees. Nick could see the branches splitting their skin, and they offered the blood and small bits of torn flesh to one another to be lapped from their bodies. The little man in the black suit stepped into view and bent toward Nick.

"Where is my box?" He hissed.

Nick didn't answer and just stared ahead.

"Do you know who I am?" The man asked.

"You're Pozerac Gemein," said Babe. "You're a piece of shit."

If Gemein was shocked to hear an outsider use his name, he didn't show it.

"I was going to say, the reaper of souls, but you are correct—miss...."

"Babe Adams, the woman who is going to kill you!" Spittle sprayed from between her clenched teeth as she strained at her bonds.

"Of course, but before you kill me, would you grant me one last wish?" He asked mockingly.

Babe didn't answer; she just glared at the frail-looking man. "Would you kindly...return...my box?" the last three words coming in a scream that reverberated as a roar across the river.

Babe drew back, partially in fear but more in revulsion at Gemein's rotting breath. The river let off an enormous blurping bubble. Gemein composed himself, and straightened his tie, and drew in a deep breath through his nose. "You have approximately five minutes to decide if you want to die quickly or be eaten alive by mother."

Gemein turned to face his minions. "Mother is coming," he said and snapped his fingers at Beatrice Kibling and Grover Horn from the town council, sending them scurrying off to the cabin.

Cyrus Tucker approached Gemein. "Mr. Gemein, if you don't mind, I have a little present for you."

"By all means, Cyrus," said Gemein.

"Abernathy, front and center boy," snapped the fat lawman.

"Boy? Did you call me, boy?" Andrew started toward Tucker with clenched fists.

"Andrew," said Gemein. "This is mother's time; we will speak with the Sheriff later."

That seemed to calm Andrew Abernathy, who walked over to the Sheriff's cruiser to lend a hand. Tucker popped open his trunk. Achak, handcuffed, gagged, and drugged, stared vacantly up at the two cops.

"Don't just stand there, boy; lift him out."

Abernathy clenched his jaw and did as he was told. The big Indian toppled to the ground and was pulled back to his feet by the two lawmen.

"Let's go, asshole," Tucker said. "Your days of making problems for me are over."

They dragged him toward the water's edge, and Babe was the first to see him. "Achak!"

"Holy shit!" Tucker exclaimed. "What do we have here? Is that you, Babe? Yeah, you and your smart-ass boyfriend."

Still under the effects of whatever narcotics Tucker had pumped into him. Achak swung his head heavily toward the sound of Babe's voice.

"Babe," he said, drool dripping from his lips, his words coming out in sloppy slurs. "Run!"

"What the fuck have you done to him?" Babe snapped at Gemein.

"What have we here?" Asked Pozerac Gemein, ignoring Babe's outburst.

"This is the asshole, who has been snooping around, and those are his friends. His co-conspirators," he said and waved a hand in Babe and Nick's direction. Tucker drove his heel into the back of Achak's knee, forcing the big man to his knees at Gemein's feet.

Gemein's jaw dropped. "Gi Aakwaadizi, gi giiyose niin?"

"What did he say?" Nick whispered to Jinan.

"He said that Achak is Aakwaadizi, the assassin who has been hunting for him."

Achak lifted his head and looked Gemein in the eyes. "Ni Achak, ondaadizi makade ma'iingan biidaashi gomaapii inendaagozi."

Without being asked, Jinan translated for Nick and Babe. "He said that he is Achak, born of Black Wolf's line and that the winds have carried him over distance and time so that he might fulfill his destiny."

***

Arriaga dragged a hay bale over to the haymow door and called for distance and windage readings from Lightfoot. Lightfoot looked out across the river. There was no movement in the trees, so windage wouldn't be an issue. He could clearly make out facial features on the people holding torches, but not so clearly on the others. Lightfoot estimated the distance at approximately 325 yards but pulled his range finder to verify.

"Got a distance of 338 yards to the cabin, 310 to the shoreline."

"Roger that," Arriaga said.

Arriaga checked the zero on his scope. At that distance, there was no need for adjustments.

"Boss," said Lightfoot into his radio. "I hope you guys are getting close. They just dragged some guy out of the trunk of a squad car. Shit's heating up."

Lightfoot swapped his rangefinder for a pair of binoculars and watched as two other members of the group walked out of the small cabin dragging a pregnant woman along with them.

"Holy shit Arriaga, are you seeing what I'm seeing?"

Arriaga had been scanning the attendants. "Yeah, is that?"

"That's Jessica Upshaw," Lightfoot said.

Lightfoot and Arriaga watched as they marched the woman toward a man in the black suit who appeared to be addressing the crowd. Directly in front of the small man was the large tattooed man that they had pulled out of the trunk of the Chesapeake Station Crown Vic.

Arriaga turned his M-40 on the little man in the black suit. "Got him lined up," Arriaga said. "You watch his hands."

"On it."

***

Gemein reached down and ripped Achak's shirt from his body. There in the light of the torches and the silver moon, Gemein began scanning the tattoos on Achak's body. There, laid out on his flesh, was the story of his creation. Throughout his childhood, Pozerac Gemein had been alone in the world. Not for lack of people; there were always people around. In fact, there were far too many. He had grown up in an orphanage with 142 other children, but even among so many other castaways, he never found one with whom he could feel some sort of kinship. The other kids bonded quickly, forming gangs and cliques, but Gemein remained alone. He was different, and he did not understand why. When he was about seventeen, he found himself standing right on the spot where he now stood. He could never explain it, not that he had anyone to explain it to, but something called him to that spot at that time. That was where he met her, the thing he called mother.

Images began flashing through his mind as if recalled from some deep unknown place, and Gemein's eyes rolled in their sockets, looking like two gray tea eggs. His body began convulsing like an epileptic in seizure and then stopped. He found himself hovering in space in the distant past, watching as a beautiful woman ran in terror through the frozen woods. She ran barefoot through broken branches and thorn patches that pierced her frozen feet and ripped at her flesh. The woman who was dragging a small child behind her collapsed in exhaustion against the trunk of a large tree and clutched the boy to her chest. He knew instinctively that he was that boy. As she trembled there, gulping cold air into her burning lungs, a pack of huge Timber wolves, all gray, save the largest of the pack, a great black beast with eyes as green as emeralds, encircled them. Chuffs of vapor escaped the woman, and Gemein could feel her terror. It was not for herself but for him. The boy had been wrapped in pelts, but he could still feel rough tree bark against the woman's skin, the cold of the snow on her bare feet. But most of all, he could feel her terror, a feeling so foreign to him, he'd never, for as long as he could remember, felt fear, but now it was so real.

The enormous wolves, their jaws dripping and snapping, closed on her, and she cried out in a language he did not understand but recognized as a dark language, a soul-speak. Then, as the first wolf attacked, sinking its teeth into her thigh; she did nothing to protect herself, there came a loud thrumming in the air. She held him up high, too high for the wolves to reach as another and another fell upon her. Their weight must have been unbearable, but somehow, she bore the weight until a large black bird with wings of leather swooped down and snatched the boy from her hands. As his rescuer soared skyward, Gemein watched as the wolves transformed into men, and, with him safely away, the woman began to fight back. The men battered the woman with knives and war-hammers and tomahawks, delivering blow after deadly blow, but the woman spun and whirled like the wind lashing out with razor-sharp nails. As the bird circled above, Gemein watched the battle. The woman fought ferociously but was no match for the numbers she faced.

Beaten, bloodied and bound, the men dragged her out to the middle of the frozen river. The river that even now ran before him. They chopped through the ice there, and after weighing her body down with rocks gathered from the shoreline, they dropped her into her watery grave. Gemein broke from his hypnotic state with his eyes filled with rage.

"It was you!" Gemein cried.

37

A disturbance in the river drew Lightfoot's attention away from the captives. Thirty feet offshore, enormous air bubbles exploded, and the ground all around began to quake and rumble. Lightfoot steadied himself as he heard a deep muffled crack and silt rose in a great spout from the riverbed.

"What the hell was that?" Arriaga asked.

Lightfoot flashed his binoculars back toward the man in the black suit and keyed his mic. "What the fuck!" Not the preferred vernacular for use over police radios, but fitting for what he was seeing.

"Check yourself, Lightfoot," Marshall scolded. "Now, tell me what's going on."

"We have several subjects tied up and—" As he spoke, the spout fell, and another huge air bubble broke the surface of the river. "And God knows what coming up out of the water! Step it up, sir; we have a situation!"

"Roger that. All teams, push hard!"

"Sir, can you green-light us so we can drop this mother-fucker?"

"You know the R.O.E. Lightfoot," Marshall chided.

Every man on the team knew the rules of engagement. Do not fire unless fired upon or to preserve life, and if it becomes necessary to fire, know what's behind your target.

"Roger that, sir." Lightfoot let his hand fall from his mic to his rifle.

"I can't believe we have to sit here with our thumbs up our asses!" Arriaga protested.

"Stay frosty; I think we're about to get real busy real fast. You see the knife, right?"

Arriaga took several deep breaths and exhaled slowly to lower his heart rate. His finger moved from the locator button on the side of his M-40 and eased onto the trigger. "I got the shot," he said.

"Roger that, stand by for confirmation," Lightfoot replied. "Marshall from Lightfoot, my shooter, is requesting the green, over."

"The green?" Marshall said, sounding more than a little surprised. "Negative on the green," he said. Marshall knew that if overwatch had time to ask to take a shot, he had time to ask why. "Gimme a sit-rep?"

"Boss, we have some shit here. The guy just pulled a knife."

"Shit!" Marshall neglected to release his talk button.

"Sir, they have the Upshaw woman and—Shit!" Lightfoot exclaimed. "Boss, we need a —" He was about to say, *call here*, when Arriaga's M-40 roared."

Lightfoot watched in horror as the man in the black suit drove the blade into the large tattooed man's neck and sawed madly. The 7.62 mm bullet left the muzzle traveling 2600 feet per second. The trip took less than a second at a hundred yards, but it never made it to its intended target as something burst forth from the river.

Arriaga slid the bolt back on his rifle and slammed another cartridge into the chamber. "Fuck it." He fired a second round.

The second round struck the same mark.

***

Gemein drove the blade into Achak's neck, ripped it cleanly through his spinal column, severing the head from the body, and dropped it to the ground. Achak's head rolled and came to rest on the ground near Babe. Babe sat back on her heels, turned her head, and retched. Jinan dropped sideways, overtaken by raw barbarous violence. For Nick, the response was different. The world he had known had ceased to exist, and with it, the rules that he thought governed all men. The zip-ties cut deep into his wrists before snapping. He'd never in his life thrown so much as a punch in anger. It wasn't that he was afraid. He'd stood up to his share of drunks in bars around campus. He played intramural rugby and had given as good as he got, but not once had he ever intentionally harmed another human being. But all of that was about to change. Nick lunged at the man who had kicked him in the guts and ripped the shotgun from his hands. The sudden appearance of the Inaki from beneath the water drew the onlooker's attention and distracted the man just long enough for Nick to disarm him. Nick swung the shotgun baseball bat style and split the side of the man's head open. He was out before he hit the ground.

Nick rifled through his pockets and, just as he'd expected, found a large folding knife. He snapped it open and cut Babe's restraints, and it was like freeing a bull from its chute. Babe splayed her fingers and launched into the air. Had Nick not grabbed her firmly around the waist, Babe would have tried to gouge Gemein's eyes out. She beat her fists against Nick's forearms, but he wouldn't let go.

"Let me go!" Babe hissed.

"I can't; I need your help with Jinan. We'll deal with Gemein." He held the shotgun out so that Babe could see it, and he felt her body relax.

"He killed him, Nick. He killed Achak," she said. Spittle flew from her lips, and her eyes flared with rage.

"I know, Babe, now I need you to focus! Help me with Jinan."

It was a cold response. He wanted to tell her how sorry he was, how, despite their initial meeting, he had come to like the big man, but he hoped there would be time for that later. He cut Jinan's ties and brought her to a seated position. Babe shook her shoulders, and Jinan responded by blinking slowly as she came back around.

"What just happened?" Jinan asked dreamily.

"Your ghost just killed Achak," said Nick.

Jinan's eyes widened, fixed on something behind Nick.

Nick turned to see Pozerac Gemein flailing his arms about like some kind of maniacal conductor. His acolytes, like a bunch of prairie dogs, stood, necks outstretched, searching for the source of the shots. A pregnant woman being dragged toward the shoreline dug her bare heels into the sharp gravel on the path that ran down from the cabin.

"Please, let me go. Can't you see that I'm pregnant? Please, don't kill my baby! My husband will pay you whatever you want!"

"That's Jessica Upshaw," Nick said, but Jinan didn't respond. That was not what commanded Jinan's attention. Nick turned his head a little further to the left, twisting as far as his muscles and tendons would allow.

***

Arriaga didn't know what he was looking at, but it filled his scope. The thing was 10, maybe 15 feet tall. It was hard to say because the thing kept moving. Perhaps it was the atmosphere or the nature of their mission, but he knew that he had to keep sending rounds into it until he put it down.

"Te envoi de Vuelta al infierno, puta madre"

Lightfoot's mic crackled. "What's going on?"

Lightfoot had one hand on his radio, and the other pressed his binoculars to his eyes. "Boss, we have a —I don't know what it is! It's like some half gator, half spider-looking thing," Lightfoot said, allowing his binoculars to trail off the monster back toward the commotion on the path.

"What? Say again!"

"Boss, they're dragging the Upshaw woman right toward that damned thing!"

Arriaga fired again. The monster roared and flung its body to-and-fro in reaction to the third shot. For one insane second in this rapidly unfolding deluge of insane seconds, Lightfoot thought of Ray Charles and how he moved his body when he played piano. Lightfoot watched as Jessica Upshaw, for some reason, stopped struggling and began walking toward the monster. It reminded Lightfoot of the women in old Dracula movies. How they would willingly walk to their doom after he hypnotized them. Arriaga seated another round, but before he could fire, a volley of shots came tearing across the river.

"Lightfoot, Report!"

Bullets whistled through the air and flitted through leaves. Several punched holes through the barn walls, but it was clear to Lightfoot that the locals were just firing in the direction of Arriaga's shot. He and Arriaga hunkered down behind hay bales to wait for a lull in the shooting, but it wasn't coming.

"Boss, we hit the monster but can't confirm the kill. The locals are laying down suppressive fire, but I don't think they know where we are."

A round struck a beam overhead releasing a shower of splinters and dust down onto Lightfoot and Arriaga, then another, and another. "Check that, boss. The rounds are hitting closer to home."

Arriaga grabbed Lightfoot's arm. "Let's go, brother; we gotta move."

"Roger, I'll put some rounds downrange to draw fire up here. That way, these idiots won't be shooting low when we break," said Lightfoot.

The bullets were still flying when Lightfoot moved to a kneeling position to provide cover fire. He squeezed off several rounds before one lucky shot punched through the hay bale and slammed into Lightfoot's thigh. The pain exploded through his body as he fell back onto the loft floor. Arriaga had already made it to the ladder when he heard his partner cry out.

"Fuck!" Arriaga ran for Lightfoot, and a bullet screamed past his ear. He dropped to the floor and crawled toward his spotter.

"Where are you hit?"

Lightfoot tapped his leg. "Here, bro," he said through clenched teeth.

Arriaga found the bullet hole in Lightfoot's BDUs and ripped the material. The blood pooled around the wound but didn't come out in spurts.

"They didn't hit an artery; you're still in this," Arriaga said as he pulled a tourniquet from one of the molle pouches on his tactical vest. Arriaga cinched the tourniquet above the wound and made a note of the time.

"Now get off your ass. We gotta move."

Arriaga helped Lightfoot to his feet, but the instant he put weight on the injured leg, Lightfoot fell back to the floor.

"Shit! I think the bullet hit the bone," Lightfoot said. "My leg is broken. You go ahead, I'll get over to the door and rain lead on these mother-fuckers."

"I'm not leaving you, bro," said Arriaga.

"Go, man! You can shoot from the ground and divide their fire."

But Arriaga was already picking his first target through his scope. All the while, Pat Marshall panted into his radio, demanding situation reports.

***

From his vantage point in the shadow of the evergreen's, Nick saw Jessica Upshaw as she stood entranced before a reptilian-looking creature at the water's edge. The image took his breath away. Nick recognized the monster. Somehow, he had seen it before, although the particulars were escaping him at the moment. He searched his mind, pulling fragmented memories together until the recollection came crashing down on him.

It was the winter after the drowning death of Joshua Ironweiler. No wonder it didn't come more easily. He'd blocked out most everything connected to that event. He remembered his mother Maggie had told him to go and call his father in for dinner. In those days, Tim Ryan had been spending most of his waking hours in his secret room. Nick put on his jacket, slipped his feet into his boots, and walked out to the garage. The snow had been falling, and it had blown up against the door making a small drift. Nick kicked the drift aside, pushed open the door, and stood at the base of the stairs where he called up to his father, but Tim Ryan didn't answer. Nick started up the stairs and was about to call out again when he saw that the door to the room was opened. It was just a crack, but it sent a chill down his spine. Tim Ryan never left the door to his secret room open. Nick drew in a breath and called to his dad again, and again there was no answer. Nick made his way cautiously up the stairs and, upon reaching the small landing, called to his father one last time in a louder voice.

"Dad, are you in there?"

Still, there was no reply. Nick was sure his father was in the room. He had to be. There were no footprints in the snow leading away from the garage. Not to mention the snow-drift. If his father had opened the door, he would have disturbed the snow. With great trepidation, Nick placed a trembling hand on the door and pushed it open. The room was dark, except for a light over one of his father's drafting tables. Taped to the board was a sketch of the thing threatening to devour Jessica Upshaw. As he stepped back from the doorway, Nick felt a hand on the back of his neck. The hand spun him around, and he stood face to face with his father. His father's eyes were filled with rage. Without saying a word, Tim Ryan drew his hand back, brought it down hard on the side of Nick's face, and then everything went black. Nick's hand went to his cheek, remembering the shock he felt that night. Not unlike the shock, he felt, recognizing that image as the monster standing by water with Jessica Upshaw.

As he returned to the present, a shot rang out. A deep and primeval scream rose up out of the creature. It was so loud that it managed to drown out the sound from the gunfire that had erupted all around.

The monster reared its head back, breaking its controlling gaze on Jessica Upshaw, but it seemed that she was too frightened to move. Nick sprinted for Jessica. As the monster writhed in pain, a strange metamorphosis began to take place. The creature folded in on itself, and in its place stood an old woman. Her soot-colored hair flowed from her head to the ground, covering almost her entire body. Nick had no time to ponder the change. He wrapped one arm around Jessica's chest and turned to run, only to find Gemein blocking his path. The frail-looking man's skin was stretched impossibly tight over high cheekbones and seemed to flatten his small, broad nose. He had small pupils, like little black marbles set into down-turned, sad-looking eyes, and making the whole picture even more off-putting, the man's head and face were completely devoid of hair.

Nick shouldered the little man to get past him, but it was like slamming his shoulder into a concrete wall. The man in the black suit didn't budge.

"That belongs to mother," said Gemein.

His tone was anything but menacing. More matter of fact, like a person addressing someone who accidentally picked up the wrong coffee cup in a coffee shop. Still surprised by the man's sturdiness, Nick turned back toward the old woman, choosing to take what he thought would be the path of least resistance. But before he could complete the turn, a hand seized him by his shoulder. Nick looked back to see a crooked, atrophied arm reaching out from the long sooty hair, ending in the gnarled hand that clamped like a vice onto his shoulder.

Gemein smiled as mother tightened her grip. Pain erupted in Nick's shoulder. He tried to pull away and realized that his other arm, the arm that held Jessica Upshaw, was suddenly free. Babe and Jinan had emerged from the darkness to pull the frightened woman to safety. Nick reared back his right fist and swung hard for Gemein's bald face. The punch connected square with Gemein's right temple, but Gemein just continued to smile. The hand on Nick's shoulder forced him down to one knee, and Gemein raised his hand to strike Nick down, but something hit Gemein in the shoulder and corkscrewed him to the ground. The old woman howled at the sight of her son's falling body and loosened her grip on Nick's shoulder. Nick felt it relax and got to his feet and ran toward Babe and Jinan, who had already started back to get him. They each wrapped an arm around his waist and started back for cover.

"We gotta get her out of here," said Nick.

When Nick made it back to the tree line, he turned to see if they were being followed. No one pursued them. Instead, he saw that a huge, black bird, or perhaps it was a bat, Nick couldn't be sure. The thing landed on top of Pozerac Gemein and wrapped him in its black wings like some demonic angel. Another shot came from across the river and struck the winged creature, but it took no notice. Nick scrambled for the shotgun that he'd left on the ground when he made his run for Jessica Upshaw and turned to fire. He tried to level the shotgun at the creature, but the pain in his shoulder stopped him. With Gemein secured, the creature bolted into the air and vanished like vapor.

"Nick! Why didn't you shoot? You let him get away!" Babe said, clawing at the shotgun.

Keeping the weapon away from Babe, Nick said, "I tried, my shoulder, I think it's dislocated."

Babe's jaw unclenched, and fear and worry filled her eyes. "He's gone, Nick. We let him get away," she said and burst into tears.

"Listen to me! If I had shot, we would have drawn their attention," he said, pointing at the heavily armed locals. "Besides, I know where it's taking him."

Babe's jaw dropped.

38

The 442's headlights cut through the mist and splashed against the front door to the Ironweiler's house. Donnie reached it first and turned the knob. He pushed the door open on its rusted hinges and was about to call out when the words caught in his throat. Merlyn was a little slower getting to the door.

"What the hell?"

"You see it too?" Donnie asked.

"Uh-huh, but I can't say I've ever seen anything like it before," Merlyn replied.

The headlights stopped dead at the door. The frame and the wall around the door were still illuminated, but the threshold was flat and black as a pit.

"You better brace yourself, son. I think we're apt to see lots of strange things here."

Merlyn stepped through the doorway and disappeared from view.

"Merlyn, where did you go?" Donnie pulled his Maglite and shined it at the black. The Maglite hit the invisible barrier and stopped just like the 442's headlights. No reflection, just stopped as if someone had cut it off midstream. "Shit, Merlyn, where did you go?" Donnie's hand flew to his radio, and he keyed up but had no idea what to say and released the talk button.

"Dammit!" Donnie paced in a small box for a moment and then steeled himself and pushed through the dark doorway.

From the other side of the black, he could see back out to the car and the mist that danced on the car's headlights, but his flashlight flickered and died.

"Glad you could join me," came a voice from deeper inside the room.

Merlyn stepped forward, holding the lit Zippo that lighted his way through some deep dark tunnels back in Vietnam.

"What the hell is going on here, Merlyn?" Donnie asked as he clicked his flashlight button nervously. "What the hell is wrong with this thing," he said, slamming it against his palm.

Merlyn tore a section of wallpaper down and twisted it into a make-shift torch.

"I can't say, Donnie. Here, hold this for a minute." Merlyn lit the torch and then pealed another section of the wallpaper down.

"Near as I can figure, that doorway is acting like some kind of portal."

"A portal? A portal to where?"

"I don't know, son."

"And what the hell is wrong with my flashlight?"

"I don't know that either. Let's just find the kids and get out of here."

Together they studied the room and called out to Frankie Waters and Kaylin Vaughn. But their calls went unheard or unheeded. A flat-topped Bornholm grandfather clock stood undaunted by time or circumstance in the corner of the living room.

"One of yours?" Donnie asked.

Donnie could see the sadness in the clock maker's eyes.

"It was a gift from Mark's parents on Mark and Sadie's wedding day," Merlyn answered. "I guess there was no next of kin to claim it."

"My parents have one like this," Donnie said as he held his torch up, reading the clock's face. "It stopped at 9 o'clock."

Donnie opened the clock's lower door, reached inside, and touched the pendulum, setting the works into motion. The clock's chimes rang out, clear as crystal, but slow as molasses; bong—.

All throughout the Ironweiler's house, long-dead light bulbs flickered to life with the sound of the first chime. The light started out dim but grew in intensity as the first chime faded, and the second rang out—bong. The second chime came louder than the first and brought with it the sound of crackling as the scrolls of old wallpaper crawled back up the walls. By the time the fourth chime sounded, all of the wallpaper was back in place, and the cracked, yellowed coloring gave way to its original, stately, blue, and gold fleur-de-lis pattern. The clock rang out again—bong, and the furniture, soiled and broken by time and trespassers, sprung to life, looking fresh as the day it was purchased. The sixth and seventh—bong, bong, were louder, almost deafening, and brought with them the overpowering smell of gunpowder, which clung like a fog in the air.

***

"What the hell is that?" Yelled Stan, sticking his fingers in his ears against the loud chiming of the clock.

Frankie clamped his hands over his ears and followed the metallic sulphury smell into the Ironweiler's master bedroom. There the gunpowder smell mixed with other, more pungent smells causing Frankie to double over and gag. As he rose back up, he saw something that wasn't there just a second ago. Mark Ironweiler sat slouched against the wall. His body convulsed, and he coughed, spraying blood across the room. His lower jaw, or what was left of it, hung open, and Frankie could see through the broken bone and torn flesh to the hole in the wall where presumably the heavy slug came to rest. Mark's left arm rested on his left thigh; his right arm outstretched with his thumb caught in the trigger-guard of the compact shotgun he used to end his life. As Frankie wretched, fighting the urge to vomit, Mark Ironweiler blinked twice, and then his lids fell to half-mast and stayed that way. The smell of shit, piss, and something musty rose up and filled Frankie's nostrils, and he turned and pushed his way past Stan, who hadn't entirely made it into the doorway of the room.

"Holy," — Stan waved his hand over his face. "Dude, did you shit your," — Stanley Howard froze on the 'p' in pants.

The eighth chime rang out after what seemed an incredibly long delay—bong. They all clapped their hands over their ears and dropped to their knees.

"I can feel it in my throat," Stevie yelled.

Lonnie nodded, "Yeah, I feel like I'm gonna puke."

The final toll thundered—bong and sucked all of the air out of the old house. They all collapsed onto the floor and gasped, clawing at their throats. Frankie gulped helplessly as his field of vision narrowed to the size of a quarter. In the second, before darkness took him, he heard a loud clicking as the horrendous crow stepped into view. It didn't fly. It had no feathers. Like boiled and cooled fat, its ink-black skin rolled in puddles from its head to the spiny stalks that made up its legs. Maggots encircled hollowed-out eye sockets that shined with black fire from deep inside the bird's body. Frankie swung his racket and connected good and hard with the left side of the thing's head, but it didn't seem to faze the bird. The crow cocked and lowered its head spasmodically toward Frankie's face. Frankie froze and felt the warm, familiar sensation of piss running down his leg, and then he lost consciousness.

***

At the tolling of the ninth bell, the floor under Donnie and Merlyn's feet crumbled away, sending them sliding deep into the bowels of the Ironweiler house. As they descended, the light from above dimmed as the final chime faded. They came to a hard stop hitting the basement floor. Donnie looked up. The soft light from above that looked a mile away flickered and died. The house gave one last and violent shudder, and all was black.

"What the hell just happened?" Donnie asked, feeling around in the darkness for his flashlight and finally laying his hand on it.

"You may have answered your own question," said Merlyn, as he snapped open his Zippo.

Donnie, forgetting for the moment that his flashlight wasn't working, thumbed the button sending its beam out into the darkness.

"Merlyn, my light, it's working again."

Donnie shined the light around. Ancient timbers, like bolt-straight roots from some great tree already here when time began, shot up from the ground and vanished in the blackness above. From somewhere in the vast space around them came the sound of rushing water and a dank, musty smell that seemed familiar, though Donnie couldn't put his finger on it.

"Shine that over here," said Merlyn, holding his lighter near the ground. "There's something here."

Donnie gripped the shaft of the light and gave the lamp housing a twist. Widening the beam, he washed it around the space and stopped it on something that glinted in the light. Merlyn worked to free the object from the hard-packed ground. He heard a loud thumping sound, like enormous wings beating the air, and with it came a sour smell.

"Do you smell that?" Donnie asked.

Merlyn sniffed at the air. "Smells like something's rotting down here," he said. "Come on, shine the light back over here."

Donnie, distracted by the smell, let the light drift off its mark but quickly redirected it.

"That's strange," Merlyn said.

Donnie held his forearm to his nose and breathed into his sleeve. "Merlyn, that smell — it's awful."

"Don't smell like roses," Merlyn said and continued digging.

"Seriously, Merlyn, I think I'm going to vomit."

Merlyn didn't respond. Seeming intent on freeing the object from the ground, he dug his nails into the dirt and pried it free.

"Donnie, look at this. It has to be hundreds of years old!"

Merlyn held the thing in the air so that Donnie could see it. It was made from the jawbone of some large animal. Some of the teeth were still in place; the forward part was wrapped in some kind of yellowing hide to make a handle. Long black strands of hair still crusted with dirt hung from the pommel of the weapon. Ahead of the handle, large, jagged cuts followed the bone's widening curve back to the jawbone's broad ramus. Strips of animal hide hung from holes bored through the bone. Affixed to the ends of the strips were barbs made of bone. Along the ramus, a bizarre joining of bone and metal formed the weapon's killing edge. Merlyn ran a fingernail across the edge and peeled a layer of keratin off in the process. There was no telling exactly how long the weapon had been buried there, but the blade was still razor-sharp.

38

"It's a bone tomahawk," Merlyn said.

Behind him, Donnie Marshall let out a scream. Merlyn held his lighter high in the air as the thing, half-bird half-bat, wrapped Donnie in its veiny wings and plunged its misshapen beak into his neck, sending spurts of blood cascading through the air. Merlyn dropped the ancient weapon and reached for his Colt, but it was too late. The creature bolted into the darkness above, carrying Donnie with it. Merlyn could see the soft glow of his light behind the things translucent wings and watched till it rose out of sight.

"Donnie, Donnie," Merlyn called out to the young officer. He squinted and strained his neck, looking to see where the thing had carried him off to, but the Zippo was a poor light source. As he reached the Zippo up as high as he could, a shot rang out from the darkness above.

"Donnie!"

A pinprick of light began falling from high above. The light grew in size and brightness as it got closer, and then Donnie Marshall's flashlight landed on the ground. Merlyn bent to pick it up and was almost struck by a second falling object. Donnie Marshall's Glock lay, covered in blood, on the dirt floor at Merlyn's feet. He popped the magazine from the magazine well, held it to the light and checked for rounds, reseated it into the gun, and tucked the Glock into his waistband. He bent to pick up the tomahawk when a third object struck the ground with a sickening thud.

Thinking it was the bird-thing again, Merlyn raised the weapon but lowered it when he recognized the silver badge on Donnie Marshall's blood-soaked shirt. His body lay bloodied and broken and drained of life, there in the basement, or whatever this place was, beneath the Ironweiler house. Sadly, Merlyn was no stranger to death in the field, but he was a long way from Kae Sanh. Merlyn did not cry out in anger, nor did he swear some oath to finding the creature and making it pay; he simply knelt next to Donnie, asked the Lord to welcome him into Heaven, and then got to his feet. Merlyn knew that he was the one who dragged Donnie into this nightmare. He knew that it was his fault that Mr. and Mrs. Marshall had lost a son, but this wasn't the time for beating himself up; this was the time to hunt.

***

Frankie opened his eyes and whipped his head around frantically for the crow. He was still a bit dazed, but the crow was gone. As he sat and composed himself, he could hear something heavy being dragged across the attic floor above. Frankie shook his head to clear it and began to wake his friends, all but Lonnie Johnson, who was gone.

"Guys, wake up; wake up, guys!"

The group began to stir.

"Come on, guys; wake up! Lonnie is gone."

Stevie Johnson got to his feet and called out to his brother, "Lonnie! Where are you, Lonnie? Quit screwing around, or I'm gonna kick your ass!"

"He's not here, Stevie. I think he's —"

Frankie didn't finish. Instead, he pointed up, directing the group's attention to the dragging sound above. Stevie began to search the landing, looking for stairs to the attic.

"How do you get up there, guys?"

In the ceiling in the hall where they stood was an eye-hook screwed into the door for the drop-down ladder; Stan was the first to see it.

"There, guys," he said, pointing at the ceiling. "There's an eye-hook."

Finn stood beneath it and jumped, but he was two feet short of his mark.

"Pick me up, and I'll grab it," said Kaylin.

Finn squatted, wrapped his arms around the backs of Kaylin's knees, and lifted her up. Kaylin slipped a finger through the eye-hook and pulled the ladder down. The old steel frame squealed on its rusty hinges as Stevie grabbed hold, pulled it down, and raced up the steps. The rest followed, and together, they all stepped deeper into the unknown.

The attic looked like any attic in any old house anywhere in the country. Dusty cardboard boxes stacked in corners; several old ornately framed paintings leaned against a black steamer trunk with brass fittings. An antique flesh-colored mannequin stood unclothed next to an armoire that had to have been assembled in the attic being far too large to have been brought up in one piece. But what made this attic different was a series of doorways, at least three from what Frankie could see, that led off down the length of the space. They walked through each doorway, finally coming to the last room. On a table sat an 8mm movie projector with a film spooled through the reels. Directly across the attic from the projector stood a silver movie screen, draped in cobwebs, waiting for someone to flash images across its skin again. Instinctively, Stan flicked the switch on the projector, and much to their surprise, the projector whirred to life, sending silent, black and white images flickering onto the waiting screen.

The light flashed and reflected off their eyes as images of a family, a mom, a dad, and a little boy sat by the riverside with fishing poles. Frankie recognized the family's fishing spot as the dock on the river where they parked the boat. The little boy turned, smiling to wave at the cameraman. As he waved, his smile faded into wide-eyed terror, then the image flickered off.

"Guys, we don't have time for this shit. We have to find Lonnie," said Stevie Johnson, his voice quivering.

As Stevie spoke, the screen lit up again. The man from the first segment stood cooking hotdogs over a kettle grill with a cigarette dangling from his lips and a baseball glove on his non-hotdog- tending hand. The man looked off-camera, raised his glove, and caught a ball without missing a beat. He set down the long fork he'd been using to turn the hotdogs, waved and smiled at the camera, and threw it. The camera followed the ball past a beautiful woman in a white blouse and into the boy's mitt. He caught the ball and turned to wave at the camera, and again, the smile faded into a look of terror, and the screen began to flicker white light again.

"How many kids did Mr. Ryan say this family had?" Stan asked.

No one answered. Instead, they all shared nervous glances as a series of flashes appeared on the screen, and the camera found good old dad standing in the garage, tying knots in a rope. He smiled a toothy grin, and the camera's perspective spun slowly into his point of view.

His hands tugged at the rope tied into a noose. The camera view moved quickly and as smooth as a marble on glass from the garage, bursting through the kitchen door into the house. It went through the house and turned toward the boy who sat curled, knees to chest, under the dining room table as it passed. The foot of the stairs came into view, and a black form rolled and surged ahead of him, beckoning him up. Up the stairs, the camera turned a corner into a bedroom where a beautiful young woman, the same woman in the white blouse, unzipped her skirt and slid it down over her hips, letting it fall to the floor. The camera panned back up to her long neck and then followed down the length of her body. A blonde ponytail hung to her bare back, which tapered down to a narrow waist. The deep slope of her back gave way to the curve of her buttocks beneath tight white panties.

Frankie felt a strange stirring in his young body. The camera continued down to nylon stockings held up by a garter belt and high-heeled shoes that stepped out of the skirt. The woman glanced back over her shoulder and batted long eyelashes at the man. Licking her lips seductively, she turned and walked toward him.

What happened next happened in a blur, and Frankie gasped. The man grabbed the woman by the throat with one hand and slipped the noose around her neck. The camera angle turned back and forth from the stairs to the woman as she was dragged down them by the rope around her neck. Frankie felt sick. The sickening jarring motion of the camera, the act that unfolded before him on the screen, and knowing that it wasn't make-believe, upset Frankie to the point of tears, but he could not look away.

Passing the dining table, the camera dipped under its edge, and an arm reached out, seized the cowering boy, and yanked him from his hiding spot. The man dragged the woman and the boy into the garage and threw the boy hard against the center support post as he tossed the rope up and over a rafter. He grabbed the boy by the back of his hair and turned his face to watch as he pulled on the rope, trapped it under his foot, and pulled again. She clawed frantically at the noose, digging her nails into the flesh on her neck, her legs kicked in desperation, and all around them, black formless shapes floated and swirled in the air. Finally, the woman looked down at the terrified boy, stopped struggling, offered a pained smile, and surrendered.

Somehow, the fact that the movie was silent and black and white made the whole thing more horrifying. The camera turned to the boy's terrified face and then hands tied off the rope around a support post. With the boy reaching and pulling on his mother, the camera turned toward the door. It moved back again across the walkway, into the house, up the stairs, and back into the bedroom. The camera showed hands loading a short-barreled shotgun, and then with the barrel facing it, a flash erupted, and the screen went black. They all reacted to the shot and turned away from the screen.

"What the hell was that?" Stan asked, being the first to break the silence.

"You know what that was," said McKenna. "We all know what that was."

"Yeah," agreed Stevie. "Now, let's find Lonnie and get the fuck out of here!"

The screen flickered to life again. One by one, they were all drawn back to see what the projector had to show them. Surrounded by black forms, a little boy walked through the grass, carrying a small stuffed giraffe. McKenna's eyes widened at the sight of it. The boy dragged his toy and blanket and walked to the water's edge, where he stepped in.

"I can't watch this," said McKenna, hiding her face against Finn's chest. Finn placed a hand on the back of his sister's head to comfort her but continued watching.

Across the river, a man was waving his arms and running toward a small rowboat. Deeper and deeper, the boy went until his head slipped below the water's surface.

The silt stirred on the riverbed and clouded the already murky water. Frankie squinted and focused harder. Rows of bony spikes arched up and out of the riverbed and then rolled back under. Frankie hoped that would be the end of it, but he knew better. The thing began to vibrate and tremor convulsively as the creature worked to free its body from the thick muck. Its front legs, covered in leathery scales, broke free, splayed their three finger-like claws out, and then dug back into the riverbed to pull its head free. The thing's head and neck were covered in the same bony spikes as its back, and when the chest rose up, Frankie could see dozens of appendages like the pereopods on the underside of a crayfish working feverishly at the bed to pull the rest of its body free. The rest of the thing freed itself from the sucking muck and launched itself with horrible grace, gliding through the water toward the boy. As it neared, a long probing tongue with sharp barbs slithered out of its open mouth. Rows of hooked teeth, hundreds or perhaps thousands, rimmed the mouth and throat and were visible as far down into the thing's gullet as Frankie could see.

The boy floated, face down, a few feet off the riverbed, and it looked to Frankie like he had drowned. He closed one eye, not wanting to bear the full brunt of what he was sure was about to happen. In a flash, the thing grabbed the boy up in its pereopods and forced its terrible snake-like tongue down the boy's throat. The boy, who seemed to Frankie to have been dead, began to wiggle and struggle like a fish caught on a hook. The thrashing lasted only a minute, and then the boy went still. The thing retracted its tongue back out of the boy, and Frankie braced himself for the inevitable, but it never came. He fully expected to see the creature shove the boy into its gullet, but it didn't. Instead, it began to auger itself back into the riverbed dragging the little boy along with it.

"No! No, no, no!" Frankie cried.

As if reading his mind, Kaylin said, "That's not what happened to Levi."

"You don't know that!" Frankie's hands were balled into fists, and tears poured from his eyes.

"Kaylin's right Frankie," Finn assured him. "What happened to Levi was an accident."

"Yeah, it wasn't that thing," Stan agreed.

"Guys? What the hell was that?" Stevie asked, not really reading the mood.

"I don't know," said Lonnie, "but it wasn't no crow."

The group spun in unison at the sound of Lonnie's voice.

"Lonnie, where were you?" Stevie asked as he grabbed his brother and hugged him tightly.

Lonnie turned his face away from his brother and pushed against him. "Get off me, you weirdo!"

Stevie cleared his throat and regained his cool. "Dude, where were you?" He asked his younger brother.

"I don't know," he said. "Here, I guess."

"Are you okay?" Kaylin asked. "You're bleeding."

The group stared at him, waiting for an explanation.

"You guys are giving me the creeps," said Lonnie.

"Lonnie, you were gone," Stevie said. "We were all downstairs. Remember, remember when we all heard the loud bells? And then—and then you were gone, dude. What the hell happened?"

Lonnie clenched and unclenched his jaw a few times, and then all of the muscles in his face tensed. Frankie thought he was about to attack Stevie. Then Lonnie's eyes rolled up and darted from side to side, like a person searching the corners of their mind for answers.

"Easy, Stevie," said McKenna. "You're freaking him out."

Then Lonnie's eyes stopped rolling and fixed on something behind the group. His mouth dropped open and hung slack.

"Lonnie, your head, it's bleeding. Are you okay?" McKenna asked.

Lonnie didn't respond. Slowly, all turned to see what had stolen Lonnie's attention.

39

abe blinked hard and shook her head to clear it, but that didn't change what she saw. Achak was standing there, right in the spot where his body dropped. His head was back where it belonged, and his blood-soaked tee-shirt was clean and white. Achak seemed unphased by the chaos erupting all around him, and when he looked at her, Babe could see the warmth in his deep brown eyes and feel the joy in his bright smile. She returned his smile though it belied the anguish she felt in her heart. Achak bowed his head in what Babe read as an apologetic gesture and stood motionless for a moment. As she watched, Achak began to move his arms in great sweeping circles as if a rod ran through his body from one hand to the other. As his arms moved faster and faster, Achak began to whirl and spin. As he turned in place, a soft light began to emanate from him. He spun faster and faster, and the faster he spun, the brighter the light became until Babe had to shield her eyes. Finally, the light softened, and when she looked again, there was something very different about Achak. Babe could see him, but she could also see through him, into him, where a small bright light grew in intensity until it exploded in a corona of pure white.

Babe shielded her eyes from the glare, and when she looked again, Achak was draped head to foot in a covering made from a black wolf's pelt. Across his chest, he wore a breastplate of brilliant white bone and deep blue stones. From his arms and legs, blue and white feathers hung and fluttered like hundreds of Blue Jays, forming a protective barrier around him as he continued to whirl. Achak began to sing in a language Babe did not understand, and his whirling became a dance. Through his sacred dance and song, he transformed into a great black wolf and flew at the now howling old woman that had crawled from the river. The wolf snapped and snarled at the water-witch as he slowly moved between her and the water, backing her farther onto land. A dozen black, brown, gray wolves emerged from the woods and surrounded the old woman. There was no path for escape. The witch lashed out with dagger-like claws to keep the wolves at bay, but it did her no good.

Achak struck first. He brought her down and tore flesh from the old woman's leg, and then backed off. The pack howled and yipped and snapped their jaws in explosive clicks. The old woman dragged herself back to her feet and moved away from Achak. A large gray wolf, larger than Achak, struck her from behind and bit down on her shoulder, crushing bones that Babe could clearly hear, even over the gunfire that continued to erupt all around her. Again, the pack yipped and howled with mad delight. The old woman got to her feet again and again was taken down by a pack member. The woman cried out in pain, and Nick raised the shotgun.

"No," Babe said and placed her hand on the barrel. "You can't shoot them."

"I wasn't going to shoot them; I was going to put the old lady out of her misery."

Without taking her eyes off of the frenzied wolf pack, she said, "Let them finish."

One by one, the wolves came in and ripped flesh from the old woman until her cries stopped, and there was almost nothing left of her. Then a white wolf, larger than any of the others, walked from the woods, lowered, and placed his head against the Achak-wolf's bloodied head. At once, the white coat of the huge wolf began to fade to a pale gray as Achak's coat turned a brilliant white. The pale gray wolf then took up what was left of the old woman in its jaws and dragged her remains deep into the woods. The Achak wolf regarded Babe with what seemed to her like a bow, and then turned and disappeared into the woods with the rest of his brothers.

In the chaos of rifles booming and killing and devouring the creature, Nick failed to see Sheriff Tucker until it was too late. Tucker raised his handgun and took aim at Nick.

"I told you I'd get you, you city, sum-bitch! You couldn't mind your own got-dammed-binnes!"

Nick's hands flew out in front of him as a shot rang out, and Sheriff Cyrus Tucker fell dead.

"Nick, are you alright?" Patrick Marshall asked.

"Pat, holy shit, am I glad to see you!" Nick threw his arms around his savior.

"Yeah," he said, pushing Nick off of him. "What the fuck is going on here?" He had to yell to be heard over the exchange of gunfire.

"Long story," Nick shouted back. This is Jessica Upshaw." Nick pointed to a pregnant woman.

"Ma'am, am I glad to see you!" Marshall said and then keyed his radio and spoke. "Lightfoot, Arriaga, check your fire. We are on the scene. Copy."

"That's a negative sir, we're pinned down."

Repeating his orders, Marshall said. "I say again, we have the scene. Provide overwatch and be advised that we have secured Jessica Upshaw and the friendlies."

Then, in a loud, clear voice directed at those gathered, "This is Commander Patrick Marshall of the Illinois State Police. Drop your weapons. You are all under arrest. The locals stopped shooting out over the lake and redirected their guns to the new threat. Andrew Abernathy pointed his rifle at Patrick Marshall and squeezed the trigger. There was a loud crack, and that was the last sound Andrew Abernathy would ever hear. Arriaga's M-40 punched a hole through Abernathy's right temple and exited, leaving a gaping wound roughly the size of a softball where the left side of his head used to be.

A few of the locals dropped their weapons, but the rest returned fire. The well-trained troopers dropped them like clay pipes in a shooting gallery. Nick, who had dropped to the ground for cover, looked up in time to see the last wolf disappear into the thick woods. Across the lake, shots continued to ring out. Standing above Nick, Patrick Marshall spoke into his radio's mic.

"Lightfoot, Arriaga, hold your fire. We have secured the area."

"No can-do, sir," said Arriaga. "We're still pinned down in the loft in the barn, sir.”

Marshall looked at Nick. “What’s the fastest way to the barn?”

“I’ll get you there,” said Babe.

Nick nodded, “She’s your best bet, Pat.”

“Saunders, you stay here and secure the prisoners and call for a medic for Mrs. Upshaw.”

“Roger that,” said Trooper Saunders.

“Nick, you and —”

“Jinan, Dr. Jinan B —” she offered and then cut herself off.

“Right,” said Marshall. You and Dr. Jinan stay here with Mrs. Upshaw,” then to Jessica Upshaw;

“You’re safe now, ma’am.” And with that, he tore off into the woods after Babe with the rest of his troopers.

***

Even at full speed, it took almost ten minutes for Babe to make it to the edge of the path that led to the old barn. About two dozen townies were trying to close in, but heavy rifle fire from the hayloft had them pinned down. Indifferent to the brutalities occurring below, the clouds floated off on the gentle breeze allowing the soft moonlight to illuminate a few of the faces in the crowd. Babe knew every face she saw. Most of them were regulars at the Triumph Diner. She had just served Saul Rupert that very morning. Two eggs over easy with limp bacon and white toast. *“Never trust a person who likes their bacon limp,”* she thought to herself.

The shotgun he was pointing toward the loft flew from his hands as his blood sprayed the leaves around him. His body dropped like a bag of wet sand. No more bacon and eggs for Saul Rupert. Jerry Ball drove a milk truck for Hann’s Dairy; he threw a Molotov cocktail that struck the north-side of the barn. It was a hell of a throw, but Jerry never got to see it hit. The round that caught him took the upper left side of his face off. He was dead before he hit the ground. But dead or not, he’d hit his mark, and the dry old barn was going up fast. Orange and blue flames climbed up the wall like a waterfall running in reverse.

Without ordering the townies to surrender or issuing any kind of warning, Marshall and his men opened fire. Some of the townies turned to engage, while others continued their assault on the barn, but none that Babe could see turned and ran. Marshall and his men moved like jungle cats through the trees and brush. Babe took cover behind an oak tree and watched the people she'd known for most of her life fall, one after another. Jerry Ball's brother Lolly worked at the hardware store. He got off a lucky shot and hit one of Marshall's men square in the chest. But even as Babe was about to start over to him, the trooper got up, first to a knee and then back on his feet and returned fire, killing Lolly Ball right where he stood. She'd known Lolly all her life.

He was always quick with a joke and had a reputation as a *'shirt off his back'* kind of guy. *"How could he be involved in kidnapping and murder?"* Babe thought. Marshall's team was making relatively short work of the townies, but the barn was going up fast, and even at thirty yards away, she could feel the heat coming off of it.

***

Smoke filled the barn, and the temperature rose quickly. It was as if the damned thing were designed to burn. At first, Lightfoot and Arriaga tried to stay low, just like everyone was taught in elementary school, but the smoke was coming through the gaps in the floorboards, and there was little air to be had. Above them, the fire rolled in waves across the ceiling. They were running out of time and air, and they had to get out. The men ceased fire and made their way to the ladder, but flames were already crawling up the rungs. The wooden floor below was also in flames. Arriaga looked at his watch and noticed that it was already past the time he was supposed to loosen Lightfoot's tourniquet.

"Joe, we gotta loosen that tourniquet, or you're going to lose that leg."

"Fuck my leg; there's no way I'm making it out of here, bro," Lightfoot said as he let himself slip, exhausted and oxygen-starved to the floor. The floorboards were hot, too hot to touch, and Joseph Lightfoot's flesh was blistering.

"You have to find a way down and get clear of this. No point in both of us burning alive."

"I'm not leaving you, Joe."

Both men's faces were blackened from the soot and smoke that engulfed them, and their words came out in coughs and gasps. Sirens rose up in the distance. Arriaga looked around and saw the opened haymow door.

"We are both going to jump for it," said Arriaga with a look in his eyes that was somewhere between determination and terror. "The fall might not kill us, but the fire sure as shit will."

Arriaga grabbed Lightfoot's forearm and pulled to get him to his feet. Lightfoot let out a blood-curdling scream as his blistered skin slid off his arm.

"Fuck, I'm sorry, man!"

Arriaga tried to release his grip, but Lightfoot clamped his hand around his partner's wrist and pulled himself up. "Let's do this."

Flames licked at their feet through the gaps, and already, small fires were blocking the path to the opening. Arriaga and Lightfoot managed a couple of steps before the floor joists gave way, and the two men fell onto the flames below.

***

Outside, burning embers danced like fireflies on the night's gentle updrafts. Some drifted onto the gravel road, where they faded like bad dreams. Others found new life in nearby trees and bushes. As she watched the barn burn, it occurred to her that a part of Chesapeake Station was being erased from the map. The very young and those born after this night would have no memory of this place and could be spared ever knowing what happened here. Babe knew that Chesapeake Station once had a lumber mill. She'd seen pictures of it at the CSHS, but she had no actual knowledge of the mill or of the experiences of the men who worked there. Perhaps one day, the history of this horrible place might hold no meaning to any living resident of Chesapeake Station.

Babe watched as Marshall and his men made one final push for the barn.

Seemingly satisfied that the barn fire would take care of the outsiders trapped within, the townies turned their rifles fully on Marshall and his approaching troopers. The townies, all avid hunters, were great shots, but they weren't used to things that shot back. The well-trained TRU cut down every last man that stood between them and their comrades in the barn in a matter of minutes. Babe saw the troopers stepping over the dead and smashing the wounded with the buts of their rifles as they moved toward the barn. It seemed harsh to her, but at least they weren't executing them. As they drew near, the troopers shielded their faces from the heat with their hands. She could hear them calling out to their brothers, and she could see their heads and their shoulders fall when no response came from inside. In almost no time at all, the barn collapsed in on itself, sending a fresh shower of sparks into the sky. The efforts of Marshall and his men were halted. The heat was too much to bear. In an act of pointless desperation, Marshall keyed his mic and called out to his overwatch team one last time.

"Lightfoot, Arriaga, come in." There was no response.

"I'm sorry, sir," Babe placed a hand on Patrick Marshall's forearm.

"Yeah, me too," he answered. "They were good men." Marshall stared into the dying fire.

"Boss, you should get back to Saunders. He's going to need your help, and there's nothing you can do here. I'll stand by for the fire department."

Trooper Mike Day was the youngest member of the TRU, but like the rest, he was no stranger to combat and battle fatigue. Mike Day's soft face didn't fit his battle-tested spirit as a decorated veteran of the Persian Gulf War.

"I can lead you back whenever you're ready, sir," offered Babe.

Marshall turned back toward the fire, and Babe read a look of such profound loss and pain that she thought she understood just a little what her father had left of himself at the Battle of Chosin.

40

erlyn hurried toward the sound of screaming children. He saw the kids on the ground and trained the late Donnie Marshall's flashlight on the monster.

"Stay down!"

Merlyn leveled his colt and fired a round striking the thing in the back. The monster reared back in pain, and Merlyn fired again. The thing spun on Merlyn, ripping gashes across Stan's chest and stomach in the process. The young man cried out in pain, and the rest of the gang scrambled over to him.

As the creature closed on Merlyn, he unloaded his 1911 into the thing, and it fell to the floor. Merlyn rushed over to the children and checked Stan in the beam of the flashlight. There were three gashes in the boy's torso. Merlyn trained the light on the wounds and pressed lightly around one of the gashes. The blood flow was minimal.

"You'll be fine, son. I've seen much worse in combat," he said and tousled the boy's hair. "On your feet, troops, we gotta find a way out of here. I think I killed that thing," he said.

Merlyn turned the light back toward the monster, but it was gone. "Shit, spoke too soon."

Somewhere in the distance, they could hear the sound of lapping water.

"I think we have to go this way," Frankie said.

"Is that you, Frankie?"

"Yes, sir," he answered.

"It's me, son. Merlyn."

"Mr. Merlyn!" Excitement rose in Frankie's voice.

"Well, just Merlyn, but yes, son, and I'm going to get you kids out of here."

The group moved cautiously toward the sound of the water and peered into the darkness looking for, but hoping not to see, the thing that Merlyn had shot. Muffled sounds of sirens grew louder from somewhere beyond. Merlyn did his best to keep the light ahead of the kids so that they could see where they were going but continued to check behind them to make sure the thing didn't sneak up on them. Before long, they could smell the river.

"Just a little farther, kids. Can you smell it?"

"It's the river," said Finn. "We're almost out."

"Stop, guys!" Frankie yelled.

The group stopped.

"Frankie, we have to keep going," Stan said.

"That thing lives in the river!"

"Mr. Merlyn shot it, Frankie," McKenna reassured him. "It probably crawled off and died in some dark corner."

"How do we know there's only one?" Frankie had a valid point.

"Maybe Frankie's right," said Stan.

"Kids, you have to get out of here. Either the fire is going to get you, or that thing will." Merlyn pulled the bone tomahawk from his belt and gripped the handle tightly. "If that one or another one shows up, I'll kill it."

The group continued on and found themselves standing at what looked like a cave pool.

"I think we have to go in and swim out," said Stevie.

Frankie looked at Merlyn. "But you can't swim, Mr. Merlyn."

"It's okay, you guys go ahead. I'll stay here to make sure that thing doesn't follow you into the water, and then I'll catch up."

"We can't leave you behind," said Kaylin.

"You're not leaving anyone behind. I said I'll follow you kids out; now get going!"

From deep in the darkness behind them came scraping and trembling, like a colossal stone dragged across the ground.

"There's no time, kids. You have to go."

Frankie hugged Merlyn. "Thank you for saving me, but if you don't come with us, I'm not going."

"I can't swim, Frankie. I'll drown."

"When was the last time you tried?"

"I've never tried."

"Then how do you know you can't?"

Merlyn looked at Frankie and then back toward the closing sound.

"Levi said that it's okay to be scared, but we have to face our fears."

"I'm so sorry about Levi, Frankie."

"I know me too. That's why I can't leave you behind. I've lost too many friends today."

"Please, Mr. Merlyn, I don't want that thing to get me."

Merlyn tucked the tomahawk back in his waistband. "Okay, kid, I'll give it a try."

The thing came out of nowhere, knocking Merlyn to the ground and locking its gaze on Stan again. Merlyn sat up, a bit bruised, but none the worse for wear. The fire had spread to the basement level now, and the whole area glowed in its light. He ripped the ancient weapon from his belt and swung the bone-tomahawk, sinking it to the haft into the monster's neck. The thing that used to be Gemein whirled around, spraying viscera and gore into the air. Merlyn drew and unloaded Donnie Marshall's Glock into the creature as it clawed at the tomahawk in its neck. The monster dropped and writhed there on the ground.

"Move!" Merlyn cried as they all plunged into the water.

"Just take a deep breath and hold it and follow us," Frankie said. "You'll be okay, you'll see. Just kick your feet and move your arms like this." Frankie demonstrated the dog paddle.

The air around them was heating up fast, and it was getting difficult to breathe. Merlyn hovered in place and dog-paddled frantically.

"Hang on, guys," said Finn. "I'll go under and see where it comes out."

Finn took in a deep breath and disappeared below the water.

"Are you doing okay, Mr. Merlyn?" Frankie asked.

Merlyn was holding his breath and dog-paddling to beat the devil. As the group waited for Finn to return, they heard the dragging sound again.

"I think we are just going to have to dive under and take our chances," Stan said.

The dragging sound grew louder.

Merlyn, seeming to have reached his limit, began paddling back toward land when Finn re-emerged from the water, sucking in a deep breath.

"Guys, it's cool, just a short swim underwater, and we're out."

Frankie locked eyes with Merlyn. "You ready, Mr. Merlyn?"

Merlyn shook his head, no. His steely eyes were wide with fear.

"It's going to be okay; I'll help you."

Frankie offered a smile, and Merlyn nodded.

"Okay, let's go."

Merlyn took one last breath and dove.

***

The Ironweiler house was fully engulfed in flames. The heat kept onlookers from getting in the way of the firefighters who battled the blaze. Engines pumped hundreds of gallons of water out of the Red Hook River and into the house to knock the flames down, but the progress was slow. Scott Waters had to be locked in the back of a squad to keep him from running into the burning structure and now watched helplessly as he lost his other son. He was sure no one could survive this. Their marriage had always been strong, but he knew Connie would blame him for moving the family to Red Hook. And why shouldn't she? He blamed himself. The whole family wanted to stay put. They could have found another school for Levi. With his arm, any one of the academies would have taken Levi the Cannon Waters, despite the number of fights he had gotten into. Besides, who could blame him for protecting his little brother? Who except for the nuns over at St. Francis, the bitches. But none of that mattered now. Scott Waters' life was over. Connie would be inconsolable, and Scott had no interest in life without her and the boys.

***

Merlyn's lungs felt like they were on fire, and it took every last bit of his resolve not to inhale. He could feel the kids tugging and pushing him along and almost lashed out at the hands-on him, feeling sure that they were trying to drown him. Finally, he felt himself relax. He could feel the coolness of the water as it slipped down his throat. Merlyn knew he was going to die, and he was okay with that. His death would mean the lives of the kids he'd saved, and it would spare Scott and Connie Waters the loss of their only remaining child. Merlyn exhaled hard. His last breath had escaped him, and peace settled over him.

"We made it, Mr. Merlyn!" Cried, Frankie. "We made it!"

***

The medics loaded Merlyn onto a stretcher, carried him up the hill to the road, and placed him into the ambulance. The kids sat on the back of the ambulance wrapped in blankets as fire personnel checked them for injuries. Chief Vecchio was the first family member to see the kids, and he rushed to embrace his niece.

"Kaylin, are you okay. Sweetie?"

"I'm fine, Uncle Chris," she said, tears streaming down her face. "Mr. Merlyn, he saved us, but—," Kaylin buried her face against her uncle's chest.

Chris Vecchio hugged Kaylin tight. "Where's Donnie Marshall, sweetie?" Vecchio asked.

"I didn't see him," Kaylin answered.

Chief Vecchio closed his eyes and hugged Kaylin that much tighter.

Scott Waters pushed past the medics and lifted his son in the air. "Frankie! Thank God you're alive, son!"

"I'm okay, Dad. Where's mom?"

"She's still waiting for the searchers to find Levi," he said, their momentary joy falling to sadness.

"Oh, son, I'm so glad you're alive. I don't know what we would have done if we'd lost you too."

Frankie knew Levi was gone, but hearing his father admit it made it all so final.

"Dad," he looked at his father. "Lonnie Johnson didn't make it either. This is Stevie," he said, placing a hand on Stevie's shoulder, "Lonnie's brother."

Scott Waters wrapped his arms around both boys and kissed the tops of their wet heads.

41

Babe barely reached the path back toward the cabin when Nick and Jinan emerged from the treeline.

"Are you okay?" Nick asked Babe.

"I'm fine, but we have to get the box and get out to that islet. Do you still have the key?"

Nick reached into his pocket and pulled the key Merlyn had made for them. "Where's the box?"

"I hid it under some leaves by an oak tree."

Nick looked around. There were oak trees as far as the eye could see. "Some oak tree?"

"Relax, I know exactly where it is."

They ran through the woods to the place where Babe stashed the horrible box. She clawed at the leaves and pulled the box from its hiding spot. When they reached the water's edge, they were presented with a new problem.

"How are we supposed to get out there?" Jinan asked.

"I'll fucking swim if I have to."

"I don't think that will be necessary," Nick said, pointing at an old rowboat tied to the Kramer's dock.

They carried the box to the rowboat, and Babe and Jinan got in. Nick stared apprehensively at the boat.

"Are you coming or not?" Babe asked anxiously.

"I guess," Nick said and stepped into the boat. "Kind of weird."

"What's kind of weird?" Jinan asked.

"For my family, this whole thing started in a rowboat, kind of like this one."

Jinan placed a hand on his and smiled warmly at him. Babe bore down and pulled on the oars. They reached the little island and pulled the boat onto the shore. They walked to the twisted tree, and Nick set the box on the ground.

"Well, here we are."

"Yep." Babe held her hand out for the key, and Nick handed it to her.

"We're sure about this, right?" Nick asked Jinan.

"According to legend, this is the only way to give these poor souls the rest that they so deserve," Jinan said.

"Ready or not, here I go." Babe slid the key into the lock and gave it a turn.

Nick closed one eye and turned his head slightly. Secretly, he expected something like the opening of the Arc of the Covenant in Raiders, but that didn't happen. It was just a box. There was nothing whatsoever special about it other than its contents. Tiny white bones. Hundreds and hundreds of tiny white bones, some smaller than others, but all rather small. Babe dropped to her knees and wept. Jinan knelt beside her. Nick picked up a couple of stones and began digging. It took some time, but they carefully laid each bone, one by one, into the hole Nick dug. When they were done, they all stood and silently said whatever words they felt appropriate to the situation. As they turned to leave, Babe noticed a small green leaf that had sprouted from the trunk. She smiled and silently thanked her father.

***

They pulled into Red Hook late that night and drove straight to the Ironweiler house only to find it burnt to the ground. Nick paused a moment, trying to imagine what had happened. He supposed that no matter what had transpired, it was for the best that the place had been wiped from Red Hook. From the burnt remains of the Ironweiler place, Nick drove to the Red Hook Police Department. Ronald Coreless was watching the desk while the records ladies were on a break. Nick had known Ron his whole life, but he'd never seen him looking more tired and run down.

"Ron, you okay?"

"Nick, what brings you to town?"

"You wouldn't believe me if I told you. Hey, what happened to the Ironweiler house?"

"Burnt down earlier today. Merlyn Greer saved a bunch of kids from the fire, but he took a lot of damage. He's over at St. Anthony's. Who are your friends?"

"Oh, sorry, this is Babe, and this is Dr.—"

"I'm Jinan," she said, cutting him off.

Ron smiled a genuine smile. "It's nice to meet you, ladies." Then the smile faded. "We lost Donnie Marshall tonight too."

The color faded from their faces. "No, not Donnie. What happened?" Nick tried to conjure an image of some distracted driver hitting Donnie but knew it couldn't have been anything so mundane, not in Red Hook.

"Lost him in the fire. He went in with Merlyn, trying to save the kids."

"Shit. So, are the kids okay?" Nick asked.

"No, Lonnie Johnson died," Coreless shook his head. "This fucking town, sometimes I swear it's cursed."

Nick didn't respond, though deep down, he thought Coreless was right. After a moment, Coreless continued.

"The Waters family," Ronald paused. "That's the family that bought your place. They lost a son. The Red Hook took him. He was out rafting with a bunch of kids and got swept into the boil." Coreless adjusted himself in his chair and cleared his throat. "Honest to Christ, Nick, you would not believe the summer we have been having. Just a couple months ago, Joe Kott went missing."

"Joe? No shit? What do you mean; he went missing?"

"Just what I said. He made a traffic stop and vanished."

"Did he ever turn up?"

"It's a long story. Stop back in town sometime. I'll let you buy me a cup of coffee, and I'll tell you a story that will curl you fucking toes."

"I'll do that. I have one for you too, buddy. Sure, was good to see you."

"You too. And it was a pleasure meeting you, ladies."

They all walked back out into the still night air.

"Next stop St. Anthony's," Nick said.

They pulled into the parking lot and walked through the Emergency Room doors. Security guards checked them in, and the receptionist gave them name tags and strict instructions to wear them at all times. Merlyn had already been sent up to a room, so they took the elevator up to his floor and knocked on his door.

"Nick, good to see you, son."

"It's good to see you too."

"I see you brought my girlfriends back." Merlyn winked at the ladies.

"You think you could handle this?" Babe said, flashing a flirtatious smile.

"Hell no! But what a nice way to go."

They all laughed, but then the mood turned serious.

"What's with all the security?" Nick asked.

"Had some maniac in here a couple months back. Guy killed a bunch of people."

"What the hell is going on?" The question was rhetorical, but Merlyn answered anyway.

"Whole damned planet is shifted out of whack if you ask me."

"What about the Ironweiler house?" Nick asked.

"You wouldn't believe it, Nick."

"People have to stop saying that. I just watched a pack of ghost wolves take down some kind of sea monster, for god's sake."

"River monster," Babe corrected.

Merlyn's eyes widened. "River monster? What'd it look like?"

Nick described the thing he saw as best he could.

"I think I killed one of those myself tonight," Merlyn said.

"Are you sure it's dead?" Babe asked.

"Can't say for sure darlin'. I shot the thing and damned near hacked its head off, and then I shot it some more. If it ain't dead, I bet it sure as shit is wishing it was. Oh, and it burned up in the fire, so, yeah. I'm sure." Merlyn took a sip of water. "Pardon me, folks, I'm a little parched. Oh, and the damnedest thing. As I was making my escape, a bunch of hands came up out of the ground and dragged it under, or at least that's what I remember.

Gotta give me a little room on that, though; after all, I did drown."

Just then, Merlyn's phone rang.

"Greer's Clock Sh—" he stopped himself and covered the mouthpiece, "Been an awfully long day. Sorry, Merlyn Greer here—well, shit son, I'm just as sorry as I can be about your brother."

"Yeah, Vecchio's out at my mom and dad's. I just got off the phone with them."

"Donnie was a good man. Pat, I have to tell you something. It's my fault your brother died. I made him go in that damned house with me."

Is Nick there? Let me talk to him."

"Sure, he's right here," Merlyn said and handed the phone to Nick.

Nick drew in a long slow breath. "Hi, Pat, I just heard about Donnie. I'm so sorry."

"It's this fucking job, Nick. Do me a favor?"

"You don't even have to ask. I'll stop in and check on your folks."

"I'd appreciate that. Fuck! He was so young."

"Yeah he was," Nick agreed.

"I'll head home as soon as I can. And hey, where did you guys get to so fast?"

"I'm sorry, but we had to take care of something back here."

"Well, I wanted to say thanks. We found Jessica Upshaw and stopped a...well, I'm not exactly sure what we stopped yet, but we couldn't have done it without you."

"You and your troopers saved our lives, Pat. It's us that should be thanking you."

"Listen, I'm going to reach out to you in a day or so, all of you. I'm going to need statements."

"You have my number Pat, just call, and we'll set it up."

"Would you do me another favor and tell Merlyn not to beat himself up. Me and Donnie, we knew this job was dangerous when we took it. Guess I just never thought anything would happen in our sleepy little town.

"Will do, Pat—you take care." Nick hung up the phone just as the night nurse came in.

"You all are going to have to leave. Visiting hours are over."

"Chris, is that you?"

"Nick Ryan? How the heck are you?"

"I'm good, well good as can be expected."

"Well, it sure is nice to see you, honey," she hugged him. "But you still have to get going. Merlyn needs his rest."

***

They drove back to 289 Sugar Maple Lane. There were six cars in the driveway, counting Gus, Nick's Bronco. Nick hopped in, and Jinan and Babe followed him back to the river where the recovery team was still at work. They sat on the grass and watched the men and women go about their solemn work. As they sat in silence, Tony Carlini approached.

"Nick, how are you?"

"Hey Chief, I'm okay."

"Sure, picked a hell of a day to come back home."

"I sure did."

We lost two children today and a damned good cop. Sometimes I wonder if there's a curse on this town."

"Me too, Chief; me too."

"You know the real bitch of it?" Carlini shook his head. "Tomorrow's the first day of school."

"Hell of a way to start off the year," Nick agreed.

"Well, I gotta get up to St. Anthony's," Carlini said grimly. "How about that?"

"How about what?" Nick asked.

"The hospital and my son have the same name. He's there tonight, you know, almost lost him too."

The chief turned and walked back up the hill.

"Funny, how we forget those guys are people too."

"What, guys?" Babe asked.

"Firemen, cops."

"Well, maybe here they're people, but where I'm from—"

"Yeah, I guess you guys have some house cleaning to do."

"To say the least." Babe let her head drop. "I guess it's over," she said.

"Seems so."

"I'm going to have to tell Achak's family that he's gone.

"Are you sure about that?"

"Well, who else is going to tell them?"

"I mean about him being gone. How sure are you that he's gone?"

"I had the same thought," Jinan said. "Seems like he's more changed than gone."

"I suppose," she said and got to her feet. Well, partner, I guess this is where we part ways. You guys have a Greyhound Station in this town?"

Nick and Jinan both stood up. Nick dug into his pocket and tossed her a set of keys. "Here you go."

"What are these for? I'm not sacking out at your place. You'll probably get all handsy."

Nick's face took on a pained expression. "Actually, I'm going to need those back."

Babe tossed them back, and Nick removed one of the keys and tossed it to her. "There you go; Gus is all yours."

"Is that because you're too cheap to fix it?"

"Funny, smart ass."

Babe threw her arms around Nick's neck and kissed him long and slow. She stepped back, smacked her lips, and ran her thumb over them. "Yep, almost enough."

"Almost enough for what?" Nick asked.

"You really are an idiot, Nick Ryan," Jinan said and took his hand.

"Babe hopped in the Bronco and fired it up. "You two have fun."

"We will," Jinan assured her.

"Congratulations, guys," Babe said and put Gus in gear.

"What are you doing for Thanksgiving?" Nick called to her.

"I don't know, are you inviting me to the big city for the holidays?"

"If you can get off work. What do you say Jinan, can we make room for one more at the table?"

"What table? As soon as you turn your work in, I'm done with you."

"Then I'll never turn it in," Nick smiled, and Jinan smiled back.

"If I liked boy's you would have a fight on your hands," Babe called to Jinan.

Jinan laughed. "Who says I'd fight you for him?"

Nick's face lit up in an expression of revelation.

"And the light goes on," Jinan teased.

Babe hit the gas and turned out of the parking lot.

Nick and Jinan walked back up the hill arm in arm.

"You know, I forgot your apartment number and had to ask several people in your building for directions."

"Really?"

"Really, and none of them knew who you were."

"Come on," he said in disbelief.

"Including two people who lived on your floor. Do you know that you have a nice Persian couple right across the hall?"

"Of course, Mr. and Mrs...."

"You really don't know your neighbors! Well, all of that is going to change."

"Is that right?"

"That's right, I'm a very social person."

He stopped and kissed her.

42

Connie Waters hung up the phone and walked into the living room where Scott sat, holding a sleeping Frankie on his lap. She handed her husband a cup of coffee and sat down next to him. Outside, the morning sunlight sparkled on the Red Hook River, and to anyone not knowing the story, everything seemed perfect.

"Thanks, honey."

"Our old apartment is still available," she said. It's going to cost us an extra $150.00 a month, but I told the super that we'd take it."

"That's fine; I talked to Terry. He said the manager at the Home Depot owes him a favor. He said he'd take me on until I could land another teaching job."

"I'm sorry, Scott, I just can't stay here."

"Neither can I, honey, and I don't think it would be good for Frankie. I'm just so sorry I dragged us out here." Tears filled Scott's eyes, and Connie leaned over and kissed them away.

"It's not your fault. It's that damned river. Look at it, like nothing happened, like it didn't steal our son away from us."

Scott kissed the top of Frankie's head. "I thank God that He spared Frankie."

Connie exhaled hard and shook her head. "The Realtor will be here with the sign this morning, and the movers said driving time from Chicago. They are handling most of the packing, but there are a few things I'm going to want to take with us in the car. I called Mr. Burton, he said he'd set some boxes aside. I would go, but I can't listen to any more people tell me how

371

fucking sorry they are."

Connie got up from the couch and walked back into the kitchen. Scott carefully laid Frankie on the couch and touched his son's head, and whispered, "Mom, thanks God that you're safe too, son."

The Waters were out of the house in Red Hook and back in their apartment by dinner time. Connie ordered Chinese from the place on the corner, and they ate right out of the cartons as the movers stacked boxes and placed furniture. After dinner, after the movers left, once things were as back to normal as they would ever be for the Waters family, Scott took some of the empty boxes to the garbage shoot and put Frankie's bed together. They were home again, but Scott knew it would never feel normal. Even as he lay Frankie in bed, the absence of the second bed, Levi's bed, was as stark a contrast to normal as Scott Waters could ever imagine. Nothing would ever be the same, and there was no point in pretending that it would be or that it would somehow all be okay. Scott looked at his arms and legs, and he thought it would be a million times easier to adjust to the loss of one or, hell, all of his limbs than it would be to adapt to the loss of his son. And a terrible thought, an unforgivable thought, crossed his mind. A thought that he would take to the grave and never speak aloud. He thought that it might have been better if Frankie died rather than Levi.

Scott sunk to his knees beside his sleeping child and shuddered as he wept. Long deep exhalations escaped his body in racking chuffs as he did what he could to release the pain and shame of that horrible thought. When he finally regained his composure, Scott stood up and felt dizzy as the blood raced back to his head from his extremities. He steadied himself with a hand on the window and noticed a blackbird sitting on the outside window sill. The bird, a common crow, was not at all common to the area, and as it turned its head and fixed Scott with one deep red eye, Scott's tenuous grasp on consciousness failed, and he crumbled to the floor.

Scott woke up the following day to a ringing phone, a pillow under his head, and a blanket over his shoulders. *Connie must have found me asleep and covered me*, he thought to himself. He answered the phone and was greeted by a cheery Janice Crenshaw of Crenshaw and Crenshaw Realty.

"Good morning Mr. Waters. Do I have news for you!" She began.

"Hello, Janice."

"Who's on the phone?" Connie came walking in from their bedroom.

"Janice Crenshaw, the Realtor."

"You mean Janice Crenshaw, Super Realtor," she said.

"What can I do for you, Janice?" He asked flatly.

"It's not what you can do for me. It's what I am about to do for you. I have a buyer. Can you believe it?"

"The house just went on the market yesterday."

"Not only that, but I got $5,000.00 over your asking price. How's that?"

"Wow, that *is* good news. How'd you sell it so fast?"

"Well, I showed the house after you guys told me you wanted it. It's not uncommon to have a deal fall through, and the people fell in love with the place. They were crushed when I told them that you had already put the earnest money down. Anyway, I reached back out to them and told them that the place was back on the market. They offered five-grand over the asking price if I promised to take them out there today. I'm confident we will have a contract by lunchtime."

"Wow, you really are something," he said, still absent emotion.

"In fact, I'm heading out to meet them now. Cross your fingers."

The sing-songy tones were just too much for Nick, and he hung up without another word.

***

Janice Crenshaw, never one to leave things to chance, left home an hour and a half before the meet time. On her way, Janice stopped at the BGS and bought a frozen apple pie. When she got to the house, she simply popped the pie in the oven and baked it. When the pie was done, she carefully removed it, wrapped it in foil, and hid it away in her car. Walking back into the house, she inhaled deeply and congratulated herself on her cunning. "Nothing makes a person feel at home like the smell of a freshly baked pie," she said to herself and took a seat on the front stoop to await the Campbells.

Like most people in the Heartland, the Campbells were punctual. They ran on Lombardi time. On-time is late; 15 minutes early is on time. Alice and Denny Jr., the Campbell twins, the dizygotic type, bolted from the car like bulls from the chute and headed straight for the river.

Despite her own self-interest, Janice cautioned Dennis and Cathy Campbell, "They really should be careful. That river can be dangerous."

"Hell, those two? You'd swear they were born in water the way they swim," Dennis beamed. "Both varsity swimmers since freshman year."

"Refresh my memory," Janice begged. "You are from the Galena area, aren't you?"

"That's right," Dennis said, "and those two have been swimming in the Mississippi since they were eight years old."

"That's just wonderful," Janice smiled ear to ear at the news. "Would you like to take a look inside?"

"Absolutely," Cathy said and started for the front door with Janice.

The house smelled wonderful, and except for a little fresh paint, it was move-in ready.

"Can I ask why the previous owners left so suddenly?" Cathy asked.

Janice felt her smile fade. "It's really very sad."

"Don't tell me; they didn't care for life in the country," Dennis boomed.

"Their son drowned."

"Oh my gosh, that's awful." Cathy clamped a hand over her mouth in automatic response.

"Yes, it really is. That's why I cautioned you about the kids by the river."

"Couldn't the kid swim?"

"No, Mr. Campbell, least not the older boy, the one who...."

"Well, who the hell would move by the river if their kids can't swim?"

"Dennis! Not another word!" Cathy scolded. "I'm sorry, men can be so unfeeling sometimes. How are the parents holding up?"

"Well, they moved back to Chicago, and Mr. Waters seemed happy when I mentioned your offer, assuming you decide to take the house."

"Oh honey, coming out here was just me being impatient to see the place again. The second you called, we knew we wanted it." Cathy hugged Janice and smiled warmly. "You didn't have to go through the trouble of baking a pie."

Janice was only a little embarrassed at being found out, and the two shared a laugh.

"I'll fetch it from the car. I have some paper plates and plastic forks if you're interested."

"Hell, yeah, we're interested," the loud Dennis Campbell bellowed from the back porch. "We can eat it back here; I think this is my favorite part of the whole damned place." He sniffed at the air. "Hey, Janice, were the last owners' smokers?"

"No, I don't believe so."

"Funny, I thought I smelled cigarette smoke."

"I'll be right back," Janice called over her shoulder as she hurried out to the car and returned with the warm pie. She set it on the counter and offered Cathy the knife to cut the first piece.

"Our first meal in our new home," she said.

No sooner had she cut the first piece when the back door slammed open and the twins came bounding in.

"Oh, pie!"

"Denny Jr. has an appetite as big as his father's," Cathy beamed.

"Mom, can we keep it?"

"Keep what, dear?"

"Gypsy Soul?"

"Whatever is Gypsy Soul?"

The other Campbell twin, Alice, dragged her mother to the back window and pointed to the old rowboat tied to their dock.

About the Author

Paul VanDorn was born and raised in Chicago's Pilsen neighborhood on the city's south side. He spent over 25 years in law enforcement in one of the cities western suburbs and draws on his experiences, relationships, and whatever random thoughts pop into his head in his writing. Aside from writing and spending time with his family, he enjoys sailing, flying, and playing music.

You can connect with me on:

🌐 https://www.coldfrontpublishing.com

Also by Paul VanDorn

Hiraeth

Officer Joe Kott settled into his cruiser prepared for another long midnight shift in rural Red Hook, Illinois. He planned on spending this night as he spent most. Listening to Todd Zeelander's weird radio show, smoking cigarettes, and drinking coffee to try and stay awake. But the driver of a dark blue 1970 Mustang Boss 302 disrupts his plans, and before day breaks, Officer Kott's cruiser is discovered abandoned, and he is left to find his way through a world that even Zeelander wouldn't believe.

Challenging Entropy

Detective Charlotte Rittenhouse of the Northeastern Major Crimes Task Force has been assigned to investigate the brutal murders of four women in northern Iowa. While it's apparent that the murders are connected, it isn't clear until a fifth woman is taken that they are tied to a series of murders that occurred in Chicago almost ten years earlier. Now Rittenhouse must enlist the aid of a disgraced US Marshal and a campus security guard if there is any hope of finding the missing woman before she becomes the next victim of the infamous Tooth Fairy.

Diastole (Book 2 in the Hiraeth Series)

Having barely survived his first journey through the brutal and unforgiving world of the Territories, Joe Kott must once again pierce the veil between the two worlds if he hopes to save the people he has come to know and care for. But as perilous as his first trip had been, it might not prove enough to get him through again. Not without the help of a dangerously gifted 12-year-old girl named Tine and a few other good souls he meets along the way. But if he manages to survive, Joe may finally bring balance to his life and peace to the Territories once and for all.

Downfall (Book 3 in the Hiraeth Series)

Downfall will follow Joe Kott as he returns home from the Territories to find his world quite different and far more dangerous than when he left it. Coming Fall, 2022